# THE TREATMENT PLAN

## ANDREW WOLFENDON

Black Rose Writing | Texas

ISBN: 978-1-68513-093-0
PUBLISHED BY BLACK ROSE WRITING
www.blackrosewriting.com

Printed in the United States of America
Suggested Retail Price (SRP) $23.95

*The Treatment Plan* is printed in Garamond Premier Pro

*As a planet-friendly publisher, Black Rose Writing does its best to eliminate unnecessary waste to reduce paper usage and energy costs, while never compromising the reading experience. As a result, the final word count vs. page count may not meet common expectations.

*This father's tale is dedicated with enormous love to my daughters,*
*Phelan and Quinn*

# THE
# TREATMENT
# PLAN

# PART I
## Intake

# Chapter 1

*At first, only flat blackness.*

*Then, points of flickering light. Shimmering, darting. Up and down. Side to side. Now collecting in a circle. Concentric rings forming, receding into space and bending out of sight, like mirrors within mirrors. A "tunnel" of light-rings.*

*A feeling of falling into this tunnel, falling* through *it. Falling, falling. Not down, but up. A dizzying release of gravity.*

*Motion slows to a stop.*

*Lids flutter open. Light blinds the eye. White, sacred, pure. Strings of golden light coalescing from within the brilliant whiteness. Endless strings of shimmering, singing light—billions, trillions of strings—intertwining and vibrating. The light is made of music. The music is made of light. Harmonies within harmonies within harmonies.*

*And then: a change. The music retreats, as if pulled into a vacuum. The strings of vibrating light freeze into shapes.*

*Walls. Ceiling. Doorway.*

• • •

My head jerks from the pillow with a neck-cracking start. What just happened? My heart feels like it's been paddled awake. What room is this? Whose house am I in?

What stupid damn thing did I do last night?

Oh. Wait. Shit.

Shit, shit.

Narrow bed with metal railings, digital gadgets on wheeling poles, hideous painting of Dutch milkmaid.

Art so combatively bad can exist nowhere but on institutional walls; this I know.

I look down at my body. It's clad in a hospital johnny—cowboy-boot-patterned for no conceivable reason—and draped in a bedsheet. From the hall come the sounds of a medical device pinging, a loud phone ringing, a speaker paging Dr. Mukherjee.

Shit, shit, shit. When was I admitted? What for?

Elective surgery? Emergency?

Not a clue. I give it a few more seconds. Still nothing. Maybe I'm coming out of... Anastasia? Anesthesia. That can take time. I wait again.

Why isn't it kicking in, my "system reboot"? My sense of me-ness? That list of daily dreads that clicks into place a moment after you awaken?

I reach up to touch my head, but my hand snaps back like a charging dog that's run out of chain. That's when I notice my wrists are strapped to the bed frame on either side. Someone thought I might try to injure myself. Or someone else.

Or that I would try to pull out tubes and needles.

*Am I intubated?* I rotate my head to one side, then the other. Equipment sprouting tubes and wires surrounds me—an IV unit, a couple of patient monitors, a sphygmomanometer—but none of it seems to be attached to me. A hopeful sign?

The fact that I know the word "sphygmomanometer" but not my own name? *Not* such a hopeful sign, perhaps.

Something feels off in my cranial region. A sense of pressure extends backward from my frontal bone—my forehead—and over my parietal bone like a cap. Bandages, tightly wrapped?

*Bandages + memory loss = head injury.* I've suffered a head injury. Right. My heart punches my ribs from the inside, one-two.

Fear tries to hijack my mind.

*Easy... easy... you're having a bad reaction to anesthesia, that's all. It happens.*

Calm down. Breathe and assess. Breathe and assess.

Okay, cognitive system seems intact. Senses seem functional—I can smell disinfectant in the air and a trace of fresh paint. (What do you call this room color, by the way—Yesterday's Guacamole?) I can hear the thump of an old Eagles tune in the wall. Someone's getting a peaceful, easy feeling.

Not I.

But still, being able to name the recording artists is a good thing, yes?

If I have a head injury, it's not a catastrophic one. I'm sure any second now I'll be *A + O x 4*—"alert and oriented" to time, place, identity, and reason for being here.

Meanwhile, why this strange sense of "second awareness"—as if I'm *living* this experience and *watching myself* live it at the same time?

A sound hooks my attention.

Rubber-soled footsteps, squeaking slightly, growing louder. My senses go on alert. A flurry of blue motion passes my partially open doorway.

The footsteps stop. A figure leans back, looks into my room. Woman. African American, size fourteen, dark-framed glasses, light-blue scrubs, burdened shoulders. She flashes a smile, but it tightens quickly.

"Well, well, do tell, look who has decided to join the living." She shuffles to my bed. "How are you feeling, Mr. G.?" It takes me a second or two to realize a response is called for. By then the moment has passed. "Do you know where you are?"

"Huff-pull," I say. Well done. My tongue feels four inches thick. "Huff-pull," I try again, going for "hospital." The voice from my throat—gravelly, male—sounds alien to my ears.

"Do you know *which* 'huff-pull'?"

I heave a random muscle in a shrug-like manner.

"St. Clownifer's in Poopdale." She looks me straight in the eye, no trace of humor showing. A trickle of unease runs through me. "Just kidding," she says, still not smiling. "Testing your responses. You are at Emblem-Triad. Does that name ring any bells?"

Emblem-Triad. Sure. Huge medical conglomerate, hospitals and medical centers all over creation. But which location I'm at? Clue zero.

"What do you remember about arriving here?"

A throat-rattle is all the reply I can manage.

"We need to get you lubricated. I'm going to fetch you some ice water. I'll be back in two shakes of a viper's tail, Mr. Greenbird."

She turns with a chirp of crepe soles and exits.

A spike of disquiet shoots through my nerves. *Two shakes of a viper's tail?* Who says that? Especially to a hospital patient who's obviously in trauma?

But that's not the main cause of my unease. No, that stems from the name she just called me. Mr. Greenbird. I know virtually nothing about myself at this point, but of this I am certain: Greenbird is not my name.

That's a mistake you don't like to see people making in a hospital setting. *Clerical error. Don't freak out. They'll catch it.* Until then, what are some facts I can nail down?

The room has no window, so no help from the outside world. I crane my neck to examine the milkmaid painting. The freakishly cheerful lass rendered in faux oil is wearing a Dutch cap and carrying two pails of milk on an over-the-shoulder yoke. She's standing outside a barn—strange, I could have sworn she was *inside* the barn—as a black cow lurks in the doorway behind her with lugubrious eyes.

*Holland*, my brain spits out, unbidden. *The Netherlands. Lowest elevation in Europe. Dikes. Tulip mania. Amsterdam. Red-light district. Former weed capital of the free world.*

Impressive. Long-term memory intact. What about short-term? What's the last thing I can remember?

I close my eyes. Nothing comes.

*Check your body. Any injuries except to the head?*

I lift my hands as far as the wrist straps will allow and wiggle my fingers; all digits functional. I open my mouth, moving the jaw joint from side to side—check. I try to bend my legs beneath the bed sheets.

No joy. My right leg doesn't want to budge. And oh, what's this? The outline of my right foot beneath the sheets is fatter than the left. A leg cast?

My heart-rate shifts from trot to canter. I close my eyes again and try to tamp it down.

From out of the mental darkness, a voice shouts, "Okay, let's get a splint on it."

*I'm sprawled on my back in rocky dirt, looking up at converging columns of green: a trio of young palo verde trees, an ocotillo plant with spindly stems, a fat saguaro cactus with a gray-brown decay hole. Flashing red and blue lights paint the plants in a repeating pattern. The smells of gasoline and burnt rubber hang in the air. I lift my left arm to find a chunk of dead cholla cactus stuck to it, a hundred of its barbs impaling my flesh like fish hooks.*

*A man and a woman crouch beside me. Blue polo shirts, medical insignias, earnest eyes. A police officer, female, stands behind them, training a flashlight on my lower body. I crane my head to look around, but the male EMT says, "Don't move, sir. You've been injured. We're going to get you to a hospital just as soon as we can."*

The memory-image goes black. My eyes fly open.

Okay, okay, quick, what have I gathered? One, I've been in a car accident. *(Where was I going? Was I alone?)* Two, I am in Arizona, somewhere in the southwest quadrant. I know this because the lower left corner of the state is in the Sonoran desert, the only place in America where the big saguaro cacti grow. My gut says Arizona is not my native home, though. And yet, the names of the plant life came effortlessly to me—which tells me I'm more than a tourist.

There are two main cities in Arizona's Sonoran region, says my inner Google Map—Tucson and Phoenix. Odds are, I am in or near one of those two cities. I mentally reel off the names of the towns around Phoenix. Chandler, Gilbert, Mesa, Scottsdale... Scottsdale feels "hot." *Scottsdale, Scottsdale.* A street lined with boutique-type shops. My inner eye homes in on a storefront, a coffee place starting with "Ca—." Before the image can resolve itself, my mind springs back in retreat, like a hand burned by a stove.

The milkmaid in the painting *grins* at me in a conspiratorial way. That's not the expression she was wearing before, damn it. What is wrong with me? I shake my head to clear the fog. Everything feels swimmy.

Could be the anesthesia, still wearing off. Or some other drug.

*Focus.* What day of the week is it? Nothing comes. Not even a specific *year* jumps to mind.

*Check for time-and-place clues.* No calendars or clocks on the walls—only beige-gray power cords and outlets. A vase of flowers sitting on a shelf has a gift tag on it. From whom? That might be the log that breaks the jam. But it's too far away. A whiteboard near the door reads, "Tues-Wed," with "Ruth" and "LaTisha" below it—nurses' names?

*Tues-Wed.* So is today Tuesday or Wednesday?

Probably should nail down the year first. The *decade.*

My hands, what do they tell me? Age spots, skin a bit crepey. I'm not in my salad days, that's for sure. A wedding ring, shaped like the branch of a tree, adorns my left hand. A vision of a woman's hand appears next to mine, wearing a similar ring. The shadow of a third hand creeps across our two. Again my mind springs away, as if afraid of being burned.

A knowing hits me. The reason I'm having trouble recalling personal data is not that I *can't* remember, it's that I don't *want* to. Some part of me—a major shareholder, I think—is terrified of acquiring the knowledge of who I am.

I glance up at the Dutch milkmaid. She grins her agreement in that leering, conspiratorial way. And holy shit, did she just wink at me? Not possible. But my heart revs anyway.

The nurse re-enters my room holding a giant pink plastic mug with a bent straw sticking out the top. Thirst hits me like a flamethrower.

"Here, let me sit you up," she says. The head of the bed angles forward, lifting me to a sitting position. The nurse holds the straw up to my lips. I pull in a mouthful of water.

It tastes like peace, love, and understanding.

"Better?"

"Beh-ah."

She allows me another drink, then pulls the mug away as if I'm trying to steal it and sets it near the flowers.

Suddenly, apropos of nothing, her eyes go wide, and she shouts, "Now if you don't calm down, Mr. Greenbird, I'm going to have to *calm* you down!"

I haven't moved or said a word, and my wrists are hog-tied to the bed.

"I *said*, calm down!" she repeats, pulling a syringe from her scrubs pocket. *What the hell is that for?* Without explanation, she throws her weight across my body as if to pin me down and slides the needle into my left arm, depressing the plunger.

What the fuck?

She rises, brushes herself off, deposits the used syringe into the sharps disposal unit on the wall, then sashays toward the door as if nothing has happened.

"All right, then, Mr. Greenbird..." She turns to me before she leaves. "The doctor will be in to kill you in a few."

# Chapter 2

My inner ear is scrambling its output signals, that's the explanation. "The doctor will be in to *see* you in a few" is undoubtedly what the nurse said. Small comfort there—the prospect of a damaged brain causes a finger of ice to trace my spine.

I'm anxious to hear the doctor's report—diagnosis, prognosis, treatment plan. What did the nurse mean by "in a few"? Is the doctor coming in a few *minutes*? A few *hours*?

I barely have time to entertain the question when drowsiness mugs me from within. My consciousness drops like an elevator weight. This isn't normal sleepiness. That injection the nurse gave me, it must have been a sedative or hypnotic. Why? I was being a good little patient. What drug is it? She gave it to me intramusc...

. . .

I awake in almost total darkness. It feels wrong, but I can't say why. How long have I been asleep/unconscious?

The sound of drumming has stirred me from sleep. A hand-held skin drum, not far away, pounds a *one*-two-three-four rhythm. It's been going on for some time, I think.

The drumbeats reverberate as if trapped in a long, narrow space.

A hallway.

I try to sit up, only to discover—*re*discover—that my hands are strapped down. And then I recall: *hospital*. Damn. Fuck. Piss.

Wait, though. Then the sound of a skin drum makes no sense. Nor does the near-total darkness. With all the LED-lit gadgetry and ambient light in a hospital, it's impossible to blacken a patient's room to this extent.

So that means what? My bed's been moved to a new location? Is that why I was drugged? My chest tightens. I force myself to breathe from the diaphragm. Belly in, belly out. *There's no reason to panic.* Unless, of course, there *is*.

*One*-two-three-four goes the drum.

Three glowing skeletons shuffle into the blackness of my room—yes, they do—moving to the beat. They stand in a semicircle at the foot of my bed.

I try to shout, but my throat closes up.

The three figures are naked humans, smeared with luminous white body paint in skeletal designs. (The designs resemble those of the Chimbu tribesmen of New Guinea—why I know this, I can't say.) Their eyes and nose-holes are black and empty, their painted cheekbones sharp and white. Grinning mouths, huge and toothy, wrap halfway around their heads.

My flesh wants to jump off my body.

The three glowing figures begin to dance to the drumbeat, which now shifts to a more complex pattern. They shimmy their shoulders in a loose-jointed way and hop from side to side in a half-crouching posture. The leftmost one has swaying breasts beneath her rib-bone paint; the other two are male, one tall and beefy, one *very* tall and thin.

As the dancers move, wavy after-traces of light linger in the air behind them, creating their own ghostly dance-show. I must be hallucinating that effect.

News flash: I'm hallucinating the whole thing.

When the rhythm hits a climactic beat, the dancers thrust their faces at me in unison, eyes wide and real mouths grinning.

Again I try to scream, again my voice is choked off—like trying to scream in a dream.

That is what's happening here, of course. I'm dreaming. The nurse gave me a powerful sedative-hypnotic, and now I'm experiencing "vivid and disturbing dreams," a side effect of many psychoactive medications.

But no. As I pull against the wrist straps, the foam lining of the cuffs digs into the pores of my skin. I can sense the pressure of the bandages on my head and feel individual drops of perspiration trickling down the hairline of my neck.

These sensory details tell me I am fully awake.

Adrenaline courses through me, electrifying the nerves in my arms and legs.

A chant arises from the dancers.

*Loo-KA-ta LEE-da-ma*

*Loo-KA-ta LEE-da-ma*

*Loo-KA-ta LEE-da-ma*

The dancers move with a fluid, yet jerky, syncopation that reminds me of those creepy black-and-white cartoons from the Betty Boop era. Then they literally *turn into* old cartoon characters. I shake my head, and they turn "real" again. Drugs are definitely involved here. The three figures point at me in a mocking way.

*Loo-KA-ta LEE-da-ma*

*Loo-KA-ta LEE-da-ma*

The chanted syllables resolve into recognizable words: *Look at the little man.* That's what the dancers are saying.

They sing and point at me. *Look at the little man.* The male dancer in the middle, the tallest and thinnest of the three, pulls an object from behind his back and shakes it in front of me. It is a tiny human form, ten inches from head to toe, also painted like a glowing skeleton. It wiggles in a rubbery way.

A wave of nausea hits me. God! The foul thing is a human fetus—in its fifth or sixth month. Once again, I try to scream but can't find my voice. From the fluid way the small body jiggles, it must be... recently deceased.

"Little man" refers to the fetus then, not me? I don't want to look at it but can't turn my eyes away. Its skull seems weirdly small. Before I can process what that implies, one of its legs contracts. Shit. It isn't dead.

*Look at the little man!* the dancers shout in crescendo. The lead male tosses the fetus, face-down, onto my blanketed body, and then the three dancers exit the room in a wordless conga line. The drumbeat ceases and the footsteps scurry away.

Blackness and silence resume. The only light in the room is from the glow of the skeletal paint on the tiny body's back.

The ten-inch body does an appalling thing; it leaps across my blanketed torso with powerful legs. I pull back in revulsion. What the hell? The body leaps again. Ah, wait. Its hump-backed shape reveals it is not a human fetus after all. It is a frog. A huge bullfrog with its underside and topside painted in a Chimbu skeletal design. For some reason, this realization fills me with greater horror than the notion that a live human fetus was tossed onto my bed.

The sweat on my back turns to sleet. I find my voice and let out a full-throated scream. Its sound waves bounce off the walls and echo down the hall.

I scream again. And again. And again.

•        •        •

I awake to find the room brightly lit again. The monitor beside my bed is beeping like an alarm clock. The nurse from yesterday—or was it earlier today?—barrels in, making a beeline for the monitor.

"People were in my room!" I shout at her, surprised to find my mouth fully operational.

She ignores me and studies the monitor with a cinched face. She makes an adjustment to a wired lead stuck to my chest. The beeping stops. Her face relaxes. She checks a needle and tube taped to my forearm. An IV drip?

"People were in my room," I repeat. The acquisition of speech is a welcome step in the evolution of *homo hospitalis.*

"Lots of people have been in your room, honey child. We do our best not to let patients croak while they're in our custody."

*Custody? Odd choice of words. Or am I just being paranoid?*

"These people weren't nurses or doctors. They were painted like skeletons. They were dancing. The room was pitch dark. They threw a live frog onto my bed."

She tosses her head back with a high cackle, her shoulders bouncing up and down. "You, my friend, were experiencing what we in the medical profession call... *a dream.*"

"No, I thought so too. But it wasn't. I tested my senses."

"Well, test 'em again. Because I ain't seen no live amphibians jumpin' around in here—unless you count Mr. Yancy in three-eighteen. Your brain is playing tricks on you, sweetie. As the doctor explained, you've sustained a boo-boo to the headbone."

"I haven't seen the doctor yet."

She stares at me, the back of her wrist curled against her hip. "Dr. Mukherjee was in to see you last evening. Moon-faced fella. Lazy eye. He sat with you for about ten minutes. Don't you remember? You asked him several questions."

"That must have been another patient."

"Yeah, you're probably right. We don't keep records or nothin'; too much hassle. It was *you*, Mr. Greenbird. Are you honestly telling me you have no memory of that conversation? Because that would be clinically significant."

"I have no memory because it didn't happen. I fell asleep a few minutes after you left... because *you drugged me with something!*"

"Are you getting agitated on me again, Mr. Greenbird?" Her hand moves toward the syringe sticking out of her pocket.

"My name is not Greenbird! And what do you mean, 'again'?"

"Are we going to have to invite *him* in?"

She nods in the direction of the hallway.

I notice, for the first time, a uniformed pant leg and black shoe just outside my door. Someone sitting in a chair. Someone of the constabulary persuasion, it appears. A cop.

"You've had a twenty-four-hour guard on you ever since you checked in to this two-star establishment."

"Why?"

"Not my place to say. Someone will be in to explain it to you."

"Who? What's going on?"

"Patience, Mr. Greenbird, patience. Meantime, fill out your meal slip." A food checklist and pencil lie on the tray table in front of me—a pencil I clearly can't use with my wrists strapped down. "Don't order the chicken pie unless you enjoy the taste of take-out coffee trays."

She heads toward the door. Before leaving, she tosses a glance at the guard near the door. "I don't think *he* would have let a trio of dancing skeletons into your room."

She patters off down the hall.

A few seconds later, it hits me. I never mentioned there were *three* dancers in my room.

I'm certain of it.

Nearly certain.

13

# Chapter 3

"Greenbird."

The silhouette of a man fills the doorframe. From the cut of his hair and the fit of his suit, I can deduce his profession. He doesn't leave me guessing.

"I'm Detective Pratt of the Carefree Police."

*And I'm Doctor Wahoo of the Lighthearted Proctologists.* Wait, he's not joking. He's referring to the *town* of Carefree. Carefree, Arizona. Near Scottsdale.

"May I come in?" Not awaiting my answer, he steps into the harsh fluorescent lighting of the room. He's a bearish man, six-one, two-fifty, with a short, dark-brown beard that probably took him all of four minutes to grow. He sports a jarringly white rack of teeth and a pair of thick, rose-framed glasses that make his eyes look googly. Something tells me the effect is intentional. "The nursing staff tells me you're well enough to talk."

*Well enough to talk? What clinical criteria do they use around here?*

"Talk about what?"

"I think you know the answer to that."

"I... don't." I really don't.

"We can play this any way you like, Greenbird. I have all day—I'm on salary—and *you're* not going anywhere. So...?"

"First things first, sir. My name is not Greenbird."

"First things first, *sir.* I have your wallet." He holds up a folded brown wallet, hefts it like a pound of meat. "With all your IDs in it."

My pulse does a two-step. "May I see it, please?"

"In due time, Mr. Greenbird, in due time."

He spots a padded armchair with a wooden frame, drags it to the bedside with an unnecessarily loud screech, and sits. He slips the wallet into the pocket of his suit.

"The more cooperative you are with me," he says, folding his hands in an affectation of courtesy, "the more cooperative I can be with you."

"Officer..."

"Detective," he corrects.

"Detective... How can I cooperate with you if I'm not even the man you think I am?"

"So that's gonna be your play here? Trot out the *gringo loco* card?"

"It's not a play. My name really is not Gree—"

"PIG-FUCKER!" he shouts, his head twisting sharply to the right. My body jumps off the mattress in shock. Jesus. What have I done to push this guy from zero to sixty in one second?

"You'll have to excuse me," he says with a flash of his neon teeth, "I have a neurological condition. It causes these compulsive verbal... *tics*."

"Tourette's?" I tender.

"The very thing. It's gotten some media buzz in recent years. Evidently, comedians find it amusing. But hey, at least the public awareness has allowed me to keep my job. Now I've got a disability instead of just being a crazy asshole. Right?"

He stares at me with a glint of *something* in his lens-distorted eyes. Amusement? Defiance? I can't tell if he's messing with me.

I shrug, noncommittal.

"So let's get down to it, Mr. Greenbird." He draws a whistling breath through his nose. "Are you aware you were injured while fleeing the scene of a crime?"

His words hit me like a sack of dimes. They can't be true.

Or can they? The desert scene with the EMTs flashes in my mind. A police pursuit gone wrong?

"Mr. Greenbird? Did you hear my question?"

15

A self-protective impulse arises from some unknown place. "If there was a crime," I say, "why aren't you reading me my..." The word dangles just out of reach. "*Miranda* rights?"

"ASS COCK!" he snaps, jerking his head as before. I flinch on the bed again. He eyeballs me for a moment, then carries on. "You haven't been 'Mirandized' because you're not under arrest. You're free to walk out of here anytime you choose."

I laugh and point my chin toward my body. "Even if my leg weren't broken, my wrists are strapped down and there's a guard outside my door. Which means I'm being detained involuntarily. Which *means* that regardless of whether I've been formally arrested or not, I'm entitled to hear my rights." I seem to have some literacy in this area of the law; who knew?

"You want to hear your Mirandy-pandas, Mr. Greenbird? Okay: You have the right to remain smiling. Anything you say cannonball be used against you in a corner lawn. You have the right to an old gurney. If you cannot applaud one, one will be divided for you. Happy?"

He stares at me with that defiant glint. What just happened here? My brain scrambles for traction. The skeletons are dancing again.

"The only real question before us," he says, "is are you going to lawyer up or are you and me going to have a chitty-chat-chat?"

The truth is, I wouldn't have the remotest notion how to hire a lawyer right now. Or what to say to one if I did. And besides, I really want—*need*—to know what cards Pratt has up his sleeve. Crazy as he might be. Or as *I* might be, perhaps.

"No lawyer for now," I say.

He nods formally—almost a bow—and leans back in his chair, interlacing his hands.

I wait for him to talk, but no, *he's* waiting for *me*.

"Okay... I remember an accident scene. In the desert. EMTs trying to get me into an ambulance. One of them said I was hurt. That's all I remember."

"So you recall being in a car accident?"

"The *after* part, not the accident itself. Lying on the ground. Red and blue lights, the smell of gas."

"Fascinating, Mr. Greenbird. A fictional *tour de force*. Five stars, couldn't put it down."

"Why are you saying that?"

"Because... SHIT MY FUCK!" Again his head twists spastically. Again I startle. He presses his hands on his thighs as if trying to contain his own wild energies. "*Because...* you were injured on a flight of stairs inside a residential property."

"What?" The good times keep rolling.

"A police officer—I probably shouldn't be telling you this part—*tackled* you when you refused his order to stop. You landed badly, fell down some stairs, hit the stone tile with your head. Hence the leg-break and the noggin blow. Do you know a Dr. Zachariah Fenton?"

I stare at him dumbly.

"Really, Greenbird? You're going to make me work for every inch of this?"

He examines my face and seems to notice something—or *lack* of something—in my eyes that softens his edge. "Okay, listen. Maybe you do have some brain trauma, maybe that's legit. So I'll spoon-feed you some of this. You tell me when bells start to ting-a-ling. Agreed?"

I toss my hand; sure, whatever.

"Friday evening, December eleventh, you and several other 'gentlemen' of local standing attended a private party at the home of one Zachariah Fenton, MD, in the Black Mountain Foothills. Two young ladies of... *negotiable affections* were on hand. An esteemed colleague of yours decided it would be 'funny' to engage one of them in a party game she wasn't interested in playing. She made her objections known. Her objections were overruled. Things took a decidedly... *unfunny* turn. Ting-a-ling?"

My stomach sours, and my pulse quickens.

"One of the young ladies dialed 911 on her cell. When the police arrived unannounced, there was a scattering of middle-aged white men, not unlike when a nest of mice is uncovered beneath a rotting sofa cushion."

I'm on the verge of panic and have no idea why. I don't remember any party—and I wouldn't have participated in the kind of scene Pratt described; I *know* it. So why the pang in my gut? My body wants to go into flight mode.

"Your injuries required medical attention, and you were brought here under police escort. There was no vehicular incident."

*No. That's not how it happened.* Absolutely not. I trawl my memory for details. My need to remember exactly how I ended up in this half-assed hospital takes on burning urgency. I replay the car accident scene in my mind, panning it for gold I can use.

"My arm!" I point to my left triceps. "Check my arm."

Pratt stares at me with all the pathos of a doorstop.

"Roll up my sleeve. You'll see marks. From a cholla burr that got stuck in my arm."

Pratt remains planted.

"Detective, please! Check it out."

He sighs, pries his ample ass out of his seat, and walks around the bed. I hold my breath as he lifts the sleeve of my cowboy-themed johnny. Relief washes over me: angry welts dot my upper arm, the skin stained yellow from topical antiseptic.

"So you were attacked by a rogue cholla bush at some point. You and everybody else who spends time in this godforsaken valley. It proves exactly fuck."

He's right, of course, from a prosecutorial viewpoint. But it proves something *to me*. It proves my memory of the accident scene in the desert is not imagined.

"Is it possible," I ask, "that *two* patients were brought in at the same time, and we got mixed up somehow?"

"Absolutely. If this was an Adam Sandler flick. I'm going to show you something, Greenbird. After you view it, I'm going to do-si-do out that door and grab some lunch. When I come back, it is my sincere hope that you're in a more talkative mood. Bueno?"

I shrug *okay*. I'm eager to see whatever card he's about to play.

He slips a finger into the wallet he claims is mine and pulls out an ID card. An Arizona state driver's license. He holds it in front of me.

My bowels clench.

That face. Fifties, Caucasian, green eyes, trim white beard, eighty-dollar haircut, tanned skin. Tumblers spin in my mind.

"Handsome dude, right? So? Ting-a-ling?"

I refuse to accept what my body already knows. Pratt pulls out his phone, puts it in mirror mode, and holds it up for me to see.

Fuck a duck. Except for the bandaged head, the face on the phone screen is identical to the one in the ID photo. Me.

Pratt holds up the driver's license again:

**Cornelius T. Greenbird**
**12 Sunrise Rd.**
**Crystal Rock, AZ 85753**

No. No-no.

"What the hell *is* this?" My voice goes high with panic. "*Cornelius?* Seriously? Don't you think I would remember running around the planet with a fucking handle like *Cornelius?*"

My words don't ring convincingly, even to me.

"I'm counting on your memory returning," he says, "*before* I lose my patience. As promised, Mr. Greenbird—Cornelius—I will leave you with your thoughts and return a few hours hence."

He slips the driver's license back into the wallet.

As he heads for the door, his back toward me, he blares out, "FUCK A CORPSE," then stops, turns to me with that I-dare-you-to-say-something gleam in his eye, and marches off.

. . .

Seeing my face on that phone has unleashed a torrent of memory fragments that churn and flash in my mind but refuse to stay put long enough to fix on. Every time the jigsaw pieces start to assemble into something cohesive, they fly apart again.

Cornelius Greenbird. Crystal Rock, Arizona.

Horseshit.

I've never even *heard* of that town. *Maybe* it's near Tucson, but I couldn't swear to it. And yet that was *my face* on the license. Looking so smug—like old Corny Greenbird was the cock of Crystal Rock.

The presence of a police guard outside my door—a guard who never seems to stretch or take a leak, by the way—is consistent with either version of events, the accident or the house party. But the accident is the version *I remember*.

At the same time, that party scene Pratt described has wormed its way into my conscience. I have no specific memory of it, but it *feels* sickly resonant.

It's as if two different stories—two separate versions of me—were gaining equal steam, like trains on parallel tracks. How could that be? My mind spins like a stripped gear.

And the frog thing. That punched me harder than anything else. That tapped into a memory that's running on a separate track altogether; a deeper, older, and more dangerous track.

And now something comes through on yet another track—faintly at first but then drawing more of my awareness. A piece of instrumental music. Playing for real, on the hospital sound system. A fiddle and a... folk harp? My gut recognizes the old Celtic tune before my conscious mind does. I want to bathe in its melancholic strains. This is the first time my *heart* has stirred since my arrival here; the first emotion I've felt other than terror and confusion.

Lyrics to the tune seep out of some forgotten vault in my mind. I sing them aloud—in a passable baritone—as the verse comes around.

*I wish I was in Carrickfergus*
*Only for nights in Ballygrand*
*I would swim over the deepest ocean*
*The deepest ocean, to be by your side*

Tears rush to my eyes. It's a sad song, yes, but this feeling is personal. A voice from my memory vault sings the chorus. *But the sea is wide and I can't swim over.* A female voice. High and lilting and achingly lovely, if a tad rough-edged. A recording artist? No. I *know* this singer. I know her and I love her. I love this singer so much.

Emmy. Em.

*My* Em.

Emmy Powers. My daughter.

My heart floods with light. Emmy's face appears, glowing, in my mind. That toying half-smile of hers. That incandescent blonde hair with strawberry highlights you can spot in a stadium crowd. Those rainforest eyes that change like the weather.

"Carrickfergus" is her favorite song, and she sings it like an angel.

Emmy Powers. Just the knowledge that she exists in this world makes all things bright and possible. The jigsaw pieces click into place. Everything comes rushing back at once.

Emily R. Powers. Daughter of Oliver and Hannah Powers, 23 Javelina Drive, Fountain Hills, Arizona.

Oliver Powers, that's who I am.

Oliver Powers, MD.

Psychiatrist. Fifty-five years old.

Preferred nickname, Liv. Not Ollie, because no.

I live in Fountain Hills and have an office in Scottsdale. Old Town. I share the building with a dental cosmetician, a gem wholesaler, and a quantum energy healer (no, I have no idea either). That coffee place I couldn't get a bead on? Cartel Coffee Lab. It's where I get my morning coffee every day. My office is a minute's walk away.

Dr. Oliver Powers, not Cornelius Effing Greenbird.

My "system reboot" has kicked in at last. I'm back in business.

Some sort of identity-theft scenario has taken place. Someone must have hacked into the Motor Vehicle Division's computer system and stolen my license photo, changed the name and address to his own...

But no. What good would *my face* on a driver's license do someone else?

And why are the police so certain I attended a house party where dirty deeds went down? And why do people around me keep acting like characters in a David Lynch film? And what about the skeletal dance crew and disappearing frog?

These things still point to brain trauma. I collapse into my pillow.

At least I know who I am, though. Yes. That's huge. Now I only need to convince *them*. And get these damn straps off my wrists and start angling for a discharge. Hallelujah.

The song on the sound system winds to a close. I imbibe its waning measures, hearing Emmy's voice sing the ending words, *"come all ye young men and lay me down."* As the final fiddle note fades away, the tune restarts—in my mind only. This time, though, it's played on a solo bagpipe.

A shadow moves across my heart.

The drone of the pipes feels like a memory—a memory I've buried hastily, in a shallow grave. The notes swell and fade, blown by the wind. An image crystalizes in my mind: a kilted piper standing on a grassy hillock.

A cold fog of dread envelops me.

My inner camera turns away from the lone piper and dollies across the fresh-cut grass in the opposite direction. "The camera" closes in on a scene my body wants to reject like cancer.

A cluster of people, dressed in muted colors, stand on a second hill, beneath the canopy of an oak with orange-turning leaves. A woman with iron-gray hair, angular cheekbones, and black-rimmed glasses—my wife, Hannah—sobs unreservedly, her nose raw and wet. She reaches into her shoulder bag and takes out a clay jar decorated with Hopi designs. She opens the jar and upends it, releasing a gray-tan powder into the wind. The powder circles once in the swirling air and then whips in a streamer toward the piper on the other knoll, thirty feet away.

No, please, no.

The powder is Emmy's ashes. My daughter is dead.

# Chapter 4

*Please let it be a bad dream. Please. Please. Please.*

Listen to me. To whom am I "praying"? Why?

I am Oliver Powers, after all. Oliver Powers, MD, author of *Spiritual Delusion: Man's Invention of Meaning in a Lonely Universe.* Oliver Powers, debunker of faith healers and New Age gurus. Oliver Powers, champion of brain chemistry and rational thought. Oliver Powers, psychopharmacologist, consultant on troublesome cases of DRC— delusions with religious content—and deprogrammer of cult victims.

And yet, behold! When brought to my knees emotionally, I, too, clutch my prayer beads like a child in the dark. *Help me. Save me. Make the bad thing go away.*

Pathetic.

Needless to say, my "prayer" goes for naught. My daughter is dead. Game, set, match. That fact is as unyielding as the nylon straps yoking me to the bed.

How I wish—not for the first time in my life—I could be one of the lucky ones. The believers. The blissfully deluded majority who are able to sell themselves on the fiction that life has a grander purpose, that there is a loving, benevolent intelligence watching over us, that conscious existence is eternal. The lucky ones, after all, are happier and healthier for their delusion. Clinical studies stubbornly prove this. Spiritual believers have less anxiety, lower suicide rates, better heart health, greater longevity...

And yet, delusion is delusion, regardless of its health benefits. My mind is incapable of clinging to a fantasy it knows to be patently false. That is my curse.

Fact: Em hasn't "transitioned to the other side." She is dead. Extinguished. As lifeless as an empty soda can. And I would toss myself into a blazing furnace to change that fact.

Emmy. Oh, Emmy.

Thoughts of my daughter flood my mind, and this time I don't try to hold them back.

*Friends and family sometimes referred to her as a "troubled soul." Hannah, my wife, would unfailingly correct them: "She is a searching soul in a troubled world."*

*Emmy didn't start out troubled, that's for sure. She was radiant from the moment her umbilical was cut. Hannah claimed all Emmy had to do was enter a room and the energy shifted to a higher frequency. I wouldn't go that far, but I do remember once, when she was eight or nine, watching her brewing a cup of tea for Hannah, who was ill. I swear I could see a physical glow, almost a halo, around her head.*

*Emmy breezed through elementary and middle school, bypassing all the usual childhood drama. She loved all kids equally and handled bullies with an equanimity world leaders could emulate. She had a bell-like singing voice and sang her way through every bath and homework session. She sketched and painted endlessly and wrote poetry bursting with insight. Hannah said she came to Earth to bring lost grace back to humanity. That's a Hannah thing, but still.*

*As light as she was, though, Em had an equally dark side, which began to emerge in high school. She would lapse into black moods that could last for days on end and sucked the joy out of everyone around her. One time she locked herself in her room for over thirty-six hours with bath towels hung over the window shades to block out every stray ray of light. Drugs came into play, and there were suspicions of self-injury.*

*As a psychiatrist, it was hard not to leap to worries of a bipolar condition, but Hannah forbade any attempts on my part to diagnose our daughter. She insisted Emmy's struggles were of an "existential" nature. (She used the term "spiritual" when talking to others but not to me.)*

*As hard as it was not to diagnose Em's mood swings, it was equally hard not to take them personally. Why? Because I bore the usual brunt of her resentment and disillusionment. It was as if I was perpetually letting her down on levels I couldn't begin to understand. Most of the big choices she made in her life felt like calculated acts of rebellion against me.*

*In college, she elected to major in Religious Studies, a decision she must have known would set my teeth on edge, especially at tuition-check-writing time. When one day I had the audacity to question her educational goals, she responded by quitting school. She then fell into an itinerant, almost homeless, lifestyle, in which she would drift into a new living situation every six or eight months, always in pursuit of some new spiritual or quasi-spiritual path—Nichiren Buddhism, Reiki healing, past-life regression... She even experimented with "plant spirit medicine"—i.e., hallucinogens made from South American plants. In between life-chapters, she would often come back home, for a month or several, to reconnect with Hannah and the cats, to belittle my life choices, and, of course, to hit me up for money.*

Today, I would give up every literal dime I owned so she could go study feline feng-shui or whatever struck her loony fancy, just to have her back on this steaming green orb for one day.

I feel my mind being dragged across broken glass, back to that awful day in September—it must have been about three months ago, if Pratt's December eleventh date was accurate—when Hannah's life and mine took the black left turn no parent's life should take.

. . . .

*"I'm not giving her four thousand dollars to study fucking shamanism!" I shouted. "Correction: 'female-empowerment shamanism.' Mustn't forget that all-important qualifier!"*

*Hannah and I almost never fight, but on this day we were making an exception.*

*"Why does this subject enrage you so much?" she countered, matching my volume. "Look at you. You're turning red, for God's sake. It's not as if she wants to study... bomb-making... or money-laundering or..."*

*"At least there's work in those fields. Shamanism! If it's such a practical career choice, let her go down to Wells Fargo and take out a small business loan."*

*"Come on, you were paying more than that for each of her courses at Merrimack."*

*"Don't remind me! Money down the toilet. I'm sorry, Hannah, but this time I draw the line."*

*"Why? Why? It's not as if we don't have the money."*

*"That's not the point. Are we ever going to stop subsidizing her 'journeys into expanded selfhood' and ask our daughter to be a functioning fucking income-earning adult?"*

*"She's an unconventional learner... with unconventional goals."*

*"I'll tell you what her goal is."*

*"Don't start, Liv! Don't even start! Her life's ambition is what? To make you miserable? Every morning when she wakes up, she doesn't think, 'What would make me happy?' she thinks, 'What can I do to waterboard my father's heart today?' You're such a goddamn narcissist."*

*"Don't use words that have actual clinical meaning. You'll hurt yourself."*

*"Oh, fuck you, asshole."*

*"No, fuck you."*

*We stared at each other in charged silence. We had both stepped out of bounds. Way out.*

*"Is she in the Dollhouse?" I asked, trying for a conciliatory tone.*

*The Dollhouse is the name Em came up with for the little outbuilding behind our house, which we converted from a pool-house to guest quarters. Over the years, when Emmy would come visit us in Fountain Hills, her request to stay in the Dollhouse rather than the main house was our cue that her stay was going to be an extended one. During such stays, she would sometimes pay us a nominal fee we laughably called "rent."*

*"I don't know," said Hannah, tight-jawed, in response to my question. "Is the Volvo in the drive?"*

*I peered out the window and saw the blue XC60 (ours) that Emmy used whenever she stayed with us, parked in the shade of the cottonwood tree out back.*

*I started for the door.*

*"Where are you going?"*

*"To talk to her." I stepped out into the deepening dusk. "Just to talk."*

*Hannah followed. "You and I are not done talking yet. Oliver, stop! I don't want you speaking to her until you've detoxified and we've agreed on how we're going to handle this."*

*Ignoring her, I approached the Dollhouse. No lights on inside. A bit odd, given the lateness of the hour, but Emmy was probably meditating or napping.*

*I knocked. No response. I knocked again, louder and longer. Silence. An empty kind of silence, though. It was then we had our first inkling of something amiss. I tried the knob. Locked.*

*Emmy never locked her door when she was home. Hannah shot me a tense glance.*

*She trotted back to the house and returned with our spare Dollhouse key. We opened the door and announced ourselves. Nothing.*

*No, we did not find the body of our daughter sprawled in a pool of blood. What we did find was the little studio apartment tidied up and cleaned as if a hotel maid had just finished her rounds. Propped against the dresser mirror was an envelope made of artisan paper.*

*Hannah tore it open and read aloud, "Mom and Dad, thanks for letting me stay and for everything. I know I don't always make things easy for you. I'm sorry we didn't get a chance to go out to breakfast and have that talk, Dad. I won't be seeing you guys for a while. It's nothing you did. It's all on me. I love you big time. Bye."*

*The words struck alarm in my chest, though I didn't know why. It was nothing new for Em to leave suddenly. But I knew in my marrow I had seen my daughter for the last time.*

· · ·

Eleven days later, I was in session with a patient when the call came in. The instant I saw "Wolfeboro Police Department" on the caller ID, my blood froze. Wolfeboro, New Hampshire was Emmy's East Coast home base.

I knew exactly what the voicemail would say before I pressed play.

I want to curl up on my side now, cover my head with a pillow, and sleep for a long, long time. Yes, I know who I am, and it's the last person on Earth I want to be. I no longer have any interest in proving my identity to anyone. I don't want to be Oliver Powers.

I'd rather be Cornelius Cocksure Greenbird. Hell, maybe I'll give *his* life a spin, see where it takes me. Everyone believes I'm him anyway.

But what about Hannah?

Oh. Hannah.

A shudder rocks my bones as I think about how I've left my wife out to dry since that blighted September day.

In the immediate aftermath of Em's death, I did a passing imitation of a decent husband. I held Hannah's hand as we planned the memorial service, as we decided it should take place in New England, where Emmy was raised and where she died in a mangled automobile. I put on a show of strength as we drove around our old haunts to choose the location—a favorite hillside of Emmy's in Wolfeboro, overlooking Lake Winnipesaukee.

But when we returned to Arizona after the funeral, I checked out. Mentally and emotionally.

I tried to work, but couldn't. So I took a leave of absence, and my business partner, Abe, graciously agreed to babysit my caseload. I began spending my days hiking in the desert mountains and going for long drives, my evenings getting drunk in Scottsdale bars—an unwise choice on so many levels.

My behavior became more and more reckless—mouthing off to strangers, driving drunk, jogging heedlessly on narrow mountain trails where the slightest slip of the foot would send me plunging me a hundred yards onto sharp rocks. As a shrink, I knew exactly what I was up to, but that didn't seem to deter me.

My leave of absence stretched on into November. And then, when Thanksgiving was drawing near, Hannah received an invitation from her sister in Gilbert to join her family for the holiday. Hannah and I were in no shape to host a feast, and since no one else wanted us—and Emmy's ghost—at their table, we accepted the invite.

I remember, the day before the holiday, setting out on a mission to Whole Foods to pick up a few items to bring, and then, seemingly the next minute, driving on the Apache Trail, a scenic dirt road in the Superstition Mountains about fifty miles in the opposite direction. That's the last thing I recall.

The Apache Trail. I don't know why I drove there.

I don't remember Thanksgiving. I don't know what I've been doing since.

But I suspect drinking and driving may have landed me here.

I look down at my wedding ring. Hannah. Oh God, Hannah. My breathing accelerates. Does she know I'm in the hospital?

Doubtful, since everyone here thinks I'm Cornelius Greenbird.

What must she be thinking? Am I officially a missing person? Does she know I've been injured? If so, does she even care?

How could I have abandoned her as I did? How could I have been so selfish? A truth springs out at me like strangler's hands: my marriage, which was already on life support, is now in critical condition. My only hope of saving it, if I'm not already too late, is to get out of this place *yesterday*.

That's what I must do, then. I must sell the Oliver Powers story—foul as it may taste—to Pratt and the hospital staff. And I must do it *now*.

For Hannah, if not for myself.

A charge of fresh energy fires me up.

# Chapter 5

"Mr. Greenbird! You don't look happy to see me."

The truth is, I'm overjoyed to see Pratt. He is my ticket out of here. I hope. "Come in, Detective."

"Oh, I was planning to, but thanks for the invite."

Pratt drags the armchair noisily to the bed, plants himself in it.

I need to play this artfully. About an hour ago, I tried to convince my favorite nurse—her name is indeed LaTisha as the whiteboard suggested—that Oliver Powers was my true identity. It did not, shall we say, "go well." She introduced the syringe to the conversation, and I backed down. So I can't afford to blow my chance with Pratt. He's going to be a tough sell, though.

"So, have you had the opportunity to reflect, Mr. G.?"

"I have, Detective, and you'll be glad to know I'm thinking much more clearly now. Memories have been flooding back in a veritable deluge."

"Funny thing, memories."

"Listen, Detective, I'll spare us both the tiresome feinting and jabbing. I'm prepared to tell you everything that happened on Friday night." A bald-faced lie, of course. "I'm prepared to give up names, addresses..."

"That's excellent news, Mr. Greenbird. I was hoping you'd see the light... now that the light has seen *you*, so to speak." He laughs, his teeth shining like a rack of knives.

"May I ask you a favor, though?" I say.

"No law against asking."

"I'm flying solo here, no lawyer, and I am about to massively incriminate myself. So before I take that plunge, I'd like you to do something small for me."

I brace myself for one of his Tourette's outbursts. It doesn't come. He folds his arms and arches a brow.

"I would like you to take out your phone."

He waits a five-count—dominance move—then sighs and extracts his phone from his pocket. "And...?"

"Go to Amazon, please." My author page on Amazon has a good picture and bio of me.

Pratt sighs, taps his thick fingers around the screen, waits for the site to pop up.

"No bueno," he says. "Hospitals can be dead spots."

"There must be Wi-Fi here. Go to the nurses' station. Ask for the password."

"'Go to the nurses' station'? What are you, my wife?"

"Please, Detective."

Again I brace for a blast of obscenity. Only a ten-second staring contest ensues.

"Fine, Greenbird. I will go to the nurses' station and ask for the Wi-Fi code. Better still, I will ask to use their computer. I hate typing on these tiny fucking phones." He stands. "And what exactly is it you want me to do on Amazon? Order Santa cookies?"

"Go to the Amazon search bar and type, 'Oliver Powers, Spiritual Delusion.' A sales page for a book will come up. Click on the link to the author's page."

Pratt crunches his brow. "Why?"

"It's simpler if you just do as I say."

"I'm not in the mood for playing games." He sits again. "Not with a guy who sees dancing skeletons and can't remember his own name. Tell me what this is about first."

"Can't you just take my word for this one thing?" Evidently not. "Fine! I'll tell you." I wanted him to visit the website first, let my photo and bio do the talking. "But I need to warn you. You're not going to believe a word I say. I guarantee it. That's why I need you to promise me you'll look on Amazon, regardless."

"Pinkie fucking promise. That's a two-way street; remember *your* promise too."

"I will." There's no way to ease into this, so I take the plunge. "There's been an identity mix-up. No joke. My name is Oliver Powers. I'm a psychiatrist and author. I serve on the staff of two valley hospitals and have a private practice in Scottsdale. I've been on CNN as a subject expert a dozen times. I live in Fountain Hills. I have a wife, Hannah, and a daugh—" I catch myself, with a fresh shot of pain. "And my address is twenty-three Javelina Drive."

Again I expect a verbal explosion, but Pratt remains calm. A nurse with stringy blonde hair schleps by in the hall. He waits for her to pass.

"Is that all?" His tone betrays nothing.

"Yes... for now."

Pratt's feet remain glued to the floor. He's not buying it. I've got to do something to move him off the fence. Here goes. "I notice your Tourette's symptoms are under control now. Let me guess. You carry a little brown vial in your pocket—maybe Haldol or one of the other dopamine blockers. It works pretty well on the tics, but the side effects are a bear; the grogginess, the xerostomia—that's why I usually try prescribing a stimulant or dextroamphetamine first. You hate taking the meds, but after your little 'fuck a corpse' soliloquy, you decided it was time to reach for mother's little helper. And now the verbal compulsions have calmed, but the fog and cottonmouth have kicked in. How'd I do?"

Pratt stares at me, his face a plastic mask.

"I'll be back in ten minutes... 'Doctor Powers.'" He turns and exits.

I exhale.

After about twenty minutes, give or take a week, Pratt's footsteps approach from down the hall. They slow as they near my door. Why the hesitancy?

Pratt steps through the doorway, smiles in a grimacing way, and folds his hands formally in front of him. Do I detect a note of sheepishness?

"I was able to borrow a laptop," he says. "That Amazon site was an eye-opener, you were right. I did some additional googling, had the precinct make a few calls. It seems we have a rather unique dilemma on our hands."

"Indeed we do."

"I mean"—he shakes his head—"I could shop this one to Hulu. On one hand, we have a veritable mountain of evidence proving you are Cornelius Greenbird, who does indeed live at twelve Sunrise Road in Crystal Rock—we checked, of course—and who possesses your exact face. On the other hand, we have this Doctor Oliver Powers..."

He pauses. I count my heartbeats.

"... who doesn't fucking exist."

Gooseflesh erupts on my back and arms. Is he joking? Not by his eyes.

"Oh, there are several Doctor Oliver Powerses out there," he says, "even a couple who are shrinks. But none with an office in Scottsdale or a residence in Fountain Hills."

"Come on, Detective. That's a load of crap."

"And none who wrote a stupid fucking book about 'spiritual delusions.' So what's *your* delusion, asshole? That you're going to crazy your way out of this? Nuh-uh. So. I'll give you one last chance. Make good on your promise and tell me everything that happened last Friday evening in the Black Mountain Foothills. Or..."

"I can't tell you what I don't know!"

He sighs. "You win, Greenbird. Or rather, you lose. I am leaving now. I am heading straight to the district courthouse in Phoenix, where I will obtain a warrant for your arrest. The instant you are cleared for discharge, I will be back here to drag your ass out the door, attached to my wrist like a Six Flags day-pass. Meanwhile, I am reinstating your twenty-four-hour guard."

The guard is no longer seated outside my door. When did he leave?

"I'd say have a nice day, Greenbird, but the young lady who filed charges isn't having a very nice day."

A chill runs through me at the mention of the girl. Why the guilt I'm feeling?

Pratt makes for the door, then stops and turns to me as he did last time. "Oh, and by the way, Greenbird. I don't have Tourette's. I don't know where you got that fuckin' stupid idea."

He departs, closing the door.

Okay. That does it. The line has been drawn. Only two possibilities exist. One, I have a brain injury that is distorting my processing of reality, or two, I am being gaslighted in a deliberate and coordinated way.

My eyes zig-zag around the room, searching for something—anything—that might help me cast the deciding vote. That's when I notice the painting again. The Dutch girl is now inside the barn, naked, on all fours, in the spot where the bovine creature formerly stood. She's flashing a lascivious grin. A carved sign above her reads, "Dutch Treat."

That settles it. Someone *is* screwing with me. Why? No idea. But I need to get out of here. Escape. And I need to do so before the new guard arrives.

Not five minutes later, an opportunity presents itself.

"Knock, knock," says a reedy voice from the doorway.

A stick-thin young woman with stringy blonde hair—the one who passed in the hall—carries a tray with a covered food dish into my room. Her skin has the salubrious glow of a career meth addict's.

"Mr. Greenbird?"

"So they inform me."

As the young woman draws near, her name tag comes into view—Cassandra R., Nursing Aide. She places the food tray on my tray-table and wheels it in front of me.

"I'm going to remove your wrist straps," she says in her thin voice, "so you can eat. Before I do that, I need your assurance that you won't try to hurt yourself or, well, *me*." She giggles nervously.

"Assurance granted. I'm harmless."

Cassandra bends and tugs the strap binding my right wrist to the bed frame. The "quick-release knot"—ah yes, I remember it well from my intern days. I've had to employ it once or twice as a hospital psychiatrist too. The knot is designed so the patient can't loosen it but the staff can undo it instantly with a tug.

Cassandra removes the padded cuff from my wrist, lays the entire cuff-and-strap apparatus on the bed, then repeats the procedure on the left side.

I'm free. Technically speaking.

I stretch my arms. My back and shoulders crack in relief.

Cassandra unveils my feast with a soulless *ta-da*: breaded chicken breast (à la Sysco Foods), green beans, tater tots, canned pear halves. My stomach rumbles despite the food's heroic efforts to discourage such a response. When did I last eat?

I'm not permitted a knife, so Cassandra cuts up my chicken. As I attack the food with my plastic fork, Cassandra tidies the room and moves equipment around unnecessarily. She's making sure I can be trusted with my hands free before she leaves.

"Someone will be in to check on you shortly," she says at last, then heads off, wheeling a cart full of trays down the hall. *Good. Go feed the multitudes, Cass.*

My golden opportunity has arrived. Of course, I can't just stroll out of the room whistling "Free Bird." Not now, not at feeding time, when the halls will be swarming with staff. But maybe I can set myself up for later...

I scarf my food down in triple time, plotting my escape strategy as I eat. The plan I come up with has about a thirty percent chance of working. But thirty beats zero.

I need to move fast. If anyone enters my room in the next minute, I'm dead.

I cover my meal plate and push the tray-table aside. I tie the left-hand restraint to the bed frame, using the quick-release knot I learned in the springtime of my career. I loop the left cuff closed, but leave it loose enough for my hand to slip into easily.

Next, I tie the strap of the *right*-hand restraint to the bed and fasten the cuff around my right wrist, securing it tightly. My right hand is now bound.

With my free left hand, I switch off the bed light and lower the bed to a reclining position. I slip my left hand into its loosely preset cuff.

I lay my head on the pillow and close my eyes. If I haven't fucked up in some grand way, it should appear I'm bound by the wrists and napping my Sysco chicken away.

# Chapter 6

LaTisha's voice approaches in the hall. She's talking on a phone. "You're early, that ain't my fault... I got two more patients, then I'll be down... Play with your phone, play with your nuts, I don't care."

LaTisha is in on the gaslighting scheme, so I have no idea if she'll bite for my possum ploy. Is she even a real nurse? Who knows?

Her crepe soles squeak into my room. They stop silently beside the bed. I sense her standing, still as a predator locked on its prey, a foot from my right arm. I can *feel* her eyes sweeping me, up and down. What is she looking at? What is she thinking?

"Now, am I losing my damn mind?" she mutters at last. I can't tell if she's talking to herself or to me. "How the hell did you get roped and tied again, Mr. Mister?"

Should I reply or continue to feign sleep?

Instinct kicks in. "The nurse's aide who fed me," I answer groggily, blinking my eyes open. "She did it. Blonde. Cassidy? Catherine?"

"Cassandra? She's just supposed to do meals. She ain't qualified to do wrist restraints. Did she take you through your range-of-motion exercises before strapping you back up?"

"Yes," I groan, hoping that's the right answer.

"Hmmm." LaTisha bends over and examines the right-side knot. "Well, looks like she knows what she's doing. Didn't see *that* coming." She shifts her eyes to the left-side cuff. I hold my breath. *Don't check too closely.* "Okay then, you won't see my fine ass till Friday." LaTisha exits, leaving the door ajar. From the hall I hear, "But I certainly hope you die before then."

*Ha, ha, hilarious. I'm on to you, LaTisha.*

Over the next several minutes, voices laugh and chatter up and down the hall. Change-of-shift time. I'll wait till the activity has subsided before trying anything. Meanwhile, I scan the room for cameras. None visible.

. . .

All seems quiet on the western front.

My intuition—that mysterious inner guide I wish I had a closer partnership with—tells me now's the time to make my move.

I slip my left hand out of its pre-loosened cuff, then roll my body to the right, pull the quick-release knot on the right side, and remove the second cuff.

Success. I am free to move about the cabin.

I sit up and push the blankets off me. I swing my right leg—the one with the cast on it—off the bed. I push my body to a stand, easing my right foot onto the floor. I don't want to put any weight on it till I get a better read on my injury.

No sooner am I upright than a rush of lightheadedness hits me like a rogue wave. I wobble and lose my balance. I slide my right foot outward to broaden my stance. The bottom of the cast slips on the polished tile and thuds into the baseboard.

I freeze in place. No one comes running. Balancing my weight on my left leg, I flex the muscles up and down my *right* leg. It feels normal, with the exception of being encased in a cast. No pain or numbness. Hmm.

I limp to the painting of the Dutch maid and lift the frame off the wall, confirming what I already suspected. It's a "virtual picture frame"—a flat-screen monitor designed to display digital images. It's one of those pricey jobs that adjust to the lighting of the room to mimic the look of a real painting. On the back of the picture frame are traces of dried paint, the same puked-avocado color as the wall.

That's when I become aware of a smell I noticed when I first awoke but have become inured to: freshly dried latex. The room has been recently painted.

I approach the vase of flowers and read the gift card on the plastic holder. "Get Well, Fuckface! From: Your Worst Nightmare." Teleflora needs better writers.

My next move is a risky one—try to get a view of the hallway without being spotted. I search the room for a small mirror or reflective object I can use to peek around the doorframe. Nothing grabs my eye.

Putting as little weight on my right foot as possible, I step-slide across the tiled floor to the area to the right of the door. Pressing my head against the wall, I peek out the door crack at an acute angle, taking in a sliver-sized view of the corridor.

No. Freaking. Way.

I *can't* be seeing what I think I'm seeing. *Can't* be.

Abandoning caution, I pull myself to the door and stick my head out, looking quickly in both directions. Holy fuck. It's true. The corridor is tiled, painted, and fluorescent-lit for only about twelve feet in either direction from the door. Beyond the painted/lighted zone is a dark old hallway with filthy walls, pocked plaster, and peeling, mud-colored wainscoting. Doorways, evenly spaced, punctuate the walls. Old apartments?

Two expensive-looking speakers sit on the floor, one on each side of my door.

I pull my head into the room and scramble back into the bed. My chest tightens as if it's trying to squeeze my heart out my throat. My mind wants to snap.

The room I'm in is essentially a movie set, a detailed reproduction of a hospital room. The building itself is an abandoned apartment building. The hospital sounds I've been hearing? Piped in on high-end speakers. The people I've been dealing with? All actors, pretenders.

I've been kidnapped and am being held prisoner.

Why? Why me? I have a few bucks, sure, but I'm not kidnap-wealthy, not by a long shot. And why the elaborate ruse? It couldn't have been cheap or easy to pull off. Clearly, my kidnappers have a lot of time and money on their hands—which means they wouldn't need to go after the modest resources in *my* Vanguard account.

Also, I *remember* the damn car accident. The EMTs. The cop. That was real. Right?

No, of course not. The EMTs were actors too. I never saw an actual car wreck or ambulance, just flashing lights.

How does any of this make sense? What world am I in? What universe?

I *must* be brain-injured—because there is no logical framework in which this staged scenario makes sense. My mind tap-dances toward the brink again.

No! I will *not* do what so many of my patients have done: mentally check out rather than deal with a traumatizing situation. I am stronger than that. I *will* face reality. No matter how fucked-up reality may seem at the moment.

But clearly this is an act first/think later situation.

I need to make my getaway while I'm restraint-free and temporarily unguarded. This may be my only chance. I sit up and swing my feet onto the floor again.

I hobble to the doorway, peek out. The hall is still empty. Squinting to see past the fake lighted area, I survey the dark corridor. The left end of the hall—the one nearest to me—terminates at a grime-encrusted window with streaks across it from an old paint roller. No apparent exit.

The hall in the other direction is longer and darker, with a wide doorframe partway down, on the right. An elevator? If so, I'm sure it won't be working. There may be a staircase at the far end, but it's too dark to tell.

My body swings into motion, choosing the right-hand path.

Moving as quietly and quickly as I can with a full leg cast, I limp out of the lighted area and head down the darker end of the hall in my open-assed hospital johnny, checking behind me for pursuers every few steps.

I pass an open apartment door with the number 316 on it. We're on floor three, then? Inside the room, a mannequin sits in a chair, wearing uniform pants and a shined shoe on its left foot. My "police guard." I fell for the old mannequin trick.

The human mind *begs* to be fooled, I swear it does.

It takes me half a minute—feels like half an hour—to reach the wide door frame on the right wall. No one's coming for me yet.

The opening is indeed an elevator. One of its double doors is missing, the gaping hole crisscrossed with yellow safety tape. An open shaft yawns beyond it—no elevator car. I hit the call button. To my astonishment, no car arrives.

I look back. No pursuers yet.

I make a burst for the end of the hall, passing a couple more shadowed doors with numbers on them. The air here feels warm and stale and has that baked-in-the-sun smell of old buildings in the desert.

The faster I move, the harder it is to keep my plastered right foot from clomping.

In the pool of darkness at the end of the hall, an even darker opening looms on the right side. It does appear to be a stairwell. I put on a burst of speed.

By the time I reach the end of the hall, I'm moving so fast, I need to throw my hands against the wall to stop my momentum. I turn around, my back pressed to the wall, and look down the hall in the direction I came from. Still no sign of movement within the lighted area. Good, good.

To my left, stairs descend into darkness. I start down.

A banister lines the right wall. It feels solid. Gripping it like a rescue line, I *feel* my way down the steps, hopping on my bare left foot and suspending my right leg in the air.

I pause every few stairs to listen for company.

I reach a lower landing where gritty floor-tile meets the skin of my left foot. A closed door gives onto the second floor. The door opens easily enough, its steel-plated base grinding in the dirt. Should I check out floor two or continue downstairs?

Instinct propels me onto floor two.

I expect to see another dimly lit row of apartments, mirroring the floor above, but no. Floor two is as bright as day—the light stings my eyes for a moment—and partially gutted. Daylight pours in from gaping window-holes. The inner walls have been removed from much of the floor. Only steel beams, pipes, and wires remain standing in the gutted area.

This is a building under renovation.

The floor is deadly still, though. No one is working today. Must be a weekend or a holiday.

*Whatever. Move. Hurry.*

I'm completely exposed in this open area, so I head toward the far end of the floor, where some of the old walls still offer cover.

Wait...

I should check outside first, see if I can get a sense of where I am, geographically speaking. Better be quick about it, though.

I turbo-hobble toward the nearest window-hole, weaving around chunks of fallen plaster. My "broken" leg doesn't hurt at all.

The window-hole looks out on a cluster of small desert mountains. In the foreground is a rounded foothill with a couple of tall cacti on it. One of them has a distinctive outline my brain insists on memorizing: a slightly hourglass-shaped trunk with three upright arms that look like they're holding a ball. The sun is starting its long descent over the mountains.

I hear no sounds of traffic outdoors, just an airliner flying overhead.

Looking down from the window-hole, I confirm I'm indeed on the second floor. Below me lies a narrow parking lot. The lot is bordered by shiny chain-link fence, the temporary type you see around construction sites. An open dumpster full of construction rubble sits on the right side of the lot. Part of an old sign sticks out of it: "OTE."

HOTEL?

Of course. This place is an old hotel—hence the picturesque location—not an apartment building.

The distance to the ground is about fifteen feet. Jumpable perhaps, with two good legs, youth, and a bit of luck. But do I have any of these things going for me? My best bet is to head downstairs to ground level. Look for an exit and then "run" like hell.

But how far would I get, lumbering across open desert terrain with a cast on my leg? And someone is bound to notice my empty bed any minute now and start downstairs after me.

Maybe finding a place to hide for a while is my best option. Yes. Hide in a safe spot till their search efforts run out of gas, *then* make my escape—by dark of night.

I scan the part of the floor that hasn't been demolished yet. A bright red object catches my eye beyond a partially destroyed wall.

I urge my plastered foot in that direction. Again it gives me no pain.

Within the shell of an old hotel room, I find a tall, red, Milwaukee-brand toolbox near the back wall, flanked by an assortment of power tools. I try to open it. Locked. In a corner, though, I spot a plastic milk crate filled with hand tools. One of them is a pipe cutter, for cutting PVC. I think I can use it to hack the cast off my leg.

Do I really want to do that? If so, should I do it here and now, or find a hiding place first?

I sit on a sawhorse to grab a moment's thought. It's only now that I start to process my situation at a higher level. It's mighty convenient that I was left alone, unguarded, with my wrist straps undone, isn't it? And that LaTisha fell for my ploy? And that no one was in the hallway when I made my run for the stairs?

In short, getting away was too easy. Which means I might be walking into a trap right now. Which means I need to do something they're not expecting.

Such as...?

Voices of alarm ring down the elevator shaft from above. Shit!

A male voice shouts, "Then how the hell did he get them *untied*? Fuckin' *fuck*, you guys!"

Maybe this *isn't* a trap. Maybe my ploy worked, straight up, and I got away for real. Or maybe the frantic shouting is part of their act too.

One thing's for sure. Whoever is yelling from above will be heading downstairs in seconds. I've got to move.

*Where's the last place they would think to look for me?* An insane answer flies back at me: in the room I just escaped from. They've already checked there.

Sneak back *into* my "hospital" room? Go *up* while they're coming *down*?

The idea has a weird allure. But no, it's plain nuts. Anyway, there's no way to get back upstairs without crossing paths with my captors.

Unless...

I make my way to the open elevator doors. In the darkness of the empty shaft, I see four thick cables running up the left side of a cinder-block wall. If I shimmy up one of the cables, I think I can swing my weight through the missing door on the floor above. I have good arm strength; I've been doing the weight machines at Fitness Plus for years.

But trying to escape by going *up*? That's what people do in bad horror movies.

I look down into the shaft. The elevator car is parked on the ground floor below. Only a short jump will land me on its roof. And look, there's a hatch on top. Or is there?

Down sounds better than up.

Again, my body makes the call. I toss my cutting tool down onto the roof of the elevator car, then slide down one of the cables like it's a fire pole. Groping around on the flat surface, I find a grab-handle on the hatch and give it a pull. The hatch opens easily, but inky darkness awaits below. The elevator doors must be closed on floor one. What if I jump down into the elevator car and can't open them? I'll be trapped like a rabbit in a well.

The idea of plunging into pure blackness lacks all curb appeal, but I hear voices shouting and feet running down the stairs. I need to vanish. *Now.* I lower my leg-cast through the hatch and plant my naked butt on the edge. Both legs dangle down. It can't be too far a fall, right?

But I'll have to land with all my weight on my bare left foot.

I toss the cutting tool down ahead of me. It lands with a rattle on a solid-sounding floor. Grasping the hatch-edge like a gym bar, I swing my body down into the darkness. After a three-count, I let go.

# Chapter 7

The plunge into blackness is mercifully short, but I don't stick the landing. The full bulk of my one-eighty-plus crashes sideways to the floor, the leg-cast receiving all the cargo.

I lie in the ink-black darkness, waiting for the wave of pain to travel from my leg to my brain. Nothing. I'm all but certain my leg isn't really broken.

I sit up, both legs out in front of me. My hand finds the cutting tool. Shedding the cast would be massively helpful. But that's not going to happen until I'm free of this elevator and can see what I'm doing.

Job one, then: get out of this black box.

Correction: job one is to stand up—which, I'm discovering, is a Cirque du Soleil feat when you have one leg in a cast and nothing to grab onto. In the pitch blackness.

I solve the physics challenge, eventually, by pressing my back against the smooth elevator doors and pistoning my left foot on the floor with every ounce of leg-strength my Fitness Plus membership has bought me.

Verticality achieved, I turn and run my hands over the metal doors. They seem to be the standard sliding kind that join in the middle. Can they be opened with the electricity off? The doors butt up flush against each other, and there's no handle or raised edge to grab onto.

Using the friction of my palms against the metal surface and pressing with all my weight, I manage to budge the left door just enough for me to jam the blade of the pipe-cutting tool into the crack between the two doors.

45

I lever the tool handles back and forth, prying the doors open further, until a gap of light appears between them. I force my fingers into the gap and pull on the right door. What I lack in hand-strength, I make up for with swearing; the door starts to slide, making gritty sounds in its track.

As soon as the gap is wide enough to slip through, I exit.

.  .  .

I find myself in the largely refurbished ground-floor hallway of the hotel. Sheetrock walls, woodwork, and an expensive tile floor have recently been installed. All that's needed here is wallpaper, varnish, and a condescending desk clerk, and floor one will be ready for business.

The individual guest rooms offer plenty of places to hide—but plenty of places to be cornered, too. I pause and listen for the sound of approaching footsteps. Nothing yet.

This cast needs to come off my leg. I limp down the hall a bit, enter a random guest room, and shut the door behind me. All the door hardware has been installed, including the electronic locks, which aren't functional yet. I'm able to lock the door manually from inside, though, and flip the security bar into place. If my pursuers want to get in here after me, they'll have to break the door down. And if they try to do that, I'll slip out the sliding glass door that leads to the rear parking lot.

This room is as safe a spot as I'm likely to find for the moment, but I mustn't get cozy. I press my ear to the door. Silence. Good. I hobble to the rear glass door and slide it open. The sweet, after-rain smell of some nearby creosote bushes wafts in. No sound greets my ears except the cry of a hawk.

I make my way to the bathroom and look in the mirror. Holy Jesus. Fifty-five and I don't look a day over seventy. When was the last time I showered? I strip the bandages off my head and examine my scalp. No scars amidst the once-thick white hair. Can I rule out a brain injury for good, then?

I return to the main room, sit on the floor, and go to work on the cast. The pipe-cutting tool, with its curved blade-catcher, is poorly designed for my purposes, but I make up for the design flaw with sheer willpower.

Chopping hard and fast, I work my way down my leg, an inch at a time, tearing and ripping at the plaster and bandages.

I free myself of the cast within five minutes—good time, but an eternity in my situation. No one has shown up at my door yet.

They could be right outside, though, waiting for me.

Time to take my liberated leg for a spin. Grasping the edge of a counter, I lift myself to a stand. No pain, no constricted movement in the right leg. There's not a damn thing wrong with it. I stretch it, bend it, move it in a circle. The movement feels glorious.

No time to audition for *America Can Dance*, though. I gather up the plaster and bandage debris and toss it into a cabinet, scattering the remaining plaster crumbs with my feet.

I spot a folded set of painter's coveralls amongst some painting supplies—praise the nonexistent Lord—and slip them on over my hospital johnny. It feels good to lose my rear exposure. Though it *will* make it harder for my pursuers to kiss my ass.

Now, back to Plan A. Find a place to hide where I can wait them out.

I can't stay here. As soon as they see a locked room-door, they'll know where to find me. Hiding outdoors would be better. A voice in my head whispers *dumpster*.

Having scoped out the big trash bin from above, I know it's full of jagged-looking construction debris; not a place anyone in their right mind would want to play hide-and-seek. Therefore, perfect for my purposes. Possibly.

I slip out the glass door into the mild December air and make my way, barefoot, along the strip of dirt between the building and the parking lot, darting past doors and ducking under windows. The hawk scolds me from above as the rocky ground stabs my bare feet from below.

The rusty, blue-painted dumpster stands about eight feet high and twenty-five feet long. A wraparound horizontal beam, halfway up, should make it fairly easy to climb, especially with two good legs. I scoot around to the back side of it and mount it from there.

The huge bin is stuffed to the brim with old wood-framing, plasterboard, and wire mesh, punctuated by lengths of pipe and rebar. Lots of nails and sharp edges. No safe entry point from here. But toward the far end, a tunnel-like opening in the debris catches my eye. I side-step along the horizontal beam toward it.

Yes, there appears to be a sizable rabbit-hole here, wending down through the junk. I swing my legs over the top and into the open space, holding on to the edge of the bin as I do. *Feeling* my way, bare feet first, down through the rubble, testing for nails, I discover a little "chamber" formed by an old bathtub lying on its side. I kick aside a week-old half-burrito crawling with bugs, lower myself into the tub, flip onto my back, and scrunch my legs up in a fetal pose.

Not exactly a day at Canyon Ranch, but a position I can maintain indefinitely.

It's unlikely anyone will search the trash bin thoroughly—at least not until they've exhausted their less-injurious options.

That's the story I'm telling myself anyway.

The sun is nearly down. I'll hide here in the old bathtub till darkness falls and the timing feels right, and then I'll make my escape in the night.

· · ·

I try to center myself internally, but fail. The whole "mindfulness" thing has always eluded me. My thought-stream is too powerful. And tonight, despite my imminent peril, that raging river of thought wants to flow in one direction only—not toward my own survival but toward Emmy.

Always toward Emmy. Even now.

Lying there in the musty-smelling darkness, I'm helpless to stop the cascade of questions. *What were her last moments like? What was she thinking? Did she suffer?*

Endless mind-loops, playing over and over.

For the thousandth time, my mind rereads the note she left us. *"It's nothing you did. It's all on me."* No, it's nothing I did. It's what I *didn't* do. Three times during her final stay with us she suggested going out to breakfast with me—a rare invite. And three times I put her off. The truth was, I was a little afraid to be alone with her, without the safety buffer of Hannah. But now it seems clear my daughter had something important she wanted to say to me.

To me alone.

*What was it? What might I have learned in that ever-deferred conversation? Would Em still be alive if only I had engaged with her? Would she?*

By the time the sun has set, the accumulated weight of my shame threatens to crush me. I'd rather face a firing squad than remain alone in the dark with my shitty damn self any longer.

I push myself out of the old bathtub.

. . .

Night has fallen.

Climbing *up* through the jagged debris is trickier than climbing down—a nail scrapes my arm—but my foot finds a plank to plant itself on. I gaze out over the top of the dumpster.

I'm facing the mountains, to the west. A faint afterglow outlines the peaks, and a fat moon sits high in the sky. Unhelpfully for my purposes, it's throwing a blanket of light on the landscape. As I put some leverage on my left foot to climb over the top, the plank snaps.

A *crack* pierces the night, echoing off the hills. Shit.

I freeze, listening.

The night air coalesces into a sound: the growl of a dog—a huge one by the size of its throat. The growl morphs into a frantic, woofing bark, growing louder and nearer. I duck down into the container, but seconds later a flurry of claws scrabbles against the side of the bin as the dog barks straight up at my hiding spot.

I've been made. This animal is not going to shut up until its handler arrives.

The barking goes on for a mind-destroying minute, and then a weirdly distorted male voice about thirty feet away shouts, "Baal! Down! Baal!"

The dog is named after a biblical demon. Sensational.

Baal stops its barking.

Silence obtains for several eternal seconds.

"Mr. Greenbird, you can come out now," says the echoey voice that sounds like it's being electronically processed. "We know you're in there. And we know who you really are. The question is... do you?"

The voice breaks into cackling laughter, which, owing to the added reverb, sounds fit for a carnival funhouse. The laugh rattles me more than the dog's bark does. I *know* that laugh, but with the electronic distortion I can't quite place it.

"Come out, come out, wherever you are, Ollie Wolls."

Ollie? Did he just call me by my real name? Fuck.

"Ollie, Ollie, oxen-free!"

That voice, that voice. If it was less distorted, I'm sure I could identify it. I think the guy's using one of those voice-changing devices they sell in Halloween stores. Or an auto-tuner of some kind.

"If I have to climb into that filthy dumpster..." The voice takes on a BBC British accent. "I'll be most cross with you." That keening laugh again, tinged with an almost tearful undertone. "And so will Baal. ... Come the fuck out!"

I have no choice but to comply.

Holding my hands up like a surrendering criminal, I rise over the top of the dumpster and look down.

My eyes aren't prepared for what I see. A tall man stands in the moonlight with a wooden box fastened over his head—it looks like part of an antique device I've seen somewhere, maybe in a book. The box has a cut-out section in the front, in the shape of an inverted U, to permit the man some vision and allow his voice to escape, but his face remains shadowed.

He is holding a massive Doberman on a leash. Baal.

"I've missed you for the past two thousand six hundred ninety-five days and two hours," the man says. "Did you miss me?"

• • •

Time freezes as my paralyzed brain tries to do the math that may clue me in to this guy's identity. No luck. I can't manage *four plus two*.

"You've been a highly disruptive patient, Ollie," says the Halloween-echoey voice from within the box, "and quite the resourceful lad. But did you really think we would go to all the expense of creating a perfect replica of a hospital room without installing a thirty-dollar webcam? We had bets on how long it would take you to make a run for it. I won, B-T-dubya."

B-T-dubya? Oh: "by the way."

"How do you know me?" I ask. My gut is already needling me with an answer.

"Alas," says the man, ignoring my question, "now that you've brought the curtain down on our Merry Merry Mind-Fuck Show, phase one of your treatment plan must come to an end. A tad prematurely—there was more fun to be had with our nurse and detective friends—but so be it. Time to move on to Phase Two."

"This is kidnapping." Yeah, hit 'em with a vocabulary lesson, Oliver. "It has to stop, right here, right now."

The box-headed man ignores me again, crouching down and making kissing sounds at the Doberman. "Who's a good Baal? Baal's a good Baal."

"Why are you doing this? Who are you? What do you want?"

"So many questions from the fretful little man," the stranger says to the dog. "But questions are good. Questions are the gateway to learning. And our guest has so much to learn. Fortunately for him, when the student is ready the teacher appears." He jumps to his feet, tossing his arms high and wide. "Presto! Here I am! The teacher! You, Awesome Ollie, are about to receive a once-in-a-lifetime educational opportunity. Better than Grand Canyon University!"

"What are you talking about?"

"The patient is being transferred to another facility."

He circles his finger in the air, doing the "rally the troops" signal. Two figures trot out of the shadows. "Nurse LaTisha" and "Detective Pratt." They're dressed in sweats and hoodies now. It dawns on me—why did I miss it before?—that LaTisha was also the "cop" at the accident scene. She was wearing aviator shades and a police hat then.

I climb out of the bin and jump to the ground; what choice do I have?

"How did you get hold of me?" I ask. "Where did it happen? The Apache Trail? Does my wife know you took me? How long have I been missing?"

"Questions, questions. There'll be more than enough time for Socratic inquiry after your transfer is complete. Phase Two of treatment will include *much* tighter security measures, B-T-dubya."

"Pratt" moves in behind me, crosses my wrists, and binds them. "LaTisha" takes a syringe from her sweatshirt pocket—some things don't change—and jabs it into my rear.

"'Transferred to another facility,'" the box-headed man repeats in his echo-enhanced voice. "Those words don't sound *quite* so hilarious when someone is saying them about *you*, do they, Dr. Powers?"

Pratt and LaTisha march me toward a dark red GMC Yukon.

# PART II
# Admission

# Chapter 8

Awakening in a drugged fog should be old hat to me by now, but as my eyesight comes into focus, I feel nauseated and disoriented.

Rough black shapes fill my visual field.

With a slight adjustment of my eyes, the shapes resolve into 3D forms: old wooden beams, crisscrossing pipes, ductwork. All painted flat black. About fifteen feet away from me.

Ah, but there are bars in front of my face—bars made of wood. Am I in a cell? For a moment I can't tell which way my body is oriented, horizontally or vertically.

Gravity supplies the answer. I'm lying on my back—in a coffin-like structure with its top and sides made of wooden bars—looking up at a black-painted ductwork ceiling. Panic rises in me, but I take a few breaths and let it subside. I think I know what sort of contraption I'm enclosed in. I remember it from my studies.

My impulse to grab the wooden bars and shake them is thwarted by the discovery that my arms are pinned across my chest by starchy fabric. A straitjacket, I suspect. Haven't seen one of these in thirty years.

A ball-chain dangles through the bars near my cheek. I twist my head, grab it with my teeth, and give it a tug. It makes a *chink* like a light-bulb switch.

From an unseen speaker comes the recorded sound of "mental patient" laughter from a 1950s horror movie, followed by a narrator's voice in the cornball style of that era. "This device, common in asylums in the mid-to-late nineteenth century, was known as the Utica Crib. Designed to manage disruptive patients as well as those with so-called 'nervous shaking,' it was also used as a treatment for war trauma, a consequence for domestic misbehavior—such as wifely refusal of the marriage bed—and a suicide prevention method. Ironically, many patients died within its confines. The Utica Crib."

A latch clicks open. I press the wooden bars with my forehead, and the cover swings upward easily as one of the sides folds down. Evidently I am free to exit. Climbing out of the barred coffin is awkward with my arms crossed in front of me, but I manage to slide my legs out over the edge and land on the floor.

Holy sweet crap.

This place is a museum. Of sorts. Well, not *exactly* a museum. More like a private collection hastily arranged to *look* like a museum; the lighting is poor, and junk is piled in corners. The musty, old-wood smell of an antiques barn hangs in the air. Arrayed about the warehouse-like room are several other "exhibits" that, at first glance, resemble torture devices but whose nature and purpose I know all too well.

I approach the nearest one. A wooden compartment, large enough to hold a crouching human, sits suspended eighteen inches above the floor on a vertical pole. The top of the compartment is connected by a metal arm to a crank that an operator turns from a higher platform. A plaque in front of the exhibit reads, "O'Halloran's Swing was designed to rotate mental patients at high rates of speed. The purpose of so-called 'rotational therapy' was to increase blood flow to the brain and thus cure insanity. The *actual* results included vertigo, anxiety, vomiting, defecation, brain hemorrhaging and death. No cures were ever recorded."

Using my knee, I push the red button beside the plaque. The hammy narrator recites the same text, complete with B-movie sound effects of a screaming patient being spun in circles.

I proceed to the neighboring "exhibit," a six-foot-tall ornate cabinet with a grimacing dummy trapped inside it. Its plaque reads, "The Clock was designed to resemble a grandfather clock. The disruptive patient was locked inside with his face displayed in place of the clock dial. The purpose of The

Clock was to coax compliance from unruly patients through the use of physical restraint and public humiliation."

All the exhibits feature outmoded forms of treatment for the mentally ill, cruel and bizarre by modern standards. I learned about some of these methods in my Inpatient Psychiatry course in med school and have seen one or two of the devices in older hospitals, preserved for posterity. Touring the room in my straitjacket, I encounter the Bath of Surprise, a huge steel tub into which patients were plunged in ice water without warning; the Hollow Wheel, a human gerbil wheel encased in wood; and the Tranquilizing Chair, an electric-chair-looking device in which a patient was restrained for hours, or days, with their head inside a box. The box is the model for the one my captor was wearing—with the inverted-U-hole.

On the far wall of the exhibit room hangs an Exit sign. Approaching it, I encounter a steel door designed to replicate a locked-ward door in a nineteenth century mental asylum. I peer out the small barred window and pull the metal handle. Needless to say, the door is locked, but my pulling action triggers a recorded announcement from the corny actor-voice. "Thank you for visiting! You're free to exit—*after* you've taken a complete tour of our exhibits."

With resignation, I resume my tour of the room, pressing the buttons as I go. There are displays on lobotomy, insulin coma therapy, "blistering," and bloodletting. Walking past a chilling contraption called the Isolation Box, I come upon an exhibit even more disturbing by its implications. It is labeled, simply, "Psychotropics." Its description: "In the latter half of the twentieth century, it became standard psychiatric practice to 'treat' patients with a variety of mood-, mind-, and behavior-altering drugs. These chemical agents rendered patients manageable, while often causing serious side effects such as blurred vision, nausea, dependency, weight gain, dulled thinking, sexual problems, and irreversible tics and tremors."

*Yes*, my mind retorts, *and they also relieve mental suffering and confusion for millions of real human beings. They're imperfect, but they can be life-changing.*

The fact that psychotropic drugs have been lumped in with all these quasi-torture techniques tells me how the "curator" of this little museum feels about my profession as a psychopharmacologist.

A final exhibit is dubbed Smile Therapy. It features a set of strap-on masks, made of glossy cardboard, depicting smiling female mouths. Its plaque claims—dubiously, in my opinion—that the masks were used with depressed women from the 1930s to 1950s as a way of coaxing them into uplifted moods.

An electronic bell dings and the Exit sign lights up. "Congratulations, you may now exit," says the recorded voice.

I approach the exit again. The steel door opens automatically to reveal a brick-walled hallway ending in a right turn. Daylight spills from an adjoining corridor. I'm sure I'm not really free to leave, but who can resist the lure of the unlocked door?

I step forward. The instant my foot crosses the threshold, an alarm sounds, a red light flashes, and the speakers shout, "Code Gray! Code Gray! Security breach!" I hear the sound of feet charging toward me from behind. Before I can turn to look, two bodies slam into me, grab me by the shoulders and take me down to the floor. With the straitjacket binding my arms, I have no way to break my fall.

I cry out in pain as I land, face down, but a rough hand covers my mouth.

All is still for half a minute.

Hard-heeled footsteps, paced two full seconds apart, approach me, echoing sharply on the concrete floor. They stop, a foot from my prone body.

"Sucks just a little bit to be you," says a distorted male voice from high above.

I twist my head to see the tall, thin man with the wooden box on his head looming over me. He's decked out in a tailored red blazer over a black turtleneck and black dress pants.

"So tell me, Ollie," he says in his still-distorted voice, "how did you enjoy your 'intake and assessment' period, abbreviated though it was? It's such jolly fun to be strapped to a hospital bed twenty-four-seven, idn't it? Gives the mind a bracing workout. And being randomly injected with unknown chemicals, that's my favorite! Almost as fun as being head-fucked by the police for no apparent reason. Or being told that the things you see and hear and know-for-sure are only hallucinations. When we trotted those Chimbu dancers out, I thought you'd pee your pants like Jimmy Reardon in my freshman English class."

He breaks into peals of laughter, altered by the voice device.

"You must have figured out by now who the man under the box is," says the man under the box.

My belly has known all along, but my mind has been holding out in denial. "No, I haven't," I lie.

"Pratt" and "LaTisha" muscle me to my feet.

The tall man in front of me ceremoniously unstraps the wooden box with the voice device inside it and lifts it off his head. The face revealed is that of a blonde man with high bangs, large forehead, and long, aquiline nose.

Fuck. Not him.

Anyone but him.

"I told you many years ago that our day of... *wreckoning* would come," he says, his voice no longer amplified. "I spelled it with a 'w' in my mind. Ha! Did you think I was joking when I said that? Merry prankster that I am?"

"Hark... How are you?" I say. Idiotically.

"Did you seriously just ask me that?"

Hark. Harkins Horvath III. The most troubled and troublesome patient I ever treated in my twenty-seven-year career. Also, my greatest failure as a psychiatrist.

Harkins Horvath III. Borderline personality disorder. With psychotic features. Poor impulse control. Anger management issues. Severe delusions. Occasional psychotic episodes. Grandiose narcissism. High intelligence.

Harkins Horvath III. Father rich as a Saudi prince. Mother dead of a gunshot suicide when he was seven. Lacking in nurturance as a child. No limits, no controls, no consequences for antisocial behavior. No life-direction as an adult. Too much time on hands. Wealthy enough—by way of Detached Dad—to get away with almost anything his wounded mind can concoct.

I treated him in Massachusetts about eight years ago. Our work together did not—how to put it?—*achieve its therapeutic goals*.

"If any further harm comes to me," I say, "even your father won't be able to get you out of this one."

"Let *me* worry about Daddy Gumdrops"—a name he has always hung on his father, for reasons known only to him. "You have your own rather considerable set of worries at the moment, I regret to inform you."

"I get what this is all about, Hark. Your messaging hasn't exactly been subtle. You think I mistreated you as a patient, and now you're trying to make *me* to suffer the same—"

"Mistreated?" Hark makes a cartoon expression of surprise. "Gawrsh, *I* thought the term was gross criminal malpractice, a-hyuck, a-hyuck. But what do I know? I'm just a layman. I'm just a lemon. I'm just a lemming..."

"So this is your form of payback. That's what this is all about."

"Payback..." He treats himself to a chuckle. "Is the tip of the iceberg. Payback is *the dust speck on the fly's wing on the penguin shit* on the tip of the iceberg. This thing is *sooooo* much bigger than you and me."

"What are you saying?"

His face flushes red. "I'm *saying*: You damage people, Powers. You damage the *world*. With your influence and your ideas and your lethal fucking prescription pad. And you need to be *stopped*." The smile creeps back onto his face. "A-hyuck, a-hyuck."

# Chapter 9

A conversation eight years overdue needs to take place between Hark and me. I would love to delay it eight *more* years—eighty, really—but there seems to be no choice but to have it right now. In case it isn't ludicrously obvious, there is bad blood between us. And some of it is my "fault," though not through any misfeasance. The crux of our tension is this: his sister and her children were murdered, violently, in their home, and he was not there to protect them because I had placed him under psychiatric commitment.

His anger at me is understandable, if totally misplaced.

"Hark, I am sorry for what happened." I step closer to him, forcing myself to look him in the eye. "I've never been able to tell you that personally. I'm telling you now. If I could go back in time, knowing everything I know now, I would handle that situation differently. I would make sure your sister was better protected."

"Well, that changes everything," he says. "I feel so touched, I could sue a priest."

"But—and you need to hear this—I wouldn't handle *you* any differently. I was following good psychiatric protocol with you. As a clinician, I have no regrets."

"And that's the nub of the matter, now, isn't it? Arrogance is ignorance. And ignorance is arrogance. And forever the dance goes on."

"I understand your need to focus your anger on me, Hark, but—"

"Whoa, whoa," he says. "Are we going to do this? Have 'the talk'? If so, I need to do a 'self-care intervention' first." He pulls from his pocket one of the smile-therapy masks from the "museum," depicting a grinning, lipstick-red mouth painted in 1950s style. He straps the smiley mask over his own mouth and says in a breathy southern "female" voice, "Do go on, Doctor."

Ignoring his theatrics, I repeat, "I understand your need to focus your anger on me, but what you're forgetting is that it was your *sister herself* who wanted you hospitalized. You were scaring the shit out of her, and she didn't know how to handle you. I know *in your mind* you were trying to protect her, but you were delusional and highly agitated, and she was terrified. Of you. She *wanted* you locked up."

"The fact remains," he says behind the cardboard smile, "if you had listened to *me*—your client, your *employer*—she would be alive now."

"Maybe, maybe not. It's possible *you'd* be dead too, if you'd been in the house... when it happened." The murder.

Trying not to focus on the absurd painted grin, I press on. "I'm going to tell you now what I told you many times back then, even if it gets me hurt: mental illness is a neurochemical disorder, not an alternative lifestyle. *You* have a mental illness, Hark. A serious one. Maybe someday you'll accept that. Your illness is not your fault; it is a predisposition of your brain's wiring and chemistry, triggered by a set of... *unenviable* childhood experiences. But as part of that illness, you suffer delusions, even in the best of times." I pause. "And those were not the best of times."

"No. No, they were not." He titters through the smile mask, but his eyes smolder. "At least we agree on that."

Hark had just come back from Peru, where, against my strong advice, he had ingested ayahuasca, a high-potency hallucinogen brewed from local vines and plants, as part of a spiritual retreat run by a native shaman. Already in precarious mental shape, he had a bad reaction to the drug. "You were suffering from a textbook case of drug-induced psychosis. Ranting about murderous demons from the 'Lower World.' Frightening Lisa's children. Frightening Lisa."

"You omit one trifling detail, doctor." Still with the stupid female voice, still with the cardboard smile. "I was *right* about that demonic entity. It was real. I was *right* about it following me home from Aguas Calientes. I was *right* that it wanted to harm my family. I was right, and you doodly-darn-well know it."

Hark's insistence that an actual demon killed his family was the final cut that severed our relationship. "What happened to your sister's family was a *coincidence*. Period. A horrible, freakish, and terribly timed coincidence. They were murdered by a *man*. A man, not a demon. A man who, like you, had a serious mental illness, coupled with a violent personality."

"The demon *assumed human form*." He rips the smile mask off and speaks in his own voice at last. "As I told you it would! As I told you it would!"

"You were psychotic."

"'Psychotic' means out of touch with reality. But I knew *exactly* what was going to happen to Lisa. And I was right. And I wasn't there to protect her. Because of *you*."

"There isn't a psychiatrist in the world who would have handled your case any differently. Not one. You were a danger to yourself and others. Period. Commitment was the only course of action."

"I wasn't even allowed to go to the fuckin' funeral."

"That wasn't my call," I say, a note of sheepishness creeping into my voice.

"Nah, none of it was your call, was it? None of it was your fault. You have no personal responsibility in this at all. You were just doing your *job*. The same thing the SS boys must have told themselves when they fired up the Jew ovens every day. Well, that happy crap might buy you a night's sleep in Ollie World, but it doesn't buy Jack Shit here."

"Meaning what?"

"Meaning..." He leads me back into the exhibit room. LaTisha and Pratt follow us inside, shutting and locking the steel door behind them. "You are here on involuntary commitment. What *you* believe doesn't matter anymore."

"What are you planning to do to me, Hark?" I try to keep my voice steady.

"What I am planning to do—I and my colleagues—is open your mind to things you quite literally can't imagine. Over the coming weeks"—

*weeks?*—"you are going to *change*, in profound ways. If and when a fifty-five-year-old man with a surgically enhanced hairline and twenty-thousand dollars' worth of veneers from Scottsdale Cosmetic Dentistry walks out the door of our treatment program—and that's a whopping *if*—that man won't be Dr. Oliver Powers anymore. He will be... a new revelation."

My heart does jumping jacks in my chest. "You'll go to jail for this. Whatever *this* is."

Hark laughs. "Seriously? You've met my father. If I was ever going to go to jail for anything, I'd already be locked up, believe me. No, Daddy Gumdrops and I have an *arrangement*. He gets me out of pickles and flows me the resources I need to pursue my 'hobbies,' so long as I hold up *my* end of the bargain..."

"Which is...?

"Stay the fuck out of his life. This building we're in? Daddy Gumdrops's. That hotel your hospital room was in? His too. When it comes to Harkins Horvath III, people up and down the food chain are paid good money to shut up and look the other way."

What he's telling me may well be true. It fits with what I know of his father.

"So put childish notions of rescue and justice out of your mind," he says. "You're *my* patient now. And today your treatment plan begins in earnest. Welcome to your inpatient treatment facility."

He strolls to the nearest exhibit—a collection of antique *trepanation* tools designed for drilling and carving "therapeutic" holes in the human skull—and picks up one of the polished steel instruments. He studies his reflection in it, then puts it down and grabs the descriptive plaque. "This room is not a museum, Dr. Powers. Not anymore. It is a *ward*." He sticks the plaque under his arm. "It is *your* ward now. How long you stay here is up to you. You can earn your way to a 'less restrictive setting,' but that all depends on how fast you are willing to accept your need for treatment."

I remain silent as he strolls around the room, collecting the other museum-style plaques.

"Time to get you settled in for the night," he says at last. "I am going to remove your designer blouse, but of course the ward door will remain locked."

He unbuckles my straitjacket and yanks it off me.

"You will find a blanket and a pillow in the Utica Crib, and some food over there." He points to a covered dish on a wheeling table. "Of course, you won't know if I've drugged it or poisoned it or jacked off in it, but it's all the nutrition you're going to get for a while, so I suggest you eat it. Good night, Doc-tor Powers. Get it—Docked Your Powers?"

He strolls out the door, whistling a tune I almost recognize before he changes it to something else.

•  •  •

I lie in the dark in the Utica Crib with the barred lid open, covered by the thin blanket Hark provided for me. I'm ferociously hungry, but I didn't even glance at the food on the covered plate. All I want to do now is think. Hard and clear. My body is beyond exhaustion, but my mind is pounding Red Bulls.

One truth shines plainly. From the moment I started to suspect someone was messing with my mind back in that "hospital room," I knew, subconsciously, it had to be Harkins Horvath III. I've never met anyone else with the resources, imagination, and relentless vindictiveness to orchestrate a stunt like this.

*How did he get hold of me?* He and/or his cohorts must have been following me, waiting for an opportune moment. The last thing I remember is that drive on the Apache Trail. It would have been easy enough for them to pull off a kidnapping out amidst the twists and turns of that remote mountain roadway. They probably carjacked me and drugged me with that knockout concoction of theirs. They must have *kept* me drugged, too, for quite some time. That would explain the gap in my memory—before waking up in their "hospital."

All those things that happened in the fake hospital room—the drugging; the bizarre behaviors of "Pratt" and "LaTisha"; the skeletal dance crew; the ever-changing painting—were obviously designed for one purpose only: Crazymaking 101. As for the elements that struck a more *personal* chord—the frog, Pratt's accusations—I can only assume they were incidental. There's no way Hark could know how those things would affect my psyche. Hark is a clever fellow, but there are limits to even his capabilities. He can't literally climb inside my head.

Hark.

Hark, Hark, Hark.

So what is his game plan here?

Is there anything in our history together that might hold a key?

Hark was a nightmare of a patient. His father hired me to treat him. That was the agreement Daddy Gumdrops and son came to after an incident in which Hark hid in the bedroom closet of Stepmom Number Two and videoed her having sex with her "secret lover"—who turned out to be Daddy Gumdrops.

Dad delivered the ultimatum: commit to getting long-term psychiatric help or I will financially disown you.

Hark did the math. He agreed to see a shrink—me, alas—but he never bought into our work together. Hark didn't believe in psychiatry—he'd been seeing shrinks off and on since childhood—and he definitely didn't see himself as in need of its services. He fancied himself a pioneer in the more rarefied realms of consciousness. Like my daughter Emily, he explored an endless array of non-mainstream belief systems and practices. But unlike Emmy, who was deeply curious, Hark's prime motivation, I believe, was to find new ways to discredit Western psychiatry—and, by extension, his father—and to justify his aimless lifestyle.

Hark used Daddy's money to travel to ashrams in India and to study with Huichol medicine men in the Mexican mountains. He dabbled in shamanism, occultism, and LSD micro-dosing (and macro-dosing). None of these pursuits were at all good for him. What Hark needed was *more* grounding in reality, not less, and "a good smack in the ass," as my mother would have said. No one had ever made Harkins Horvath III do one single thing he didn't feel like doing.

The only true aptitude Hark ever displayed was in making trouble for people. He had that borderline-personality knack for finding chinks in the armor of caregivers and authority figures, coupled with the high intelligence to make their lives miserable in creative ways.

That was the story of our working relationship. Hark constantly kept score on me, testing my knowledge, writing down anything I said that wasn't strictly by the books, threatening to sue me every other week or file a complaint against me with the Board of Psychiatry. Sometimes he would lapse into red-faced rages and threaten me in less strictly legal ways.

The only person in the world he really loved, and who somehow managed to love him in return, was his sister Lisa—and her two kids. Lisa would often allow Hark to live with her after he had burned all his other bridges. She took zero shit from him, and from what I could tell, he seemed to treat her and the children with love and respect.

So it was no surprise that his world imploded after the tragic events of about eight years ago. Hark had gone on that ill-advised ayahuasca retreat. Its purpose was to combine shamanic journeying—already a risky practice IMO—with the ingesting of ayahuasca, in order to trigger a deep encounter with "non-ordinary reality." The retreat was designed for advanced shamanic practitioners skilled at navigating altered states of consciousness, not for at-risk people like Hark.

During his first ayahuasca session, Hark had a bad trip. A severe psychotic episode. He left the retreat, highly agitated, and returned to the states on a private jet supplied by Señor Gumdrops. He showed up at his sister's house and proceeded to tear through the place, closing window shades and hanging "protective" amulets on the doors. He burned bundles of sage and instructed his sister and her kids to huddle together in a middle room, telling them they were in grave danger.

His sister, terrified, called me. I signed a "pink paper," a Section 12 form, authorizing the police and EMS team to pick him up and transport him to a psych unit of a local hospital. Hark was taken into custody, kicking and screaming (and, of course, threatening to sue the cops).

The next day I went to the hospital to assess him. He was *extremely* agitated, and his right eye had a burst blood vessel from punching himself in the face. After I spent fifteen minutes calming him down, he told me about his ayahuasca experience, recounting his meeting with a demon in the "Lower World"—a demon he said threatened grievous harm to his loved ones.

Those who have never borne witness to a human mind's descent into madness have no idea how unsettling an experience it can be. Psychosis has a powerful magnetism that wants to pull you in. I had to fight, with all my inner resources, to appear unruffled as he described the features of this monster his mind had conjured up—its teeth, its smell, its voice. The details were so vivid and convincing that, even now, my mind rebels against recalling them.

Hark begged me, on his knees, to release him from the hospital so he could return to his sister's house to protect her and the children from the alleged demon. He implored me to at least put a twenty-four-hour police guard on Lisa's home. But of course, I had no basis for requesting such a thing and would have been laughed out of the police station had I tried.

What I did instead was transfer Hark to a more secure facility, one that was better equipped to handle dangerous and self-injurious patients. In short, I did what any competent treating psychiatrist would have done.

Less than a week after his commitment, an ex-convict with mental health issues, high on PCP, broke into Lisa's house in an attempt to flee the police after a B&E. He held the family hostage for several hours, during which time he became convinced Lisa was his dead ex-girlfriend. He proceeded to stab her and her children to death and "modify" their bodies with power tools he found in the basement—before ending his own life with a nail gun.

In the aftermath of the horrific tragedy, I made one attempt to visit Hark in the acute ward of Harbor Estuary Hospital, the private hospital-by-the-sea where I'd had him committed. He attacked me violently, requiring four strong Mental Health Technicians to pull him off me, and made highly specific threats on my life. After that, I decided, for the good of the patient (ahem), I would make no further attempts to see him in the hospital. In fact,

I transferred his ongoing treatment to a colleague—to whom I gifted a bottle of Jameson Limited Reserve in a carved wooden case for Christmas that year—and told his father I would no longer serve as his shrink.

I was free of Harkins Horvath at last.

Or so I convinced myself. Guess Hark's not the only delusional one.

# Chapter 10

I'm back at work, in my office in Scottsdale. No idea how I got here.

This doesn't feel like a dream. It's too detailed, too concrete, and it's been going on far, far too long. But it doesn't seem exactly real either.

The room I'm in is not my actual office; it's a duplicate office in the basement, below the real one. The only light coming in is from a grate over my head and from the computer I'm working on. As I peer up through the grate, I see my real office up there—the waiting and reception area.

*Emmy* is in the waiting room of my upper office—alive and real; I can hear her voice and see her red boots moving about—and she's insisting she needs to talk to me. My receptionist keeps stalling her and saying I'll be with her in a minute. I want to shout up and tell Emmy I'll be right there, that I *want to talk*, but each time the impulse strikes, a pair of yellow eyes comes aglow in the darkness across the room.

I'm being watched by a malevolent presence that does not want me to communicate with Emily. I'm terrified of that presence.

I feel like I've been trapped in this room forever. I know time can be distorted in dreams, but not to *this* extent. Why am I here? Why is Emmy here? How? Why can't I talk to her?

I glance up at the grate for the billionth time. This time something is stuck between two of the grate-bars. A folded-up paper! Emmy taps it with her boot, and it falls with a rattle onto my desk. I surreptitiously unfold it, watching to see if the yellow eyes light up in the darkness.

By the glow of my computer monitor, I read Em's note: "Dad, you're not dreaming. The experience you're having is a—"

. . .

My skin is stung by a thousand bees.

I scream, but the only sound I hear is a bubbly ringing in my ears.

Ice water. Not bees. Ice water.

I'm under ice water.

Burning me, stinging me, stabbing me.

I'm in full-body shock.

Panic strikes. I try to leap to my feet. My body is strapped down. Underwater.

Lungs on fire.

I almost pull in a breath, but instinct seals my mouth against the water.

*Hold breath, don't inhale.*

*Hold it...*

*Hold it...*

*Hold it...*

I'm about to surrender to drowning when my body starts to rise with a metallic ratcheting sound. My face breaks the water's surface. I gulp in oxygen and blink my eyes. Warm air rushes in, swaddling me like a blanket.

"The Bath of Surprise," announces Hark, standing beside the tank of ice water from which I've just been pulled. He wears a white doctor's jacket and holds an empty syringe. "Didn't take a leap of imagination to name *this* puppy, right?"

My brain scrambles for traction. I feel like I've been yanked from one altered state to another. The harsh outlines of the room feel ominous and hateful. My lungs wolf air.

"The Bath of Surprise was designed to shock patients out of 'mental distraction.' A dunk in the tank was often followed by a tablespoon of tartrate of antimony to induce vomiting." Hark tosses the syringe aside, pats the pockets of his white jacket. "Fresh out of tartrate of antimony, I'm afraid, but don't worry, we have plenty of other ways to make you puke. As you'll soon see."

"What the *fuck*, Hark?" I say through chattering dental veneers. I'm strapped, it appears, to a stretcher of sorts, attached by steel cables to an overhead winch. I can't see my quivering body, but I feel naked except for maybe a pair of briefs.

"We've diagnosed you as mentally distracted. Thus, it would have been inhumane of us to withhold treatment from you. How's that for a rationale? Sound familiar? Would you like another dunk in the ol' polar cola or are you ready to move on to grander adventures?"

My brain struggles to process his question. Apparently my reply doesn't come fast enough. Hark pushes a release-lever, plunging me back into the ice bath.

I'm better prepared for the shock this time, but still the freezing water stings like acid.

Ten seconds after I've used up every atom of oxygen in my lungs, the winch hauls me out again, dripping and shaking and pulling in wheezy breaths.

"Mental Distraction," continues Hark, his train of thought unbroken, "takes many forms. In every case, though, its cause boils down to one thing: man's endless—what's the word?—*propensity* to be hypnotized by the contents of his own mind. You are a deeply hypnotized man, Ollie Polliwog. That's your new name, by the way. Ollie Polliwog. Olliwog for short. Like it?"

I don't reply. I'm shaking like I have jungle fever.

"Novitiates are given a new name as a symbol of the new life they are embarking on. And you *are* embarking on a new life, Olliwog, make no mistake." He leans forward and flicks a drop of water from my nose. "Have you ever heard the Zen fable of the professor and the teacup? ... Or are such tales too full of 'spiritual delusion' for your taste?"

*What is he asking? I'd better answer him.* "I've c-come across it in my research."

"I've c-come across it in m-my research-ch-ch," Hark repeats in a SpongeBob SquarePants voice. "Why don't you tell it to me, then? 'The Professor and the Teacup.' Go ahead, spin me a yarn."

I don't seem to be in a storytelling mood; go figure. Hark reaches for the winch release.

"All right!"

He pauses his hand. My mind churns to recall the parable. "Professor goes to interview wise Zen master. Zen master pours professor a cup of tea, keeps pouring till cup overflows. Professor says, 'Stop pouring, no more tea can fit in.' Zen master says, 'You are like the cup, so full of knowledge, nothing new can enter.'"

Hark pulls his hand back from the release-lever. "D-minus for delivery, B-plus for content. *You* are that professor, Olliwog. You have vital lessons to learn, but your cup is too full to learn them. Not full of *tea* in your case, but old shit juice from the bottom of a state-park toilet hole. But full just the same. And so, it falls upon *us* to empty your cup."

I'm loath to seek clarification on that point. I feel so dizzy, so disoriented.

"And the way we are going to do that—for starters—is by acquainting you with the hardware in this room. We think it's only fair that the tools of your own profession should be the instruments of your enlightenment."

"If you're talking about torture, Hark, you'd better—"

"I'm *talking* about mental health treatment, as practiced in *your* hospitals and asylums. The objects in this room are... expressions... outpourings... *manifestations* of the same grand tradition of thought that still shapes your profession as you practice it to this day."

"This stuff has nothing to do with modern psychiatry. This stuff is barbaric!"

"You only say that because it's out of fashion. If you'd been practicing your craft in earlier times, you'd have been cheerfully turning the cranks and drilling the skull-holes."

"The *hell* I would," I say, but my protest falls short of full-throated.

Hark laughs. "That's what everyone tells themselves. '*I* wouldn't have owned slaves. *I* wouldn't have turned on the gas ovens. *I* wouldn't have performed lobotomies.' Yes, you fuckin' would have. A hundred years from now, people will be saying, 'Did you know they once treated people in spiritual crisis by pumping them full of chemicals and zapping their brains with electric current?' And people like you will be saying, '*I* would never have done such a thing.'"

"I believe in psychopharmacology. I've seen the results. I've seen medication change lives. Is it a flawless science? No. But I believe in the work I do."

"You *believe* in a lot of things, Ollie Woggles. Therein lies the problem. There are truths that need to flow into your life—Buddha-under-the-Bodhi-tree-type truths—but they can't get past the shit clogging up your cup. And so it's time to get to work!"

"I repeat, if you're planning to torture me—"

"Not torture, *therapy*, as defined by your own—"

"If you're *planning to torture me*," I shout over him, "you might as well kill me right now. Because if I live, I will dedicate my life to holding you responsible. I will make sure you never spend another *minute* outside a locked facility for the criminally insane."

"Let's be clear on something, Wogs. Our treatment probably *will* kill you. I mean, if you make it to our Final Lesson—and that's a whopping *if*—you'll see what I mean. Your odds of getting out of *that* one alive are *yikes!* But the fun we're about to have in *this* room? Nah. Won't kill you. ... Prob'ly. Ha! But it *will* kill some of your arrogance, some of your pride, some of your resistance. And that's where we need to start."

"You crazy fuck. You crazy fucking fuck."

"Nice talk, doc." He pushes the release-lever, plunges me into the ice-bath again. He leaves me underwater till I feel myself turning blue and panicky, then pulls me out to drain like calamari in a fryer basket. I quake in big convulsive movements.

I hate him for seeing me this vulnerable.

"Listen to me, Ollie." Hark folds his hands and softens his face in an almost kind way. "The things we're going to do in this room have a purpose, and in the end you'll agree they were necessary and... *for your own good*. I promise. But for now..." The smarmy glint returns to his eyes. "Buckle your seatbelt, 'cause clang, clang, clang goes the trolley! Woo!"

• • •

I'm on my third go-round in O'Halloran's Swing. "Detective Pratt"—whatever the hell his real name is—stands on the upper platform, turning the crank that spins the wooden cabinet I'm crouching in. I'm light-years past sick. I'm being spun at RPMs no human body should endure. The blood is being pulled to the front of my head through centrifugal force. I'm seconds away from a hemorrhage or a stroke. Needles of pain shoot through me. I want to scream for mercy, but pride freezes my tongue.

At blessed last, the spinning cabinet squeals to a stop. I toss my feet out and stagger into the waiting arms of "LaTisha." She grabs me, but I crumple to the floor. "Pratt" holds a bucket in front of me. I try to vomit but manage only dry heaves.

"This is a crime. All of you," I call out, my voice slurring drunkenly. "What you're doing is a serious crime."

"It's *called* rotational therapy," says Hark, standing near the spin-machine in his white lab coat. "And I'll repeat what I said before. All you need to do to stop this intervention is admit you need treatment."

"Like the Salem Witch Trials, huh? Admit you're a witch and we'll stop dunking you—but then we'll burn you at the stake?"

"Precisely," Hark replies. "Like *every locked ward in every mental hospital*: 'If you want to be discharged, first admit you need help. What's that—you need help? Well, then, we'd better keep you locked up!'"

"It's not like that," I fire back, but my rebuttal finds no traction.

"It *is* when you're under psychiatric commitment—fucked if you ask for help, fucked if you don't. Especially..." He pauses pointedly. "... when the shrink holding the key to your freedom has a hidden motive for *keeping* you locked up."

Something tightens in my gut. "What are you saying?" I slur. "What hidden motive did I have?" My head is still spinning in tight circles. "What are you talking about?"

"Search your feelings, Luke Skywalker."

"No, tell me what the hell you're talking about."

"We are not even close to being ready to have that discussion. Your cup is *way* too full. But we will. We will talk about it, rest assured. So... What's it going to be, admit that you need treatment or... back in the ol' Maytag for another spin cycle?"

"Fuck you, Horvath."

"The patient requires additional rounds of rotational therapy."

My next round is even more painful than the last. I'm sure a blood vessel has burst in my head. "STOP! STOP! STOP!" I scream. Pride has flown out the window.

Pratt stops cranking, and the spinning slows to a stop. As Pratt and LaTisha lift me from the wooden cabinet and lower me to the floor, I say, "If you do that to me again, I will die!"

Hark: "Then say it."

"Say what? What are the words you need to hear?"

"'I'm sick and I need help.'"

The thought of begging Harkins Horvath nauseates me almost as much as the machine has, but I *can't* go back in that box again. I force myself to parrot the words he wants to hear, "I'm sick and I need help."

"I'm sorry, did you say something?"

"I said what you asked me to."

"Did you? Hmm. See, Wogs, it's not so much the words themselves as the *feeling* behind the words I'm looking for. The *delivery*."

"I'm sick and I need help, for fucksake."

Hark looks at his two helpers and says, Ryan Seacrest-style, "H-h-how does America vote?"

LaTisha gives it two thumbs down.

"A wooden performance," Pratt declares. "One and a half stars."

Hark shrugs: *the judges have voted.* Pratt and LaTisha drag me toward the machine again. I try to resist, but my legs are wet noodles. I call out, "I'm sick and I need help," in what I hope is a more convincing tone. I still can't seem to hide a note of defiance, though.

Pratt and LaTisha pause in their dragging of me.

"Judges?" says Hark.

"Still no credibility as a character."

"Two stars," votes LaTisha. "Meh."

My captors share a laugh. Pratt and LaTisha toss me into the cabinet for another spin.

*No!* I need to say the magic words in a believable way. Like a Method actor, I dig for an emotional truth I can use to enliven my delivery. It occurs to me I truly *am* sick—from spinning in this goddamn machine—and I truly *do* need help; from someone, anyone, who can stop these goddamn psychopaths.

"I'm sick and I need help!" I cry in a raw voice, letting my private emotions drive my words. "I'm sick and I need help! I'm sick and I need help!"

Hark makes a surprised "o" with his mouth and turns again to his fellow "judges."

Pratt frowns, tilts his head left and right, then flips his thumb upward.

LaTisha says, "He had me that time."

Hark approaches me, arms wide with compassion. "So... Olliwog. Finally admitting you need help. And guess what? We believe you." He turns to his cohorts. "He needs help, poor chap. What can we do to help him?"

They all pause "thoughtfully," then Pratt shrugs and says, "Rotational therapy?"

"A smashing idea."

Pratt dashes up the steps to the cranking platform, chuckling.

"Fuck you! Fuck you! Fuck You!" I shout as the cabinet begins to spin again.

# Chapter 11

La Tisha and Pratt finally pull me from the rotating machine, and I fall as if magnetized to the floor. The room spins like a rooftop restaurant gone haywire, tipping wildly on its axis. My inner gyroscope is shot. Logic tells me the floor is horizontal, but it feels more vertical. My left leg pistons in air, trying to push me to a stand.

Hark's feet approach. His body pitches in all directions like an inflatable punch toy that's just been punched. He looks twenty feet tall. I have no words, no coherent thoughts, not a literal leg to stand on.

Tower-Hark clucks his tongue at Pratt and LaTisha. They grab me under the armpits.

"Stand up," Hark orders.

There *is* no up. I pedal my legs in random directions.

"Stand up," repeats Hawk.

"Can't," I say.

"You mean *won't*."

"Can't."

"As your clinician, it is my judgment that you *can*, but you're refusing to cooperate."

I flail my feet as Pratt and LaTisha tug at my armpits.

"The patient is being noncompliant," Pratt declares.

A tired "fuck you" spills from my mouth.

"Fortunately, we have an excellent clinical intervention for noncompliance," says Hark. "It will help with the patient's proprioception deficit as well."

*Proprioception deficit?* Where did Hark pick up a ten-dollar term like that? Proprioception refers to a person's sense of bodily balance and spatial orientation. And yes, mine is certainly in deficit.

"Clem, Joanna," orders Hark, using his helpers' real names for the first time, either by accident or because he thinks I'm too disoriented to notice.

Clem and Joanna—aka Pratt and LaTisha—lift me to my feet and hold me upright, my arms across their shoulders like a Friday night drunk's. They walk me to a nearby contraption, the one called The Clock. Hark pulls a handle on the ornate, grandfather-clock-shaped cabinet. Its front swings open like a door. Clem and Joanna shove me into the narrow space.

Hark closes the old hardwood cabinet with a heavy *clack*. Claustrophobia wells up. The device was designed for someone shorter than me; I need to scrunch down to align my face with the round clockface-hole.

"There, that ought to help you get your legs back under you." Hark tugs the lapels of his white jacket.

The spinning floor *is* starting to settle. Still motion-drunk, I look out at the other devices in the room, dreading my encounters with each of them—particularly the lobotomy and trepanation tools. How far does Hark plan to take this?

As I'm scanning the room, I spot two new people standing in the shadows about ten yards away. One male, one female. Middle-aged bodies. Both wearing wooden boxes on their heads, the type with the cut-out front that Hark wore—inspired by the Tranquilizing Chair.

Who the hell are they? Why are they here?

"The Clock," announces Hark in a professorial tone, "was an early tool of your trade, long before *dignity* and *human rights* were even a gleam in the eye of modern psychiatry. As you may recall from your museum tour, The Clock was used for punishment and restraint, but it also had a therapeutic purpose. Pop quiz: what was that purpose?"

I groan internally but keep my face expressionless.

"Humiliation," supplies Hark. "Now, by today's 'enlightened' standards, humiliation of mental patients might be considered inhumane, but perhaps your peers of old were on to something. Perhaps they knew that pride is a powerful barrier to growth." Hark struts in front of me, gesturing like a lecturer. "Alas, it is an extremely stubborn barrier to penetrate. To cure pride—especially pride as... *intransigent* as yours—requires dedicated interventions. And so..."

He walks up close to The Clock and leans over me, his eyeballs inches from mine. "When I count to three, you will please sing 'I'm a Little Teapot.'"

My mind does a double-take. What? "I don't know what that is."

"Yes, you do," says Hark.

"I don't."

"You do, Olliwog. Everyone does."

"*I* don't."

He blows out a sigh, looks at the floor, then at me again. "It is a song schoolchildren sang back in your day. It is still in usage. You know it, so sing it."

"I don't know it!"

"You're lying, Wogs."

He's right. I am. And I hate him for knowing that. I hate him even more for having pushed me up against the edge of my pride with such crude tactics. Still I insist, "I don't know the damn song!"

"He needs more time in the spin cycle," Hark pronounces wearily. Clem and Joanna march toward The Clock, preparing to grab me for another go-'round in O'Halloran's Swing.

"All right! No! No! I'll try it."

Hark glares at me with impatience, waves off his helpers.

"On the count of three." He holds up his hand. "A-one and a-two and a..."

Over the next several minutes—with Hark coaching me to "put a little Carol Channing in it," and "add some squeals of delight"—I manage to belt out a version of "I'm a Little Teapot" worthy of a community theater star in a small Minnesota town.

Not good enough for Hark. "It needs more... personality. Name a famous cartoon character."

I blurt out Betty Boop—prompted, no doubt, by my hallucination during the skeleton dance. Big mistake. Hark finds an image of the 1930s vamp on his phone and instructs Joanna to make up my face to resemble her. She approaches me with a makeup pouch and applies white, red, and black clown paint to my face in big, rough strokes.

Hark and company force me to sing "I'm a Little Teapot" in the voice of Betty Boop, adding a *boop-boop-be-doop* after every line. Whenever my "creative energy" wanes or the smile fades from my face, Clem invokes the threat of pepper spray and a high-speed romp in O'Halloran's Swing.

Hark starts to appear bored but then gets a "divine inspiration." He composes a set of X-rated lyrics, beginning with, "I'm a little crack whore, hear me grunt," and forces me to sing it, sexy-Betty-style. After a couple of run-throughs, he decides it will be funnier to release me from The Clock so I can *dance* the number as well as sing it—adding shoulder shimmies and other Broadway moves the memory of which I shall repress till my dying day.

Hark gleefully directs, and I perform, until all trace of dignity has been burned away. All the while, the two mystery figures wearing boxes on their heads watch the show from a distance, betraying nothing.

"Okay, enough," says Hark at last, holding his belly with laughter. "Wow, you pulled things from yourself that should never have been pulled. Woo! *That's* something I can never unsee or unhear. Tell me, though—and be honest—don't *you* feel better?"

I hate—with all the force of nuclear fusion—to admit it, but I do feel somewhat lighter. Is it from tossing off the shackles of shame so utterly or from plastering a lunatic grin on my face for so long? When you smile, even artificially, you release endorphins that go straight to the mood centers of the brain.

Or does my inner brightness perhaps stem from the redoubling of my commitment to see Harkins Horvath III rotting in a hospital for the criminally insane for all eternity?

Yeah, probably that last one.

"No, I don't," I fib, in answer to his question.

"Liar." Hark sighs in disgust, then turns to his colleagues. "Judges?"

"I thought it was a little pitchy," opines Joanna/LaTisha.

"Didn't think he connected with the lyrics," says Clem/Pratt.

"Congratulations," Hark tells me, "You're through to the next round... of rotational therapy, that is!"

Damn these people to fuck.

. . .

Clem and Joanna drag my board-stiff body toward the O'Halloran device. Hark stops them at the last moment, saying, "No, not that one. He needs to work on a different axis this time." Hark nods toward the device called the Hollow Wheel, from the late eighteenth century. It turns on a horizontal axle rather than a vertical one.

Clem and Joanna drag and drop me near the indicated machine, which is nothing more than a human-sized hamster wheel encased in wood.

"Work on a *different axis?* Get it, Olliwog? A little psychiatric diagnostic humor. Axis I, Axis II... like in the DSM-5! Hyuck, hyuck! Well, *I* thought it was funny. Okay, get inside the wheel."

No point fighting him. I crawl toward the device, feigning stoicism. As I open the three-foot-high entry door on the side of the wheel, I smile at him. "What's that sound I hear, Hark? Plop, plop, plop. Oh—must be the sound of criminal charges piling up."

I climb through the low hatch and stand up within the narrow inner space. From the light spilling in through the small open door, I can see that the curved surface is crisscrossed with wooden slats every foot or so—treads for turning the wheel. The Nordic Track circa 1789.

Hark bends to look up at me through the low doorway. "The Hollow Wheel, or Hayner's Wheel, was used on mental patients for punishment, exercise, persuasion, and, oh, just general shits and giggles. *Treatment*, in other words. So here is *your* treatment goal: you will turn the wheel *x* number of times. If you succeed, you will receive a reward; if you do not, you will be punished. What is the value of *x*? As the patient, you are not privy to that information."

Hark shuts the small door and latches it. I find myself in almost total darkness.

"Let 'er rip, Hamster Boy!" he shouts, thumping the outer wall twice.

*Die, Asshole.*

I actually feel pretty well equipped for this particular challenge. I can run five miles on the treadmill at Fitness Plus without breaking a sweat.

Bring it on.

. . .

Call it off.

After less than three minutes of churning the big wheel, which isn't terribly heavy, I'm spent. I can't explain why. Maybe I was in that fake hospital bed longer than I know and my muscles have atrophied. I slow to a plodding march. A stitch of pain forms in my gut, and I place my hand on my belly. Something feels odd there. That adorable spare tire I've been carting around for the last decade? It's gone. *What?*

"Come on, Olliwog!" shouts Hark from outside, "Speed it up. You're nowhere near your quota. Pretend you're milling wheat for your daily bread."

*Bread. Food. Yes. I want to eat. Anything and everything.*

I try to run faster, but there's nothing left in my legs and no reserves in my cardio system. I slow to a plod again.

"You're not even close to *x*," shouts the voice of Hark from outside the dark chamber.

Sue me. I drop to my hands and knees. The momentum of the wheel carries me backward for a few feet, and then the wheel stops and resettles in the other direction. I collapse, chest down, on the treads. I'm finished. Why is my tank so empty?

"Olliwog," says Hark, "you're letting your treatment team down. We're starting to think you're not serious about getting well."

"Fuck you," I reply in the dark. Can't beat the old standards.

The little door opens, letting in light. Hark pokes his head in. "Tsk, tsk. Your reward for hitting the target number *was* going to be a bucket of chicken from KFC..."

My stomach explodes in a symphony of gurgles. I'm not usually a fan of battered bird parts torched under a heat lamp for hours, but a bucket of KFC sounds like pure heaven.

"... But unfortunately you didn't earn it. So you get the booby prize instead."

• : •

I'm back in The Fucking Clock again.

What humiliation awaits me next?

My captors—including the two box-headed spectators—left the room about twenty minutes earlier, and I've been trapped in this thing, alone, hearing only their muffled voices from beyond a distant wall.

At last, a whistling Hark returns, carrying a tablet device. "Oh did I mention?" He holds the tablet in front of my face. "We were videoing your whole performance. I edited together all the best bits."

He taps the play arrow and unleashes a video of me singing and dancing "I'm a Little Crack Whore" a la Betty Boop, with cartoon sound effects added. Rage and shame *explode* within me. It is the most humiliating spectacle I've ever laid eyes on.

And Hark has possession of it.

It's settled, I am going to kill this man, first chance I get.

I try to turn away from the screen, but then I notice something in the video that supersedes my anger. My bone structure. Beneath the clownish Boop makeup, my face looks weirdly gaunt. My body too. I've definitely lost weight. A lot of it.

How is that possible? I remember looking in a bathroom mirror back in the old hotel. That was only yesterday, right? I appeared to be my normal weight then.

"Noticing the Jenny Craig effect?" Hark says. He opens The Clock and releases me. "There's something I've been meaning to tell you. Let's walk... and talk."

Hark puts his hand on my shoulder and we cross the room together. "You probably noticed your stamina lagging in the ol' wheel o' fun. And your hunger spiking into the red zone. Well, that's because..."

We arrive at the Isolation Box. It is exactly what it sounds like: a wooden box, not much larger than a crate for a big dog, too small to stand in. It features a feeding hole in its front door, with a sliding metal slat covering it.

"... actually, you might want to sit for what I'm about to tell you..."

He opens the door, gestures me into the box. Like a beaten dog, I duck inside and sit on the small bench within. Hark locks the door and addresses me through the circular feeding hole.

"I'm afraid you haven't eaten in a while. Sixteen days, to be exact."

*Sixteen days? What is he talking about? I ate yesterday in the "hospital."*

"You're not starving yet, but you're close. You weigh a buck-sixty-two at the moment. Like I said, not a Feed the Children poster but a good ways from your former one-eighty-six."

I inquire politely as to how in the ass-ripping fuck such a thing could be possible.

"Here's all you need to know for now: food and a *much* nicer habitat await you, once you prove to us you're ready for your next phase of treatment. How long that takes is up to you. But given your current nutritional status, you might want to step it up a bit." He starts to leave, then turns back to me and adds, through the hole, "As to where those sixteen days went, you'll have plenty of time to cogitate on that in your new home: the Isolation Box. I call it the iBox! Adios for now, Olliwog. There's a jug of water right there and a bucket to shit in. And here..."

He tosses a travel-pack of moist towelettes through the hole.

"Wipe that makeup off, you look like a friggin' idiot."

He pulls the slat down over the six-inch hole. Darkness descends.

# Chapter 12

In the blackness of the iBox, the question *How did I lose sixteen days of my life?* becomes my dark star, the gravitational mass around which all thoughts revolve.

How could it have happened?

When I looked in the mirror in that renovated hotel room, I was at my normal weight. Therefore, the weight loss—and time loss—must have occurred after I was moved from the old hotel.

It could only have happened before I awoke in the Utica Crib the first time or after I fell asleep in it later. Probably the latter. I remember Hark, before he left, urging me to eat, telling me I might not get any more food for a while. I also remember being in that semi-conscious state I knew wasn't a dream for what seemed like a *long* time, much longer than one night.

I must have been in some kind of artificially induced coma.

People who recover from comas often report having lived an alternate version of their normal lives the whole time they were comatose. They get up every day, eat breakfast, go to work—but in coma-reality. However, coma-reality also has weird differences from real life. Like my Emmy/office "dream" did.

As a physician, I know it's no easy task to keep a person unconscious for long periods. The risks are high. You need to know what you're doing— that's why anesthesiologists earn the BMW bucks—and you need to have access to some highly restricted drugs and special equipment. But if anyone would have the resources to pull such a thing off, it would be Hark.

Yes, some kind of coma inducement must have occurred. That's the only explanation for my sixteen-day alternate reality experience. By contrast, my earlier time lapse—those missing days between my Thanksgiving Eve drive on the Apache Trail and my awakening in their fake hospital—was a pure blank.

Why would Hark want to starve me, though? Easy: because he wanted me in a weakened, needy state before starting his "treatment plan" in earnest. So I'd be Play-Doh in his hands.

*Well, surprise, Ass-wad, you may have handed me the key to victory.*

What if I *play into* Hark's expectations?

What if I lull my captors into thinking I'm already broken—in body, mind, and spirit—and resigned to passive acceptance? If I can do that convincingly, they'll eventually let their guard down. And then I can make a move, using the element of surprise.

Yes.

I'll play the traumatized zombie. But behind my glazed eyes I'll be watching them like a cat watching a mousehole, waiting for my chance to spring. And when I spot that chance, I'll grab a tool or weapon, or... whatever possibility suggests itself.

And I'll seize the upper hand.

Somehow.

It's not exactly a plan, but it's an *angle*, a chance to turn the tables so that *I'm* playing the meta-game, not Hark—that crazy-assed son of a blue-tailed fuck.

I grab the wipes and start cleaning the makeup off my face.

• • •

Sitting in the dark iBox, I think about the Zen Warrior mindset I'll need to achieve to pull off my surprise attack. I will have to be more alert, more observant, more mindful than I've ever been in my life. Am I up to the challenge?

I don't know. But I certainly have time to practice.

Sadly, there's nothing to focus on, here in the Isolation Box. Nothing but blackness and silence.

Well, let's see about that.

Turning up my hearing up to a 10 and holding it there, I become aware of a tapestry of ambient noises I hadn't noticed before: the drone of a fan motor, the ticking of the old building's timbers, the running of water through a pipe. These sounds were present earlier; I just didn't perceive them.

I switch my focus to the visual. The darkness in here isn't total, I realize. Tiny flecks of light shine through a hundred imperfections in the iBox's wooden door. One nail-hole at the bottom is letting in enough light to create a four-inch streamer on the floor. I focus *all* my attention on that little dot of light and its tail. The light becomes my entire universe.

Time disappears. I am The Watcher of the Light. I am the witnessing presence, nothing more.

A shift happens—I feel like I'm floating up and out of my body. A wave of bliss washes through me. What am I doing to myself?

Meditating, that's what. Like a damn Tibetan monk. Holy crap. I've never been able to do this before! Hannah does it regularly. Em tried to teach it to me. My partner Abe swears by it. But I've never been able to meditate for even ten seconds. Now I *get* what all the fuss is about.

Alas, the *realization* that I'm meditating kicks my thinking-mind back into gear, and I crash out of the meditative state. But I still feel its residual bliss. And I'm still more alert, more attuned than I've been in decades. My senses are *jacked*.

Over the next few hours, I'm able to regain that pure witnessing state two more times, for longer periods—once by focusing on that swatch of light again, once by focusing on the distant sound of the fan. Single-pointed focus is the key.

Single-pointed focus.

*Watch out, Ass-wad. I'm coming for you.*

A smell awakens me from sleep—something delectable sautéing in butter. Garlic and some exotic ingredient. My stomach lurches to life, churning and squirting in its weeks-empty state. I lift my head and shoulders only to uncork a massively stiff neck and a bladder in need of emptying.

But all is subordinate to that smell. That ambrosial smell. It seems to be coming from only feet away. My soul, my soul, my mythical soul for a bite of whatever is cooking.

Wait. This must be Hark tormenting me. There is no kitchen nearby. He's deliberately creating this smell, somehow, to drive me crazy. He knows I'm starving.

My suspicions are confirmed. The slat covering the six-inch feeding hole slides up to reveal Hark's grinning face, three feet away. The smell pours in, stronger now. It fills my being, making every lysosome in my body stand at attention.

Hark beckons me forward. I'm eager to learn the source of the smell, but I remind myself to play "dead." I lean toward the hole, my face slack and emotionless.

Hark sits in a folding chair outside the iBox, wearing a napkin at his neck. In front of him is a wheeling table bearing a single-burner propane cooker. A Mauviel copper-core frying pan heats on the burner, and within the pan, gently bubbling in butter, are roundish slices of a coral-patterned, musky-smelling ingredient, sprinkled with minced garlic and sprigs of a green herb. My stomach squeals like a party favor.

"You've been sleeping *really* soundly," says Hark. "Careful. Someone could take advantage of you in that state. Drug you. Rape you. What-not. Especially the what-not, gotta watch out for that."

He looks down at his table, at an array of polished hardware laid out like silverware. Trepanation instruments. I recall with a stab of anxiety what the tools are designed for.

Hark selects one with a curved, hatchet-like blade.

Wielding the instrument in one hand, a fork in the other, he cuts a piece of the maze-like, marbled ingredient from the pan and places it in his mouth. He closes his eyes and chews with orgasmic delight.

"Do you remember that scene in *Hannibal*," he says, "where Lecter is sautéing slices of a certain... *delicacy* and feeding them to Ray Liotta while Liotta sits there smiling like a happy jackass?"

I shrug emptily. I know there was a famous scene like that, but the details elude me. And I don't want to show interest. I'm Bud Zombie.

"Do you remember what that delicacy was?"

The chef in question was Hannibal Lecter, so I'm guessing it wasn't fairy bread. I shake my head no, keeping the glaze in my eyes.

"*Think*, Olliwog, think. In the scene, Ray Liotta has been surgically altered in a very striking way. If you remember how, you'll remember the answer." He gives me a few seconds. "Jodie Foster refused to be in the movie because of this one scene." He pauses again. "Give up? Lecter was feeding Liotta slices of... his own brain."

My heart jerks in my chest and my hands dart to my head.

Zombie act blown. But at least my skull cap is still attached.

Hark laughs, stomps his feet, and points at me in a *gotcha* way. "That scene was awesome. I think of it whenever I'm cooking white truffles. That's what I'm having for breakfast this morning. I would love for you to join me—this stuff is way too rich for one person—but, regrettably, you haven't earned high-level privileges yet."

He makes a show of cutting and savoring another truffle slice. My stomach feels like it's flipping inside out.

"Fortunately," he says, "I have some company to help me." He turns and gestures behind him. Two figures roll into view on wheeling chairs—the man and woman who were standing in the background when I was locked in The Clock, the ones with the wooden boxes over their heads. They're still wearing them. I feel a stir of dread in their presence. They fold their arms, their box-shadowed faces aimed toward me.

"I told you I had colleagues," Hark says as he prepares a small plate for each of them. "Did you think I was referring to Clem and Joanna— 'Detective Pratt' and 'Nurse LaTisha'? Nah, they're just employees—exundercover cops with 'appetites' that got them in trouble and rendered them highly employable by someone like *moi*."

Undercover cops. Makes sense. To survive in that job, you have to be an Oscar-level character actor. Your life might depend on it.

"The *real* members of your treatment team," Hark continues, gesturing to the pair with the boxes on their heads—"have a much more... *personal* stake in your treatment."

He hands Box-Head Man and Box-Head Woman their food dishes.

"Listen carefully, Olliwoggles. It's important you hear this *now*, while my teammates' identities remain anonymous. Soon you will learn who they are, and you will become irrationally terrified and confused. You will be convinced that the only reason we are putting you through this 'process' is that we *want* to see you suffer. And while there may be a *soupçon* of truth in that—ha!—you need to believe me when I tell you: your pain and suffering are not our ultimate aim." He turns to his box-shrouded colleagues; their boxes nod once. He looks at me again. "It's important you understand that—while you're still capable of rational thought.

"So..." He sets his fork down and claps his palms together. "Shall we commence the day's festivities?"

My impulse is to fight like a wild chimp when Clem opens the door to the iBox to let me out. But I remind myself of my game plan: play the shell-shocked meat-puppet and watch for opportunity. I may have blown my act once, but it's still my best hope.

Opportunity arises almost instantly. As Clem is pulling me out of the box, I see he's going to walk me right past the trepanation tools on Hark's table. If his attention wavers for even half a second, I will lunge for one of the tools and put it to Hark's neck. I'll threaten to kill him unless the others do as I say.

I'll *actually* kill him if I have to. I will.

Hark seems to read my mind. He looks at my eyes, then at the tools, and tells Clem, "Watch his hands. Put him in the snuggy jacket and bind his feet."

Clem and Joanna strap me into the straitjacket and tie my ankles together with a foot of rope between them so I can't walk faster than a shuffle. My hopes of being able to spring like a cat have been put on hold.

Watch and wait, then.

• • •

The longest day of my life proceeds to unfold. I won't describe it in detail, but suffice it to say it is Hark's magnum opus in his fine art of sculpting human misery.

The day includes all the "treatments" I endured yesterday—the Bath of Surprise, O'Halloran's Swing, the Hollow Wheel—interspersed with a whole new assortment of thrilling surprises from the annals of institutional mental hygiene.

Hark seems to understand, either by intuition or study, a principle the great tormentors of history have always known: the surest way to break a mind is through a combination of forced helplessness and unpredictability.

After stripping me naked and bombarding my body with alternating blasts of hot and ice-cold water, a form of "hydrotherapy" used on mental patients in the early 1900s, Hark and company lead me to the most dreaded location of all—the trepanation chair. Hark spends ten minutes fitting my head into the vise-like contraption designed to hold the trepanation drill steady as it bores through the skull, only to tell me he's "just kidding" and release me.

He starts to lead me away, then pushes me right back into the chair. This time, after securing the drill guide on my head a second time, he actually commences the drilling process, lightly puncturing the skin of my scalp before declaring, "Just kidding *again*."

Hark next leads me to the Insulin Coma Therapy "exhibit" but then slaps himself on the head. "What am I thinking? You've already *had* this treatment, but I suppose you've figured that out by now." I hadn't, but I do now. Prolonged insulin shock, an old treatment for schizophrenia, must be the means by which Hark kept me comatose for those sixteen days. Patients in the 1940s and '50s were kept in insulin comas for up to six weeks. To pull me out of *my* coma, Hark must have given me a shot of glucose along with the Bath of Surprise. That's why he was holding a syringe when I first emerged from the ice water.

For the next illuminating session, we make our way to the Bloodletting area, where Hark informs me my "humours" are in need of rebalancing. An actual leeching treatment ensues. Yes, a dozen parasitic pond-worms are attached to the skin of my chest and back for half an hour. It's every bit the rip-roaring adventure it sounds like.

The amount of thought, expense, and preparation Hark has put into this whole process provides a terrifying window into the man's state of mind.

As hour follows relentless hour, I strive to stay mindful and alert, watching for an opportunity to make a move. But my captors remain vigilant, guarding me at all times and putting the straitjacket back on me between "treatments."

The watchful state of mind I'm practicing has a side benefit, though. By staying fully focused on my present-moment experience, I'm able to prevent fear from sinking its hooks in me. I'm simply accepting whatever happens, without judgment. Oddly, I feel quite liberated.

This freed state of mind prevails until about midday, when a particularly agonizing spin in O'Halloran's Swing turns my mind into a knot of fear again. And then, as Hark is strapping me onto the stretcher-board for a no-longer-surprising dunk in the Bath of Surprise, something snaps. The fear drains out of me all at once—not because I'm back in Zen Warrior mode but because mental collapse has occurred.

I have no fucks left to give; do what you want to me. I'm a water balloon with eyes. Game over, I lose. The very state I was trying to fake.

Hark notices my internal change immediately. He stops strapping me onto the board and leans in close to me, studying my eyes. "Welly, welly, Wellington, Master McWoggles, are you finally *there*? Have you achieved surrender?"

He unbuckles the straps across my body.

"We'll know soon enough. We have one more intervention for you. Unlike the others, it's not drawn from history. It's sort of my own invention. I think you're going to like it immensely. Which is to say, not one tiny bit."

# Chapter 13

"You've heard of ECT..." Hark adjusts the electrode headset on my skull. "*Heard* of it? What am I saying? You've *administered* it. To hundreds of unsuspecting patients."

For the record, I've never once administered ECT, better known as shock therapy, to an "unsuspecting" patient—my ECT patients have always requested the treatment with open eyes and signed waivers—but I have no urge to argue with Hark.

"Yep," Hark continues, "you love to fire the ol' joy juice into their skulls until they're so neurologically traumatized they forget to be sad. Beats listening to their whining, right? Ha! ECT—brought to you by the good folks who invented rotational therapy."

Again I could mount an argument. I could point out that today's ECT is administered humanely, under general anesthesia, and can relieve the stubbornest symptoms of major depression in suffering patients who have not responded to other treatments.

But I'm done arguing. Done caring.

I'm seated, in a padded armchair, at one end of a table in a small conference room, my head hooked up to a device that does crudely resemble an ECT console. I'm strapped down, of course—what else is new? Hark sits at the console and adjusts a dial. At the far end of the table, opposite my seat, is a conspicuously empty chair.

ANDREW WOLFENDON

Terror should be my dominant emotion, but my pulse is trucking along at a mellow sixty-five bpm. I don't know if this is monk-like detachment or PTSD.

Hark resumes his spiel. "Yes, you and ECT are old pals, but are you familiar with EC-*double* T? Probably not, since I made it up and you're my first patient. Hyuck, a-hyuck-hyuck! ECTT—Electroconvulsive *Truth* Therapy. How does it work, you ask?"

I don't.

"Well, I'll tell ya, gol' dang it, settle daown! Here's how: The patient is asked a series of questions to which he must reply honestly. If he tells a lie, negative reinforcement in the form of Ben Franklin's Bottled Lightning is delivered smack to the patient's brain-box. Each false answer results in an increase of voltage until honesty is achieved. Any questions?"

None. The idea of pain doesn't frighten me anymore. It really doesn't. If pain happens to this body, I'll experience it as an observer, not a participant.

"You're probably wondering," Hark goes on, "how the administrator of the test *determines* whether the patient is answering truthfully."

I'm not.

"Hold your horses, Mr. Anson D. Pants, I'm gittin' thar." He texts a one-word message on his phone. The door opens and the mystery woman with the wooden box over her head walks in and sits at the end of the table opposite me. She's wearing a patterned green shirt and appears to be in her fifties or sixties, not in terrific shape. "Do you remember in *Meet the Parents* when De Niro did the human lie detector routine?" Hark inquires. "Well, we have our own human lie detector right here on staff. If you lie in response to any question I ask, she will know."

Translation: welcome to another mind-fuck session.

"Shall we begin?"

I nano-shrug a shoulder.

Hark takes a folded paper from his white doctor's jacket, opens it. "I'll ask the questions, you give the answers. We'll start with an easy one: If, as your book claims, there is no intelligent meta-consciousness organizing the

95

cosmos, how do you explain the prevalence of miracles—meaningful synchronicities entailing chains of trillion-to-one coincidences?"

Is he serious? Damned if my sixty-five-bpm pulse doesn't giddyup a bit.

He stares at me for three seconds, then slaps the table and laughs. "Just kidding. Okay, real question." He does the voice of the bridge troll in *Monty Python and the Holy Grail*. "*What...* is your favorite color?"

I wait to see if *this* is a joke. Guess not.

"Blue."

Hark looks to the box-headed woman. She nods once.

"Ding-ding," says Hark. "You dodged Old Sparky! Earned a lollipop too." He tosses a bargain-store yellow lollipop onto my lap. It actually looks delicious, but with my hands strapped down I can't grab it. "See how easy this is? Just answer honestly and you'll be zappage-free. Next question..." He refers to his notes again. "When you were in our 'hospital,' did you begin to doubt the soundness of your own mind?"

My ego rebels. I don't want to admit to Hark that his fake-hospital ruse was the least bit effective on me, but I choose the safe route, truth. "Yes."

Hark looks to Box Head. She nods.

"Ding-ding. Two for two. Way to go, Woggles. No lollipop, though, till you finish your first one! Okay, question three: Did you believe you had sustained a brain injury?"

My mind wants to deny it, but again the truth comes out. "I started to." I strive to keep my voice emotionless. "Yes."

A nod from Box Head.

"Ding-ding *again*. You're crushin' it, ma boy. I spelled that *b-o-i* in my mind, like on da Internets. Ha! Next question: Did you *actually* have a brain injury?"

"No."

Quick nod from Box Head.

"Ding. Wow, these high-priced jumper cables are all revved up with no one to 'lectrocute. You're so honest! Next: So you didn't *factually* have a brain disorder but your stay in our hospital convinced you that you did?"

"You could say that."

"I just did. Would *you* say it?"

"I suppose so."

"You *suppose* so? Okay, so listen, Woggums, I forgot to mention something. Hesitant or evasive responses also earn a ride on Uncle Twitchy's Lightning Train. Bear that in mind. I'll give you one more chance to answer directly."

"Yes," I amend my answer.

Box Head nods.

"Ding-ding. Guess my itchy trigger finger ain't gonna get a workout today! Next question... cue *Jeopardy* music..." He looks at his paper. "Isn't the reason you accepted a false narrative about your own mind because of the power of institutional authority—the hospital setting, the nurse, the detective with the badge—to shape human belief?"

"What had me believing a false narrative," I reply evenly, "was the fact that you were drugging me and lying to me and manufacturing fake and contradictory evidence."

"And institutional authority played no part in your false belief?"

I don't answer.

"Evasive," Hark declares. "Time to light up Christmastown! Yee-haw! Clench your teeth and reel in your tongue!" He flips a switch on the control board.

*Holy Fuck!* My head—my whole body—ignites in shock like a finger in a light socket, times five. I scream through my clamped teeth. Pain isn't even the right word for this.

Hark kills the current. Relief is instantaneous.

The smells of ozone and burnt hair waft around my head. Good God. That crap I was telling myself about being detached from physical pain? Forget it. I don't *ever* want to feel that current again.

I sit up, eyes wide. Hark has my damn attention.

"Oops," he says, "Might have had the dial turned up a bit high for a first dose. Donnie Doofus here. Remember that scene in *The Green Mile* where the guy-in-the-electric-chair's head is blowing smoke and his eyes are bulging out 'cause the guard is messing up the procedure? That's me, totally! Let's try again: Did institutional authority make you believe you had a brain disorder you did not, in fact, have?"

"It played a part, yes."

Hark turns to Box Head, the mystery woman who inexplicably holds my fate in her hands. After a pause, she nods.

"Ring-a-ling-a-ding-dong-ding. Back on the winning track. Next question: As a psychiatrist, *you* wield institutional authority, do you not?"

"I suppose I do." I catch my noncommittal answer. "Yes! Yes, I do."

"So *you* have the power to create narratives for others?"

"I... Yes."

"And have you ever—ever in your career—abused that power by creating a narrative to serve your *own* needs, rather than the patient's?"

Whoa. Where did *that* question come from?

I want with all my heart to say no, but "Yes" spills quietly from my mouth.

"Good golly, Miss Ollie, *that* answer was mighty close to the surface, wasn't it?" Hark looks again to Box Head. She nods solemnly.

"Ding," says Hark. "Hmm, we seem to have hit on a fruitful line of inquiry. Shall we dive into that topic now or save it for later in your treatment, when your teacup's a little less shit-filled? Tell ya what, let's put a pin in it. We'll switch tracks for now. Let's see how you fare in the *emotional* honesty department. Oooo, this should be fun. Ready? When you were our patient at St. Clownifer's—good one, Joanna!—what emotions were you experiencing most strongly?"

Where is he going with this? "Confusion," I reply. Easy one.

Box Head nods.

"Anger."

Box Head nods again.

The next one is obvious too, but a bit harder to admit. "Fear."

Another nod from the judge.

"Ding-dang-dong on all three," says Hark. "Follow-up question: I think I can surmise where the confusion and anger were coming from—ha—but what about the fear? What was the source of that?"

"What do you think? I was afraid I had a brain injury. I was afraid of being drugged. I was afraid of being physically harmed. I was afraid the police really believed I was someone named Greenbird and I might be under arrest."

Hark and Box Head look at each other. She nods but adds a tiny shrug.

"Madame Eight Ball says all those things are true, but you're holding something back. So, what else? What scared you the *most*?"

I've given them enough, damn it. No more. Box Head isn't *really* reading my mind; she's using some form of educated guessing. "I can't think of anything else."

Box Head swings her boxed head from side to side.

Fuck. Hark flips the switch again.

*God, that current!* It's stronger this time. My jaw, neck, and shoulders clench together like a fist. Through my locked teeth, I yell, "AAAGH! FUCK! ALL RIGHT! ALL RIGHT! THE FROG!"

Hark kills the juice. My muscles unclench.

"The frog," I wheeze out. "The thing with the frog scared me the most."

Box Head nods. Who the hell *is* this woman and how is she reading me so accurately? I must be giving her a "tell" of some kind in my eyes or body language. Maybe she can detect micro-changes in human expression. Dogs can do that; surely some people can too.

"And why was that?" inquires Hark.

How truthful do I need to be? "Because I have a fear of frogs. A phobia, I guess you'd say. An old one."

"And...?"

"And I had the feeling the skeleton dancer, the tallest one, knew about it somehow. But that's not possible, because I've never told anyone about it, not even my wife. So I was afraid—I don't know—that my mind was being... *probed.* In some way."

Hark looks to Box Head, who nods, but again only slowly.

"Ding. She's saying that's true, but there may be more. Let's move on, though. Oh, B-T-dubya—that tall dancer? That was lil' ol' me. The other two were Clem and Joanna."

Of course. Should have known. The thought that it was Hark himself who threw that frog onto my bed sends shivers through me for reasons I don't even *want* to comprehend.

Hark grins. "Took us an hour to wash that body paint off. So. What other emotions did you feel in the 'hospital room'?"

I'm tired, I'm drained, I'm weak with hunger. I want this over with. "Guilt," I offer him.

"About what?"

I'm not giving him Emmy, no way. "About something skeevy the fake detective accused me of being part of. I knew I wasn't present at the event he described, but I felt guilty anyway."

Long pause from Box Head, then a small nod.

"Again, the truth but not the whole truth," says Hark. "But let's press on. What other emotions were you feeling?"

I throw him one more. "Self-pity."

"Poor little Ollie. What else?"

I spread my palms. Nothing else.

"That's all you can come up with? Final answer?"

"Final answer."

Box Head gives the "no" sign and Hark hits the switch. *God, the voltage.*

"STOP! STOP! *GRIEF!* GOD DAMN IT! GRIEF!" I yell through locked teeth.

Hark kills the juice. My body un-tenses once again. As it does, I feel—and almost *hear*—a crack inside me, from the base of my spine to the top of my head. My psychological armor drops away, releasing its grip on me like a doomed climber letting go of a rock. Leaving me raw, naked, exposed.

"I didn't hear you," says Hark.

"Grief. I was feeling grief... My daughter died in September. She drove through a railing and off an embankment. The weather was clear, there was no sign she braked." The words pour out of me as if lubricated, words I have been unable to speak since that bleak September day. "It was suicide. My daughter killed herself. She killed herself in a car."

My head slumps forward, my chin resting on my sternum. I try to buttress the dam holding back the reservoir of tears. *Try* is the operant word. What kind of psychiatrist—what kind of *father*—misses the signs of suicide in his own daughter?

Hark observes me in my broken state for a minute, then wheels his chair toward me, moving almost respectfully into my personal space. "That's all for now, Olls." His voice is soft as he leans his head into mine. "You've reached a milestone in your treatment: truthfulness with yourself and your treatment team."

He stands, laying a hand on my shoulder. "Just so you know, the current we've been running through you? Barely enough to light a broom closet; not enough to kill you. The current that's running through you *now*, though? *That's* the one with the real power. *That's* known as emotional honesty. Get used to it. You're going to need it for the next phase of your treatment."

Hark and Box Head consult each other with their eyes. She nods.

"Congratulations, Olliwog. You're being moved to a higher-level setting."

# PART III
## Transition

# Chapter 14

My kidnappers have been kind enough not to drug me for this road trip, but they have blindfolded and handcuffed me. They've fed me a take-out meal, too, from a fast-food Mexican place, which I devoured so fast I bit my tongue three times. They've also installed a GPS monitor on my right ankle—the kind paroled prisoners wear.

We've been on the road a while now, well over an hour I'm guessing.

We seem to be doing a lot of mountain driving; the transmission of the GMC Yukon whines for long stretches, pulling uphill duty. My inner compass tells me we're driving east—against the movement of the sun. If so, that would likely put us on Route 60 or Route 87. That's assuming we were even in the Phoenix area to begin with.

Clem is driving. Joanna is not with us. I'm in the backseat with Hark, who's being eerily silent. The long ride with a full stomach in relatively non-life-threatening conditions allows my mind to return home to Hannah.

*What does she know about my situation? Have my kidnappers communicated with her? Is she worried about me or glad to be rid of my sorry ass?*

I fear the answer may be the latter, considering the way I've been treating her since we returned from Emily's memorial. How could I have let things go the way I did? I love my wife. She is better than me in every regard. And now I'm on the cusp of losing her, if I haven't already.

As the car powers up another mountain, I make a private vow: if I get out of this mess—and that's far, far from guaranteed—I will do everything humanly possible to win her back. And I will give her my full heart and presence every day going forward.

I feel a surge of energy rise from the base of my spine. Yes. I needed a power-thought to fire me up, to put the fight back in me, and that's the one that does it. Hannah. Again.

I *will* figure out a way to escape Hark's clutches and reunite with my brilliant, beautiful, extraordinary wife. And I *will* make Hark pay for his actions.

Provided he doesn't kill me first.

Right, so that.

Mustn't let it happen, then. Must stay sharp and watch for opportunity.

*Have my captors left an evidence trail behind?* I wonder. *Are the police following it?* My brain strains for details, trying again to remember the circumstances that preceded my capture. I distinctly remember abandoning my Thanksgiving-Eve Whole Foods quest and heading out to the Apache Trail. What prompted me to do that?

When recalling that drive, I have a clear memory of feeling *lured* along Route 88, past the funky old Tortilla Flat (pop. 6) settlement, and onto the twisty mountain trail beyond. Something was drawing me, pulling me, in a mysterious way. What was it? It must have been set up by Hark somehow—my drive down that scenic dirt road is the last thing I remember before waking up in his faux hospital—but how did he do it? What trail of breadcrumbs did he lay out for me, and why did I follow it?

And if the Apache Trail was indeed the location of my kidnapping, what became of my car? Have the police found it?

The car I'm *currently* in brakes sharply, pulling my attention back to the present moment. We turn onto a road with a low speed limit and continue on it for five minutes or so. The road surface then changes to dirt for several miles, and we take a couple of turns. At last we make a swooping left and stop. I hear the clink and hum of an electric gate. We proceed down a gravelly drive, and the tires grind to a stop.

Hope we're not at the body-burying location.

Someone opens the car's back door—Joanna, here to greet us—and a blast of crisp, pine-scented air rushes in. Joanna grabs the sleeve of my sweatshirt, pulling me out by my handcuffed arm. A cool mountain breeze ruffles my hair; we're not in the Valley of the Sun anymore.

"Your new residence," announces Hark. "... Unless you fuck up."

Clem whips my blindfold off. I'm standing in the front yard of a spacious home of rustic design—log-cabin boards stained a woodsy brown, with dark green trim. The yard is large and grassy, and the long gravel driveway curves back to the electric gate we just passed through. A post-and-rail fence borders the property. Beyond the fence, dense pine forest.

A second car—black Nissan sedan; smacks of a rental—is parked in front of the house. The fading daylight says the hour is five or five thirty on this Arizona winter day.

The location seems carefully chosen. Though we're in high country, this particular spot sits in a bit of a hollow. There are no views of the larger landscape, no vistas by which to identify telltale mountain peaks or other landmarks.

*What are some high-elevation, pine-forested locations in Arizona? Flagstaff? The Mogollon Rim? We weren't in the car long enough to reach the Grand Canyon National Park to the far north.*

"This is your transitional group home," Hark says. Ah, I get it now. I'm being treated to the full psych-patient experience: first a general hospital admission for initial evaluation, then a commitment to a mental hospital, and now a community residence.

"Joanna will give you the grand tour and show you to your room. After you've settled in, come see me in my office." His *office*? Cripes. "Don't make me wait too long—we don't want to start your new chapter off on the wrong foot. Bienvenido, Tio Woggles! Welcome!"

Clem removes my handcuffs, and he and Hark head inside, leaving me on the gravel drive with Joanna. She smiles in a disarming way and says with an almost shy laugh, "Sorry about all that Nurse LaTisha stuff, just doing my job." She looks younger when not in a nurse or cop uniform, and her edges seem softer. "Come on, I'll show you around."

Sure. May as well go along with this charade until I get a better read on things.

I follow Joanna through the house as she plays tour guide and I play camp newbie. The house is furnished in brand new Crate & Barrel furniture—semi-homey/semi-institutional. "These are the common rooms." Joanna spreads her hands. "The rec room..." We enter a room with a virginal pool table. "... and the living room, where we have our house meetings." Two sofas, a coffee table, a couple of armchairs, a huge TV. All pristine, unused. "Mr. Horvath's office is over there." She points to a doorway down a short hall off the living room.

*Mister Horvath.* Strangle me.

"And over here..."—I follow her again—"is the kitchen. Dinner and lunch are eaten as a group." *Group? What group?* "Breakfast is fend for yourself." A computer-printed banner on the wall reads, "Daily Activities/Weekly Goals." Hanging below it is a clipboard with a spreadsheet on it bearing the name Oliver P.

Fuck, what am in for now?

Joanna leads me upstairs and shows me through the first door on the left. "This is your room. Bathroom's down the hall. Why don't you make yourself comfortable, take a shower if you want, and then go see Mr. Horvath?" She smiles again in that unexpectedly personal way. My mind is already lighting up with thoughts of grooming her as an ally. But her sweet new smile is probably as phony as her nurse routine was.

She leaves me alone to examine my bedroom. Crate & Barrel bed; Crate & Barrel end tables; Crate & Barrel dresser, wardrobe, and bookcase; Crate & Barrel chair.

Or maybe it's Ikea. Who gives a fuck?

The single window looks out on pine forest. The bookcase houses the usual suspects—Patterson, King, Rowling, Roberts. In case I feel like relaxing with a nice novel. I open the wardrobe and find several button-up shirts and a jacket on hangers, a pair of slippers and a new pair of Nikes at the bottom. My factory-fresh chest of drawers contains some new tee-shirts, underwear, socks, jeans, sweatpants. All in my size. A tray of toiletries tops the dresser.

Beats the Utica Crib, I guess. And a shower sounds like a hot slice of heaven.

Scrubbed and decked out in clean jeans, a fresh tee-shirt, and slippers, I feel surprisingly renewed. I'm as ready for my meeting with "Mr. Horvath" as I'll ever be.

I'll need a new strategy for my group-home existence, that's for sure. My defeated-zombie act isn't even worth trying here. The game has changed, and I'd better adapt.

So what's my game plan? How do I play this sit-down with Hark?

Meeting hostility with hostility hasn't worked. At all. Of course not; even a white-belt ju-jitsu student knows that pushing *against* an opponent creates push-back, which only strengthens the opponent. So I need to stop creating conflict. I need to play a higher-level game. I need to think like a general, not a soldier.

How? I'll have to figure it out as I go. I *am* a psychiatrist, damn it. I know a thing or two about human interactions. Hark may temporarily hold all the cards when it comes to my physical freedom and wellbeing, but he will *not* win the psychological war. That is *my* terrain.

Deep breath. Let's roll. I head downstairs.

As I turn to walk through the living room toward Hark's "office," I spot someone sitting in one of the spanking new armchairs, facing away from me. It's a woman, from the shape of the brown-gray hairdo, but it's not Joanna. My footsteps slow.

Her hand is resting on the arm of the chair, revealing a green patterned blouse. Shit. This is the woman who sat in on my "ECTT" session with Hark. The one who wore the box over her head and played human lie detector at my expense.

She's not wearing a box on her head now.

My feet turn to manhole covers. On a primal, neurochemical level, I dread learning this woman's identity. Something propels me forward, though, and as I near the middle of the room, she swivels to face me.

"Dr. Powers. Long time no see."

It takes me couple of seconds to recognize her, so changed is her appearance. And then my jaw drops like a tractor bucket.

"Mary? Mary Matheson? What are *you* doing here?"

"You better talk to Mr. Horvath first.'"

# Chapter 15

Mary Matheson.

My mind scrambles for a logical handhold as my knees fight to stay beneath me.

Mary was a patient of mine in a small psych hospital in Pennsylvania over twenty years ago, when I was still wet behind the ears as a shrink. She's much heavier now and seems to have developed a stubborn "tongue-rolling" tic—a side effect of psychiatric meds. There's *no way on Earth* she and Hark should know each other—or should even have crossed paths.

The fact that Hark has somehow found Mary and teamed up with her tells me the game we're playing isn't poker anymore; it's three-dimensional chess.

And I don't know the rules.

"Come in, Dr. Powers, come in," Hark calls out, before I can run the other way.

I walk down the short hall and step into his doorframe. Hark sits behind a large blonde-oak desk with a tiny bottle of spring water in front of him. He smiles at me in a parody of warmth.

I enter his office, wearing a studiedly blank expression. I want to ask him about Mary, of course, but I don't want to betray how much her presence has thrown me.

"Close the door, would you?" Hark says. "And have a seat."

I oblige, moving slowly so as to buy myself time to reset my brain. *Forget Mary for now. Focus on Hark.*

"Water?" He shakes his mini-bottle.

"No, thanks."

Hark leans back in his wheeling chair and folds his arms. I seize the chance to speak first. "It's not too late to call this whole thing off, Hark. With no charges filed. I'm willing to call it even. An injury for an injury. Here is what I propose we do..."

"Whoa, whoa, whoa there, Wogglesworth. Did you receive an RFP? Then what made you think I was accepting *proposals*? This is not Olliwog *talk* time, this is Olliwog *shut the fuck up* time. Are you sure you don't want a water? We might be here a while."

"I'll take a water."

"Oops, fresh out. Okay, listen, Wogs, we have a lot of ground to cover. We're only going over this stuff once, so you'd better shake the potatoes out of your ears, as my mother used to say—before she ate a bowl of Smith & Wesson for breakfast, that is! I am going to explain the rules of the road, so we're all on the same page and you have the best odds of success. I want you to succeed here. You may not believe that, but I do.

"First," he goes on, "let me set you straight on where things stand vis-à-vis you and the world outside these walls. I imagine you're curious to know how you ended up as our guest?"

Why deny the obvious?

"We took you into physical custody on Route 88, in a little parking area out near Roosevelt Lake"—the Apache Trail, so I was right—"a number of days before you woke up in our little hospital.

"*How* did we do it?" he asks rhetorically. "Well, you see, I and my colleagues have at our disposal a rather exotic pharmacopeia of massively illegal compounds. These drugs can produce a wide variety of effects, though not always with predictable precision. We rendered you unconscious to subdue you, but—dang!—we had trouble bringing you back to the land of Pizza Huts and Piggly Wigglys. We almost lost the patient before the fun even began!

"Once we finally had you conscious and stable, we introduced another intriguing cocktail to your bloodstream, one that renders the subject extremely *receptive* to suggestion. Brainwave-wise, the patient enters a high theta state, but appears alert, pleasant, and coherent to others. Chatty, even. And then, later on, *niente*. No recall of the events at all. Almost like a blackout."

I've heard rumors of drugs that can produce the effects he's describing. From a pharmacological and neurological POV, I'm skeptical, but let's see where he's headed.

"While we had you in this pliant state, we drove you to your local bank in Fountain Hills, where people know you. We instructed you to withdraw thirty-thousand dollars in cash and meet us in a parking lot a block away. We weren't sure how you'd act or how the bank people would *react*. But you pulled it off without raising an eyebrow. That money is yours, B-T-dubya; we're holding it for you. We're not thieves!

"The next thing we did was log onto your email account on your phone—for which you cheerfully provided the password. We composed an email from you to your lovely wife."

*What?* A spike of adrenaline hits my bloodstream.

"Would you like me to read you that email? I forwarded a copy to myself."

I remain mute.

"I'll take that as a yes." He flips through some screens on his phone, finds the email, and reads: "Hannah, I'm so sorry for vanishing on you. I couldn't do the Thanksgiving thing. I went to a motel instead and got drunker than I've ever been. I hate to be such a coward and tell you this by email, but I've taken thirty-thousand dollars from our joint savings. I can't use credit or debit cards because I don't want you or anyone else trying to find me. My plan is to vanish. Maybe for a few months, maybe longer. I don't know. What I *do* know is that I can't live my old life anymore. I tried. Can't do it. Abe will take over my cases for now. Don't try to find me, and don't wait for me; I'm not worth it. Bye, Sweet One. Till whenever. Or not."

*Fuck.* So that's where things stand in Hannah's mind? I hate Harkins Horvath with a white-hot razor's edge. I *need* to get out of here. I *need* to fix this.

"So as you can see," Hark says, "no one is looking for you. And the police have no grounds to hunt you. It's not illegal to ditch your wife and take a road trip with your own car and a pocket full of your own cash."

He pauses for a moment to let me absorb these new twists.

"Your car is in storage, B-T-dubs, at one of Daddy Gumdrops's properties. No one will find it." He leans forward, laces his fingers. "The upshot, Wiggle-Waggles, is that you are our guest for as long as we decide to... *host* you. And that will depend on the progress you make on your treatment goals."

He waits for me to say something. Fuck him.

"Treatment goals?" he repeats. "Yes, your treatment plan is shifting into high gear now. Don't let the relaxed, open-door environment here fool you. This is where shit gets real. This is where you either make the grade or don't. Your treatment program, you see, is pass/fail. And if you fail, well... we can't very well let you waltz out of here and shoot the breeze with CNN, can we? You can identify us, and there's a *lot* of charges you could file—and there'll be plenty more by the time we're finished. You were right; even Daddy Gumdrops couldn't get me out of that one. So failure is an outcome... to avoid. I just spelled 'a void' as two words in my mind, FYI. Tee-hee.

"If, on the other hand, you succeed and 'graduate' from our program, you will be such a transformed little cowpoke, you won't bear us any ill will. You will have learned so much about yourself and about, well, *everything*, you'll be washing our feet with your grateful tears.

"I must warn you, though, success is a long shot. The smart money is on you failing miserably. But I have high hopes for you, Olliwoggums. Always have.

"So... tomorrow we'll explain how the program works. For tonight, all you need to know is that three other people will be residing here with you. The purpose of their presence is to provide a therapeutic group dynamic. Don't mistake them for your peers. They'll just *a-peer* to be, ha! Clem and Joanna, as always, will serve as the disciplinary team. Questions?"

*Yes, where's the nearest potted cactus I can jam up your ass?*

"One of your co-residents has already arrived. Mary. Shall I introduce you? Oh, that's right," he says with a twinkling eye, "you've already met. The other two will be arriving over the course of the evening. So our work won't start till morning. It's around six-thirty now. Take the rest of the evening off. Chillax, watch some TV, help yourself to a snack, sit outside, enjoy the stars. I hope I don't have to remind you you're wearing the ankle bracelet. Any attempt to 'discharge yourself' from the program will be met with— what's that term they use in those old 'Nam flicks?—*extreme prejudice*. Hyuck! Tomorrow we dig in, full bore."

Is he done? "Okay, Hark, you've had your say. Now it's your turn to listen to—"

"SHUT YOUR GODDAMN MOUTH!" He springs out of his seat, red-faced, causing me to jump backward. I throw my hands up in peace.

He calms instantly. "Sleep tight, Ollie. Don't let the bedbugs bite." I stand and turn toward the door. "Feed 'em, give 'em plenty of water, but don't let 'em bite. Hyuck!"

My heart is still hammering when I reach the living room. Mary is planted in her armchair, watching black-and-white Turner Classics. Shit. That eliminates the hang-around-and-watch-TV option. I march through the room, giving her a tight smile as I pass. I have no interest in talking to her till I've done some internal reconnaissance.

"I'm watching an old movie, Dr. Powers," she calls after me. "*Gaslight*. I think you'd like it."

Pretending not to hear her, I head upstairs.

• • •

Half an hour later, I'm climbing the walls. Pacing my bedroom floor, biting my nails.

I creep downstairs to the kitchen—unoccupied, good—to scope out the food situation. Though I inhaled that big meal from the Mexican place, my body is still craving replenishment after its long, involuntary fast. I score some Nature Valley Granola Bars and three chocolate Pudding Snacks and take them upstairs to my room.

After snacking, I reach for the bookcase only to discover that the three rows of books are a façade. A hollow row of spines.

So I have nothing whatsoever with which to occupy (distract) myself for the remainder of the evening. And it's already driving me buggy. I'm pacing a groove in the Crate & Barrel rug.

In normal life, what I would do is read or watch TV. Or do some online research. Work on one of my journal articles. Write some case notes. Play with my phone or iPad. Or chat with Hannah. Or go to the gym. Or, or, or... But I don't have access to any of those options.

I don't know how to do *nothing at all*. I literally don't. I am what the New Agers call "a Human Doing, not a Human Being."

I recall a quote by Pascal that used to hang over Hannah's desk: "All of humanity's problems stem from man's inability to sit quietly in a room alone." I hear ya, Blaise. Pathetic, isn't it? Fifty-five years old and a ball of anxiety at the prospect of spending quiet time alone. I've always been that way, truth be told, but tonight the anxiety is at fever pitch.

How will I get through the evening? Pace myself to exhaustion?

No, I have skills. Thanks to my time in the Isolation Box, I know how to meditate now. Yes! This is a perfect opportunity to work on that practice. Diffuse the anxiety with inner stillness.

I sit in the Crate & Barrel armchair and close my eyes. I shift my breathing from the upper chest down to the abdomen. Focusing on the white noise of the HVAC fan, I'm able to move my consciousness from the turbulent, freak-out level to deeper waters.

The deeper waters are quieter, but peace still eludes me. My heart wants to gravitate to its default pain spot—Emmy. My guilt, my failure, my regret. As I run my mind along the sharp contours of that familiar pain, an insight dawns: my self-flagellating about Emily has become a form of *comfort* for me. Dark comfort, to be sure, but comfort no less—like a traumatized teen who cuts her skin because it's easier to deal with self-inflicted pain than the *other thing*.

What is the *other thing* I'm so keen to avoid?

Well, how about a marriage that's on life support and that I'm powerless, at the moment, to save? How about my captivity at the hands of a hair-triggered psychopath who is outwitting me at every turn? How about...

No. Not really.

Distressing as those things are, they aren't the *true* cause of the gut-sickness that's threatening to eat me alive tonight, are they? *That* anxiety—the one I'm truly *desperate* to avoid—runs deeper and has more ancient roots.

And tonight it wants to crawl out of the shadows and bare its teeth.

Normally, my mind doesn't let me *near* this thing—it lives in the darkness of my belly only—but that beatdown I took in Hark's House of Horrors has shattered my inner defenses. I seem to have lost my ability to push bad things underwater and hold them till they stop kicking.

The ancient fear that's needling me tonight—it has to do with a sleeping... *something* that has been hiding in the corners of my psyche for as long as I can remember. A thing with a vague and slippery shape I've glimpsed only in flashes. A thing I refuse to let my mind's eye fully take in. It has a *feel*, a frequency, even a *color*, though, this thing, this lurker in the shadows. And it began stirring in its sleep when that frog was thrown onto my bed. It stirred again when I talked to Hark about his ayahuasca experience.

And tonight, something has caused the monster to sit up in its lair, wide awake, and sniff the air. And that something, I know, is Mary. Why?

Why is Mary's presence shaking me to the core?

I am petrified to find out. I fear if I do, a great unraveling will occur. An unraveling of every tightly stitched thread that has been holding my life together as long as I can remember.

But Mary is sitting in a chair downstairs. She is a flesh-and-blood reality that can't be denied. Why is she here? After twenty-plus years? *How* is she here? How does Hark know about her, and her connection to me?

I think the shadow-demon knows the answers to all these questions, and I think it's flexing its limbs in the dark right now, laughing and licking its chops.

# Chapter 16

*"Come in, Ms. Matheson," the 32-year-old version of me said to the furtive-looking young woman shifting on her feet outside my office. Mary was dark-eyed and raven-haired, and as she stepped into the light of my doorway, I was floored by the magnitude of her beauty—a trait I knew, as a professional, I must studiously ignore.*

*"Please, Mary, come in and close the door." My office was just a few yards down the hall from the busy common room of the small psych-hospital unit.*

*Twenty-seven-year-old Mary Matheson slunk around the doorframe with her back to the wall and closed the door behind her, staying as far from me as the room would allow.*

*"Welcome to Oakridge," I said, "and to my humble abode." This was my first real office of my first real job in the field—following my four-year residency. Oakridge Psychiatric Hospital was located in a "tranquil" pondside setting in northeastern Pennsylvania and was known for working with long-term and treatment-resistant patients—those who would have been labeled "chronics" in slightly less enlightened times.*

*Mary remained pressed against the door, staring at me with her huge deer eyes.*

*"Please sit down, Mary. If that's okay with you. May I call you Mary?"*

*"Are you a priest?"*

*"No, Mary, I'm a doctor."*

*"I can see that from the sign on your desk. I ain't retarded. Doesn't mean you can't be a priest too."*

"Good point. I'm afraid I'm not a very spiritually inclined person at all. I hope that won't be a—"

"Neither are most priests," she cut me off. "So... are you?"

"A priest? No, Mary, much to the disappointment of my mother, I am not." A glint of humor—or was it something else?—shone in her eyes. "Please, have a seat."

She slid into the "patient" chair like it was a baited trap.

"So Mary, this first meeting between us is just so we can get to know each other a little. What's your understanding of why you're here at Oakridge?"

"Who cares what I think all of a sudden?"

"I do. Very much. So... why do you think you're here?"

"I don't think; I know. I know exactly why I'm here."

"And that is...?"

Long, calculating pause. "Because I scare the shit out of people. With my mouth. And they want to stitch it shut."

"You 'scare people'? What do you mean by that, Mary?"

"Which part was in Chinese? Why do you guys always act like you don't understand English?—'What did you mean by that?' 'Please explain that.' 'Why do you say that?'"

She folded her arms and pressed her back against the chair. I remained silent. Silence can be a therapist's best friend. People feel a compulsion to fill it.

"I scare people because I tell the truth," she said at last. "People hate that. I scare men the most. Men want to lock me up and throw away the key. After they fuck me, that is."

Her eyes scanned me for a reaction. I kept my face neutral. I knew that sexual provocativeness—especially so early in session one—was a "proceed with caution" sign. I would need to choose my words and body language carefully.

"Why do you think men are scared by you, Mary?"

"Because I can see into their souls. I know their secrets. Like you. Want to know your secret? Besides the fact that you want to fuck me too."

"I assure you, Mary, I do not." Wrong move. Don't respond to her delusional content.

"Ha! Liar! So that's how we're going to start things off? With you lying? Are you seriously going to claim there's no part of you that wants to grab my ass and go to town?"

I knew exactly what she was up to, but still I couldn't deny a quickening of my pulse—so easy to walk into a trap with this kind of patient. "First of all, we're not here to talk about me, we're here to talk about you. Second, that's a neat little trick you pulled there, Mary. You know full well you're a very attractive woman. And you know that most men respond to your looks on some level. That doesn't require mind-reading. So I think when you throw out that 'you want to bleep me' stuff, it's your way of putting people on the ropes. What I'm interested in knowing is why you feel the need to do that."

"Good one, Dr. Powers! You avoided the question."

"And I'm going to continue to avoid it. Because we're not here to talk about me, we're here to..." I give her the chance to fill in the blank. "... talk about you."

"You have other secrets too, Dr. Powers. Worse ones than wanting to get in my Tommy Hilfigers."

"That's an easy trick too, Mary. Everyone, including me, has secrets— things they would prefer others didn't know about them. But let's talk about Mary today. How did you end up at Oakridge?"

"Read my records if you're so friggin' curious. I've been here, like, five times, as I'm sure you know."

"I don't, Mary. I don't put a lot of stock in records. I prefer to meet the person first." That was a lie; I'd read her records. Twice.

"How I ended up here—how I always end up here—is I pissed off the wrong people."

"Who? Who did you piss off?"

"My landlord—this time. He was being a total dick-ass about the rent, so I told him the secret I knew. About him."

"Which was?"

"That one time during a camping trip with his big bro's family, he slipped into his eleven-year-old niece's sleeping bag and said hidey-ho. That made him lose his shit—wham, bam, thank you, ma'am—and then he accused me of losing my shit, and who do you think the cops believed?"

"That's a serious thing to accuse someone of. Did you have any evidence?"

"I don't need evidence, I have her."

"Her? Who? The niece?"

"No, her. In here." She touched her fingertips to her left temple. "Inside my head."

Now we were getting into the thick of the schizophrenia. Good. "You have someone living in your head?"

"Not someone. Not a person. She's... Oh, fuck off. You're not going to believe me anyway, so why should I tell you?"

I replied with silence again.

Again, she dutifully filled it. "You know about demonic possession, right?"

"I've actually done some writing on the topic, yes. From a psychiatric perspective."

"Well, did you ever hear of angelic possession? It's a thing. It happened to me. My angel's name is Gadriel. She's this dot of white light that lives inside my head. She tells me whenever people are lying. Like you when you said you didn't read my records. Her light turns red. She knows the secrets men keep too. She whispers them in my ear. She's never wrong."

"How would you know that, Mary? Unless you followed up on every—"

"Because people always freak-the-fuck-out when I tell 'em what she says. People don't freak-the-fuck-out unless a thing is true. She's whispering to me right now. Something about you. Should I tell you what she's saying?"

"We are not here to talk about me."

"Something about a fun night out you had when you were still a med student."

My pulse started hammering. "That's enough, Mary."

"Whoa, doc. What's the matter? All of a sudden you're dying to end this conversation."

"I'm not, but I am eager to shift the focus back onto—"

"Red light! Red light!" She rose halfway out of her seat, her hands clenching into fists. "Gadriel's lighting up red. Blood red. Blood of Christ! Blood of Christ!"

Instead of recoiling, as I wanted to, I leaned toward her, across the desk, to show her I wasn't afraid of strong emotions. I wanted her to feel safe, contained. "So your 'angel' is communicating with you now? Tell me what that feels like."

*"Ha. Nice try, doc. Look at you, squirming in your Underoos. Fruiting up your Looms. You want me to get the fuck out of here. Just like they all do."*

*"That's not true, Mary, I promise you."*

*"Red light! Liar! Liar! I'll make it easy for you. Just tell the truth—admit you want me gone—and I'll walk out the door. Nice and quiet, like a good little Catholic girl. See no evil."*

*"I do not want you to leave, Mary. What I want—"*

*"Red light! Red light! Liar!"*

*"What I want is for you to calm down so that we can continue—"*

*"HE'S GRABBING MY TITS!"* Mary stood up, flailing her arms. *"HE'S GRABBING MY TITS! HE'S GRABBING MY TITS!"*

*My hands shot up in the universal I-didn't-do-it sign.*

*Carla, the head nurse, came charging in, sloshing a cup of take-out coffee. Her trained eyes assessed the situation, noting the wide desk between me and Mary.*

*"Mary?" said Carla, brushing liquid off her arm.*

*"Just kidding," Mary replied. "He didn't grab 'em. He wanted to, but I didn't let him."*

. . .

That was my first encounter with Mary. Things didn't get a whole lot better between us after that.

I'm pacing again in my "group home" bedroom. Meditation has flown out the window. Thoughts of Mary attack my mind from all directions. *Why is she here? After all this time?*

I could go downstairs and ask her, I suppose.

Sure.

Around ten o'clock, the twin beams of a car's headlights sweep across the pine trees outside my window. I tiptoe across the hall to an unoccupied bedroom and push the window shade aside, hoping to catch a glimpse of the late arrival.

An ice-blue MINI Cooper wagon parks near the other cars, bringing the vehicle count to three. A man climbs out of the driver's seat and stretches his arms. Husky guy, paunch, bushy salt-and-pepper hair, tracksuit. Around my age maybe. Can't see his face in the dark. A woman who looks quite a bit younger emerges from the passenger side. She wears a long robe of Indian style. A kurta? Saree?

The front door of the house opens. As the two approach the doorway, the light from the foyer illuminates their faces for just a second. Panic assails me. I dash back to my own room and toss myself onto the bed, eyes bugging.

The new guests can't be who I think they are. Can't be.

Either I'm wrong about their identities or I'm back in brain-injury land.

Up till now, I've been hoping Mary's connection to Hark would turn out to be the result of coincidence. Two mental patients who ended up in the same ward somewhere and got to talking, realized they knew someone in common. Could happen. But if these two new houseguests are who I think they are, something more nefarious and complicated is going on here.

I step back into the hallway. The murmur of voices drifts up from downstairs—a confab in the kitchen. The group erupts in laughter, and, sure enough, I recognize the two new voices in the mix.

Sleep? Yeah, not gonna happen.

# Chapter 17

Sometime after five-thirty a.m. on the longest night of my life, unconsciousness finally takes over. A rap awakens me at seven twenty-five.

"Morning meeting, eight o'clock," says Clem through my door. "Don't be late."

I sit up on the edge of my bed, exhausted, and stretch my starved-thin arms.

So... Am I going to do this? Saunter downstairs and play along with whatever new demented horseshit Hark has dreamed up? Or am I going to take a stand? Gandhi his ass, maybe—curl up on the bed, refuse to participate.

Nah, better to play the game for now. Whatever game it is. Gather intelligence, watch for opportunities. Play the long hand. General, not soldier.

Voices echo from the kitchen below. Folks communing for fried eggs and Froot Loops. As if this were a damn ski chalet, not a hostage venue. No way I'm going down there one minute before required. The lure of food is almost erotic, though.

I do have a couple of leftover Nature Valley bars on my dresser.

I wash, dress, and granola-inhale, and then, at seven fifty-nine-plus, I head downstairs.

Wallpapering a flat expression on my face, I stroll into the living room, where Clem and Joanna stand guard and four other people occupy the sofas.

When the faces of the two new arrivals come into view, I dive for the nearest armchair.

I was right about their identities. This nightmare has officially shifted into gonzo gear. I nod at the two new guests, making only brief eye contact. There *is* no appropriate social behavior for a situation like this.

My left leg starts jumping up and down as if it thinks I want to play the spoons.

Hark claps his palms together. "So! Here we all are." He beams out his caricature of a smile. "Welcome to Odyssey House." The place has a name now. Awesome. "Morning meeting is called to order. First, I want to thank you all for being here. Many of us have met, at one time or another, but we've never been in the same room together as a group. So let's go around the room and introduce ourselves. And please—do share how you know our guest of honor."

I've unwittingly planted myself in the "hot seat"—the hypotenuse of the right angle formed by the two sofas. All four men and women face me directly.

"I'll start the ball rolling," Hark offers. "I'm Harkins, as you all know. Dr. Powers was my psychiatrist in Massachusetts about eight or nine years ago." As if recounting that we once worked together at Best Buy, he says, "I went on a sacred-medicine journey in which I was warned that my sister and her kids would be murdered by a demonic entity. Dr. Powers dismissed my claims as delusions and committed me to a locked facility. During my lockup, my sister and her family *were* savagely murdered, as I knew they would be, and I couldn't do a thing to help. But I guess you all know *that* story, hyuck! Who's next?" He turns and signals to Mary.

I grasp my chair's padded arms.

"My name's Mary Magdalene. *Matheson*, I mean. Dr. Powers was my doctor out east in the Eighties. Back when I was young and fuckable. He didn't like the angel I had living inside my head, so he tried all kinds of meds to shut her up. He finally found one that worked, but it had wicked side effects. He forced me to take it anyway." She pauses for a moment as her tongue rolls around in her mouth of its own volition. "Now I'm fat and ugly and have tardive dyskinesia and don't have a single thing to live for."

Well, this is going nicely so far.

"But I *am* off the meds," Mary adds, "and my angel is back." She looks at me with a sharp-edged glint in her eye. "So I guess that's one thing."

"Thank you, Mary," says Hark. He signals to the husky guy with the bushy gray-black hair. "Bruce?"

Bruce Costa. I now realize he was the second anonymous box-wearer back at Hark's House of Horrors. Same somatotype. Same Rolex. Bruce was also a patient of mine back east. When he fired me as his doctor, he made several threats on my life and wellbeing. Threats that never materialized. Until now, perhaps.

"My turn?" Bruce flashes a car salesman smile. "So I met the doc here about thirteen-fourteen years ago as a private patient in Newburyport, Mass. Here's how big of a dumb-ass I am. I actually went to see him because things were going *too good*. You guys remember *The Secret*? Well, this buddy of mine turned me on to it. The whole Law of Attraction thing. I jumped in with both feet. Learned how to raise my vibration, work a vision board. My life turned around like *that*..." He snaps his finger with a firecracker sound. "Overnight. Suddenly, I was on *fire*. I had the Midas touch, I was on a freakin' roll.

"Money, you kidding me? Earlier in my life, I only *messed around* in the stock market, piddly stuff, lost more than I made. Now, all of a sudden, I couldn't *make* a bad investment. I was in the Vortex, man. Running hot. People were literally lining up to hand me their life savings to invest. I'm buying up houses, apartment buildings, parking garages, bam, bam, bam. My wife starts freaking out. *Whoa, Hunnybun, this is too much, too fast. What if we lose it all? What if your luck runs out?* She's afraid I'm being 'grandiose,' losin' my grip on the ol' handlebars, so she makes me go see the doc here.

"Well, he sure cured *me*! Got my head out of the clouds. Right, doc? Then pow! Everything came crashing down. I lost it all. The investments, the wife, the family. Went eight mill in the hole. A hole I'm still trying to climb out of. ... So. That's how *I* met the doc. How ya doin' there, Dr. Powers?"

He gives me that big, icy smile that chilled many a night for me.

I smile back tightly. I want to point out that what destroyed Bruce financially was the fact that he went into the manic phase of his bipolar illness at the same time a rascally rabbit called 2008 hopped onto the scene, sending him and a million other wannabe Warren Buffetts crashing back to Earth. And that what destroyed his *marriage* was the massive cocaine habit he developed when his house of cards started tumbling.

But I hold my tongue. I'm still trying to process what in the exact living fuck is going on here.

"Thank you, Bruce," says Hark. "Anvita?"

Hark turns to the Indian woman, in robes, next to him. She is only 25 and has a glow about her that reminds me of Emmy. How do I know Anvita's age? Because I met her when she was 17, during the same period I was working with Hark. I was called in, as an expert on delusions with religious content, to consult on her case at a Chicago-area hospital. The fact that she is here, now, has my mind plunging over Niagara Falls in a cardboard box.

"Dr. Powers," she starts in, with her gently rolling r's. "I have no bone to choose with you. I bear you no ill will and do not wish to see you suffer. But... at the same time, I feel no duty to spare you from the karmic consequences of your life choices. In that regard, I view this... *retreat* we are on... as a glorious opportunity for you to do some karmic cleansing that might ordinarily require many lifetimes."

Karmic cleansing. Lovin' the sound of that.

"Anvita is being modest," says Hark. "She's light years ahead of the rest of us, spiritually speaking. What she's failing to mention is the fact that when she was a teenager, she was on her way to becoming one of the great spiritual teachers of our time. You, Oliver Powers, robbed her of the opportunity to bring her message to the world, and you robbed the world of the opportunity to hear it. Millions—hundreds of millions—of lives might have been changed by her message. World events might have shifted. But you cut her flowering short."

Is he actually accusing me of being a force of global destruction? Small thing, but it hurts. He's vastly overstating the role I played in Anvita's life.

"Yes, unlike the rest of us, whose issues with you are a bit more... personal," Hark goes on, "Anvita's issues are, well, *cosmic*. Suffice it to say, we all have a vested stake in—"

"Getting revenge on me," I say, fighting the nascent wobble in my voice. "Making me pay for my 'crimes.' It's obvious that's what this is all about."

"Of course you *would* see it that way, given your current level of consciousness," replies Hark. "But no, that's not it at all." He laughs to himself. "Okay, full disclosure, vengeance *was* an initial motive for some of us—still is, perhaps—but Anvita has helped us broaden our mission. Thanks to her, our goal for you has become much more... *evolutionary*."

"Uh-huh. Right. Excuse me."

I charge out of the room before Clem or Joanna can stop me, making for the nearest bathroom. I lock the door and collapse to the tiled floor. The urge to vomit rises up and passes.

The absurdist drama unfolding in the living room has no earthly explanation.

I shake my head, literally trying to reset my brain—back to the time my life last made sense. When was that? When was my last *sure thing*?

It was that moment, back in the hospital room, when I realized I was brain-injured. That was a reliable thought. Everything since then has been nothing but the cascading symptoms of a wounded, hallucinating brain.

I close my eyes and try to transport myself back to that hospital bed.

*Come on. The bed, the bed. The nice, warm bed in the nice, stable hospital.*

I wrench my eyes open. No luck. I'm still sprawled on the floor of the bathroom of "Odyssey House." Still stuck in this impossible scenario.

Why do I say *impossible*? Well, perhaps a little background is in order here.

A painful truth about psychiatry is this. Every shrink who has practiced their craft as long as I have has notched a few "bad" cases. Cases they got wrong. Cases they'd like to take back, do over, recuse themselves from. Cases that gnaw at their guts on long, sleepless nights.

I imagine the same is true for judges and surgeons.

*I* have a few of those cases in my past. Four, to be precise. Not bad, really, for a twenty-seven-year career. But four more than I would prefer.

Hark, needless to say, is one of those cases.

The other three—*the other three*—are sitting in the living room of this house right this minute. Mary, Bruce, and Anvita. All under one roof:

Mary, keeper of the angel who knows the lies men tell and the secrets men hide.

Bruce, former vision-board master, who blames me for his financial ruin and is the only other patient, besides Hark, who ever gave me serious concerns about my safety.

Anvita, would-be spiritual guru who came closer than any other patient to making me question my atheistic faith.

Their presence, together here, is causing my brain to short-circuit. For multiple reasons.

First of all, I am extremely conscientious about patient confidentiality. I have never spoken to anyone, not one living soul—not even Hannah—about any of these patients, except in the vaguest and most anonymous terms. *No one* on this planet could possibly know the private thread that connects the four people sitting in the other room.

Second, I treated all of these patients at different times of my life and in different places. Mary was a patient of mine twenty-three years ago in rural Pennsylvania. Bruce worked with me in the brief period from 2007 to 2008 when I had a practice in Newburyport, Massachusetts. I treated Hark a few years after that in Andover, Mass, and Anvita as a one-off consultation case in Chicago. The odds of the four of them connecting by chance are nil.

They have been brought together by design.

*Whose* design? Hark's, no doubt. But how? How does he know about them?

To learn about the others, he would have had to access confidential patient records in several states and interview a thousand patients to find the few who had axes to grind with me. Or else he would have had to create an anti-Oliver Powers forum on the Internet—in which case I would know about it. I am nothing if not a passionate googler of my own name. Even if he *had* done either of those things, and even if he had hired the CIA itself to dig into my background, he still couldn't know the effect these four individuals privately had on me. I've *never talked about it*. To anyone. The significance of these four people, as a group, exists in my mind and my mind alone.

Yet here the four of them sit, in a real house. In rural Arizona.

What is the damn explanation? There must be one.

And I need to know what it is—before my mind dances off the edge of the world.

I stand up and march back to the living room.

# Chapter 18

"Okay, how did you do it?" I say to the group, straining to keep my voice even. "How the hell did you find each other? How did it happen? Somebody say something."

"Sit," commands Hark.

I want to disobey him, but four pairs of eyes drill holes in me. I find my seat.

"Rule number one," he says. "You don't ask questions of us. Ever. You are here to *answer*. Rule number two: *gratitude* is the only sentiment permissible from your lips."

Right. I'll be sending that Edible Arrangement along any minute.

"There are those among us," he continues, "who would have preferred to settle our... *differences* with you in a much cruder and more direct manner..."

"Amen to that," adds Bruce. He laughs and cracks his knuckles. Subtle. Get a job in a Guy Ritchie film.

"... but cooler minds, and spirits, prevailed," continues Hark, with a glance at Anvita. "And so we are generously offering you an opportunity you don't deserve. An opportunity to participate in our residential treatment program and transform into a new person. If you succeed, rewards beyond your wildest dreams are possible. If you fail... Well, we've been over that. Bruce, would you be so kind as to explain how the program works?"

"Sure." Bruce cracks his knuckles again, keeping his eyes on mine. "Your 'enrollment' here at Odyssey House lasts for three weeks, max. That means you've got three weeks to become a changed man. Heh. During your stay with us, you'll be participating in structured daily activities and working on weekly goals." He picks up a clipboard with papers on it—the one with my name on it that was hanging in the kitchen. "That's what your little chart here is all about. Bottom line: Do good on your goals and behave yourself, good things happen for you. Do bad on your goals and act like an asshole— i.e., like *you*—bad things happen."

"Reward and punishment, simple formula," says Hark. "Positive and negative reinforcement. The Lord giveth and the Lord taketh away. And at the end of your program, you either graduate or... not. Entirely in your hands."

Straining to keep the sarcasm out of my voice, I say, "As one 'treatment professional' to another, may I point out a tiny flaw in your program design?"

"I so wish you wouldn't, but go ahead."

"You say it's based on rewards—but you have nothing to reward me with. Except to give me back what you took away: my shitty life with a dead daughter and a marriage that's circling the drain. Is *that* the carrot-on-a-stick that's supposed to spur me to the finish line?" (Hark needn't know how badly I long to see Hannah.) "If so, I'll save us all three weeks of grief." I stand up. "You'll find me upstairs in my room. I'll be the hundred-sixty-two-pound lumpfish on the mattress. You can do whatever you want with me; I won't be participating."

I head out of the room.

"Actually, Dr. Powers..." Anvita halts my momentum with the sharpness of her voice. "We have something *quite extraordinary* in store for you. Something you *do* want. More than life itself."

I pause in the doorway. Hark has hinted at something similar. I know it's grade-A bullshit, but still...

"She ain't lying, Doc," Mary adds, a secretive spark in her eyes.

"What could *you* possibly offer *me*," I say to the group, "that I want more than life itself?"

The four engage in a silent eye-consultation. *How much should we share with him?*

Bruce breaks rank: "What if we told you we could arrange for you to see your—"

"Bruce! No!" snaps Anvita. "He is not ready!" She turns to me. "Herein lies our dilemma." She draws her palms together and lowers her head. "The *nature* of the reward we have planned for you is such that you are presently incapable of accepting it. In fact, we cannot even *tell* you about it yet, because you would become enraged at us for even claiming such a thing was possible." Her head lifts. "Your current belief system would not permit it."

"Do you see the pickle that puts us in?" Hark tilts his head. "The reward we're planning is one that would motivate you to scale Mount Everest in flip-flops. But your primitive little consciousness can't grasp it yet. That means you'll have to trust us for now. It also means, sadly, that the only tool we have for motivating you in the short term is... negative reinforcement."

"The good old billy club of life," says Bruce, doing his Guy Ritchie-thug laugh.

Hark takes the clipboard from Bruce. "We've set a Week One goal for you. If you achieve it, you will be a giant step closer to receiving the gift-that-cannot-be-named. If you fail to achieve it, well, then I'm afraid... the billy club comes out."

"Meaning...?"

He hands me my phone, which I haven't laid eyes on since my kidnapping. On its screen is an email, cued up and ready to send. The sender's address is mine and the subject line reads, "EMERGENCY: PLEASE OPEN!" The body of the email contains a link with no explanation.

My blood starts to simmer.

"When you unlocked your phone for us," Hark says, "you unlocked all your contact lists. You're quite the popular fella, turns out. Over a thousand addresses. Friends, family, professional colleagues, publishing and PR contacts, the good folks at CNN, even a couple hundred of your patients... Why don't you go ahead and click the link?"

I stare at him with icepicks in my eyes. He stares back.

Clem and Joanna join the stare brigade, outnumbering me.

Fine. I jab the link with my finger.

Oh God no. *You fuckers.* My Betty Boop-painted face fills the screen, and my voice sings, in Cyndi Lauper Brooklynese, "I'm a little crack whore, hear me grunt, here is my asshole, here is my—"

I throw the phone at Hark, hard. It bounces off his shoulder. He blinks, not reacting to the blow. Clem and Joanna move in on me like lightning.

"Assaulting staff, one demerit," Hark says, calmly marking an X on my Goal Chart as his goons restrain me. "Consequence: for lunch today you get a slab of bargain-brand bologna, no bread, no condiments, while the rest of us eat lobster-salad croissant sandwiches and handmade kettle chips. See? Positive and negative reinforcement."

Hark bends over and picks my phone up off the floor, holds it in front of me wordlessly. His implicit threat is clear. If I don't achieve my Week One goal, he'll email that Boop video to everyone on my contact lists—my patients, the CNN team, the Board of Psychiatry... Hannah. And there'll be no putting *that* genie back in the bottle. Ever.

"Feeling motivated yet, Olliwog?"

I stifle the "fuck you" forming in my mouth. *Play General, not soldier, damn it.* "And what, may I ask, is this Week One goal I'm supposed to achieve?"

Hark hands me my Goal Chart clipboard, face-down. "Take it to your room and read it in private, so you can give it due consideration. You'll find your daily schedule on there too. As you'll see, our first group activity begins in about twenty-five minutes. You'll want to get ready for it."

He claps his hands. "Meeting adjourned. Let's meet back here at nine o'clock sharp, ready to roll."

• • •

I return to my room and sit on the bedside chair, my head ringing from the fresh blows I've been dealt. If that video goes out... Oh my Christ. I can't even...

I shake my head and turn my attention to the clipboard, dreading to see what demented "goal" Hark and company have cooked up for me. The top page is headed, "Weekly Goal and Daily Activities for Week One." My

Week One Goal reads, "Olliwog shall achieve a state of spiritual humility and openness to the truth."

Is this a joke? Apparently not. Hey folks, want me to take a crack at world peace, too, while I'm at it?

I look at the next page to see what my "structured daily activities" are for today. A grid is laid out for the week. In the Monday column:

Group Nature Hike – 9:00 to 11:30
Lunch – 12:00
One-on-one with Mary – 1:00 to 2:00
Spiritual Counseling with Anvita – 2:30 to 3:30
Personal Prayer/Meditation Time – 3:30 to 4:30
Dinner Prep with Bruce – 4:45
Dinner – 6:00
Group Meeting and Closing Prayer – 7:00

Drive a lobster fork through my brain, please.

The spiritual slant to all this stuff is what really has my hair on end. What's that all about? If these guys think they're going to pull a "come to Jesus" or "come to Krishna" thing on me, they'd better think again. Better minds than theirs—including those of my wife and daughter—have tried to effect a spiritual awakening on me, to no avail. I am what I am.

Oh and by the way, people, exactly how does one achieve a state of "spiritual humility and openness to the truth" under threat of public humiliation and/or death?

Scanning the rest of the week's schedule, I see several additional "one-on-ones" with Hark, Mary, and Bruce, and "Spiritual Counseling" sessions with Anvita, as well as activities like Group Therapy, Drum Circle/Journeying, and Manifestation Lessons—whatever that means.

The whole day on Friday is blocked off for a Sweat Lodge Ceremony. Whoa. Nope. Not gonna happen. I got roped into doing one of those a very long time ago, and once was enough for a lifetime. Besides, I have zero faith that Hark, or anyone else in his motley crew, has the expertise to conduct a sweat lodge safely and properly.

Oh well, that's another worry for another day. The demands of the present moment are all I can handle for now.

Which means I'd better suck it up and get dressed for our "nature hike."

Do they know I'm a highly experienced and conditioned trail hiker? Let's find out, lads and lasses, shall we?

# Chapter 19

At nine o'clock we gather in the living room. Everyone's wearing sturdy shoes and warm outerwear. Clem and Joanna are armed with knapsacks; guess they'll be our pack mules.

I stand among my former patients, looking down at the floor, avoiding eye contact.

Hark enters the room, wearing a seriously idiotic outback fedora. "Okay, so listen up," he says. "This morning we will walk in nature and try to receive whatever messages the spirits of the Earth have in store for us." Gad, I despise New Age drivel—but especially coming from a head-case like Hark. "Olliwog, you will be allowed to walk free, but we'll be watching you. If you make the slightest attempt to 'diverge from the pack,' you will be placed on a dog leash and 'I'm a Little Crack Whore' will drop *today*. And remember, you are wearing the ankle device, and I'm carrying the receiver. Enough on that note, I hope. Onward, Christian soldiers!"

Hark strikes off through the kitchen toward the back door. We follow, like city kids on their first day at camp.

The mountain air is crisp and cool—mid-fifties—as we step out into the dewy grass of the backyard. The piney breeze carries memories of New Hampshire and weekend getaways with my family. Emmy would talk to the birds and trees like they were people. My heart does its daily death-dive as I remind myself I'll never see her again.

Hark leads us to the back of the property where a gate in the post-and-rail fence gives onto a woodland trailhead. "I'll ask everyone to remain in silence for the first part of our walk," he says. Works for me. "Try to open your receptivity centers."

Receive *this*. I picture my foot punting his testicles into his chest cavity. *Stop it, Oliver. Play the high-level game. Eyes and ears open.*

We hike down the trail in single file, up a small hill, then down into a sweet-smelling hollow padded with pine needles. The sparkling air awakens my senses. The terrain is mostly pine forest, punctuated by small maples and scrub oaks. We could almost *be* in New Hampshire if not for the scattering of agaves and prickly pears, looking like Phoenix tourists lost in the woods.

We walk in silence for seven or eight minutes, and then Hark leads us off the main trail toward a rock formation fifty yards to the right. As we circle the massive rock pile, we pass a sight hidden from the view of the main trail: a pile of dirt with two spade-handles sticking out of it, bordering an oblong hole in the ground, about six feet long. We file past it mutely, but Hark can't resist a glance over his shoulder to make sure I'm receiving its message.

I am. It isn't subtle.

As we loop back toward the main trail, I am gobsmacked once again by how much work, expense, and forethought Hark has put into orchestrating this whole lunatic plan of his. And as over-the-top as his overt actions have been, it's his behind-the-scenes maneuvering that truly unnerves me. Somehow he tracked down Mary, Bruce, and Anvita. With all the confidentiality rules and HIPAA regulations that psych facilities operate under, how the hell did he pull it off? And again, how could he know the significance of *these three particular patients* to me? How?

The heel of my shoe crunches a piece of plastic. I stop and kick the pine needles aside to reveal a discarded syringe. Nice—beer cans on the moon.

Wait, though. Have I stumbled on my answer? Drugs.

Drugs, yes. Damn. I've been dismissing the idea that Hark could have probed my mind, but maybe that's exactly what he did. I know Hark and his henchmen used drugs to kidnap me on the Apache Trail. I also know—if Hark was telling the truth—that they plied me with another chemical that made me "cooperative" enough to give them my phone password and withdraw thirty grand from the bank on their say-so. So if Hark was able to render me *that* malleable, via drugging, isn't it possible he also coaxed me into spilling some closely held secrets?

The more I think about this idea, the more sense it makes.

"Come on, Olliwog!" shouts Hark.

I hustle through the pine needles to catch up.

As a shrink, I've often theorized that all of us, on some level, yearn to share our secrets with someone. Keeping secrets is a lonely enterprise. And a burdensome one—not only because of the effort required to keep our lies straight, but also because a shameful truth held inside comes back to torment us over and over. But if we release it to someone else, or to the world at large, its power dissipates. It is no longer our burden alone.

I think we all crave that freedom.

So it's no huge stretch to imagine that Hark may have loosened my willing tongue in some chemical way. There are drugs known to produce such effects—the "truth serums" popularized in spy movies of the '60s: sodium amytal, sodium pentothal, scopolamine... They can't really *force* someone to give up guarded secrets, like in *The Man from U.N.C.L.E.*, but they can certainly lower the chattiness threshold for someone who *wants* to talk.

Maybe Hark used one of those drugs, or a newer, more persuasive chemical, on me. And under the effect of such a drug, maybe I told him about my longtime guilts and fears, including my frog "issue." Maybe I also revealed the identities of Bruce, Mary, and Anvita.

Yes. That's it. He found out about the others from me.

From *me*. Not from doing sophisticated detective work.

God, if he "probed" me that deeply, what else might I have told him?

I haul in an audible breath and step up my pace.

The drug theory, I realize, would explain some other things. None of the other three patients—Mary, Bruce, or Anvita—seemed to be present at the *start* of Hark's caper, when I was still in the "hospital room." That's because

Hark didn't know about them at first. It was only after he drugged me and grilled me that he learned about them. And then it would have taken him some time to locate them, convince them to join him in his insane quest, fly them to Arizona, et cetera.

That's the real reason he put me in the insulin coma. To buy him some time to get the others together. Yes. My starvation was only a side benefit.

My new theory doesn't tie *everything* together with a bow, but it has one supreme advantage: it's plausible. And sane. Gloriously sane. And thus far, nothing else has been. The mountain air suddenly tastes sweeter, and my step becomes lighter.

A piece of the jigsaw puzzle has snapped into place, I feel it. I fall into rhythm with the others.

. . . .

Hark leads the party up a steep, scrub-pine-covered hill. It's a challenging five-minute climb. Bruce and Mary stop more than once to catch their breath, hands on hips.

When we reach the flattish hilltop, a fresh wind is blowing clouds across a cobalt sky. Hark instructs us to stand in a circle. He points to a pattern of old stones embedded in the ground. They're arranged in a cross-like shape, with a rough circle of larger stones around them.

"This is an ancient medicine wheel," Hark explains. "Anvita is going to try an experiment here. If it succeeds—Spirit willing—we will get a priceless kickoff to the week ahead. Let's close our eyes and open our hearts to Spirit."

I close my eyes and open my heart to thoughts of lunch. Hark as a spiritual guru? No, thank you.

Hark leads us through a short ritual in which we face each of the four directions and ask for permission to conduct a "communion ceremony" on this hill.

I'm hoping bargain-brand bologna isn't really on the menu for me.

Next, following Hark's instruction, we sit in a circle around the perimeter of the medicine wheel. He tells us to close our eyes and invite "Spirit" to join the circle and guide us.

I invite a lobster salad croissant to join *me*.

Hark finally breaks the silence. "Olliwog."

I open my eyes. He takes a deck of cards from his pocket and shows it to me. "These are power animal cards." They look like the kind of overwrought novelty item you can buy in a Sedona gift store—$21.95 for two bucks' worth of printed cardboard. McShamanism at its finest.

He fans the cards out, face up; there are several dozen cards in all, each featuring the name and image of an animal. He lets me study them for a few moments, then collapses the deck, shuffles it, and fans the cards out again, this time face-down.

"Close your eyes, ask Spirit for guidance, and pick a card."

I close my eyes, think about flaky pastry stuffed with lobster meat, and pick a card.

"Don't look at it, just slide it into your pocket."

I do as he says.

"Anvita will now lead the rest of the ceremony."

Anvita steps to the center of the stone circle. She sits on the hub-stone of the "medicine wheel" and turns her palms upward. "Let us close our eyes, and take slow, cleansing breaths through the nose." The others comply.

"That goes for you too, Olliwog," says Hark. "Don't blow this by being *you*."

"Slow, cleansing breaths," Anvita repeats. "Open yourself to the ground of being. Clear your mind of expectations, and be thankful for whatever manifests."

Fine, I'll play along.

Breathing through my nose and focusing on the sound of the wind whistling through the pines, I find myself—almost involuntarily—falling into a meditative state. It feels good, damn it; as if I've joined a special club I was excluded from all my life: people who know how to meditate. A pleasing ball of vibrating energy moves up from the base of my spine. My mind wants to offer resistance and anger, but instead I feel inexplicable peace. *Gratitude*, even, for the circumstances that have brought this moment to me. Whatever else may happen, this moment—this timeless moment—is mine. And I shall savor it.

Against my own fuckin' will.

· · ·

Time does pass; I'm not sure how much.

A horse-like huff of breath in front of my face reawakens my thinking mind, but my eyes remain closed. A musky odor wafts past me, and a heavy foot crunches the dirt. Anvita makes a clucking sound I interpret as a signal to open our eyes.

My brain needs a moment to register what I'm seeing. Standing in the middle of the stone circle, its head dipped toward Anvita, is a magnificent creature with a rack of antlers four feet high and six feet wide. Moose? Mule deer? Oh my God, I've never seen a creature this large and beautiful so close up, in the wild. Anvita's hand rests on its muzzle!

I look at Hark in wonder, completely forgetting our enmity for a moment. He smiles, apparently forgetting it too, and silently mouths, "the card," pointing to my sweatshirt pocket.

I pull the power-animal card I randomly selected from my pocket.

It reads, "Elk."

# Chapter 20

"Talking is permissible now," Hark announces as he leads the group into a dense grove of pine.

A few minutes earlier, after we opened our eyes, the elk looked at each of us in turn, nodded its majestic headpiece, and then wandered off, seemingly as mystified by its presence among us as we were. We departed in awed silence, filing down the hill and along the trail.

With each step we've taken, though, my state of wonder has receded, as my critical mind has crept to the fore. *They must have set the whole thing up somehow.*

"Who'd like to speak first?" says Hark.

"I will," I reply, finding my footing amongst some scattered rocks. "Nicely done back there. You almost had me. Let me guess how you pulled it off. You had the elk—the *domesticated* elk—waiting on the blind side of the hill, tied up. Hark, you tricked me into picking the Elk card, like a Vegas street hustler, and I fell for it. After I closed my eyes, Clem—or was it you, Joanna?—went and fetched the animal, led it into the circle."

God, it's fun being me. I can't begin to tell you.

The others stop in their tracks and look at one another. As if on cue, they burst into laughter—the kind of unhinged gut-laughter that comes from sharing a cosmic joke beyond words. After a moment, I join in too. I mean, I'm *gone*. I'm laughing so hard I'm bent over and gasping for breath, tears pouring from my eyes. I know a lot of this is stress release, and I know I'm the butt of the whole joke, but I can't help myself.

The laughter peters out and we stand in uneasy silence. Anvita finally says, "Any other observations, Dr. Powers?" We burst out laughing all over again. My head feels so light I'm about to tip over.

Hark gets us moving again.

The elk experience, followed by the shared laughter, has created a sort of bond with my fellow hikers. I mustn't allow that. These people aren't my friends; they are my kidnappers, my tormentors. I can't let Stockholm syndrome kick in. I need to retain my detachment, my anger, my edge. I need to stay battle-ready.

Bruce obligingly lights the fuse for me. "So, Powers, I read your book," he says, plodding along. "Well, *skimmed* it, anyway; it wasn't exactly *To Kill a Mockingbird*. Tell me, which category of 'spiritual delusion' did we just experience up on that hill?"

"I never claimed, in my book or otherwise, that life doesn't sometimes offer us mysterious experiences. Seeming 'miracles.'" I look down at my walking feet; miracles in their own right, some might say. "The point my book makes is that we don't need to leap to supernatural explanations like a bunch of rainforest tribesmen spotting their first airplane. We can explain them on the basis of what science knows."

"Explain away, Bill Nye," says Bruce. I still can't believe Bruce is here. In Arizona. Hiking in the woods with me. This is the weirdest goddamn thing.

"Okay." I set a confident pace with my feet. "I will. The human brain is a... meaning-seeking missile. It looks for meaning, patterns in everything. Connections. That's how we make sense of the billions of data points that bombard us every second. And when an event occurs that seems to connect an unusually high number of data points, our parietal cortex is stimulated. Our brains flood with oxytocin, which boosts our mood, creates a sense of awe, and overrides logic and ego. We call it a spiritual experience. These experiences tend to make us more engaged with life and community, thus contributing to human survival. We're literally wired for delusion."

Boy, did that sound better in my head.

"Holy crap, Doc." Bruce stops on the trail. "Did you just say that? I'd laugh at you again, but I'm all laughed out." He walks on.

"At least it's rooted in science, not magic. I realize 'science' has become a dirty word in this era of alternative facts and born-again flat-earthers, but I like Occam's Razor. The simplest explanation, with the fewest assumptions, tends to be correct."

"*That* was the simplest explanation?"

At this, everyone does laugh again.

"It's better than assuming the intervention of some grand supernatural force outside ourselves."

"Doc," says Bruce, as if to a kid. "Hark asked you to pick a random card. You picked Elk. Anvita said a prayer to the forest. An elk showed up. What the fuck does that have to do with brain chemistry?"

"I guess you're right," I fire back with more zip than intended. "There must be some big white-bearded puppeteer up in the clouds pulling the strings."

"Is that what you think people mean when they say they believe in God?" Anvita asks, emerging from her silence.

"Isn't it? On some level?"

"That may be what *some* people believe." She glances up at a puffy cloud that has just rolled in. "They require metaphors to grasp the ineffable. But what about you?"

"What *about* me?"

"You just had... an *elevated* experience up on that hill. And yet, when asked to explain it, you become agitated and leap to attacking large bearded fellows in the sky. Why do you avoid addressing your experience directly? Why is this subject so threatening—so *personal*—to you?"

I feel like I'm sparring with my daughter all over again. "It isn't personal. It's just that I reject arguments that rely on—"

"Oh, it's personal with you, Dr. Powers," Mary says in a low voice, bringing up the rear.

I feel chastened by her words but don't know why.

"Listen to the smart lady," says Hark.

We walk in quietude for a while. Hark leads us along a ridgeline spanning a series of small hills.

The morning chill is giving way to midday warmth. Scanning the forest to our left, I spot a cluster of buildings—houses?—nestled in the woods, lower down from us, about two or three hundred yards away. I angle my head for a better look, but the view is too obstructed, too distant. We're not far from civilization, though. Noted.

"So tell me, Doc," says Bruce, refusing to let go of the topic, "that elk showing up, how do you wedge that into *your* belief system?"

"I don't *need* to wedge it. That's the beauty. It was a natural occurrence. Coincidental? Yes, hugely so, I admit. But *natural*. We didn't see a pink unicorn, we saw a creature native to the Arizona mountains. And I still suspect one of you 'encouraged' it to make its appearance. So until proven otherwise, I'll stick to Occam's Razor."

"You cut my throat with Uggam's Razor," mutters Mary.

I let her statement go unchallenged. But as we trudge on wordlessly, the air around us seems to thicken. I sense the others feeding assent to Mary's accusal.

"All right!" I snap at last, stopping in my tracks and forcing the others to stop. "Let's get it out on the table. Right here, right now. I don't care if you punish me or torture me; we're doing this. Now. *Why the fuck are you all here?* Why are you holding me against my will? What huge and unforgivable sin have I committed?"

"Sin is *your* word, not ours, Dr. Powers." Anvita smiles. "Perhaps *you* should tell *us*."

"No, no, enough with the mystery and evasion. Something motivated all of you to put your lives on hold and travel thousands of miles to screw with my life. By the way, Hark, I know how you found out about the others—Mary, Bruce, and Anvita. You got me to spill some very private beans when you had me drugged. But what I really want to know is what's motivating the rest of you to cooperate with him." I'm surprised Hark isn't shutting me up. "You clearly have a huge collective axe to grind with me, and I'm entitled to hear what it is. What. Exactly. Am I. Accused of?"

"The real question is, how long will you continue to feign ignorance?" Anvita says.

"I'm not feigning a damn thing except patience and civility."

"Lie. You're lying right now." Mary points to her head. "Gadriel just said so."

"I don't need to hear from the angel in your head, Mary, I need to hear from *you*. From *all* of you. Come on, out with it. What is my goddamn crime?"

Hark starts to speak, but Anvita silences him with her hand. He's oddly deferential to Anvita, I notice. "Let me ask you a question," she says. "Let us say for a moment your theorized scenario is correct. Let us say you *were* given a 'drug of truth.' Why was it that *our* three names popped out of your mouth?"

The obvious question, but it hits me unprepared.

Fine, damn it. Maybe it *is* time to stop feigning ignorance.

"Okay, I'll say it. I know all of you have issues with me, with the work we did together. In a couple of your cases, I might even agree with you; I may have made clinical mistakes. Okay? In other cases, I stand by every damn treatment decision I made. But one thing's obvious—you're all righteously pissed. At me. I get it.

"Is that it, then?" I go on. "You think I'm a bad psychiatrist? Well, join the club. Every psychiatrist makes enemies. Turns out we're human. *Mea frickin' culpa.* But I'm happy to discuss each of your cases with you—in private—and explain why I took the steps I did. And if apologies are in order, to give those too. So are we done here? Can we go back to the house, set up some individual meetings, and put an end to this whole ridiculous criminal enterprise?"

No one speaks. Hark grunts and hikes onward. The other five follow. I shake my head and do the same.

A hundred yards later, Anvita wheels about, facing me and blocking my path. "When you come to *really* understand how and why we are here—and accept it—then you will be ready to graduate from the program." She walks on.

Thanks. More pseudo-meaningful horseshit from the Hindu princess.

Little does she know, I have no plans to "graduate from the program." I intend to make my exit, dead or alive, by the end of the week. I've already come to that decision. If by Thursday night at the latest I haven't worked out a better escape option, I'm going to bolt in the night, try to outrun them before they can GPS me. I think I've got a decent shot at reaching those houses we just passed, or finding a closer house, before they could track me down electronically.

And if I fail? If they catch me and kill me? So be it.

Why Thursday? What Hark doesn't realize is that I have a private incentive for getting free before Friday, one that supersedes my fear of his releasing that video or even killing me. That is, I *refuse* to participate in that sweat lodge—I'm never doing that again, period—so I've chosen late Thursday/early Friday as my final cut-off time.

The midnight-run option is a last resort, though. I'd still vastly prefer a cleaner, safer, and earlier getaway. So I must work as many angles as I can, watch for opportunities, and seize my first viable chance.

As if in response to my thoughts, a flash of yellow appears up ahead—a piece of paper, trapped in a bush, just a foot or two off the trail. A burger wrapper from a take-out joint. And not Mickey D's or Burger King, so maybe a locally owned business.

As we walk past the bush, I quietly snag the paper. A minute or two later, when everyone's busy looking up at a colorful green bird in a tree, I read the print: "Buffalo Bob's Burgers. Route 87, Payson, AZ."

People don't travel far with take-out burgers.

That means we're near Payson. Very near. For some reason, this knowledge fills me with hope. For the first time since my capture, I have a clear sense of my physical coordinates on planet Earth. I've actually visited Payson a few times, hunting crystals at Diamond Point with Emmy and Hannah—well, playing Words With Friends in the car while *they* hunted crystals.

Payson diamonds, they call them.

Payson, you're *my* diamond now. Shine on.

# Chapter 21

We arrive back at the house around eleven-forty.

"Clem went to pick up our sandwiches," Hark announces as we file into the kitchen from outdoors, shedding our jackets and packs. "It'll take him at least forty minutes. So let's meet back here at twelve-fifteen for lunch. Till then, free time."

I'm hoping Hark has forgotten his earlier threat about my all-bologna lunch or has decided to show me some clemency. Right now, I could eat an elk. So to speak.

With half an hour to kill, I head for the rec room.

I want to shoot a few racks of pool and do some thinking. I was a pretty fair player in my youth and have always found pocket billiards a great way to focus my mind.

I've got a lot to focus on.

During the whole return hike, my mind was in overdrive, trying to come up with as many potential escape strategies as possible before my Thursday-night cut-and-run date. I want to collect those thoughts and flesh them out so I can start putting together an action plan.

I rack the balls on the pristine pool table and chalk up one of the polished maple cue sticks. I aim, draw back my arm, lean into the motion, and break.

*Crack.* I get a good spread of balls, potting the nine and the fourteen.

The one-ball is lined up for an easy side-pocket shot. I'll start there.

Enumerating my potential strategies as I shoot:

*1. Get hold of a phone. I'm guessing everyone here is carrying one, though they're being coy about it. I've seen Joanna and Clem using theirs privately, and I know Hark has one. He has mine too. That's at least four phones I know of. I'll bet there are more. If I can grab one for even sixty seconds, I can call Hannah, call 911.*

I sink the one ball, using bottom English to draw the cue-ball back for an angled shot on the six. Perfect positioning. I aim again. Potting the six in the corner, I bank the cue-ball off the bumper with a bit of right English. Haven't lost the touch.

*2. Steal one of the cars. There are three vehicles on premises. If anyone becomes careless with their keys, or leaves them unguarded at night, I can snatch them and make a break for it. My captors will hear the car drive off, of course— or the alarm triggered by my ankle bracelet—and they'll be right on my tail, but I'll have the jump on them. Payson can't be far.*

*There's the electric gate to contend with, too. I don't have the code or the remote for it—at least not yet—and might not have time to wait for it to open anyway. Might have to drive right through the post-and-rail fence. In that case, Bruce's MINI wouldn't be the ideal vehicle. The Nissan either. Unless I can find a spot where the thick rails are weak.*

I study the green expanse of the pool table. Can I make a long shot on the four-ball, nestled against the rail? You need to hit the sweet spot between the ball and the bumper with precision and *just enough* force.

Four-ball down. Yesss. Three for three. I'm on a roll.

Escape options 1 and 2 are simple and direct, therefore appealing. But I need to consider every possible angle.

*3. Get someone to "defect" from Hark. Fact: Hark is eminently unlikable. The only way he's getting people to cooperate with him is through threats and bribes, I'm sure. But such methods wear thin when people dislike you. You make enemies. Clem or Joanna might be my best shot at forging an alliance. Hark claims they're former undercover cops—with predilections that got them into trouble. But maybe, as former cops, part of them still hates bad guys and resents being part of a criminal plot. And working for a sadistic psychopath.*

*Forging alliances takes time, though.*

Alternatively...

*4. Take a hostage. I could overpower one of the women—Mary or Anvita, not Joanna; she's too buff—and threaten to kill her unless Hark releases me. Nah, too risky. Hark might call my bluff, and then what?*

I sink the five and ten ball in rapid succession, then execute a delicate combo to shave the twelve into the side pocket. Haven't missed yet. Burnin' down the house.

Say now...

*5. Burn down the house. That is an option, isn't it? Start a fire. When everyone is asleep or occupied. I wouldn't want to kill anyone, even Hark if I could help it, but a fire could cause temporary chaos. I could slip away during the panic or just hide somewhere and wait for the fire department to show up, throw myself on their civic duty.*

*Potentially doable. I'll need to keep an eye open for accelerants and flammables.*

Surveying the seven remaining balls, I wonder, *Can I run the table?* Hmm.

Fifteen-ball, *down*. Three-ball, *down*. Eleven-ball, *down*. I create a fantasy contest in my mind to sweeten the stakes. If I make every shot without missing, I win.

The prize? I beat Hark and go free.

Of course, beating Hark *for real* remains my most compelling option— but my most daunting one as well.

*6. Defeat Harkins Horvath. If I can find a way to take Hark down directly, I can put a stop to this insanity for good and, yes, enjoy the satisfaction of besting him.*

But so far he has remained one step ahead of me.

Why do I still get the sense he knows things about me he couldn't possibly know? Things I barely know myself. It's probably just his combination of borderline personality and high intelligence—borderline clients have a way of making you feel they're on to your deepest insecurities. Either that or I spilled a lot more beans than I thought when he had me drugged.

But what cards do *I* hold, as a psychiatrist? I step away from the table, tapping the cue stick on my forehead. What do I know about Hark, and how can I leverage it? Number one, the borderline personality thing. Borderline folks have major attachment issues and fears of abandonment. In Hark's case, those fears are well-grounded. His mother shot herself at the kitchen table when he was seven. Daddy Gumdrops never liked Hark, even as a toddler, and was wildly unpredictable in his doling out of affection. He did the rich-dad shuffle—bought his son off with material things; hired a parade of coaches, counselors, and caretakers as stand-ins for himself. Hark, of course, drove them all away with ruthless efficiency. That's what borderlines do. They don't wait for you to abandon them, they grab the wheel and drive you away first.

*I* was probably the stablest long-term relationship with an adult male Hark ever had, the closest thing to a real father figure in his lonely, neglected life. Clearly, I've underestimated the importance of our relationship to him.

Borderline clients tend to have intense emotions, which they have trouble regulating. That's certainly true of Hark. Anger has always been his biggie. But one thing that's true for all of us—not just borderline people—is that anger is a measure of emotional investment. We don't get passionately angry at people we don't care about. Everything Hark has been doing to me thus far has been an expression of his anger.

And what could possibly push a person to such extremes of anger?

Answer: a commensurate level of caring.

On some level, I *matter* more to Hark than anyone else on Earth does. Therefore, on some level, I still have something he *wants*, emotionally. I mustn't forget that.

Hark believes I abandoned him after he attacked me at Harbor Estuary. That must have caused him grievous pain. He has transmuted that pain into anger, but the pain is still there. And like a child that's been abandoned by a parent, deep down he still wants that parent's acceptance.

Deep down, he wants the "parent" to make things right again.

Could that be the key here? Could that be what Hark—what all my captors—*really* want from me? They believe I let them down, yet they've chosen to *bring me back into their lives*. Because they still want something from me. They still want me to fix things. To set their world back on its axis again. The world I left askew for them.

Maybe on some level the lunatics *don't really want* to be running the asylum, to use an inelegant phrase. Maybe they want the grownup to seize control. If that's true, then I need to adopt the mindset of the psychiatrist-in-charge, the stable one, the rock. These people have serious mental illnesses, and I need to act like the one who doesn't.

Ultimately, *that's* the approach that will save us all.

Question: Am I capable of playing the take-charge therapist even as I'm actively plotting my own escape? Can I internally walk and chew gum at the same time?

We'll have to find out.

I scan the pool table. A long bank-shot on the thirteen ball, at the upper end of my skill range, seems to be taunting me to try it.

I chalk, aim, and shoot. And miss by a Payson mile.

And now the cue-ball is buried behind the eight.

. . .

Clem arrives with lunch. Six lobster-salad croissant sandwiches with sides of homemade kettle chips, as promised. He must have scored them in Payson. After handing out a Styrofoam take-out box to each member of the team, he reaches into the bag and tosses me a brown-paper-wrapped packet from a supermarket deli counter.

"Yours, champ."

I tear into it. It's a chunk of bologna, unsliced. No bread, no condiments. Did I mention I detest bologna? When I was in Catholic school, one of the nuns caught me throwing a bologna sandwich in the trash and forced me to eat it in front of the class. To save the starving kids in India. I've never been able to look at bologna since.

Is it possible Hark knows about that too?

As the scent of lobster—my favorite food on the planet—suffuses the air, I'm already feeling my antagonism rise again.

No. Be the sane one here. *Be the rock.*

I glance at the clock. Twelve twenty-five. Thirty-five minutes till my "one-on-one" with Mary. Me and Mary, alone together? Christ. The smell of the lobster turns nauseating.

*Be the rock.*

Get the hell out of here. Before Thursday.

*Be the rock, be the rock, be the rock.*

# Chapter 22

"What shall we talk about, Mary?" Much as I've been dreading this interaction, I want it to proceed on *my* terms, not Mary's or Hark's. So I've made the opening move.

"Maybe I don't feel like talking to *you* right now, Dr. Powers."

Mary and I are seated in a small room near Hark's office. The only furnishings are four armchairs and a coffee table scattered with pens and legal pads. Clem and Joanna escorted me here and are standing guard inside the door like corrections officers on visiting day at Sing Sing.

"Well," I reply to her, "we *could* use this time for playing tic-tac-toe. But I don't think that will serve either of us very well, do you?" I give Clem and Joanna an imploring look. To my surprise, they step out into the hall, closing the door, granting us privacy.

My first thought in their absence is to grab Mary and threaten to puncture her windpipe with a pen unless Hark sets me free—not very Brené Brown of me—but I've ruled out hostage-taking as an option.

No, I need to be the rock. The axis of reason. Find out where things stand with Mary and use my skills to get her working *with* me instead of *against* me.

Tricky, when every muscle in my body wants to run for the hills.

"Why don't we start with your anger, Mary? The very fact that you're here, cooperating with Hark, tells me you're holding a lot of anger. I suggest we try to get to the bottom of it. What do you say?"

Mary shrugs, staring at the wall in insolent silence.

"Nothing to talk about? Come now, Mary. You go to the extraordinary measure—*after twenty-three years*—of flying cross-country and joining Hark in this violent act of kidnapping, but now that we're alone together, you have nothing to say to me?"

"*I* didn't kidnap nobody," she mutters.

"Aiding and abetting is a crime. You're as guilty as Hark now, hate to say. Unless you help put an end to this. And one way you can do that is by telling me exactly why you're here and what's going on. With you and the others."

"I ain't allowed to talk about that stuff with you."

"Gag order from Hark?"

"You're supposed to figure things out for yourself. That's the deal. If you keep asking me questions like this, I'll have to report you to Hark. And you won't like what happens next."

"So that's your position? You have nothing to say to me? As your former psychiatrist and present hostage? Not a peep?"

She folds her arms and stares into space. But I can see the rage simmering behind her eyes. I know she *wants* to say something, and I know her impulse control is poor.

"Okay. I'll assume you and I are fine, then," I say. "No issues. So you won't mind if I use this time to do some thinking on paper?" I start scribbling on a legal pad, pretending to shut her out.

... Wait for it...

... Wait for it...

She lunges from her seat, unleashing an animal roar—GRAAAAGH! I pull back reflexively. She gestures at her body in red-faced fury. Her meaning is clear: look at *this*. Look at the abomination I've become.

She *is* a sobering sight. Not only has she gained sixty pounds since we worked together, but her skin has become doughy and pockmarked, her features gnarled. And the tongue-rolling tic is ever-present. There is nothing left of the preternatural beauty of her youth. The tragedy is not so much in the loss of the beauty—though I think the world *is* diminished when beauty the caliber of Mary's departs—but in her apparent belief that she no longer possesses intrinsic worth now that her days of effortless male bedazzlement are over.

Of course, what her angry gesture is *really* saying is *I accuse YOU of this.* She settles back into a simmering silence.

"Okay, Mary, since you're not going to use your words, I'll take a stab at this. Nod if I'm getting warm... You think I'm to blame for the side effects of your medications."

She stares at me as if I've just said *water is wet.*

"You're right," I grant. "I do share some of the blame. I was the first doctor to prescribe Stelazine for you. But I'm also guessing that many other doctors have prescribed it—or a similar neuroleptic—in the years since we worked together."

Her non-response confirms my theory.

"Why do you suppose they all—*we* all—did that?"

"Because you're a scared little boys' club made of scared little boys. A truth-telling angel that can see inside men's souls? Can't have that. Gotta stomp *that* out with big fat army boots."

"Or... could it be because the Stelazine *worked*, where no other medication did?"

"Worked. Right. For who?"

"It controlled your symptoms. *Your* symptoms, Mary, not mine."

"You mean, it shut Gadriel the fuck up."

My chest does a little rat-a-tat. "The 'angel's voice' you heard in your head was an auditory hallucination, a symptom of schizophrenia, which you suffer from."

"That's what *you* say. But you're not inside my head, so you don't know. *I'm* the only one who knows what Gadriel really is—she's *back*, by the way, in case I didn't mention. She ain't no hallucination. She's an angel, and she's real, and she's back."

"If she's real, not a symptom of your illness, then why did she go away when the medicine started working?" *Careful, don't put her on the defensive.*

"She didn't *go away*. I just stopped being able to hear her 'cause the meds scrambled my brain so bad. Gadriel was what made me special in the world—not my tits and ass, you freakin' pervert—and you took her away from me.

"You needed the medication."

"No, *you* needed me medicated. I tried to refuse the pills; you wouldn't let me."

"Mary, I'm a firm supporter of a patient's right to refuse treatment. If 'Gadriel' had been a *benign* symptom, one that brought you pleasure instead of suffering, I would have left well enough alone. But she was part of a complex of hostile symptoms, including your habit of punching female patients in the face and accusing every male that glanced at you of sexual assault. When we got 'Gadriel' under control, we controlled the problem behavior as well."

"Convenient."

"If there was a price to be paid for accomplishing that—the side effects—I'm sorry. I truly am, Mary."

"'*A price to be paid.*' Like it wasn't personal. It *was* personal. And *I* paid the price. Not you. You put me under guardianship. You *forced* me to keep taking a bad old medication you knew had horrible side effects. A medication you never woulda gave your wife or daughter."

Her accusation stings. "I prescribed it for one reason and one reason only: because it worked, where others didn't. It was my duty to protect you and the people around you."

"It was your duty to protect Oliver Fuckin' Powers."

"Your mental illness prevented you from being able to make sound decisions about your own treatment. A judge heard the clinical arguments and granted the guardianship order."

"Yeah, but why did you *really* do it? Force the meds on me?"

Again the rat-a-tat inside. "Mary, my decision to prescribe trifluoperazine—Stelazine—was consistent with the highest standards of professional care."

"Ha! See what you did there? Danced away from the question. 'Cause you know Gadriel is listening *right now*, and you don't want her to call you a fuckin' liar."

"I'm not concerned about the opinion of an angel in your head."

"You sure cared about her opinion when you were strapped to that electricity machine."

My neck hairs stand on end. Mary's ability to read me during that "ECTT" session with Hark was uncanny, no doubt, but there is a rational explanation for that. It wasn't an angel in her head, that much is certain.

"I'll ask you again, Dr. Powers: Why did you really put me on those meds?"

Who's grilling whom all of a sudden?

"Round and round we go, Mary. Just like in the old days. You would try to shift the focus onto me, and I would say *we're not here to talk about me.*"

"You just did it again. Dodged the question. And guess what? We *are* here to talk about you. Things are different now, asshole." She rises from her seat. "You ain't my shrink anymore, and you don't make the rules. *I* do. *We* do." Power streams from Mary's eyes, a power I've never seen in her before. "You want to get hooked up to that electricity machine again? Hark brang it in the car."

I lift my hands; no I don't.

"Then answer the god-damn question. Why did you really put me on those meds?"

The tables have turned with dizzying speed here. She has me backed into the ropes. My shirt collar burns. "It was a sound clinical decision."

"That ain't what I asked! Why did *you* put me on those meds? *You?*"

"Because I wanted to help you!"

"Liar! Gadriel is turning red. Red, red, red!"

How is she doing this? How the *hell* is she doing this?

She's reading my tell, my micro-expressions, must be. She can't possibly know I *did* have an ulterior motive for wanting to control her symptoms. Only *I* know that. Only *I've* had to live with that knowledge for twenty-three years.

But she *does* know. Damn her. She knew it back then, and she knows it now. She has always known. Somehow.

"This is unproductive," I say, my voice catching in my throat. I stand up, as if to leave. I'm in full, shameless retreat now. But where do I think I'm going? Clem and Joanna are waiting outside the door. There's nowhere to escape to.

I reach for the door knob but freeze in place.

Enough, damn it. Enough dodging, enough running.

It's time to end this. Isn't it?

As if in an act of surrender, I raise my hands and place them on either side of the doorframe.

I stand, statue-like, facing the door. A ten-count passes.

"Look at you," she says, "posing like *you're* the one on the crucifix."

I blow the air out of my lungs.

"I did want to help you, Mary." I shake my head, my back still turned to her. "That part is true."

"What about the other part?"

The other part. The other part.

My theory about secrets is about to be tested. Perhaps holding onto them does have a cost. Perhaps the secret-keeper does crave an unburdening.

What I told Mary was true. My decision to put her on Stelazine twenty-three years ago was clinically defensible. Clinically *indicated*, in fact. I believed that, or I wouldn't have done it.

But... it was also sullied by another motive.

I think back to my very first meeting with Mary. *Gadriel's whispering to me right now*, she said. *Something about you. Something about a fun night out you had when you were still a med student.* Alarms went off in me when she spoke those words. And she knew it. She could sense it. And so she continued to bring up this "fun night," over and over again, in every session we had, constantly using it as leverage, coming at it from different angles, extracting more truth about it by reading my reactions.

It was an incident she had no way of knowing about but knew about anyway.

And I was afraid of who she might tell. That's the revolting truth.

Am I going to do this, then? Open this can of snakes? This can I've kept hermetically sealed for decades? Am I going to talk about "the night in med school"? If I do so, I will lose deniability (to myself, mainly). I will have to own this.

I sit back down in my chair. This was not how I envisioned this session going.

"All right, Mary, I guess you deserve to hear this. You seem to know it anyway, but you deserve to hear it from my mouth. Please understand, though: I would have put you on the Stelazine, regardless. Nothing would have changed."

"Except maybe everything."

"At first," I say with a mirthless laugh, "I thought you must have been there. At the party. That maybe you came along with the dancers and I just didn't notice you. But no, I checked your records. You were in a hospital in New Jersey at the time; your first stay. So I can't figure out how you knew about it."

"I *told* you how I knew. Gadriel told me about it."

"Yes, well, I don't believe in truth-telling angels that live in people's heads, so we'll have to agree to disagree on that point, shall we?"

I massage my eyeballs with my finger pads and release the story from its cage. "It was the end of my second year of med school. I was sharing a house in Somerville, near Boston, with three other med students." Long breath. "End of year two is huge. We'd just taken our boards—board exams; they're rough—so we were all feeling a need to cut loose.

"This third-year guy, Todd, was getting married and having a big blow-out. I didn't really want to go. Everyone loved this guy—big-man-on-campus type—but I thought he was kind of an asshole. My housemates wouldn't take no for an answer, though. 'You *need* this,' they said, blah, blah. So I dragged myself along.

"This was in the pre-MeToo era, okay? Bachelor parties were old school. There was a *lot* of drinking, and there were strippers, two of them. So they were doing their thing, and some of the guys were getting pretty rowdy. But these gals were handling it; they were pros. They even let Bachelor Boy Todd join in their act a little and were fake flirting with him and all that. But then when they took their tops off, Todd decided it was open season and grabbed the shorter one's breasts, weighing them in his hands and mugging the crowd. She was *pissed*. She pushed him away and yelled, 'Yo, what the fuck, jagoff?'

"*That's* when I should have done something. Right then. I should have spoken up and put asshole Todd in his place. I should have made it safe for the ladies to gather their things, collect their pay, and leave. I probably should have called the cops too. But I didn't. Neither did anyone else. Too much testosterone in the air.

"The other dancer, the taller one, tried to smooth things over and keep the party mood going. She made a joke like, 'All hands, no dick.' Not exactly Sarah Silverman, but everyone laughed. Not Bachelor Boy Todd, though. He turned *purple*.

"'Don't forget who's signing your check, bitch,' he said.

"Well, *that* killed the mood. I went out into the backyard to smoke a joint, and when I came back inside, the strippers were gone—I thought— and I was feeling pretty woozy. I went upstairs and found a bed to pass out on. I woke up a little while later when I thought I heard a woman yell, but her voice was muffled."

Here's the part I have to pry out of memory with a crowbar.

"I went down the hall and around the corner—it was a big house—and that's when I saw a 'private party' going on in the home gym. Some guys were sitting in a circle, and in the middle of them the two strippers were... 'performing' on Todd. A couple of guys were standing over them in a... aggressive-looking way, so I'm pretty sure it wasn't a voluntary situation.

"I took off. Didn't watch. Didn't participate. But I didn't stop it either. For the second time, I didn't stop it. I ran down the back stairs and out the back door as if the place was full of tear gas. I didn't want anyone seeing me or knowing I was still there."

It suddenly becomes clear why "Detective Pratt's" accusations landed on me so hard. Hark must have talked to Mary before writing that little script.

"You already knew most of the story," I say. "Now you know all of it."

"Do I really?"

A pause before answering. "No."

# Chapter 23

"What else, Dr. Powers? ... *What else?*"

"After it happened..." I look down at the table, not at Mary. "I tried to put it out of my mind. But then, a few years later—around the time I started working with you, actually—I heard Todd had joined a medical practice up in Vermont. I found out he was practicing... gynecology. Of all things. This guy was spending time behind closed doors with women."

"So what did you do about it?"

"I didn't know what to do. I told myself I wasn't sure what I saw that night. And it's true, I wasn't. Maybe the dancers were sex workers, maybe he had an arrangement with them. I couldn't swear for sure it was... a forced situation. I only glanced for a second. Did I have a right to ruin someone's career over a maybe?"

"Oh right, can't ruin those boys' club careers. Plus you'd have to admit to your blushing bride that you saw what you saw. And did dick to stop it."

"You don't need to convince me to feel guilty, Mary. I've handled that part just fine on my own. But you've known that since the first time you met me. You have some kind of hyper-sensitivity to male shame, and I had it shooting out of me like a leaky firehose. So I was an easy read for you."

"That was Gadriel reading you, not me."

"Whatever. But you're right about the main thing: I did want you to stop talking about it. I didn't want to have to deal with the whole Todd situation. I swear, I didn't let my personal needs cloud my professional judgment—at least I don't think I did—but I do admit that shutting

'Gadriel' up was a welcome fringe benefit for me. You know what the biggest irony is?"

"I don't know what that means."

"The sickest joke, the weirdest twist. ... In my desire to cover up one source of shame, I created an even bigger one. I've never been able to forgive myself for the way I treated you."

"Well don't look at *me* to forgive your sins. 'Say ten Hail Marys and three Our Fathers.' I ain't no priest. I'm the one whose life got ruined."

"Clinically speaking, Mary, I *did the right thing*. The fact that other doctors prescribed you the same meds for years is proof of that."

Mary folds her arms and stares at me.

"Can I ask *you* something now?" I venture.

She doesn't reply.

"I've bared my soul to you here. Can you give me a bit of honesty in return? Can you tell me how you and Hark got connected? Was I right— did he drug me, get me talking? Or was it something else?"

Mary looks at me for a second, then bursts out laughing—a coarse braying sound. "Bared your soul? Is that what you just said? Bared your soul? Are you going to pretend that was an honest-to-God Act of Contrition?"

"That *was* the truth, Mary. Do you think I enjoyed admitting those things?"

"I went to Catholic school, same as you," says Mary. "What did the nuns always tell us? A half-truth is even worse than a lie. Because it uses truth as a tool of deception."

A half-truth? What is she talking about? But even as I ask myself the question, a sick flutter in my chest tells me there *is* more to this story, stuff I'm *still* not admitting.

Enough, though. This has gone far enough. "You love to point out when other people aren't being honest, Mary. That's your *thing*. To catch people off guard, rattle them, make them defensive. It keeps the focus off you. Why don't *you* try being honest for a change? Why are you here, committing crimes with Hark, instead of happily living your own life?"

"I told you, you don't get to ask about that!"

"Why are you letting someone like Harkins Horvath manipulate you? Why do you refuse to call out *his* lies? What fantasy world has he pulled you into? What has he tricked you into believing you'll gain from all of this?"

She bursts into that coarse, open-mouthed laughter again, then straightens her face. "You still think Hark is the one pulling the strings here?"

. . .

I storm out of the room, expecting a rebuke from Clem and Joanna for ending my session early. But they're not standing guard anymore. I lean against the wall, taking deep breaths. I need to process what just happened in there—my ego feels like it's gone ten rounds with Mike Tyson.

But "processing" is a luxury I can't afford right now. Not with Clem and Joanna gone. I need to seize this guard-free moment.

I allow myself two more deep breaths, then shake my head and hands a few times, casting off the emotional residue of my session with Mary. Feeling somewhat reenergized, I soft-foot toward the living room. According to the clock there, it is only one-fifty. Forty minutes till my next scheduled activity, my "spiritual counseling" session (kill me now) with Anvita.

No one in sight. Where did everyone go?

I start toward the second-floor stairs, when I hear Hark's raised voice behind me. It's coming from within his closed office. I step back into the short hallway to listen in.

I can't make out all the words but pick up snatches such as, "don't care what you do on your own time, but when you're working for me..." and "you can go back to being a mule for the Barsamian brothers, but I don't think they'll be too..."

A voice rises up in self-defense—Joanna's—but I can't make out her words. She is receiving a dressing-down from Hark. Clem is probably in there with her. This spells opportunity for me.

I hustle through the deserted living room. No one's in the kitchen, I note. Through a window, I see all three cars parked outside. Everyone's still on site.

That means Bruce and Anvita, and possibly Clem, are either upstairs or outside. I slink up the stairs. Cell phones and car keys are my main quarry, though I'm sure everyone is treating those items guardedly.

There are five bedrooms, counting mine. And there are seven human beings here. I still haven't figured out the sleeping arrangements, although I know Hark has the master bedroom at the end of the hall. Some of the "guests" must be doubling up—cozy—or else there are additional sleeping quarters in the house.

All the bedroom doors are shut, except mine. The door knobs have key locks. I wasn't given the key to mine, but the others probably were. Has anyone left their room vacant and unlocked?

I approach the door across the hall from mine and knock with a feather touch—just loudly enough for an occupant, but no one else (I hope), to hear.

No response. I tap again. Nothing. I slowly turn the knob clockwise. It stops at the one o'clock position. Locked.

I return to the top of the stairs and listen for movement on the ground floor. All quiet. I proceed to the door of the room next to mine. Again I tap with my knuckle. No reply. I turn the knob. Locked also.

I cross to the opposite side of the hall. This time, when I feather-knock, the voice of Bruce answers from within, "Yeah?"

"I was just looking for Anvita," I lie.

"Try the chapel. That's where your session with her will be."

There's a *chapel* in this house too? How the hell big is this place? It's like a horror-movie mansion.

"Okay, thanks." Thanks, my ass.

The only remaining bedroom is the master. Hark's room. I'm sure *that* one will be locked, but, knowing Hark is busy downstairs, I try the knob anyway. I'm surprised when it turns freely. The door pops open.

My heart does a little drum flourish. Dare I take a quick peek?

I estimate it'll take Hark at least twenty seconds to get up here from his office. So I'll do my snooping in fifteen-second bursts.

I dart into Hark's room, heading straight to the far right corner. I open the closet door—a few button-up shirts on hangers, a small digital safe. Locked, of course.

I step to the nightstand and open the top drawer. Hark's cell phone!

I've reached my time limit already, though.

I tiptoe out of the room, look down the hall, and listen. Everything's still quiet. I pull in a breath, dash back inside, grab Hark's phone, and touch its screen. Password-protected. Of course! Like every cell phone on the planet. What was I thinking? That I could just pick up someone's phone and call an Uber?

Passwords are going to be an issue. Damn.

I fish around some more in the nightstand drawer, searching for *my* phone. I look under the mattress, under the bed. Time's up.

I exit again.

Hallway still deserted. I wait a few seconds, then slip back into Hark's room.

This time I head for the area to the left of the bed, where a tall dresser stands. I open the top drawer. Underwear and socks. The next two drawers, clothes only. In the bottom drawer, atop a pile of sweaters, sits a book: *The Way of the Shaman* by Michael Harner. A classic on shamanism. Emmy owned it. I've encountered it in my research too. Something about the book cover makes my gut twinge, but I don't have time to analyze what it is.

I shut the drawer, dash out into the hall again. Coast still clear.

Or not.

Bruce's doorknob turns.

Shit! I duck back into Hark's room, heart thumping, praying Bruce doesn't check in here. (Why would he? But still.) I sense him moving down the hall, away from me, toward the stairs. Instinct tells me to return to my own bedroom—*now*.

Good instinct. Less than ten seconds after I enter my room, I hear Hark huffing up the stairs, muttering as he passes my partially open door.

The door to his room opens and closes. I half-expect to hear him roar, "Who's been in my room?" but all is still.

Okay, Hark is now *up*stairs and accounted for. So I'll head *down*stairs and do some reconnaissance.

I expect to encounter Bruce on floor one. Or Clem and Joanna, now that their meeting with Hark is over. But the downstairs still seems unoccupied. Where is everyone?

It strikes me that arming myself—with a knife, perhaps—might be a wise idea.

I head to the kitchen to see what I can find. The utensil drawers are locked. The cabinets too. Figures. I notice, for the first time, a door on the far side of the kitchen. Leading to the basement? Yes. I flip the light-switch and creep down the stairs, trying not to creak the wooden steps.

The basement is divided into two large unfinished rooms with a poured concrete floor. Not much to see. A collapsed patio umbrella, a ladder, a water heater. A wall of shelves in the far room—nothing on them but a few cans of paint.

But what's this? A gas-powered generator. Bolted to the floor. A red plastic gas can sits near it. I give it a shake. Empty.

I remove the gas cap from the generator. There's fuel in the tank. Two or three gallons, looks like. Duly noted. If I can find something to use as a siphon hose, I might be able to drain some gas from the generator tank into the plastic can.

The start-a-fire option is not my go-to choice, but I'll resort to it if necessary.

I slink back up the stairs and am about to open the door when I hear voices. A hushed conversation in the kitchen. Crap.

I press my ear to the door.

Joanna's voice spits out, "psycho motherfucker"—a reference to Hark, no doubt.

Clem replies to her. His first words are muffled, but then I make out, "not the one we really need to worry about, is he?"

*What? What does he mean by that?*

"Yeah, well, fuck this shit anyway," Joanna answers. "I didn't sign up for this."

"*Yeah* you did," says Clem. "It's *exactly* what you signed up for. But believe me, I'm not thrilled about it either."

"I got a kid I need to think about," says Joanna, "and if Hark thinks..." She lowers her voice to a whisper, then she and Clem move out of the kitchen. I think.

So... what intel have I just gathered?

First of all, Joanna is not happy with Hark. What is he asking of her that she's suddenly bristling at? She was okay with kidnapping and torture. What line has now been crossed? I shudder to think.

And what's this about Hark not being "the one we really need to worry about"? I think back on the last comment Mary made: *You still think Hark is the one pulling the strings here?* Are Joanna and Clem working for someone higher than Hark?

I'm struck again by the almost subservient way Hark behaves toward Anvita. Is she the uber-boss here? Is Anvita really running the show?

No. Not her.

Damn. A more obvious answer has been staring me in the face all along.

Hark wasn't the only one who lost family members when that violent criminal on PCP did his thing eight years ago. Daddy Gumdrops lost his daughter and two grandchildren. Does Gumdrops know exactly what's going on here?

Why wouldn't he? This *is* his property we're using, no doubt. Just as the warehouse and old hotel were his.

Shit. Is Harkins Horvath II—the father—behind all this? Is he just letting his crazy son serve as the front person? So the insanity card can be played if everything goes to shit? Is *Dad* the one who signs Clem's and Joanna's paychecks?

If that's the case, then defeating Hark and escaping from here isn't going to solve my problems. If Harkins Senior has it in for me, I'm a dead man wherever I go.

*Easy, Oliver, this is all conjecture. You don't know anything yet.*

# Chapter 24

Clem finds me in my bedroom, hiding out, and drags me downstairs for my next "structured daily activity."

There is indeed a small chapel here at Odyssey House. It's tucked away in a back section beyond the rec room. A non-denominational affair, it features a rose window, a generic altar, a couple of kneelers, a half-dozen candleholders of varying heights, and several pillows with tasseled corners strewn on a carpeted floor.

A PrayStation-360. Can I get a hallelujah?

My Spiritual Counseling session with Anvita is scheduled to start now, at two-thirty, so here I sit, ass on pillow, ready to receive words of wisdom.

Right. Blow me.

I have no idea what to expect from this session—I still don't get why they're cramming this spiritual crap down my throat; I was their shrink, not their priest—but I intend to maintain control. I can't let this session get away from me like Mary's did. I'll start things off by explaining my past treatment decisions to Anvita. She deserves that, in spite of her newfound criminality. And then I'll stay on the offensive.

Anvita glides into the room, wearing a cream-colored sari with a red sash. She bows before the generic altar and sits on a pillow facing me. The energy in the room seems to shift in her presence, I can't deny it. She has that same vibe Emmy sometimes had when she was younger.

Why is someone like Anvita involved in such a lowbrow criminal act?

She looks at me with no trace of hostility, but no trace of warmth, and says without preamble, "We will begin our session by deconstructing your assumptions."

Whoa, hold on a sec. "Really, Anvita? You don't think we need to clear the air first? Say what needs to be said to each other?"

"No clearing of air is required."

"I disagree. You and I have a history, which has clearly caused you some injury—real or perceived."

"When I told you this morning that I bear you no ill will, I spoke truthfully. Our interactions in the past happened exactly as karmically ordained. Sanchita. Prarabdha. Agami. I harbor no resentment toward you in even the smallest way."

"Come on, Anvita. The fact that you're here, joining forces with a psychopath like Hark, tells me that's a lie."

"You know nothing of my motives, Dr. Powers. From your current vantage point, you could not *possibly* know."

"I know you're carrying rage toward me, even if you cover it with a veneer of spiritual serenity."

"If there is rageful energy in me," she says, "it is not of the vengeful sort you imagine."

"Oh? Do enlighten me."

She pauses, seeming to deliberate whether I merit a further explanation. "Are you familiar with Kali the Destroyer?"

"Hindu goddess? Blue skin, crazy eyes, wagging tongue?"

"Your disrespect does you no service. Yes, her. You are familiar with her image, but do you understand her nature?"

I shrug.

"She comes to the realm of Man to destroy whatever stands in the way of enlightenment. She is fierce, feral, elemental. Full of violence."

"And this would be relevant because...?"

"Our helpers on the path to awakening do not always come in the form of gentle teachers and kind sages. Kali stands naked on the piled corpses of her enemies, drenched in their blood..."

As she's saying this, my mind plays a trick. Anvita's voice becomes distant and echoey. Her skin turns a dark black-blue, her eyes yellow, her tongue long and bright red. Her *rudraksha*-bead necklace transforms into a string of tiny, screaming heads, and her breath takes on a wild-animal stench—causing the ground within me to shift.

My heart wants to leap out of my chest. And then, suddenly, she is Anvita again.

"... and offering no comfort whatsoever," she continues, as if nothing has happened. "Kali comes to clear the way for you, murdering your pride, murdering your arrogance, murdering your illusions. She *is* an ally, but of the most ferocious kind. Not the kind with whom you share a Budweiser beer."

What is she telling me? That she herself is Kali?

I find myself in full mental retreat, as I did with Mary. I mustn't allow that to happen. No. The Kali vision was a mental hiccup. That's all. I need to stand my ground, seize control.

"Anyway..." I slap my thighs. "Back to business. You may claim you have no residual feelings about what happened when you were in Bridgeview"— the psych unit where I first met her—"and I'm forced to take your word for it, but there are things *I* cannot allow to go unsaid."

She drops her shoulders as if to say, *speak your mind and get it over with*.

"Your *parents* were the ones who flew me to Chicago to consult on your case, did you know that? They didn't want to tell you at the time. They were extremely confused. They didn't know whether you were the next coming of Krishna or a highly psychotic young lady. They only knew they had no idea how to manage you."

Anvita gives no trace of a response.

"Do you remember the way you were acting at home? Spending hours every day in the garden, 'talking to God,' completely unresponsive. You refused to go to school, refused to bathe, refused to take care of yourself. You *had* no sense of self."

*But*, I remind myself, her folks also swore she could "make things happen" around her—unexplainable things—so they weren't sure mental illness was the explanation for her oddness. Still, they decided to have her hospitalized.

"When you started giving your little *talks* at Bridgeview," I go on, "you gained quite a following. Even some of the staff started listening in. But there was also concern that you were exacerbating some of the other patients' symptoms."

During her stay at Bridgeview, young Anvita would give daily "sermons" in the common room. The staff was divided as to whether these lectures should be viewed as an expression of religious free speech or a hindrance to collective healing. After all, many of the other patients were folks who had trouble getting a handle on reality and establishing boundaries. And here was this intense, persuasive young woman telling them reality was a veil of illusion; that all was one, and life was a dream.

"Your parents—and the staff—wanted an outside opinion. Were you ill or enlightened? So they called me in to examine you. ... I concluded your issues were psychiatric in nature. I thought you should be medicated and kept at home until your ego boundaries returned."

Anvita is just waiting for me to shut up.

"The seizures," I continue, "were an unexpected side effect." Anvita had a prolonged and debilitating reaction to the meds I prescribed. "I'm sorry you had to suffer those; I truly am. But, in retrospect, maybe they were a blessing in disguise. When you recovered from them, your healthy sense of ego returned. You were able to finish high school and go to college. That was a good thing, right?"

"Are you through defending yourself?"

"You're not going to comment? Clearly you have feelings about what happened. My intervention changed the course of your life. For better or worse."

"We are wasting precious time." She closes her eyes, shimmies her body as if to rid it of bad energy, then starts afresh: "We will begin our session, as I said, by deconstructing your assumptions. May I make an observation?"

I flip my palm open. I've said my piece.

"The atheistic stance you assume in your book and psychiatric practice is the most striking example of religious fundamentalism I have ever encountered."

I laugh. Wasn't expecting this. "Oliver Powers MD, a religious fundamentalist?"

"Oh, absolutely. Your rigid insistence that there are no dimensions beyond the material plane keeps your mind closed to all signs of their existence."

*You want to get into this, Anvita? Fine.* "My mind is wide open, I promise you. Show me evidence that spiritual dimensions exist, and I will change my tune. *Evidence*, not wishful projection."

"That is what people of your ilk always say. And yet the evidence abounds—studies that prove prayer can improve the health of total strangers and the growth of plants; that loving thoughts can transform the *physical structure* of water; that collective meditation can lower crime rates around the world... The list goes on and on."

"Questionable, unsubstantiated stuff."

"Quite the contrary—peer-reviewed studies that follow good scientific protocol. But you don't credit them, because you *know in your mind* they cannot be true. You are like the scientists of Galileo's day who refused to look in his telescope because they *knew* he was wrong. No amount of proof will ever be enough for you, because your mind is made up."

"I challenge you on that," I say, but my voice rises slightly at the end.

"Even *direct experience* of the 'miraculous' is not enough for you. You saw that elk on the hill. You saw *Kali the Destroyer* appear before your eyes!"

She *made* that happen? The effect wasn't just in my own mind? She must have used a magician's trick of some kind. Some sort of flash-hypnosis thing, maybe.

"You dismiss even what your own eyes show you," she says. "Because you prefer to dwell in ignorance and superstition."

"Superstition?" I laugh again. "So now I'm not just a religious bigot, I'm also superstitious?" The pattern of colored sunlight from the rose window has crept onto my leg. I shift six inches to my left.

Anvita chuckles. "Quite primitively so. You embrace the Superstition of Materialism."

She's using the term to be provocative. I refuse to bite.

"Do you believe in the physical universe, Dr. Powers? In matter, time, space, dimension?"

"Is that a bad thing now? To believe reality exists?"

"And do you believe the universe came into existence through an event called the Big Bang, and that billions of years later, after the planets cooled, life arose, by lark, in a previously lifeless universe, and consciousness was born? An observer incidentally came into being?"

"I think we've pretty well established that's how it went down."

"Is that so?" Anvita's eyes twinkle. "This scenario you endorse is a creation myth of the most magical sort—trillions of *galaxies* erupting from a point the size of nothing? That's no better than 'turtles all the way down.' And yet you accept it without proof. The humorous thing is that it does not even comport with what science itself has known about consciousness for the past century." I wait for her to elaborate; she shifts tack. "You claim in your book that we should always proceed from the known and avoid making assumptions, correct?"

"Correct." *What kind of trap is she laying here?*

"Very well then, let me ask you a few questions." I vowed *I* would be the one asking the questions, but fine, let's see where this goes. "When was the last time you experienced something outside your own consciousness?"

"What? What do you mean?"

"Just what I said. When was the last time you had a direct experience of reality, unmediated by consciousness?"

"Experience is always mediated to some degree," I reply. "Obviously. Our senses interact with the environment and feed data to the brain, which interprets the data."

"How do you know your senses exist, and that they are interacting with something *out there* called the environment?"

"It's self-evident."

"Is it? When you experience the wetness of water, the redness of a rose, the hardness of a rock, where do you experience it?"

"Well... in my brain."

"Quite so," she says. "Well, actually, in your *mind*—your brain, too, is a theorized construct—but you see my point. None of the qualities I described, or any other qualities, exist *in the object itself*, they exist in consciousness. Literally *every single thing we have ever known and experienced* is an event in consciousness."

"Based on data fed to us by reality."

"That part—the claim that there is a world 'out there' beyond our perception—is pure hypothesis. Speculation. *Superstition*. Do you ever read the work of your advanced physicists?"

"I don't have time for Schrodinger's cat. My wife's cats are handful enough."

Ba-dum. Hold for laughs.

"For over one hundred years," she says, "they have been telling us what the sages have always known—that material reality is an elaborate illusion. The observer is so entwined with the observed that it is impossible to talk about the universe *even existing* without a consciousness to perceive it. And so your physicists have been forced to ask the question I now ask you. How do you *know* anything exists beyond the one and only dimension we have literally ever known: consciousness itself? Should you not be placed on medication for suggesting such a thing?"

She's got me trapped logically. I bounce back with, "*You're* talking to me, so clearly *you* believe I exist outside your consciousness."

"I believe you exist *within* my consciousness. You are a fan of Occam's Razor, are you not, Dr. Powers? The idea that the explanation with the fewest assumptions is typically best?"

I shrug assent.

"All the paradoxes with which your physicists struggle—wave/particle duality, non-local interactions, the problem of quantum entanglement—are resolved when we stop *assuming* the existence of a physical world beyond consciousness. When we simply say that consciousness *is* reality and reality *is* consciousness. No difference."

"Come on, Anvita. Reality exists. Out there. We all know that intuitively. When I run into a wall, it stops me. Every time. It stops everyone else too."

"When you run into a wall in a video game, it stops you also. Does that wall, therefore, have an independent, three-dimensional existence?" Before I can answer—I don't really *have* an answer—she says, "Let us pause here and meditate on what we have discussed so far."

Meditate? But we're in the middle of—

A high-frequency vibration moves into me through the top of my head. *Whoa.* It spreads downward like a tingling wash, warming and enlivening every nerve and cell in my body. Where did *this* come from? It's as if I suddenly possess an inner body made entirely of light. I *remember* this feeling. From when? Is Anvita causing it somehow?

She stands. Using a lighter that seems to materialize in her hand, she lights three of the tall candles and pulls a shade over the rose window, darkening the room. She sits again and says, "Close your eyes and focus on your breathing."

I do. Within seconds, I feel myself lifting, as if rising above the floor.

# Chapter 25

With a rush of vertigo, I seem to fly up out of my body, through the upper floors of the house and the roof, past the treetops, and up over the lush pine forest. The town of Payson and the Mogollon Rim, a two-hundred-mile-wide geological feature, recede below me at impossible speeds.

Seconds later, I'm hovering thousands of feet in the sky, looking down on the land as if from an airliner. And then, *whoosh*, I'm up and out of the atmosphere. Earth recedes to a dime-sized object in space. My heart floods with the insight—usually the province of astronauts—that Earth is a single organism and that all the separateness we humans traffic in is pure illusion.

For a flash of a moment, I know *everything*.

And then I begin the roller-coaster descent back to Earth. As I near the ground, I swoop into a banking maneuver over a striated rock formation. I'm in a new location, not Payson anymore. I'm still in Arizona, but now I'm surrounded by rocky desert mountains. I soar along as if on the wings of a bird, tacking in the wind and steering a course above a dirt road.

The Apache Trail.

I lock my sights on a car below me as it grinds along in the dirt. I feel heart-swelling love for that car. It's a Land Rover Discovery, metallic teal. The car belongs to Oliver Powers, MD. I fly out ahead of it in bird form, alight on a barrel cactus, and watch it drive past me, kicking up twin streamers of dust.

Suddenly I am at the wheel of the car, back in my "own" body again, driving along the Apache Trail, feeling confused, urgent, pulled like a magnet.

My analytical mind kicks in again. I know the scene I am reliving: that day-before-Thanksgiving drive, just before I was kidnapped.

I'm on the brink of remembering. Remembering *everything*. Why I drove out to the Trail. What clues I was following. What happened next.

*If only I can pull these details from memory,* an inner voice tells me, *all my questions will be answered. My path forward will be clear. I will understand Hark's motives, and I will know how to take his power away.*

*Remember*, damn it, *remember*.

But no. Straining for the memory only kicks it farther away, like a can down the road.

My mind tumbles and crashes back to nuts-and-bolts reality. I feel the press of the pillow beneath my earthbound ass. I'm back in the chapel again.

Back in rational-thinking mode.

Anvita bows and exits the room, leaving me aghast. She *gave* me that experience, somehow. More than that, she did what I have not allowed any other person to do: defeat me in an argument about my own bread-and-butter topic. I still believe my version of reality is correct, but I'm surprised at my inability to defend my position against an able opponent. And I'm wondering, frankly, why I have always chosen this topic as the hill I want to die on. Why have I invested so much passion in being the "anti-spiritual" guy, even at the cost of alienating my own daughter? And wife.

Why?

The answer to that question lies at the heart of why I am here, in this house, with these people. I know this in my bones. And the thought makes me physically ill.

• • •

"Chop this, asshole," says Bruce, plunking a grapefruit-sized onion and a chef's knife on the cutting board in front of me. We're on to a thrilling new segment of my scheduled day, "Dinner Prep with Bruce, 4:45." It promises to be every bit as entertaining as the Mary and Anvita sessions were.

I feel the eyes of Clem and Joanna boring in on me as I pick up the knife. The two thugs sit perched on the edge of the kitchen table, watching Bruce and me like wolves at feeding time.

"Do me a favor, by the way," says Bruce as I flip the onion to cut off its ends. "Please, please, *please*, come at me with that knife. Give me a fuckin' excuse."

I actually *consider* attacking Bruce with the knife, but harming or threatening him won't get me to a happy place. I need to be more strategic.

*After my session with Anvita, my schedule called for an hour of "Personal Prayer/Meditation Time" in the chapel. I did not pray during my allotted time. No. I used the hour to flesh out my escape options—car keys, phones, house-fires.*

*I began by mentally focusing on the gas can in the basement. After wringing my brain dry for a quarter of an hour, I came up with a pretty good idea for siphoning gas from the generator into the gas can—an idea I hope to try at the earliest opportunity.*

*Then I moved on to phones. As I was wrangling with the problem of password protection, a mind-punching realization dawned: every cell phone has an emergency bypass key on its passcode screen. All you need to do is tap the icon and you can call 911 without needing the phone password. I could have called 911 when I had Hark's phone in my hand! Crap!*

*My fuckup hit me like an uppercut. On the heels of my disastrous sessions with Mary and Anvita, it felt like yet another defeat. I needed a win. With Bruce. I needed to turn the tide in my favor somehow.*

"What are we making?" I ask Bruce, trying to keep my voice light.

"Oliver-dick stew," he says, not missing a beat. Boy, he had that one cued up. "Just need to harvest the main ingredient." He snips a pair of kitchen scissors in the air, widening his eyes. Effing with me.

"You're a humorous man, Bruce. Don't let anyone tell you otherwise."

"Fun fact," he adds, putting the scissors down. "Oliver-dick stew technically qualifies as a vegetarian dish, because there's so little meat in it."

"Ah, I see what you did there." I start peeling the onion. "You imputed smallness to my penis. See, I'm on your waggish wavelength. Soulmates in jocularity, you and I."

"Still an asshole after all these years, Powers. How do you keep it up?" He bends down and pulls two pots and a frying pan from below the counter. "Chili. That's what we're making. The quick kind. Here, mince this when you're done with the onion." He tosses a fat head of garlic onto my cutting board. "And don't fuck around; use the whole thing."

"Well, at least we see eye to eye on one thing. Garlic." Setting the bulb aside, I chop my onion without speaking for a while. "What do we have for other ingredients?"

"I took care of that, don't worry." He snaps the side of a brown paper supermarket bag with his finger. "Life's too short to eat crap chili."

Gastric juices explode within me as Bruce pulls groceries from the bag: poblano peppers, fresh Italian parsley, dried Hatch chilies, red wine, tubs of fresh-made stock, and more. The man came to cook. He points to a locked cupboard, and Joanna unlocks it with her keys. He takes three big cans of crushed tomatoes and a bottle of olive oil from the stocked larder, then fetches a pack of butcher-shop ground meat from the fridge.

"We're making two batches." He fires up the burner, waits for his pan to heat. "One for vegans and one for normal people."

Trying to forge a connection, any connection, with him, I say, "They sell vegan meatloaf at my Whole Foods, with vegan gravy. Hold me back. Notice they never do it the other way? Like, fake watercress salad made of ham."

At this Bruce actually laughs. "My wife used to eat vegan pizza. Christ, just stab me."

An olive branch from Bruce? I decide not to push things. He plops the meat into the pan with a sizzle. We work in agreeable silence for a while; two dudes cooking.

Then it hits me: nothing about this situation is normal. One of the most dangerous faculties of the human mind is its ability to normalize the abhorrent. There's no time for that. I need to shake things up, create an opening, make a move.

"You know, Bruce, I've been thinking. I acknowledge I've made some mistakes as a psychiatrist. But..."

"You're making one right now, Powers. *I'll* tell you when it's time for you and me to talk, man to man. Till then, just slice and dice."

I make a few obnoxiously loud chops on the board. Bruce shoots me a dirty look. He steps away from the stove, rinses the parsley under the faucet and tosses it onto my board. "Trim the stems off those, too. Then mince the leaves." He goes back to browning meat.

I commence trimming the parsley. "I've made some mistakes as a psychiatrist," I repeat, not retreating. "But your case wasn't one of them."

"Seriously, Powers. You're going to want to shut your mouth if you don't want me to shut it for you."

He flicks his eyes toward Clem, who meets his glance with a ten-pound brow. The power dynamic in the room becomes clearer. Clem is reminding Bruce he doesn't have the authority to get rough with me. I guess only Hark is permitted to initiate physical abuse.

That gives me some elbow room here. Maybe.

Eyes on my chopping, I say, "I've been reviewing your case in my mind, Bruce. I don't have my records handy because, oh yeah, I'm *kidnapped*, but here's what I recall." I avoid looking at him—that way he can't warn me off with a glare. "You went into a manic phase at a time when the markets were going nuts. You made some daredevil investments and got lucky with them. That fed into your mania. You tossed a little cocaine into the mix. Your whirlwind started spinning faster and faster, till you thought you were God in Gucci loafers. But I *told you* you were headed for a crash. I didn't know it would be *the* crash—2008—but I knew one was coming. For you. And it did. And it kicked your ass. Case summary: I correctly diagnosed you. I offered you medication and short-term hospitalization. You ignored my advice, you lost a fortune, your life went to shit, and now you want someone to blame for it all. Me."

Bruce steps away from the stove, sliding the pan off its burner. His face reddens. We square off, gladiators in striped aprons. "*Here* are the facts, Powers. I *was* invincible at that time. I *was* God in Gucci. I was tapped into Source, and I was in the fucking miracle zone. And that scared the shit out of you. Your only option was to bring me down to your level. And *that's* when everything fell apart for me. Working with you was the biggest mistake of my life."

"Then why did you do it? Work with me?"

"You know why. My wife insisted."

"*Why* did she insist? Why was she convinced you needed a shrink?"

"Because she didn't get what was happening with me. And she didn't know how to deal with my success. Some people can't handle unlimited abundance. They become—"

"Or maybe she knew *exactly* what was happening with you. Why did you listen to her if you knew she was wrong? Why did *you* make an appointment to see me?"

"Because she said she'd divorce me if I didn't."

"Bruce, you're a strong-willed guy. You don't do anything you don't want to. You wouldn't have shown up in my office unless there was some part of you that knew you were coming untethered and needed to be brought back down to Earth."

"I went to see you because I promised my wife I would. I was riding so high, I had no fear of someone like *you* destroying the roll I was on. In fact, I saw you as an amusing challenge. Little did I know the fear I would trigger in you. And how dangerous that fear would make you."

"Fear? In *me*? Nice try, Bruce. Listen to your own words: 'riding so high,' 'roll I was on.' You were on a manic carpet ride, and you knew it, and it terrified you. You wanted help, but you didn't want to admit it. So you put that onus on your wife."

Bruce barks a sound between a laugh and a cough. "A man knows, on a gut level, when the man sitting across from him is in animal fear. Whenever I'd walk into your office, I could feel your hackles rising, your balls retracting, your defenses going up. Not because you were afraid I was crazy, but because you were afraid I *wasn't*."

My knife-hand starts jittering as if with its own power source. I return to my chore, converting the motion into chopping energy. So much parsley, so little time.

"What's the matter, Powers? Suddenly not enjoying this conversation? You started this; let's finish it. Put the fuckin' knife down." Clem and Joanna snap to attention. Bruce signals, *don't worry, it's all good.* "Look me in the eye and tell me you were a hundred percent convinced I was manic and not in a state of divine grace."

I look into his eyes but can't quite hold his gaze. "I made a good diagnosis, Bruce."

"You're fuckin' pathetic. And a god-damn liar."

"Think whatever you want."

"I will," he says. "Because I know something you don't *know* that I know. You see, Dave Barrows is a friend of mine."

My chopping hand freezes, and my scalp breaks out in hot-spots. "Who?" My voice goes *just* a tad too high.

Bruce laughs and shakes his head. "You know damn well who. Office in Newburyport, over the fossil shop. Dave Barrows, 'Last of the Great American Stockbrokers.' Him and me had a chat. About an interesting visit you made to his office."

My hand nearly drops the knife.

# Chapter 26

"I met with Dave Barrows *once*." I accent the word with a chop of the blade. "And made *one* investment with him. A modest one."

"Modest, huh?" says Bruce.

An alarm goes off within me. *Is this the part where the kidnappers reveal they are seeking ransom money after all?*

"Do you happen to recall where you got the inspiration for that particular investment?" Bruce casts an eye at Clem and Joanna.

Mincing my words along with my greens, I reply, "I admit that talking to you—about the stock market—made me realize I hadn't been aggressive enough with my retirement fund. I decided to take a chunk of money I could afford to lose and make a play with it."

"So you took investment advice from a crazy person you thought should be on meds?"

"I didn't 'take investment advice.' Talking to you got me thinking, that's all. Thinking independently about my own investment situation."

"I see. So just an independent train of thought?"

"What?" My face flushes. "I don't have the right to play the stock market? Just because I'm in the helping professions? Did Bruce Costa invent the concept of investing in stocks? Do I owe you a commission for sparking that idea in me?"

"Watching you squirm," he says, "is like watching an octopus on *Blue Planet* running from a shark. You dodge, you dart, you change color, you squirt ink, but you know Mister Shark's gonna git ya."

"Don't injure yourself on those metaphors, Bruce." I make a show of surveying our cooking supplies. "Are we going to puree those dried chilies? Shouldn't we get some water boiling for that?"

"There goes Mr. Octopus, dodging and darting."

He turns back to browning his meat, making loud stabs with the spatula. *Stab... Stab... Stab... Stab... Stab...*

I slam my knife down. "Is that really what you think? That I owe you something because I made an investment, a successful investment, during the time we were working together?"

"What stock did you invest in, Powers?"

"What difference does it make?"

"You know exactly what difference it makes, you octopus-fuckin'-weasel-fuck." He stops cooking again, pivots toward me. "You knew it the second the name Dave Barrows came out of my mouth."

I did. I did know.

• • •

*Friday, August 28, 2008, was one of those crystal-sky New England days when the first hint of autumn steals into the air. Downtown Newburyport was bustling. Through the leaded-glass window in my office door, I saw Bruce approaching our reception area from the second-floor lobby of Port Place, the professional building where I rented my space. He greeted Tracy, my receptionist, with a huge smile, and pulled a wad of bills from his pocket. The two of them had an exchange in which Tracy held her hands up in laughing protest—no, I can't accept that—and then Bruce whispered something in her ear and shot a glance at my door, eyes aglow with manic fire.*

*I braced for our session.*

*"Doc!" said Bruce after I ushered him into my office and into his favorite armchair. "Do you know what I spent my morning doing?"*

*"As I was not following you and don't have psychic powers, Bruce, I do not." I said this with a smile.*

"Handing out hundred-dollar bills on the waterfront boardwalk. Real hundreds, coin of the realm; I got a big fat wad of 'em right here. Do you know why I was doing that?"

"I have my theories, Bruce, which hopefully we'll get into today."

"Because that which we give freely unto others returns multifold unto us. It is law. You would not believe how many people out there refused my gift. Walked around me like I was a leper. Typical human self-sabotage. We block the gifts Source tries to give us by insisting on limitations. Do you know why I'm in such a fantastic freakin' mood right now, Doc?"

"Are you going to keep asking questions, Bruce, or might I wedge a few in?"

"I'll give you a hint," he said, ignoring me. "It's not because I made two-hundred-nine grand in one afternoon yesterday—although I did do that. It's not because the trees and water are glowing with freakin' God-fire today, although they are. It's because I found a five-dollar bill on the boardwalk and another twenty on the sidewalk right out front. Who finds cash on the ground twice in the same morning? That twenty-five bucks is worth more than yesterday's two-hundred grand to me. You know why? Because it shows the eye of God winking at me."

"Or the eye of chance."

"Listen to you, Doc, livin' in your limited little bubble. Believing you're unworthy of miracles. You know what's so funny? I could change your life today, if you would open your mind, but you won't. You're just like those people on the boardwalk; you wouldn't take a gift if Source handed it to you wrapped in Snoopy wrapping paper."

"And how, pray tell, would you change my life today, Bruce?"

"I could tell you a securities purchase to make. And you could walk across the street, after our session, buy some shares in this small biotech firm, and you would become wealthy. Sure thing. But you won't do it. Why? Because you believe more in scarcity than abundance."

"I'm not here to get investment advice from you, Bruce. Even if I believed you, it would be unethical of me to take stock tips from a patient."

"Yeah, well, I'm in the mood to give, give, give today, baby, and you can't stop me! So I gave my pick to Tracy out front. Maybe she'll be smart enough to cash in on it and buy a ticket to the miracle zone."

"Yeah, good ol' Dave Barrows," says Bruce, taking a step toward me under the watchful eyes of Clem and Joanna. "He told me you bought three-thousand-some-odd shares that day. Of a little stock called GenSyn."

"Barrows had no right to tell you anything. That was un—" I cut myself off.

"Were you about to say *unethical*?"

"No," I fib, "I was going to say—"

"Spooky word, *unethical*, ennit?"

"Bruce, if you're implying that what I did—making that investment—was somehow improper, you're wrong. I weighed the ethics carefully. It's not like you were the only one saying 'buy GenSyn.' Motley Fool had it as a pick. That guy with the glasses on Bloomberg, he mentioned it. I did my own independent research."

"So you would have gone out and invested—what?—twenty grand in GenSyn purely on your own research, your own instincts?"

"We're all influenced by the people around us. None of us exist in a vacuum. We can't insulate ourselves from—"

"He dodges! He darts!"

I grab the head of garlic, break off a clove to peel. "Okay, did your comment to Tracy about GenSyn have *some* effect on me? It probably did. But only insofar as to pique my initial curiosity. It was one of several stocks I looked into. When I gave Dave Barrows my short list, he liked that one best. So really, *he* picked it. Did he mention that part?"

Bruce lays his spatula on the edge of the pan and looks at Clem and Joanna with a hard-to-read expression. The two goons slide off the kitchen table, and a complicated three-way eye exchange goes down. Evidently I misread the power dynamic. Whatever authority the two ex-cops have over Bruce, he also has some authority over *them*.

"We need to go take care of something," says Joanna. "You two gonna be okay if we leave you alone for a few minutes?"

Bruce holds up his hands in peace. I shrug; what does "okay" even mean anymore? Clem and Joanna exit the room, Clem shooting us a warning glare as he goes.

It's just the two chefs alone in the kitchen now.

The air is thick. I wait for Bruce to stir it.

"So," he says in a soft, I'm-not-going-to-hurt-you tone, "you really don't see an ethical issue with what you did?"

"I didn't ask for your financial advice, Bruce. In fact, if you recall, I *tried to stop you from giving it to me.*"

"And I didn't give it to *you*, did I? I gave it to Tracy. Which means you must have gone and asked her for it."

"She was my paid staff person. I was privy to any information my patients shared with her."

"But why'd you do it?" Bruce steps closer to me, undaunted by the knife I've unconsciously picked up again. "Why'd you ask her about my stock pick?"

"I did not put myself in a compromised position with you, Bruce. I made one trade of a public security you happened to mention to Tracy. It had no effect on our work together."

"But correct me if I'm wrong. Didn't you think I was suffering from a mental illness?"

"You know I did. Bipolar disorder. Manic phase."

"And when I advised Tracy to invest in GenSyn, wasn't that an *expression* of my mental illness—at least by your way of seeing things?"

"So?"

"So," he steps closer, "you think it's okay for a psychiatrist to profit from his patients' mental illness?"

"Of course not, but I—"

"But isn't that what you did? If a shrink is acting on tips from a patient in a disturbed state of mind, doesn't that give him a financial incentive to *keep* that patient in a disturbed state of mind? Isn't that a pretty damn big conflict of interest?"

"It would be," I say, unconsciously stepping backward, "*if* that was what was going on. But I didn't invest in that stock *because* you told me too, I invested *in spite* of you. And it was a one-time thing. And I didn't try to keep you ill. I fought tooth and nail to *curb* your mania."

"And you sure succeeded, didn't you? You made me doubt my instincts, put me in a financial panic. I sold off my whole portfolio during the house fire of 2008. For pennies on the dollar. When I should have been scooping up more bargains."

He takes another step closer to me. I hold my ground, but uncertainly.

"What about you?" he says. "What did you do with your GenSyn stock? Did you sell it after it tripled or quadrupled in value, buy yourself a Benz? Or did you hang on to it?"

"My financial life is none of your business, Bruce."

"*Did* you, Powers? Did you hang onto that stock? 'Cause if you did, then by my reckoning your twenty-K is now worth over a mill."

Something in my expression tells him he's scored a bullseye. The truth is, my wildly successful GenSyn stock has become the cornerstone of my retirement portfolio.

"So let me paint this picture in neon pink." He paces around me. "While I was losing my shirt and the extra buttons that came with it because you were telling me not to trust my intuition anymore—that it was all grandiosity and mania—you were sitting back, making bank on the fruits of my 'illness.'"

I blink twice. Twice again for good measure.

Wait a minute, though. We're back to money again. So maybe that *is* Bruce's motivation in all this. Money. This may be an opening I can exploit. I need to play my cards wisely. And *fast*, while we're alone in the kitchen.

"That wasn't the situation, Bruce, I promise you. But I can see where it might look that way to you. So... what? Do you want me to make you whole, is that it? Because I can do that. There was no wrongdoing on my part, but I'm willing to share some of the returns on that investment with you." Bruce doesn't speak. I take that as encouragement. "I mean, you're right, I wouldn't have thought of buying GenSyn if not for you. So, yeah, I guess a commission is arguable. What do you think is a fair amount? I could go as high as twenty percent." No answer. "Thirty?" Nothing. "Thirty-five?"

I don't know how to interpret his silence, but at least he's not stopping me.

"I have all my investments with Vanguard," I say. "All in one place, one website. Super easy to manage. GenSyn's in my brokerage account. If I had a phone, I could execute the sell order on that stock, have the money sitting in my settlement fund within minutes. From there, I can transfer the funds to anyone's account I want. Like, today. *Now*. So what do you say?"

He gives me a little smile and turns his thumb upward. My heart races.

"Is that a yes, or a 'go higher'?"

He holds his pose, thumb up.

"Okay, we can go forty." I just want to get my hands on his damn phone. If I can punch in three quick digits, 9-1-1, the police are required to trace the call, come out and investigate in person, even if I don't say a word on the phone. "But before I transfer the money to your account, I need something from you." He'll be suspicious if I don't play an angle. "A guarantee that you'll help get me out of here. That's *my* demand, no negotiating."

His silence seems to indicate we have a deal. Or not.

"I just need your phone to get on the Vanguard site."

"Mm-hmm. And exactly how fuckin' stupid do I look to you, Powers?"

"Obviously you can watch everything I do. It's just... I can't tell you my password verbally; I only know the sequence by touch. That's the truth."

Bruce stares at me, distrust oozing from every pore, but he reaches into his pocket and pulls out his phone. He studies the screen, punches a series of keys, waits a few seconds, then extends the phone toward me, keeping one hand on it, even as I tighten my grip on its case.

I grab the phone, then drop and do a barrel-roll across the floor. My aim is to run for the nearest bathroom, just beyond the kitchen, lock the door before he can catch me, and call 911 from there.

I spring to my feet and charge toward the kitchen doorway, just as the door is blocked by a wall of bodies: Clem, Joanna, Hark.

I bounce off Clem and fall backwards to the floor. I lift Bruce's phone to my eyes. It shows a text from Bruce to Hark, sent just before he reached me the phone: *He tried it. Come now.*

# Chapter 27

"Refresh my Clozaril-addled memory," says Hark. "Did I, or did I not, tell you there are only two exits from Odyssey House? One is through the front door, with a shiny diploma in your hand. The other is via the six-foot hole in the ground out back. It seems you've made your choice."

Bruce pokes my rib with his shoe. "Did you really think you were going to bribe your way out of this, Fuck-Patrol?"

"I thought maybe *you*, Bruce, of all these deluded... individuals, had enough brains to do what was best for yourself. Take the money and run. But no, you insist on being manipulated by a psychotic puppet who is himself being manipulated by someone else." I watch Hark to see how this last comment lands with him. Nothing shows.

"Stand up," Hark orders.

Hark and I face each other eye to eye, Hark using his height differential to full advantage.

"You've forced us to an inflection point, Woggles. We must decide whether your treatment program ends tonight, via the back-woods exit, or whether you will be granted a conditional reprieve. *My* mind is made up, but we'll have to see how the rest of the jury votes."

"Killing me would play right into Daddy Gumdrops's hands, wouldn't it?"

He leaves my bait untaken. "Here is what's going to happen. You will finish making dinner with Bruce. After dinner, we will have our house meeting, as scheduled, at seven o'clock. And you will plead your case. You will either convince us you have made sufficient progress on your goals to warrant an extension of your stay, or you won't. If you fail to make your case—no more subtlety here, Wogs—Clem and Joanna will bind your hands and feet, stuff your mouth with dirty rags, drag you out to the woods, and bury you alive in the hole you saw earlier."

Ice water rushes through me, but I stand tall. "*Here* is what will happen if I die. You will rot away in a facility for the criminally insane, while your father sits back in his brushed-leather Eames recliner, sipping Macallan 18 and picking pan-seared scallop from his teeth. He'll get his revenge on me, you'll get put away forever, win/win for Gumdrops."

"Your trial starts in..."—Hark glances at his watch—"ninety-seven minutes. I suggest you start preparing your defense as you cook." He turns on his heels, almost like a Nazi soldier in a WWII movie, and marches out of the room.

"I know you're not really in charge here, Hark," I shout after him. He keeps walking. "Your lackeys aren't as discreet as you think." *That* puts some tar under his feet. "I know who's paying Clem and Joanna's salaries."

"By the way," Hark says, stopping but not turning toward me, "You've probably deduced this already, but you won't be dining on the food you're preparing. Your meal tonight will be prime cut of Safeway bologna, no fixin's."

He adds, "hyuck, hyuck," in a monotone and continues toward his office.

• • •

Seven-o-five p.m. My "trial" is set to begin. I'm seated, as I was this morning, in the single chair in the middle of the living room, with the two sofas angled toward me. Clem and Joanna flank me, striking formal postures that would be laughable if not for the piece of rope and grimy rag each holds in their hands. The four "jurors" haven't arrived yet. They seem to be stalling their entrance to ratchet up the drama.

As I wait for the next act of this two-bit Pinter play to unfold, I remind myself that *I* am the psychiatrist, *I* am the professional, *I* am the stable one.

I know how to work group dynamics, and I *will* find a way to steer them to my advantage.

Of course, that didn't go too well for me at dinnertime.

Dinner was quite the joy-fest indeed. I sat alone, gagging on my off-brand bologna while my ex-patients, plus Clem and Joanna, sat together, enjoying the fruits of my culinary labors. My two attempts to speak were shut down with bullet speed.

My captors tried to act like mutual friends, but clearly they weren't very comfortable together. They talked about alarmingly mundane things—the Oscars, the Super Bowl, what everyone did for Christmas. The one helpful nugget I was able to glean was that today's date is somewhere near New Year's. That was my best guess anyway, but it's good to know I was right.

Now as I sit here awaiting "trial," I find myself wondering how Hannah spent Christmas. Did she see her family? Did she miss me? How is her life in these days of spousal abandonment? I can *feel* our marriage dying with each passing hour.

The "jurors" file into the room: Mary, Anvita, Bruce, Harkins, all wearing blank expressions. Here we go. They take their seats.

"As you all know," says Hark after everyone settles in, "our regular house meeting has been preempted so we can hold this emergency meeting of the treatment team. The patient has violated house rules, and we must decide whether he will be terminated... from the program or allowed to continue in treatment. I will begin the proceedings by advising the patient to wipe that cocky fucking smirk off his face and reminding him that, thanks to his ability to identify us to the police, his likeliest route out of Odyssey House is live burial."

Jesus, no cutesiness this time. I look to the others, to see how they react to his unvarnished death threat. They seem unperturbed. "What about you, Anvita?" I say. "You can't be okay with this."

She meets my eyes, unblinking. Okay, then.

"You may make your opening statement now." Hark waves his hand at me.

"Opening statement?" I wasn't prepared for this. "So we're really going to play out this farce?"

"If you think we're being even a tiny bit farcical"—Hark flicks his eyes at Clem, who flexes the rope in his hand—"you are approaching these proceedings in the worst imaginable mindset. Commence."

I have no idea what words will issue from my mouth. What I do know is that smarminess will not serve me here.

"I think you all know," I begin, scanning their sober faces, "that if anyone should be on trial here, it's Harkins Horvath III, for planning and executing this criminal abduction, and all of you for serving as his accomplices. So please don't act as if you have any moral high-ground here. Did I try to bribe my way out? Hell, yes. Anyone in their right mind would've done the same." A rash impulse kicks in—to make a last-ditch play to win people over to Team Oliver. "And that's the key point here. I *am* in my right mind. Hark, on the other hand, has a diseased mind and has used his powers of persuasion to pull the rest of you into his delusional system. That's why I'll make you this one-time offer: work with me here and I'll make sure you're treated with leniency when the *real* trial happens. In a *real* courtroom."

The expressions on the four faces tell me my gambit was a fool's play.

Hark lowers his head, shakes it twice. "Olliwog, Olliwog, Olliwog." He does a weary thumbs-down and looks to the others, who require *zero* time to render their verdicts. They point their thumbs downward in almost perfect unison.

Clem and Joanna grab my armpits. They yank me out of my seat and, with military efficiency, slam me to the floor, face-down. In one swift motion, Clem straddles my back and pushes my wrists together. Joanna drops her full weight onto my legs and lashes my ankles together with a couple of swift loops of the rope. She then comes around to tie my wrists.

As I think about what's coming next for me, the whole scene plays out in my mind in full Sensurround: the crunching of Clem's and Joanna's heels in the dead pine needles as they march along the woodland trail holding my bound body from both ends; the clasp of their finger-bones in my flesh as I wriggle and scream through the oily rags stuffing my mouth; the bone-rocking blow of the four-foot drop into the burial hole; the tang of the loamy dirt raining down on my face, covering my eyes and nostrils...

"No! Wait!"

Clem shoves his dirty rags into my face. "No! No! Please!" I shout through the muffling of the cloth. "Give me another chance! One more chance!"

"Clem," Hark orders.

Clem eases up on the rags. I tug for air. Hark stares at me, expressionless, for what feels like a calendar era, then nods at Clem to back off—a bit.

Clem withdraws his hands by six inches.

I need to save my life, right this second. Fuck dignity. The next words out of my mouth may be the most important ones I'll ever speak.

"I deserve to be on trial. I admit it. I made some mistakes in my treatment of all of you. I see that now. No! Mistakes are when you spill a cup of coffee. I did things that... merit your outrage." This next part feels almost physically painful coming out of my mouth: "I allowed myself to be ethically compromised as a psychiatrist."

Hark rolls his eyes as if to say *more intellectual horseshit from Powers* but signals his thugs to lift me back into the chair. They do so, in a rougher way than strictly called for. A stay of execution, however brief? I'd better make the best of it.

"Spending time with each of you has opened my eyes." I gaze at my captors one by one. "Much as I disapprove of you kidnapping me, you've made me face some things I wouldn't have faced otherwise. Things I've been denying and rationalizing for years."

Hark plays the air violin: *quit the speechifying and get to the meat.*

"Mary..." I meet her eyes. "Putting you on Stelazine was a decision I made for *me*, not you. You had dirt on me, plain and simple. I don't know how you got it, I only know that when the voices were under control, you stopped telling those stories about me. I should have tried harder to find a newer medication, one that had milder side effects, but I didn't. Why? Because I liked you on Stelazine: quiet and docile. I'm sorry for what I did to you."

Mary starts to say something. Hark holds his hand up.

I move on. "Bruce, you were right when you said I wanted to take you down a few pegs. The truth is, I was jealous of you. Money is the ultimate alpha-dog badge. You were doing amazing things with money, and it pissed me off. I wanted some of what you had. That's why I took your stock tip, even as I was telling you you were deluded and grandiose. You *were* manic, that was true. But the reason *I* took issue with your success was personal. I'm sorry for that.

"Anvita." I turn to the young woman in the sari. "I shouldn't have recommended you be put on meds. I did it for your parents, I did it for the psych ward staff, I did it for the other patients whose recovery you were affecting. I did it for my reputation. Not for you. If I'd known the meds would cause seizures—and knock you off your spiritual path for years—I certainly wouldn't have prescribed them. Aham Ksantavya. I think that means 'I'm sorry' in Sanskrit."

I hope it does. I turn at last to Hark.

"Hark, I don't know how I could have handled your treatment any differently. You *needed* to be removed from your sister's house and committed. But I should have paid more attention to the depth of your terror. I should have arranged for a guard on Lisa's house, just to make you feel safer. Your father could have afforded it. But the simple truth was, I didn't want to look like I was giving credence to the rantings of a psychotic patient. I was more worried about saving face than about you. The other simple truth was... I enjoyed having power over you. Saying I'm sorry isn't enough. To all of you. I am ashamed of my actions."

I hang my head, not wanting to look in anyone's face. I wait for Hark to speak and my final verdict to be delivered.

Hark sighs. "Are you done with that half-assed attempt at an opening statement? If so, let your trial begin."

*Begin?*

# Chapter 28

"The prosecution will now examine the witness." Hark stands, holding his hands behind his back. "The witness is advised to respond to our questions as if he were hooked up to the ECTT machine at full voltage—because that can be arranged. Mary, would you like to begin?"

"Yah." Mary sits up straight, her eyes tuned to a surprisingly clear channel. She has come prepared. "Doctor Powers, you told me your decision to put me on Stelazine was a good one, and you said the proof was that the doctors that treated me later made the same decision, right?"

I guess I'd better play along... for now. "That's right. Your other treatment providers continued to support my choice of medicine."

"Is that another half-truth?"

"No."

"Really? Isn't there something else you want to tell me about that?"

I start to say "no" again but my mouth stays shut.

"Like, did you put a note in my patient record?"

I pull against the ropes binding my wrists and ankles but can't escape the question. "Yes." My voice flattens. "I put a treatment note in your file, advising future clinicians not to vary your medication and saying that to do so might put you at risk."

"So it wasn't really *their* decision to keep me on Stelazine, was it?"

"It was still their decision, Mary. I had no authority to dictate their clinical choices."

"Yeah, but Dr. Tejwani—he was two shrinks after you—said your note made it seem like you tried a bunch of other meds and they had bad effects. That way other doctors would be nervous about changing my meds."

"I did try other meds," I say. "And I *wanted* other doctors to be nervous. That's why I wrote the note. I wanted them to stay with what worked."

"Why? Why did you care so much? Why did you want to keep Gadriel quiet *even after you left Oakridge*?"

"I cared about *you*. You were better off without her. Without the symptoms."

"You didn't care about me."

"I did, Mary. I do. That's the truth. Whether you believe it or not."

"You were afraid of *her*. Gadriel."

"I already admitted that. How low do you want me to sink? I can put the Betty Boop makeup on again if it'll help."

"You weren't afraid of what Gadriel was saying about you, Dr. Powers." Mary's eyes shine like inquisitors' lamps. "Well, not *just* that. You were afraid of what she *was*, what she *is*. You were afraid of being on the same planet with her."

I pull at my bindings again. "*She* is a psychiatric symptom, Mary. I've told you that five hundred times."

"You don't believe that."

"I do."

"Powers!" Hark shouts in warning from the sidelines. "You lie, you die. How much clearer do I need to be?" His thugs inch closer to me with their ropes and rags.

"You were afraid Gadriel was real," says Mary. "You *knew* she was real. You know it now!"

"I *treat* spiritual delusions, I don't believe in them."

"Liar. Red light. Part of you does. Part of you does believe."

"That's *your* delusion, Mary."

"What about the test?" she says. My breath stops short. "Did you think I forgot about that?"

"What test?" My heart flutters like a trapped bird's wings.

"You know what test. The envelope test. Why don't you tell everyone about it, Doctor Powers? Tell 'em about the envelope test."

Fuck.

*After I put Mary on Stelazine, her schizophrenia symptoms abated, and Gadriel—her "angel of truth"—fell silent. But then Mary began to suffer symptoms of depression. A month or so later, lo and behold, Gadriel was back in business and Mary's mood brightened.*

*We discovered Mary had begun "cheeking" her pills—pretending to swallow them but spitting them out later. When confronted about this, she became belligerent. She refused, outright, to take the medication, and issued a formal challenge to the Oakridge staff. She insisted that by chemically depriving her of the Gadriel experience, we were interfering with her religious rights. An intriguing argument, I had to admit.*

*She and I discussed the matter at length and came to an agreement, one I never should have made: if she could prove to me that Gadriel was real, I would allow her to remain medication-free; if she could not, she would resume the Stelazine.*

*I designed what I considered a fair and objective double-blind test. I wrote seventeen statements that were indisputably true on seventeen slips of paper. On thirteen other slips of paper, I wrote thirteen false statements. I then asked a staff member to seal the thirty slips in thirty identical envelopes and shuffle them, out of my sight.*

*I invited Mary into my office, handed her the envelopes, and instructed her, with Gadriel's guidance, to sort them into two piles: truths and lies. Without opening them.*

*Mary gave me a cocky toss of the head and set to the task. She quickly created two piles of sealed envelopes on my desk. Striking was the fact that she placed seventeen envelopes in one pile, thirteen in the other.*

*I hadn't told her the number of truths versus falsehoods.*

"Okay, Doctor Powers." *She gestured to the piles.* "Rip 'em open."

*She leaned back, waiting for me to open the envelopes. I found myself unable—or unwilling—to comply.*

"What's the matter?" *she asked.*

"I'm... to be honest, I'm having second thoughts, Mary. I'm afraid I've allowed myself to be talked into a very unprofessional arrangement here. I'm sorry. It's my fault, not yours. But I don't think we should open the envelopes."

"Not open them? Why not?"

"Because I think it's wrong for us to play games of chance with your mental health. Here's the thing. We don't know the extent to which luck may have played a role in your choices. And the fact is, even if your results turn out to be accurate, that still doesn't confirm the hypothesis that you have an angel living inside you. There could be a hundred other explanations. This whole thing was a mistake—pinning your treatment decisions on the shuffle of a deck. Shame on me. And so, I think the best thing we can do is..."

I picked up the two stacks and deposited them into the wastebasket beside my desk, unopened.

Mary leapt from her seat, protesting my action and demanding I come up with another test. She became wildly agitated and had to be forcibly (and conveniently) removed.

After she left, I sat for a long time in my chair, unmoving. Then I reached into the trash and removed the envelopes—I'd placed them at cross angles to preserve her stacks.

As I confess the story to the group, the knot of resistance within me loosens further. I'm inching toward a truth that's been walled off for decades, and I'm losing the ability to fight it. Terror and relief are braided together in a tight weave.

"And what did you do after I left your office?" asks Mary.

"I'm sure you can all guess the answer to that." I flash a pinched smile. "I opened the envelopes. I'm sure you can all guess the next part too. Mary scored perfectly."

"That was Gadriel, not me."

"She identified all thirteen lies without having seen inside the envelopes."

"Lies have a vibe," says Mary, "that's what Gadriel tells me. They're like cancer. That's why they eat away at people. Right, Dr. Powers? What did you do next?"

What I want to do *now* is study the weave of the carpet on the floor, but I reply, "I petitioned the court to have you placed under guardianship so I could administer the meds to you intravenously without your consent."

"Why did you do that?"

I can't come up with words to defend myself.

"Maybe I can answer for you." Mary drops her voice to a near-whisper. "The little Catholic boy in you was scared to death. You *knew* Gadriel was real. You knew it in a place deeper than your brain. You didn't know *what* she was—angel or demon—but you knew you wanted her gone from this world. For *your* sanity, not mine."

*A memory cracks open. The little Catholic boy. Me. Attending Sunday mass at Sacred Heart with my parents. Sensing the presence of God in the gold-trimmed arches and domes, but also sensing the peering eye of the Devil. Obsessing over a stained-glass window on the wall—one depicting a white-robed Christ giving blessings to a crowd while a pack of demons grinned and giggled in the corner of the frame. Loathing those demons and their inexplicable hyena-like necks. Wondering why they were in the same picture with Jesus—in a church. In my church. Fretting over the notion that a loving God would allow such demons to exist.*

*The memory feels like sickness in my gut.*

"Perhaps *I* can help you find your words, Dr. Powers," says Anvita, speaking up for the first time and pulling me back to the present. "Do you recall the evening of your first day at Bridgeview?" The Chicago hospital where I consulted on Anvita's case.

Weariness floods my veins. I want to sleep. For days on end. To dissociate, the way I've seen many a patient do.

"You had spent the whole day in consultations," Anvita goes on. "You met with me, with my parents, with the treatment team, with my staff psychiatrist. And you left the hospital late in the day, around six-thirty. But then you came back. Why?"

A sigh leaks out of me. "I wanted to see you one more time before writing my report and making my recommendation."

"Why?"

"Instinct. Intuition. I don't know. I wanted to be sure."

"And what happened next?"

"The staff let me into the unit... and I went down the hall to your room. The door was partially open, and your room was dark. I looked in and..."

"You can say it, Dr. Powers."

I *can*, but I don't want to. "You were sitting in a corner of the room with your eyes closed, in the lotus position... a foot above the floor." I want to walk this statement back with a tagline like, *at least that's what it looked like at the time* or *it was probably a trick of the light*, but I don't. "You were levitating. I saw it with my own eyes."

"And what did you do then?"

"I left. Quietly."

"Did you report to anyone what you had seen?"

"No."

Something inside *me* feels like it's come unmoored and is floating in air.

"Why not?" Anvita asks.

"We've already established I'm a shitty human being and the world's worst psychiatrist."

"May we assume it was for the same reason you tried to silence Mary? *Fear.*"

"*I* don't have to assume anything," Bruce breaks in, ending *his* silence, "because I've seen the fear first-hand. We had a running joke, didn't we, Doc? Every time I'd walk into your office, flying high on Source energy, some weird little... *manifestation* would happen. Remember? The lights would surge or a book would fall off a shelf. And we'd laugh it off as 'divine intervention.' But you didn't think it was very funny, did you? Your laugh was always kind of hollow. So one day, I pressed you on it."

He leans forward in his seat, forcing me to meet his gaze full-on.

"It was one of those stormy days on the coastline when the gray clouds press down like a flatiron," he says, "but the minute I stepped into your office, the clouds parted and the sun came out. You joked, 'Was that *your* doing, Bruce?' I looked you right in the eye, like I'm doing now, and I said, 'Yes, it was. It *was* my doing. And do you know why? Because I *am* God. I am pure Source energy, the creative power of the universe.' You didn't like that. One bit. Your mouth smiled but your eyes flashed like you wanted to punch me. Then I said something you liked even less. I said, 'And you are too. And you fuckin' damn well know it.'"

I flinch, as I did that day, but my eyes remain locked on his.

"You should have seen your face," he says. "You flushed red and I could see the pulse pounding in your neck. Why? If you thought I was full of shit, why would my words get to you that way? And if you *did* believe me, why would you feel fear instead of joy?"

"*I* can give you a reason," says Hark, seizing his cue to join the dance.

Crap. I dread what *he* has to say most of all.

"And it's the reason my sister, my niece, and my nephew are fattening the grave-worms right now instead of celebrating the new year."

# Chapter 29

Hark locks eyes with me. "Remember that entity I encountered during my ayahuasca journeying?"

Here we go again, digging up ancient history. His ill-fated trip to Peru. "The hallucination?"

"The *entity*. In the Lower World. That thing that told me it was coming here, to *this* world, to do harm to the people I loved?"

"I remember you... referring to it."

"*Referring* to it? *Referring* to it? Is that what I did? *Referred* to it?"

"You were clearly upset by the experience."

"Hmm, yes, now that you bring it up, I think I *was* a bit irked. A tad *nettled*. Asshole. Do you remember what I told you about the entity?"

I want to say no. But Hark will see through my lie. The truth is, I remember that hospital meeting with him—when I went to assess him after having him committed—like it happened five minutes ago. It was one of the most disturbing experiences of my life. Hark took me through his whole ayahuasca experience in detail.

• • •

*"The ceremony started, like they always do—with prayers and intentions,"* Hark said, his eyes wide with a vulnerability I'd never seen before. *"You pray for safe passage and for the plant spirits to show you a beneficial truth that will*

*help your growth. I guess I didn't pray hard enough, huh, Doc?" He tried to smile, but tears welled in his eyes.*

*"We drank the plant medicine, and after the puking was over and the medicine kicked in, the* curandero *started drumming and told us to begin our journeying.*

*"So I did. I journeyed down through this long, twisting tunnel and came out through some tree roots into the Lower World. The Lower World is a real place, Dr. Powers. All shamans know how to go there. Look it up—it's not imaginary. You can only get there by shamanic journeying, but it's real."*

*I nodded noncommittally. Hark was working hard to remain calm and lucid. I wanted him to stay that way.*

*"I could still hear the curandero's voice. He told us to summon our power animal—that's the first thing you do in the Lower World. My animal is an owl. So I called out to it, and it came swooping in, telling me to follow it.*

*"It wasn't my normal owl, though. It didn't seem... right. It had this... trickster energy about it, but I followed it anyway—against my gut. Big mistake. Never ignore a spiritual red flag, Dr. Powers. Never.*

*"The owl led me along a path through this meadow and pine forest I knew really well, but all the leaves and flowers had these nasty black spots forming on them. I wanted to turn around and run the other way, but the path was disappearing behind me with each step I took. So I kept going.*

*"We ended up in a clearing where there was a... cage, I guess you'd call it, made of yellowed bones with chunks of rotting meat stuck to them. The whole thing stunk like an old meat locker and was covered with flies making this buzzing sound that drilled right into my brain.*

*"Inside the bone cage was this... thing, this creature, this entity, that made me crap myself with fear. It had four legs and it was shaped kind of like a hyena—tall in the front, low in the back, with a long neck. Its jaws were all twisted and full of jagged teeth that didn't fit together right."*

*My stomach and intestines felt like they'd dropped right out of my body.*

*"The really awful thing about it, though..." He struggled for words here. "...was that it was* made of darkness... of absence... of negative matter. Except for its eyes. They were yellow, like jaundice. And its breath smelled like death.*

It was a bad, bad thing. Standing before it, all I could feel was confusion and fear."

I struggled to keep my face neutral and cover up the churning that was going on inside me.

"The thing spoke directly into my mind and offered me a 'deal.' I could either let it eat my power right out of my body—in shamanism, power is everything, Dr. P.; it's your soul, it's your energy, and you only have a limited supply of it for a lifetime—or else it would..." He looked at me with pleading eyes. "Or else it would... follow me back through the Lower World, into the Middle World, and into my everyday life. And it would terrorize the people I love and kill them one by one.

"I couldn't stand the thought of giving up my power. I was selfish. I panicked. I turned and ran. I ran and ran through the tangled forest. Everything was decaying all around me, turning black and rotten. I had no path to follow, I just ran and ran, and all I could hear was the sound of the entity shouting after me, in my mind, telling me awful things..."

Hark began slapping himself in the face, and I signaled the staff to restrain him.

"Do you remember the last thing it said to me?" Hark asks. "The entity?"

"Shut up!" I shout at him, surprising myself. "Shut up, Hark!"

"It said something you never reported in your clinical records. I know; I read them all. As is my right under the law."

"Shut the fuck up!" I rise out of my seat. Clem pushes me down by the shoulder.

"It said your name." Hark points at me. "The thing said *your name*."

I strain against Clem, against the ropes, snarling like a dog. I want to charge at Hark and take him to the floor. Joanna presses a heavy hand on my other shoulder.

"And it told me to say hello to you." Hark's jaw muscles jitter with tension. "And said it would be seeing you soon. And I reported that to you. And when I did, the blood drained from your face."

"Fuck you, Hark! You were psychotic. I was your treating psychiatrist. It's no surprise my name came up in your hallucination. Happens all the time."

"Then why were you so terrified?"

"I wasn't."

"You were."

"I was reflecting your fear back to you. It's basic therapy technique."

"Your pupils turned to *manholes*. And then a curtain came down over your face. I saw it. That was the moment your decision was made, that I was going to be locked up and medicated, and there wasn't a god-damn thing I could do about it."

"I locked you up because you were scaring the crap out of everyone around you, including your sister. Because your behavior was out of control."

"That thing that killed my sister and her kids," Hark says, "was something *you knew* because you had encountered it yourself. But you pretended not to know. You're still pretending not to know."

"Your sister's family was killed by an ex-con on a bad PCP trip!"

"That was the *avenue* it used. They always find a real-world avenue; I told you that. But you didn't want to hear it. So you shot me full of chemicals to scramble my connection to the truth and shut me up. Kill the messenger."

"That's why you drugged me, too," chimes Mary from her end of the sofa.

"Myself as well," adds Anvita, beside her, sitting rod-straight.

"You *tried* to drug me," says Bruce, "but I wouldn't let you. So you beat me over the head with—what did you call it?—'logic-based therapy.' Until doubt sank its claws in and wouldn't let go."

I force my eyes to meet Bruce's. "If your state of spiritual... empowerment, or whatever you want to call it, was real, I wouldn't have been *able* to talk you out of it."

"Not true, Dr. Powers." Anvita shakes her head, steady in her gaze. "Spiritual confidence can be stronger than an ironwood tree, but it comes in as a pale seedling. It needs time to grow. Logic is a... bull-tractor that crushes it before it can put down roots."

"Paging Dr. Bull-Tractor," Hark says with an icy smile.

"You stomped mine out of me," Bruce goes on, getting in my face, "and I've never been able to get it back! It was the best thing that ever happened to me. I don't care about the frickin' money. I want my *power* back."

"Why, Dr. Powers?" Anvita pleads. "Why did you need to take what we all had? Our connection to spirit?"

"I wasn't trying to *take* anything." I squirm in my chair, squirm in my *skin*. "From anybody. That wasn't my motivation."

"Then what *was* your motivation?" Anvita rises from her seat.

"I was trying to protect—" I stop mid-sentence. I want to say "you"; it would be true, on one level, but it would sound like a lie. Because it would be a half-truth.

"Protect what?"

"Protect what, Dr. Powers?" Mary says.

No answer I give them will be honest on every level.

"Protect what, asshole?" presses Bruce.

They're all standing now—my four ex-patients, a wall of glaring eyes, moving in on me. Anvita reaches her arms out, inviting the others to join hands with her. They do, and the energy in the room shifts to a different frequency. I feel it in my chest, in the air.

"What were you trying to protect?" Anvita's eyes turn yellow, Kali-like. Hark's eyes do the same. I can't tell if it's the gold of divine light or the jaundice of the demon.

"What, Dr. Powers? What?" Anvita says again. Now *Mary's* eyes turn yellow. Bruce's too. At least that's what I think I'm seeing. The whole effect might be in my mind. In my soul.

"What were you trying to protect?" Mary and Anvita say together. The other two join in. Four voices in unison. "What were you trying to protect?" The Chimbu dancers are at my bed again, chanting and shaking the frog. Madness incarnate. "What were you trying to protect?"

Their words turn wobbly, losing substance, losing meaning. Their eyes glow a brighter yellow. Their faces quiver, as if they're about to split apart and reveal things I can't bear to see. My mind wants to explode. Make it stop, make it stop.

"What were you trying—?"

"MYSELF!" I yell. "I WAS TRYING TO PROTECT MYSELF!"

I dive to the floor in a hopeless bid for escape.

"From what?" Anvita looks down at me from on high. Kali the Destroyer.

"FROM *THIS*! FROM THIS FUCKIN' INSANITY! I want it OUT, goddammit. Out of my mind. Out of my life. Why won't it stay OUT?"

"What, Powers?" says Hark. "Why won't *what* stay out?"

"This!" I scream, punching at the air. "This fucking... *chaos*. This black fucking... *malignancy* that lurks behind everything. Trying to break through. All the time. Laughing at me. Jeering. Grinning in the shadows. I want it *out*. But it always comes back. It always finds me."

The faces of my four captors glare down at me from an impossible height, stone gods of Olympus, crafting terrible verdicts.

"You want a confession?" I shout. "I'll give it to you. I'M CRAZIER THAN THE BUNCH OF YOU. I'm bat-shit fuckin' looney. That's why I became a shrink. To drive it away. Put it in a cage. Lock it up. The goddamn fucking chaos."

My captors stare. I can't meet their eyes.

I turn to the carpet, pressing my face into it, clawing at its fibers. I want to crawl through it into another dimension. I want to wrap it around me, force it to comfort me. I writhe, I kick at the floor. I toss, I twist, I churn.

At last my body collapses, a dead fish on a pier.

After half a minute, Clem lifts me, forcing me to sit up. The others still stare relentlessly at me. They're not going to let me out of this till I push through to the end. So be it.

So be it.

I expel the air from my lungs.

A minute passes. I breathe in again.

"When I was a kid... I was a believer. Ha. Here's how nuts *I* was: I actually took the words of Christ seriously—'These things I do, you will do even more.' I believed it. ... I would go out and *intend* things, and they would happen. A free donut from the baker? Boom. A rainstorm to break a heat wave? Boom. I could *feel* the angels working with me, organizing the details on my behalf. It felt completely natural to have my thoughts impact the world.

"I would also wish *bad* things. On people. And *they* would happen too. That's when the demons would go to work. That scared me. ... People told me I was nuts, that what I was doing was magical thinking. You can't live in a world like that, they said. They were right. So one day I just... shut it down. Bam. Closed the door."

I pause, hoping to end there. But more words flow, like siphoned water.

"And I felt better. For a while. Kept my nose down, did my reading, writing, and 'rithmetic. Watched *The Bionic Woman*. Stuck to the nuts-and-bolts stuff. I found I *liked* living in a world free of angels and demons, where your thoughts didn't leak out of your head and make shit happen. Part of me did miss my... power. That light inside. That connection to the source of things. But then I found a new way to shine. By kicking ass with my brain. By going for the good report-cards and the scholarships and the praise.

"By the time I got to college," I go on, "I'd forgotten all about my childhood 'adventures.' Packed them away. I took a Religious Studies course, just to fill an elective, but the guy who taught it, he was a lit-up dude. Dr. Overtree. He *knew* stuff. He had that glow in his eyes. Like you, Anvita. Like my daugh— We'd talk after class, and he'd encourage me to break through my mental barriers and tap into the 'ground of spirit.' Discover my true nature. I felt the old *stuff* awakening in me again.

"He invited me to a... ceremony, a ritual. I let my guard down. That door I'd closed inside me long ago opened again. Suddenly I was on fire—just like you were, Bruce. 'Riding the wave.' The angels were on my team again. Money started showing up out of nowhere. Creative ideas were bombarding me. Essays were writing themselves; all I had to do was hold the pen. Beautiful women jumping into my bed, miracles happening every hour...

"But then... I pushed it too far. The balance tipped. Bad things happened."

"What bad things?" comes Hark's voice from a galaxy away.

"Someone... died, a classmate. Things turned wobbly. The terror came stealing back. My mind got shaky, and suddenly I was tumbling toward a black hole that wanted to devour me." I pause. "I pulled out of it somehow—out of the black hole; it took all my strength to do it—and I slammed the door behind me. Again. Locked it tight this time. Pulled myself together. Told myself I'd had a brush with major mental illness. Put my rational mind back in the driver's seat.

"Later on, the significance of what I'd accomplished hit me. I'd pulled *myself* out of a nervous breakdown. Solo. And I thought I could help others do the same. That was when I switched majors and decided to become a shrink."

"That is why you work so hard to keep the walls up," says Anvita, in a tone not devoid of compassion. "To the point where you deny what your own eyes and ears tell you. Do you still believe mental illness was the true cause of your breakdown?"

"Yes... No. Sometimes."

"And do you still believe all four of us are victims of mental illness?"

"Part of me does."

"What about the other part?" asks Bruce, echoing Mary's words of earlier. "Doesn't part of you know damn well that when I was on my roll—when you were on *your* roll, when Anvita was floating on air in that ward in Chicago—that we were tapped into something a fuck-ton bigger than mental illness?"

"Yes."

"So what's the truth, then, Dr. Powers?" says Mary. "What is real?"

"I don't know." Those three little words crystallize into solid objects in my mind—tumbling down into some ancient, bottomless shaft within me, echoing like stones in a well, at deeper and deeper levels. They may be the most honest words I've spoken since this ordeal began. Since birth. "I don't know. I don't know. I don't know."

I truly don't. I don't know one damn thing.

Except this: I'm finished for today. My sacrament of confession is complete.

I sit on the carpet, drained of feelings, drained of thoughts. An empty vessel. I'm vaguely aware of my captors consulting in whispers a few feet away.

"Clem, Joanna," says Hark at last, his voice soft.

The two henchpersons gently lift me off the floor, placing me back in my chair. I make the minimal spinal adjustment to remain upright.

Hark approaches. He lays his hand on my chair and leans over me. "You've earned your reprieve, Dr. Powers, congratulations. In fact... you're progressing by leaps and bounds. I mean that, no screwing around. You've accomplished in one day what I thought—optimistically—would take a week or two. Or not happen at all."

It *has* been quite a day, no arguing that. Christ on a cracker.

"That's why I'm thinking," he goes on, "that I want to rearrange the week's schedule. I want to move our sweat lodge up to tomorrow. You're ready for it."

*What?* My nerves and muscles spring to life again.

"But that's going to take some doing," he explains. "A sweat lodge requires a lot of prep. I've got a team that handles it for me. I'm going to go make some calls, see if I can get them here mañana. Meanwhile... you all should take this time to do a little attitude readjusting."

He crouches, looking at each of us in turn.

"Here's what we *all* need to understand," he says. "Oliver's treatment program has entered a new phase. If he is going to progress from here, it can't happen in an atmosphere of hostility and distrust." He glares at Bruce. "We need to holster our weapons, all of us, and move forward in trust and cooperation... dare I say, love?"

I look to the others. How are they reacting to this? Their hostility seems to have retracted a bit, but we're all having trouble making eye contact.

"Wish me luck with my phone calls." Hark stands and smacks his palms together. "Let's see if we can kick this pony into the home stretch—woo!"

He strides out of the room, leaving the rest of us stewing in one of the most complicated silences I've ever endured—and I say this as a shrink.

I surprise myself by being the one to break it. I know I'm pushing my luck, but I say, "I've been honest with you all. It took a while, but I got there. So... if we're going to move forward in trust, it would help me enormously if you were honest with me too."

Defenses rise again, a slight charge in the air.

"You *have* to tell me. How did you connect with each other? How do you know so much about my private... conflicts? I've never spoken to anyone about this stuff. Not my family. Not a friend. Not a therapist. *No one*. Something very strange is going on here, and if you don't tell me what it is, how will trust ever be possible?"

No one responds for a long count, and then Anvita says, "You *will* have the answers to your questions. You *can* trust us on that. But it is not our role to hand those answers to you. It is your role to reveal them to yourself. Patience, Dr. Powers."

Sure. What Anvita doesn't realize is that patience is a virtue I do not hold in great supply. See, if Hark moves the sweat lodge from Friday to tomorrow, Tuesday, that means tonight is the night I must make my escape. Why? What I didn't tell the others is that it was a *sweat lodge* ceremony that my college professor—Dr. Overtree—roped me into. It was that sweat lodge that triggered my manic expansiveness and near breakdown as a young man. It was that sweat lodge that opened doors within me, old childhood doors, that I've been trying to nail shut ever since.

Suffer the lodge again? Never. I've fought too hard putting my mind back together. I'm not going to risk shattering it again. That is where I draw the line.

And so, if Hark succeeds in moving up the sweat lodge to tomorrow, I must depart tonight. I still believe I have at least fifty-fifty odds of outrunning their GPS system.

And if I fail, I am prepared to face the consequences. Even the direst ones.

What I am *not* prepared to face is the lodge.

"Good news, everyone." Hark reappears in the doorway. "The sweat-lodge crew is coming tomorrow at the crack of dawn! Woo-hoo!"

# PART IV
# Discharge

# Chapter 30

The house is dead silent. Not even white noise from the heating and cooling system stirs the air on this cool winter night. It is one-thirty a.m. As jarring as the day's events have been, I've packed them away for now. My mind is focused like a tractor beam on the single task ahead.

I sit on the edge of my bed, studying my ankle monitor in the moonlight streaming through the window. The device consists of a two-inch-square black box strapped to my lower calf by a black band of some high-tech polymer. The material looks military tough but not impregnable. A good blade should be able to slice it.

I'm sure it's designed, however, so that any tampering will trigger an alert. So even if I had a knife, I couldn't cut it here and now. I'll have to do it at the right time and place.

Of course, I'm assuming the damn device is even real. It's entirely possible it's fake and Hark has been using it to control me the way an Indian mahout uses a ring of rope around an elephant's ankle. But I must proceed as if it *is* real.

In that case... what? How do these things even work? How far do I need to stray to trigger an alarm? My guess is I'm on a pretty short leash. But Hark did say I was free to use the backyard, so it doesn't trigger from that nearby.

Okay—even assuming the alert gets triggered the second I cross the property line, I'll still have a running lead by the time it does. I estimate I'll have about a two-hundred-yard head start before my captors wake up, throw some clothes on, and take up the chase.

And thus far, my estimations have been bang-on. Ha.

Here's a crucial point: I don't know what I don't know. The device may function in ways I'm not aware of. Maybe, for example, it delivers an electric shock the moment I stray past my electronic bounds. There are small batteries nowadays that can deliver an astounding wallop. The more I think about it, the less confident I am about outsmarting or outrunning the device.

That means I'll need to create a distraction, boost my odds. The idea I keep circling back to is to start a fire. If I can get a blaze going and set the fire alarms off, that might keep everyone confused and occupied long enough for me to gain some real distance from the house; perhaps make it to a neighbor's house and call 911 before they can track me down.

A fire won't help me if the ankle device is a shock-delivery system, but otherwise it's my best hope. Here's the idea I came up with earlier: Under every household sink are hoses that connect the tap to the hot and cold water pipes. One of those hoses might be just long enough to siphon gas from the generator into the gas can. Behind the house, I've seen a set of locking pliers serving as a makeshift handle on an outdoor spigot. I should be able to use those pliers to detach a hose from under one of the sinks.

Then, after I use the hose to fill the gas can: Spread gasoline in the kitchen and onto the stove. Light a burner on the stove, igniting the gas. Dash outside and wait for the fire alarm to sound. (I don't want to kill anyone, so I do want to make sure the alarm goes off.) Make my run for it and hope for the best.

Is that a plan, then?

I guess. A bad one, full of potential holes, but a plan nonetheless.

I open my bedroom window—the night air is chillier than I thought—and toss my Nikes and jacket out. I'll retrieve them when I get outside. For now I'll stay dressed in sweatpants, slippers, and a tee-shirt; they'll pass for sleepwear if anyone sees me before I make my getaway.

I turn my bedroom door knob noiselessly and step out into the night-lit hallway. I stand still for twenty seconds. Nothing stirs.

I tiptoe down the hall, listening at the doors, testing the knobs. All locked; stillness in every room. But where do Clem and Joanna spend their nights? I don't know.

I head back to the stairhead and descend.

The downstairs is silent, faintly aglow from the LED lights on various appliances and devices. No sign of Clem or Joanna. First piece of business: do another search for a blade of some kind to cut the ankle band.

This time I try *all* the drawers and cabinets on floor one; no luck—they're either locked or empty. Ah well.

I head to the back door off the kitchen. Is it alarmed? I turn the knob. Cool air rushes in. I wait thirty seconds to see if an alarm, silent or otherwise, brings anyone running. It does not.

I slip outside. Man, it's cold out here. The gibbous moon is fairly bright, but the back side of the house is cloaked in night shadows. Swishing through the wet, overgrown grass, I look for the spigot. I pause for a moment, shivering in the cold, letting my eyes adjust to the darkness.

That's when it hits me, I don't even have an escape route planned.

If I run on the road, I can make good speed, but Hark and company will be able to chase me down by car.

I'll have to use the trail system, then, the one we hiked on earlier. The woods look inky black, unpenetrated by moonlight. I doubt I'll be able to run very fast on a dark trail, but if my fire-setting ploy buys me some time, maybe I can make it to that cluster of homes I spotted this morning before anyone catches me.

Pretty huge *maybe*.

I grope along the clapboards and find the outdoor faucet. The locking pliers are still clamped onto the valve stem. I pop the tool free. It feels cold in my pocket.

Should I grab my Nikes and run right now?

No, stick to the plan. I re-enter the house and shut the door behind me with a burglar's touch. The warmth inside feels inviting. Am I a fool to leave?

I make my way to the small bathroom in the back of the house—beyond the rec room, next to the "chapel." It has a pedestal-style sink, which should make its hoses easy to access.

It does. From a kneeling position, I'm able to reach behind the sink, shut off the water supply, and, without too much trouble, detach the hot-water hose.

I step out of the bathroom, listening again for any movement in the house. Coiling the hose in my hand, I skulk back into the dimly lit rec room.

Joanna is standing on the far side of the pool table, staring at me from the shadows.

Fuck. I'm dead. Every hair on my body fires an electric charge.

Any attempt to drop the hose or hide it would be pointless. She's already seen it in my hand. My mind scrambles to invent a story. "Couldn't sleep. Heading back upstairs now." I fake a yawn. "Oh, the sink in there was spraying water—this was the culprit." I proffer her the hose, wondering how to explain the fact that the bathroom isn't actually wet.

Joanna ignores my offering. Instead—most inexplicably—she places her forefinger on her lips and rolls her eyes toward the corner pocket of the pool table. She holds her stare there for a full five seconds, then turns and slips away in her sweatsuit, a night phantasm.

I approach the pool table as if it's electrified and look down into the hole. It takes me a second to register what I'm seeing. Nestled at the bottom of the latticed leather pocket is a keychain, loaded with keys and a car fob. My heart leaps.

Either I'm being lured into the most obvious trap ever set or Joanna has grown a conscience—or perhaps has simply grown weary of working for a narcissistic psychopath who treats her like something he scraped off his shoe.

My impulse is to grab the keys, jump in her car, and flee. But no, *think this through*. I fish the keys out of the pocket and study them: a Nissan door/ignition fob, three house/door keys, a couple of unmarked electronic fobs, and several smaller keys of unknown purpose.

Here's my dilemma. Even if I make it out of here by car—assuming one of the fobs opens the electronic gate—I still have the ankle monitor on. As soon as I drive away, an alert will trigger. My captors will run downstairs, jump in their bigger, faster, four-wheel-drive SUV, and track me down by GPS. The bumpy dirt roads out here are not Nissan-sedan-friendly. And at one forty-five a.m. in rural Arizona, it's likely Hark and company will be able to catch up to me and overtake me without causing a stir. That means I still need to set the fire to buy myself some extra time. And I still need to get the ankle device off. But how?

A thought. Joanna was opening locked cabinets with her keys earlier this evening. And now I have those keys.

I slink into the kitchen and head for the locked knife drawer. Instinct guides my fingers to the smallest of Joanna's keys, a silver one. It works! The drawer unlocks to reveal a collection of German-made Wüsthof knives in a mahogany case. I select the chef's knife I used earlier, along with a thinner-bladed paring knife and a slicing knife with a serrated edge. If one of *these* puppies can't cut the polymer strap, nothing can. I wrap the knives in a kitchen towel.

Revised plan: Forget the fire, I'll take my chances with the car and the knives. But first I'll need to run out to the locking gate and test the electronic fobs—so I'll know whether a gate-exit is possible or I'll have to smash through the fence in a *Dukes of Hazzard*-style escape, banjo music included.

As for the ankle bracelet, that remains problematic, even with the knives. I can't cut the bracelet off *now*, because that will trigger the tamper alert. So I'll have to cut it off *right after* I drive through the gate. And do it quickly.

After that, I'll make my way to a main road as fast as I can and then break every speed law known to man—hoping to either get pulled over by the cops or make it to a safe location.

Okay, time to act.

My body doesn't move. Not sure why. A mystery paralysis has gripped me.

I center my thoughts on getting back to Hannah. And avoiding the sweat lodge.

My feet kick into gear.

I exit again into the chill night air, carrying the towel-wrapped knives. Tiptoeing around the back of the house, I retrieve my tossed items of clothing from below my window. I put on my jacket and running shoes and leave the slippers behind, then head out toward the gate to test the electronic fobs. As I'm stepping through the grass bordering the gravel drive, a sound arrests my feet and nearly arrests my heart as well.

A tune, softly whistled.

I walk back toward the house, approaching it from a different angle. Hark's window comes into view. It's partly open. The whistling is coming from his room. I step closer. The moment I recognize the melody, my blood temperature drops. All the tumblers that have been spinning wildly in my mind since I was lying in that fake hospital bed clink into alignment.

A forgotten detail from my past leaps from memory. I know exactly how my captors came together and how they know my inner terrain so well.

# Chapter 31

The tune Hark is whistling is "Carrickfergus."

*But the sea is wide and I can't swim over...*

That was the tune he whistled on my first night of my captivity in his House of Horrors, too. I shoved it out of my mind at the time, amidst all the other merriment that was consuming my attention.

And here's something I only now realize. Hark was the one who played "Carrickfergus" on the "hospital" sound system too, the instrumental version that triggered my first memory of Emmy and broke the dam holding my identity back. When I heard it, I was still under the illusion the hospital room was real. And so I assumed the tune was just a random selection from an institutional playlist. But thinking back now, it was clearly hand-chosen. By Hark.

Because he knew the effect it would have on me. He knows it now.

Is he aware I'm standing below his window at this moment? Is his whistling aimed directly at me?

"Carrickfergus" is not an *obscure* tune, but it is uncommon enough to convey its grim implications: Hark knew Emmy in some way. He spent time with her. At minimum, he talked to her, had some kind of non-superficial interaction with her.

He knows this was her song.

Jesus, no.

Hark and Emmy, *together*? Did he kidnap *her*, too, before she died?

Standing in the moonlit grass, an even grimmer thought breaks through. Is it possible—no, I can't think it—that Hark...?

Emily's death was adjudged a likely suicide, but there were no eyewitnesses. Has Hark already exacted his perfect revenge on me? By killing my daughter? Has the rest of this charade been mere foreplay, a prelude to his triumphant revelation of his *piece de resistance*?

The possibility gels to near certainty in my bones. I don't know how he could have done it, framing it as a suicide, but he is clever enough to have figured out a way.

My mind blanks, and my body locks on a single intention: strangle Hark. I march toward the house, jaws tightening, hands already flexing for the deed.

Wait, though. A thought stops me in my tracks.

What if the contact occurred the other way? What if it was *Emmy* who reached out to *Hark*?

I allow that possibility to percolate. And that's when the forgotten detail from my past—the key to the whole puzzle box—crashes through to my awareness like a car through a living-room wall.

I've been saying all along that I never spoke to another living soul about my four greatest failures as a psychiatrist. And that is true; I never *spoke* a word about them.

But I did *write* some words. For a brief time in my life, I kept a journal. That fucking journal. Of course.

Years ago, when we were living in Massachusetts, I went through a period of intense... *self-questioning* in the wake of Hark's sister's death. My rational mind knew I had done the right thing, clinically, with Hark, but my conscience wouldn't let me off the hook. For the better part of a fall season, I sat up late into the night and wrote vodka-fueled journal entries, sifting and resifting my guilt and failure around Hark's case. Those midnight soul-purgings soon expanded into the cases of the other three patients who lie sleeping only yards from where I stand.

Emmy even walked in on me one night during my journaling. She must have been 18 or 19. I was holed up in my office, drinking and scribing feverishly. She entered without knocking, and I covered the page with my hands. We argued about something—of course we did—and she stormed out. But she saw the journal. She knew it was a secretive thing.

I don't know exactly what I wrote in that journal. I was always pretty boozed up when I did my writing, and I never read it again afterward. Didn't want to. Too painful, too vein-opening. And *reading* it was never the point. All I know is that I filled hundreds of pages in a pretty short time. I processed *a lot* of doubt and guilt, did a *lot* of self-flagellating.

Anyone reading those pages would be treated to a grand tour of the darkest tunnels and alleys of Oliver Powers' tortured psyche. That person would also know the myriad ways in which these four cases—Hark, Mary, Bruce, Anvita—have rattled my core and shaken my bedrock beliefs.

Though I've never read that forgotten diary, I did take it with us when we moved to Arizona six years ago. I stashed it in my study, laying it flat against the back of a bookshelf, behind a row of old clinical textbooks that I knew no one, including me, would ever crack again.

Emily must have gone snooping for it during one of her visits. There's no way she could have stumbled upon it accidentally. Shame flushes through me like an acid bath. The thought of my daughter reading those private pages makes me cringe and almost growl aloud.

Hark's open window reminds me to keep my mouth shut.

Anger flares up, replacing shame. Reading that journal was a gross violation of privacy. Emily—if she did this thing—learned things about me no one else on Earth was ever meant to learn. And she learned confidential things about my patients no one had any *right* to learn.

Anger gives way, in turn, to confusion: but how did *personal contact* occur? Even though my secret pages contained confidential facts about Hark and the others, I'm sure there wasn't any *identifying* information in there. I wouldn't have used their last names or any other details that would have allowed Em, or anyone else, to track down these people in the real world.

The answer comes almost instantly. My patient records. Since launching my career over a quarter century ago, I've kept electronic backups of all my clinical notes and records, even when the official records were stored elsewhere. A wise psychiatrist always does this—in case of misconduct accusations, malpractice lawsuits, clinical or legal questions about old cases, and so forth.

A motivated person could have *cross-referenced* the stuff in my journal with my official records—which *do* contain identifying information—and thereby tracked down the actual patients. It wouldn't have been easy, but it wouldn't have been surpassingly difficult. Emmy and Hannah—no one else on Earth—knew I kept my patient records on a portable hard drive in my home-office desk.

The bigger question, of course, is *why*. Why would Em go to the effort of tracking down Hark—I feel certain he's the one she would have approached—and sharing my journal with him? She and I had issues, yes. But did she hate me to the extent that she would knowingly put me through an ordeal like *this*? Or worse?

What is her connection to these people?

For half a minute I stand stone-still in the cold, looking down the gravel drive at the electronic gate, letting the night breeze ruffle my jacket.

Then I turn back toward the house.

I walk to the outdoor spigot and replace the locking pliers on the valve stem.

I find my slippers in the grass and put them back on my feet.

Quietly, I reenter the house, carrying my shoes and the towel-wrapped knives.

I lock the Wüsthof knives back in the kitchen drawer, put the car keys back in the pool table pocket, replace the water hose on the sink by hand, and head upstairs.

I enter my bedroom and close the door.

. . .

Sleep does not come easily. I lie on my back with my eyes closed, giving my mind free rein to rove where it will.

It wants to rove to Em.

She found my old journal, of that I am certain. But when? It could have been years ago—I haven't laid eyes on the thing since hiding it in my bookcase when we moved to Fountain Hills—or it could have been fairly recently. Did her reading of the journal have anything to do with her death? I don't see how, but I *feel* a connection there.

Were there signs at any point? Signs that would indicate she had read what was written in those journal pages?

I skim back across the highs and lows of our relationship over the years. Despite our perennial friction, we did have periods of closeness when we'd do things together, like watch nature shows or hike in the woods. Or cook. Tide-pooling, that was another thing we loved to do together, when we lived in New England. God, to have just one of those silent, sacred mornings back—Emmy and me and the starfish and the sky.

But our pockets of peace would inevitably rupture. She would start needling me, goading me. Her recurrent theme was that I was narrow-minded, arrogant, fear-driven. Silly rabbit. She often invited me to participate in events in her "alternative" world—Buddhist chanting sessions, drum circles, psychic fairs. She always picked the most out-there venues, knowing full well I would refuse her invites and then using my refusal as ammunition in her ever-mounting case against me.

A scene from about five or six months ago flashes in my mind. Emmy was staying with us in Fountain Hills for that final time, living in the Dollhouse. She had emailed me a brochure about a five-day "San Pedro Cactus Visioning Retreat" in Ecuador, suggesting—facetiously, I assumed—that the two of us do it together. It was not the first time she had urged me to partake of "plant-spirit medicine." She and Hark, two peas in *that* pod.

.  .  .

*A day or two after she sent the email, Emmy and I were in the kitchen of the main house doing meal cleanup duty. She had joined us for dinner. I was pre-scrubbing a broiling pan, she was loading the dishwasher, and she asked me if I'd given any thought to her invitation.*

"*You were serious about that?*" I replied. "*Come on, Ems. Why would I spend fifty-five hundred dollars to fly us to Ecuador for five days of destroying our brain cells with substances science hasn't even begun to figure out?*"

"*I don't know,*" she said, leaning into our Thermador dishwasher as if it had teeth. "*Maybe to spend time with this inconvenient stranger who seems to think she's your daughter. Maybe to actually—no, no, this is really swing-from-the-chandelier stuff—learn something.*"

"*How are you supposed to learn anything if you're high on cactus juice all day long?*"

"*I've told you fifty times...*" She turned toward me, a knife unconsciously upright in her hand. "*This isn't recreational drug use. This is not five days stoned in the mountains. This is about doing serious inner work.*"

"*I'm all for serious inner work. But you don't do that baked out of your gourd.*"

"*Nobody's going to be bak— Jeez, you don't hear a word I say, do you?*" She tossed her knife into the silverware rack and shook her hair back in disbelief. That was when I got my first full gander at the new tattoo—a large, multicolor etching of a tropical bird, high enough on her neck that not even a turtleneck could hide it. Great, she was now fully committed to a lifetime career as a Starbucks barista. I decided—wisely, for a change—not to comment on it.

"*Emmy, I hear you,*" I said, scouring my pan with contained energy, "*but I've had patients who've tried to convince me that plant hallucinogens are the doorway to higher consciousness. And they've ended up in... bad places. Very bad. Inner work requires sobriety, seriousness of purpose.*"

"*It also involves taking risks.*" She racked a wineglass more forcefully than necessary. "*You don't change your state of consciousness by paying some shrink to listen to you talk for four years about how your mother emotionally abandoned you when you were twelve.*"

"*Glad, as always, to know how much respect you have for the work I do.*"

"*I'd have a lot more respect for it if it was informed by a wider perspective. Why are you so afraid of any road to the truth that might take you somewhere you haven't already been?*"

"*And why are you so afraid of reality?*" I continued to scrub, regulating my temper with the measured strokes. "*Why are you always trying to escape it?*

*With chemicals and meditation and... and shamanic drumming and God knows what else? Why can't you try to master this reality first? What scares you so much about being real?"*

*"I'm not afraid of being real, Dad," she sighed. "I'm bored with it. I've seen enough of this reality to last me forty lifetimes. I'm ready to move on. You're the one who lives in terror."*

*"Maybe I know things you don't know." I handed her my attentively scrubbed pan. "Maybe in my fifty-four years I've seen things you haven't seen in your twenty-five. Is that possible? Maybe I know how delicate the human mind is. How easily it can go down rabbit holes it can't climb out of. How dangerous toying with consciousness can be."*

*"What's dangerous is buying into The Matrix." She tossed my pan into the dishwasher at a deliberately haphazard angle. "Any way we can break out of the hypnosis of consensus reality is a good one, as far as I'm concerned."*

*"You need to get real, Emily!" I snapped, glaring at her new tattoo. "Stop fucking around and get real with your life!"*

*"I will, Dad." She closed the dishwasher with a thud. "And don't worry, I won't invite you on any more adventures." She strode out of the room in silence.*

Lying in my bed, I have to fight to breathe. Three things jump out at me from this memory.

First, Emily's comment about being "ready to move on" from reality. Was this a clue about suicidal ideation/intent? Did I miss it in my zeal to win an argument?

Second, a realization: given the subject of our conversation, if she had read my journal entries about Hark's ayahuasca experiments and subsequent hospitalization, she would have betrayed that knowledge in some way. She would have let something slip. So she must have read my journal *after* that. Toward the end of her visit. Right before she upped and left. That feels significant.

Third, and most important, a terrible insight. Emmy wasn't trying to be *provocative* with me in her endless attempts to get me to partake in her New

Age adventures. She was being sincere. She was trying to get closer to her father by including me in the things she held meaningful. Yes, and maybe testing my love a bit, too, but bottom line: she wanted me to be part of her world.

And I methodically rejected her, each and every time.

I didn't think the truth could bring me any lower than it did a few hours ago, when I was crumpled on the floor of the living room. Guess I was wrong.

# Chapter 32

I had hoped a night of reflection would bring me wisdom on how to confront the others about their connection to my daughter. But morning finds me only steeped in grief. I'm missing Emmy with every tiny ray of consciousness beaming from every cell of my body; wishing I could spend a year doing nothing but accepting her wild invitations—to vision quests in the desert, to "light-healing" workshops in Sedona, to silent vigils on Machu Picchu...

One thing my captors have helped me see is that my daughter was right about me. I have built a life and career around fear. Emmy was always the one trying to break through my fear-wall. And now I long for the impossible. To be able to say *yes* to her. To open my ears and heart. To listen.

To *listen*, for God's sake. Would it have killed me to do that just once?

"Emmy, show me the way," I say to the empty bedroom. No response comes, of course. I wasn't expecting one. But I do feel a lightening of sorts, a crumbling of inner barricades.

Perhaps that *is* her response.

Defenses down, then. A posture of openness. That is how I must approach the others. They—or at least Hark—interacted with Emmy before she died. And I must sponge up every drop of information I can about those interactions—which likely took place during her final days on Earth. I will not gain that information by accusing and threatening. My captors hold all the precious cards. I must be open and humble with them so they will share those cards with me.

Grant me grace.

The smell of frying bacon drifts under my door. My stomach rumbles awake. I put on my day clothes and head downstairs.

Hark stands at the kitchen stove, wearing an apron and tending three huge pans of sizzling food—bacon in one of them, scrambled eggs in another, potatoes and colorful veggies in a third.

"Good morning," he says with apparent sincerity, not looking up.

"Good morning," I reply, trying to send good will in his direction.

What universe am I walking into today? What rules will apply?

Bruce and Anvita sit at the small kitchen table, Bruce reading an actual paper newspaper, Anvita reading, of all things, a Megan Miranda thriller. They acknowledge me with head-nods. Bruce points to a rack of coffee mugs. I grab one.

Mary stands at an open window, drinking coffee and looking out into the backyard, where smoke billows from a freshly dug fire pit. The smell of burning wood drifts into the kitchen and mixes with the breakfast smells, carrying me back to a father-daughter "discovery camp" I did with Emmy in Vermont when she was ten.

Sweat lodge day is here. Out beyond the fire pit, two wiry men are using vines to tie together long, thin tree branches, supple and green, at cross-angles. They're building the bones of the lodge. I still don't intend to do the sweat ceremony, no sir, but I don't know how I'm going to Houdini my way out of it. Ah well, that's a problem for later-me. A more urgent agenda drives now-me.

As I fill my mug with coffee, Joanna enters the kitchen. Her eyes widen slightly—surprised to see me still here, perhaps? I give her a tiny nod, trying to signal, *don't worry, the car-key thing is our secret.*

Hark invites everyone to sit at the large table, set for seven, in the dining area off the kitchen. He brings out two baskets of breads and pastries, then goes back to the kitchen to fill serving platters with the vittles he's been cooking. Hark is playing chef *and* host this morning. *Noblesse oblige*, I guess.

Joanna fetches Clem, and the seven Odyssey House occupants gather around the table, chattering. The food smells absurdly good, and my stomach howls like a coyote at sunset, but I notice it only in a detached way—a body somewhere is hungry.

The platters and baskets go around, and everyone digs in. I let the feeding frenzy run its course for a while, knowing that what I have to say may be a meal-stopper.

After the symphony of silverware has settled into a steadier rhythm, I lay my knife and fork down and place my hands in my lap.

"I tried to leave last night," I announce, weeding emotion from my voice. "My intention was to make a run for it, see how far I could get before you GPS'd me. But then, standing outside in the cold, all the puzzle pieces came together. Finally."

The rhythm of forks on stoneware stalls for a moment, then continues apace.

"I knew all along you must have gotten 'inside information' about me from somewhere." I'm keeping my tone as non-confrontational as possible. "Hark, I thought maybe your dad had used his power and connections to turn my life inside out, or that you'd plied me with drugs, like I said. Then it hit me who your *real* informant, your *real* silent partner, was. My daughter. Emily. You talked to her before she died."

Quiet descends on the room, but still no one looks up.

"No?" I move my eyes around the table. No one speaks.

At last, Hark clears his throat and makes a show of laying his silverware down. A wry smile creeps onto his face. "Well done, Olliwog, well done. I must say, it took you long enough. And I practically had to hand you the key—literally as well as figuratively."

"What do you mean?" The meaning is pretty obvious.

"Oh come on, Woggles." He whistles a few notes of Carrickfergus: *but the sea is wi-i-ide.*

"You knew I was standing outside your window last night," I say—a statement, not a question. "You knew I was trying to escape."

"Wogs. We know everything. When are you going to get that through your benighted brain-bone?" He wipes his mouth, lays his cloth napkin on the table. "Did you really think Joanna was going rogue when she put those keys in the pool table?"

Yes. Yes, I did. World-class authority on the human mind that I am.

"We *handed* you a way out, for a reason," he says. "Because we've come to the phase of your treatment plan where you must *choose* to be here of your own free will. Where you must *want* what we offer. Is that what your return last night signified? Have you turned that corner?"

I'm not prepared to answer his question. I pick up my fork and pretend to eat again.

"How did it go down?" I venture. "With my daughter? How did you get in touch with her? Who contacted whom?"

"Not the important question," replies Hark.

*All right, then, how about this one?* "Did you harm her?" I work to keep the edge out of my voice. "Did you threaten her? How did you get her to cooperate?" No reply. "Did you have anything to do with her death?"

Fidgety silence around the table.

"We told you, Dr. Powers," says Anvita, sliding her chair back a few inches, "that we had a gift of enormous value for you, but that you were not yet ready to receive it. You have made remarkable progress, but you are still not nearly ready."

"I *am* ready, Anvita. If it's about Emily, I'm ready to receive anything. To *know* anything. However painful it might be. Even if it means facing the possibility that it was Emmy who approached *you*. Whatever you can tell me, I want to know."

"You *think* you want to know," says Hark, "but that's because you haven't heard it yet."

"I *know* I want to know. What you-all don't realize is that I've already hit bottom. I'm already living with the worst pain a father can endure. I may not have caused Emily's death directly, but I killed her in my own way. It doesn't get worse than that. So when I tell you I can take whatever *you* dish out, I mean it. Please. Anything you can tell me."

Hark's eyes meet the others', one by one.

He takes a long breath, pays it out. "Very well. You're right about your daughter. That she was the one who reached out to *us*. You're also right that we spent time with her. Well, two of us did—me and Anvita. But you're wrong about one part. One very big part..."

"Tell me."

"He's not ready, Hark!" Anvita lunges forward, her hands splayed on the table.

"... The part," he continues, "where you said, 'before she died.'"

*What is he saying? That she's not dead?* A wrecking ball of emotion hits me, crazy hope and animal fury mashed together. The thought lights up in me, *I never saw my daughter's body.* Hannah was the one who flew to New Hampshire and identified her; she insisted on doing that grisly job alone, and I offered only token resistance. The wake was a closed-casket affair, and the body was cremated.

The raw truth is that I do not have firsthand knowledge of Em's death. I have only the word of others. Granted, those others include a state medical examiner, a funeral director, and my wife Hannah, the person I trust most on Earth. Nevertheless, it is *possible* that...

"Is she alive?" I ask, losing my volume control. "Is she here with you?"

Dead air wraps around the table.

"Tell me!"

"Those two questions," says Anvita, "have very different answers."

"She *is* alive, but she's not here?" I spring from my chair, blood rushing to my face. "Then where have you taken her? Where is she?" *Rein it in, Oliver. You need their cooperation.* "I'm sorry." I fold back into my seat. "But please... if you're holding her somewhere... If you know where she is, you have to tell me. You have to take me to her. I'll do anything you ask."

"Oliver." Hark looks at me with a species of pity I'd pay anything not to be witnessing. "Oliver, Oliver, Oliver... You've got the answers flipped around."

"So she's *not* alive, but she *is* here with you." I let the absurdity of the statement speak for itself. But sober expressions meet me around the table.

I'm confused. What are they telling me? Not alive, but here. So... *they stole her corpse?* Why the hell would they do such a thing?

"I'll say it once more." Hark picks up a strip of bacon, examines it on both sides. "And I know you will have trouble digesting it: we *have* spoken with your deceased daughter at length. ... But not *before* she died."

*After?* Is that what he's saying? They talked to her *after* she died? Oh God, what new freak show have I wandered into?

"Death," says Anvita, sitting upright, hands folded, "is not what most Westerners imagine it to be. Death is a function of linear time. But linear time exists only in perceptual reality, not in the eternal field."

I wait with mounting anger for what she's going to say next.

Anvita reads my eyes. "I told you he's not ready for this, Hark."

"Well, he better damn well *get* ready." Bruce thumps the table with his fist. "'Cause I'm running out of fucking patience." He fixes me with a glare. "One of Anvita's many gifts... is that she can communicate with those on the 'other side.'"

Christ, here we go. The circus is coming to town. Grab the safety bar.

"Technically speaking, there is no *other side*," Anvita says, "but yes, I sometimes make contact with... the non-corporeal. Your daughter reached out to me a few weeks after her death. I was a receptive channel, and she knew of my connection to you. She asked me to get in touch with Harkins. She wanted to speak with him. Well, she *wanted* to speak with *you*, but she knew—I imagine you are growing tired of hearing this—you would not be ready."

"So she settled for me instead." Hark strikes a pose, fluttering his eyelashes. "Yep, ol' Eminem and I have been carrying on quite the enlightening convo. Through Anvita."

I should have followed my impulse to strangle him last night. "Come on, Hark. Get a grip. You want me to believe you've been talking to my *dead daughter?*"

"I'm long past wanting anything from you, Olliwog. From now on, all the wanting must come from you. I'm just presenting the facts."

"The *facts*? That's rich." I laugh, but it rings hollow. I stare down at my plate of food. It looks fake, made of acrylic—a museum exhibit. I don't think I'll ever eat again.

"She knew it would take a lot of work to *get* you ready," Hark says, returning to Anvita's point, "and she knew that I—well, I and my all-star team here—would have the means, the motivation, and the... *creativity* to break through your layers of armor and bring out the raw thing inside you. The thing still capable of learning."

"I refuse to believe this horseshit."

*But you want to believe, don't you, Oliver? Just like those poor slobs in a John Edward Crossing Over audience, hoping against hope for a sign that their dead loved ones are still live-streaming from the Great Beyond.*

"She provided us a great deal of... insight and information about you," continues Hark, "which helped us plan. But when it came to taking action, she gave us free hand to conduct your treatment as we saw fit."

"The non-corporeal try not to interfere too heavily in material matters." Anvita taps the tabletop with her fingertips. "This is not their domain."

"If it makes you feel any better," Hark says, "the one thing she insisted on was that we not hurt you in any serious way. So you've never been at any real risk of physical harm. Of course, as you well know..." He looks out the window at the blazing fire pit. "That hardly means you're out of the danger zone, does it?"

# Chapter 33

I'm in psychological freefall again.

Every time I lower my guard with these people, they hit me with some new roundhouse punch. Talking to Emily from beyond the grave? Good freaking Lord.

Here's the deal. I'm prepared to admit the universe is a more mysterious place than I've granted it to be. I accept that, I do. I know there are people, like Anvita, who possess abilities I can't explain. I saw her levitating with my own eyes, for crying out loud. I saw that elk appear in the forest, matching the card in my pocket. I've seen haloes around my own daughter's head, and I've had "non-ordinary" experiences in my own youth. Fine. Acknowledged.

But still, my dead daughter communicating with the living? That is a bridge too far. That is a walk in the land of tent-show psychics— *"I'm picking up the letter 'e.' Does anyone know someone who has passed over whose name contains an 'e'?"*

Death is death. The dark and dreamless sleep. The void. Would that it were not so. But it is. To entertain any other possibility is to wish upon a star.

Lading my voice with sarcasm, I say to Hark across the table, "When you were shooting the breeze with my dead daughter, did she happen to mention how she came into possession of intimate facts about me I never discussed with her?"

"You think the dead don't have access to knowledge we mortals aren't privy to?"

"So that's your answer—the dead just magically *know stuff*?"

"And what if it *were* my answer? You'd have to accept it, wouldn't you? But as a matter of fact..." He pushes his chair from the table and walks to the window, forcing me to wait for his next words. He watches the sweat-lodge team working in the yard. "She did mention something... about a book."

My skin freezes.

"A book of private writings. A journal of sorts."

I feel myself turning bloodless and white. But then a thought rushes to my aid: she could have told him about my journal *before* she died. This isn't evidence of trans-death communication.

A memory swoops into my brain from out of the ether. A crucial memory, perhaps. I let it play on my mental video screen.

Aha, yes, of course! Occam's Razor rides again.

I let out a laugh that sounds strangely soulless.

"What's so comical there, Olliwoggles?"

"Oh, nothing. Just remembering a little... incident that happened this past fall—I can tell you the exact date, in fact. October ninth. Ring any bells? It's my wife Hannah's birthday."

"Is that supposed to mean something to me?"

"Maybe it will in a sec." As my mind assembles the details, I move potato pieces around on my plate, forming a pattern. "I took Hannah out to dinner in Scottsdale that evening. She didn't want to go, didn't want to celebrate, what with our daughter having just *died* and all, but I insisted we mark the day, in a quiet way."

I lay down my fork and rise to my feet.

"Our 'dinner date,' needless to say, was a towering disaster. But when we came home, we both sensed something *off* when we walked in the door." I step toward Hark, where he stands at the window. "As if someone had been in our house and my home office. As if things had been moved around and put back in their place, almost—but not quite—perfectly."

He tosses his shoulders—*why are you telling me this?*

"Hannah said to me, 'Do you think it was Emmy? Do you think her ghost was here?' No, I didn't think that. My theory was more earthbound—that someone had combed the place. Not robbers; nothing was missing. Sophisticated operatives of some kind. Looking for dirt on one of my patients, perhaps. I've treated some high-profile clients. But here's what I'm realizing now. Those snoops were exactly the kind *you* could afford to hire. You or your dad." I stare across the window frame at Hark. "They got hold of my journal that day, didn't they? My patient records too. You learned everything you needed from those two sources. You've never met Emily, you didn't have to. You're lying about that. To fuck with me. As usual."

I await his reaction, ready to seize his throat if he confirms my suspicion. But I don't see a *you-got-me* in his eyes. Rather, he stares at me like I'm a little kid who doesn't realize how funny his mad-face is. His shoulders start to bob up and down. He's *laughing*. He slides to the floor, his back to the wall, covering his face with his hands and gulping air.

"You know what the funny part of all this is, Olls?" he says between laughs. "And there *is* a funny part... Before Anvita searched me out, I had actually forgotten about you."

He sighs and brushes the cloth of his pants, as if whisking away the levity. His tone sobers up. "It's true that for a time I had quite the vendetta going against you. In my mind. During those thousand-odd nights in the locked wards—as I tried to sleep, with people screaming around me like they were being skinned alive—the thought of getting revenge on you was the one thing that kept me going.

"When I finally got discharged, I was on a mission. That's when I went out and acquired the... *hardware* you came to know so intimately. Not easy items to shop for, B-T-dubya. I was going to open a museum, I really was. The Museum of Psychiatric Abuse. But first I was going to force *you* to endure its *hospitalities*." He looks up from his place on the floor. "But guess what? I got over it. Found myself a place in the country. Met a girl. Tried some new meds. Chilled out. Wrote some poetry. Godawful stuff, but it calmed my demons down.

"It was your daughter who came along—through Anvita—and... *remotivated* me. She persuaded me to go off my meds. She knew that was the nudge I'd need to rekindle my fire and get the band together. She's the one who made every bit of this happen."

"I don't believe you."

"I don't ca—" Hark cuts himself off. "Ha. I was about to say I don't care what you believe. But obviously that isn't true, is it? No one goes to the lengths I've gone with you unless they care, in some deep way. I'm sure, as a shrink, you get that."

As a matter of fact, I do.

"For reasons I've not been able to fully plumb," he continues, "you matter to me. That doesn't mean I don't hate you too. Violently at times. But *hate*, as you know, is not the opposite of love. *Indifference* is the opposite of love. The fact is, God help me, I am invested in your 'treatment.' So is your daughter. *So is your daughter*, Powers. And she *is* here with us."

We lock eyes, man to man. I study every line of his face in the lucent morning light, looking for traces of deceit.

"If you're lying to me, Hark, fuck you. Fuck you to the depths of your being."

Injury flashes in his eyes, but he covers it by slapping his thighs and blowing air out of his cheeks. He stands up and walks away from me, exiting the house and letting the door slam behind him.

I follow him outside. He wanders out onto the grass and watches the team assembling the sweat lodge. I come up behind him and stand without speaking.

"All right, Ollie," he says to me at last, "all right. You win. I'm going to give you something I *really* should not give you."

"Hark..." shouts Anvita in a tone of warning. She has followed us outside. She seems to sense what he has in mind.

"Anvita doesn't approve of this sort of thing," he explains to me, "but..." He casts a glance at her.

"But what, Hark?" I say. "What are you going to give me?"

"Proof." He turns and faces me, eyeball to eyeball.

"Proof?"

"That your daughter is here with us. Think of something we can ask her about. A detail from your past. Something private, that only you and Emily would know about."

"Hark, no." Anvita draws up near us in the grass, barefoot. "The departed do not approve of being used as parlor tricks."

"This isn't a parlor trick," he replies. "This is critical business."

"*She* may not agree with that." Anvita glares at him.

"Then *she* can tell us so."

The *she* they're referring to, of course, is my dead daughter. The freakishness of my new reality knows no bounds.

"So, Ollie." Hark brings his hands together as if to pray. "What should we ask her? What would serve as indisputable proof for you?"

My heart races. Am I really going to do this? Of course I fucking am.

Talk about a moment of truth. The shape of my entire future may turn on the answer I receive to this question. Better make it a good one.

I close my eyes and let the smoke-infused air fill my lungs. An image comes to me. I know the question to ask. "Four or five years ago, Emmy and I went to the Boyce Thompson Arboretum together. We laughed ourselves sick on the bench up on the high trail. What were we laughing at?"

Hark and Anvita exchange a look. As if on cue, they turn and walk toward the house.

"Where are you two going?" I fall in line behind them.

"To the chapel," he says over his shoulder, "to speak to your daughter. To ask her your question." He signals to Clem through the screen door. Clem steps outside, blocking me from entering.

"Why can't you talk to her out here?" I ask, leaving the "where I can see you" part unsaid.

"So now *you're* the expert on talking to the dead?" Hark turns to me as he opens the door to go inside. "*You're* going to tell us how it's done? We have a process. Wait here. We'll be back with an answer. Or we won't."

Hark and Anvita step into the house. Before I can try to follow them, Clem grabs my arm, whisks me about, and escorts me to the backyard picnic table.

I sit, awaiting the answer of all answers.

．．．

I try to keep my mind blank, but my eyes are magnetized to the three Native American men working on the sweat lodge. One of them, a smooth-faced twenty-year-old with a bandana around his head, tends the fire pit, where rounded rocks have been piled—the hot stones that will be moved inside the lodge to create the steam. The other two men—older, weathered, denim-clad—are putting the finishing touches on the lodge itself. Animal hides have been laid over the "bones" of green willow branches to create a five-foot-high domed dwelling with an entry hatch in the front.

That black entry hole gapes like an open maw, waiting to devour all who enter. An awareness arises within me, of how all the tiny threads of my life have been groping toward each other since the day I was born, to deliver this moment. The next truths I learn, the next decisions I make, the next actions I take will be fate-sealing—like turning left or right at a fork in a river. This I know.

That lodge, that fucking hateful lodge, *will not* sink its teeth in me, though. Not like last time, when it came within a hair's breadth of gobbling up my sanity. My lungs pull in a shuddery breath. I fight the memory that insists on coming...

．．．

*I was the only student asked to participate in Dr. Overtree's sweat lodge—an honor, I was told. Overtree, an affable, leather-elbow-patch kind of guy in the classroom, took on a different stature out here amongst his peers on this remote wooded estate in North Andover. He was the leader of some kind of spiritual/personal development group with indigenous roots whose nature I couldn't quite grasp. But clearly he was revered by the six or seven other lodge participants. He stood taller out here, spoke more deeply, and wore an elaborate ceremonial robe marked with symbols.*

*"Lose all expectations now," he said, preparing us for the experience. "The lodge* will *change you. Not in ways you want or anticipate, but in ways you need. Sometimes the change will happen within the lodge, sometimes it will happen later. But it* will *happen."*

*I don't remember much about the ceremony itself. Time disappeared, the world disappeared. I remember drumming and chanting. I remember naked people drenched in sweat. The smell of tobacco. A burning in my lungs. I remember scalding heat, and I remember surrendering to the heat. Other than that, it is a blur.*

*It's the* after *part I remember most. When we emerged from the tarp-covered shelter, I was in a magnified state. No earthshaking revelations, no rapturous insights, just a presence and awakeness I had never felt before. I slipped away to my car, though I'd promised not to drive for at least an hour after the sweat. Feeling guided by an intelligence bigger than mine, I drove straight to the Godwin College campus, parked in the back lot, and walked out into the woods, to the frog pond where I sometimes went to think.*

*I sat on my favorite rock and gazed at the water. It was glowing with inner light and bursting with new spring growth.*

*A bullfrog perching on a rock made eye contact with me.*

*Looking at that small being, I was struck by a tidal wave of insight that we were one and the same, the frog and I. We both had two eyes, two nostrils, and a mouth. We both had two "arms" and two legs, fingers and toes, a tongue, a heart, a liver, a stomach. He was a little man. I was a big frog. It was only words, concepts, that divided us. We were the same. We were one.*

"Look at the little man." The dancers chanting. The horror I felt when they tossed the frog onto my bed.

*When that feeling of oneness with the frog came over me, the creature responded by winking at me and lifting its "hand" in a little wave. A zoologist, of course, would say it was just hydrating its eye and stretching its forelimb. But it was winking and waving at me, saying, "I see you"; I know it was.*

*And then the frog dove into the water, and as it did, I somehow dove with it. My being fused with the frog's being, and my mind took a plunge from which it nearly never came back. I was bombarded by a billion overlapping images of every life form that had ever existed on Earth, and I felt myself hurtling backward through time and space—*

"Oliver!" Hark snaps me back to the present. He stands beside the picnic table, looking down at me. "We were able to talk to your daughter, ask her your question."

A small voice escapes me. "And...?"

"The answer she gave us was..." He cocks his head with a tiny smile. "'A hummingbird shat on his thumb.'"

My mind wants to take the same plunge it took when the frog dove off the rock all those decades ago. I steady myself, pressing my hands on the bench. Solidity, please.

*That day Emmy and I visited the Thompson arboretum, a hummingbird landed on my thumb as we sat admiring the glowing landscape. Em was in awe. She said, "Birds are messengers from the spiritual plane, Dad. You need to pay careful attention to whatever message it gives you."*

*The tiny bird proceeded to take an itty-bitty dump on my thumb and fly off. Emmy and I collapsed in gales of laughter, maybe the richest laugh we ever shared.*

I laugh now, internally, at the memory, which I've never shared with anyone. Then I turn toward the sweat lodge. Its dark mouth seems to be laughing too, but in a way that is anything but mirthful.

Emily, my dead daughter, has just spoken to me. What now?

# Chapter 34

*Occam's Razor, for fucksake, Occam's Razor.* Emmy hasn't spoken from "the other side." She has spoken from Verizon Wireless. Or from right inside the house. That's why Hark and Anvita refused to conduct their five-dollar "séance" in front of me.

Emmy is alive—*flesh-and-blood* alive. And with us now. On site. I recall the copy of *The Way of the Shaman* I saw in Hark's bedroom. The reason it struck a chord in me was that the vowels in the cover's title had been colored in with a red ballpoint pen.

Just like on Em's copy.

*Just* like it.

I rise from the picnic table bench and march across the grass, into the house. Clem follows, an arm's length behind me. Heading straight for the living room—the center of the house—I call out, "Emily! Come out! Show yourself! Please!"

No answer.

I head for the chapel. A hint of sandalwood incense—a staple of Emmy's teen years—hangs in the air, mingling with the scent of freshly extinguished candles. I call my daughter's name again. Nothing.

I tear through the rest of the downstairs, then the basement, shouting for her. Clem tails me, step for step, but doesn't try to stop me.

Next, I bound up the stairs to the second floor with all its mysterious locked bedrooms. I try the doors, one by one. All locked, except mine. I pound on each door, shouting Emily's name. She might be holed up in one of these very rooms. She might have been here this whole time, mere feet from where I've been sleeping.

No. I would have picked up on that. Dense as I might be, I think I would know if my allegedly dead daughter were sharing a house with me, bright-eyed and bushy-tailed.

I don't sense her presence.

Okay, then. Only one other possibility: she's been talking to them by phone.

With Clem dogging me step for step, I storm down the stairs and out the back door. I head, like a guided missile, toward Hark, who still stands near the picnic table with Anvita. "Hand me your phone!" I shout, surprising him into a one-eighty turn.

"Look who's giving orders now." Hark regards me with an amused smile.

"I mean it, Hark. Let me see your phone. Yours too, Anvita."

"First of all... um, no," says Hark. "Second of all, *Clem*..." He glares at his henchman.

Clem moves in on me from behind. Before he can grab me, I wheel about, drawing my arm back like a fastball pitcher's. Surprising myself even more than Clem, I unleash a blow, slingshot-fast and full force. I've never punched anyone in the face before, but somehow my fist connects with his left eye and temple. He crumples in a heap as my knuckles cry out in pain.

I spin toward Hark. A glimmer of fear shows in his eyes. He has six inches and two decades of youth on me, but I have a father's rage and two decades of gym workouts on him. And judging by the punch I just threw, my strength is back. All that nutritious bologna, I guess.

"Give me your fuckin' phone!" I order him. "I need yours too, Anvita. Don't make me hurt you. Phones! Both of you. Now!"

Hark holds his hands up in mock surrender. "I don't have mine on me. It's inside."

"Mine as well," says Anvita.

The three sweat lodge workers fan out in a semicircle behind Hark. They'll help him if need be, but their eyes say they'd rather not.

"Well, let's go find them." I jerk my thumb behind me, toward the house.

Hark lifts his hands comically high and grins compliance—but in a way that says *you'll regret this.* He walks toward the house. I turn to follow him.

The moment I turn, I'm knocked clean off my feet by a driving, linebacker-style tackle. I fly backwards through the air and land smack on my back, a small rock digging into my flesh. A microsecond later, a man is atop me, his fist high in the air. It's Bruce, not Clem. His fist connects with my face in almost the exact spot I struck Clem. Fireflies swarm my vision-field.

"I've been waiting fourteen fuckin' years to do that!" Bruce draws his fist back again.

"Bruce, enough!" shouts Hark.

Bruce pretends it's too late to stop himself. He pile-drives his fist into my face a second time—same side, lower down. Cartilage cracks. I taste blood. Good God, the pain. My jaw joint feels like it's come loose.

Hark presses a hand on Bruce's shoulder. Bruce relaxes, lowering his fists. He slowly dismounts me, locking eyes with mine, and moves away. Using both my hands, I click my jaw back into place with a fresh shot of pain.

Hark moves into view, towering over me—a POV I've become all too familiar with. "We've been wasting our time on you, haven't we?" His voice is flat, his face placid. "Your inner needle hasn't moved one fucking millimeter. You've just been playing us this whole time. Proving once again, people are not capable of change. What was I thinking? Me and my doe-eyed optimism? Clem..."

Clem looms into view above me, rubbing his temple and looking like he wants to filet me with a butter knife.

"Go get the cutter," Hark orders him.

*Cutter?*

Clem shoots me a look of *you and I aren't finished yet, pal* but obeys Hark. A few seconds later, Mary appears where Clem was standing, wiping her mouth with a paper napkin and gazing down at me like I'm a weird species of insect. She balls up the napkin and lets it roll from her hand. It bounces off my face. She walks away.

I sit up. Clem reemerges from indoors, holding a small tool that looks like a scalpel with a Y-shaped blade. Joanna is right behind him. Clem crouches at my feet, grabs my right foot, and glides the Y-notch of the twin blades through the strap of my ankle monitor, slicing the GPS device off my leg.

Why are they removing it? Oh, right. Burying a body with a live GPS transmitter on it wouldn't be too savvy from an evidentiary standpoint.

Hark gestures *get him the hell out of my sight*, and Clem and Joanna bend to grab me. The image of being carried through the woods to my grave plays in my mind again, but the two flunkies surprise me by hoisting me to my feet instead. They march me in the direction of the road, not the woods. We stumble past the house toward the driveway. Clem and Joanna, each holding one of my arms, perp-walk me down the long driveway toward the electric gate, which slides open as we near it. Hark's footsteps follow in the gravel behind us.

We reach the mouth of the driveway. Clem and Joanna give me a shove, propelling me past the open gate. I stumble out onto the dirt road, almost falling but catching myself. The gate closes, with me on the outside looking in.

Okay, what are they up to now?

"Right," I shout at Hark. "I'm supposed to believe I'm free now? Like I can just sashay into town for a burger at Buffalo Bob's?"

Hark approaches the gate from the other side, places his hands on the crossbar. "Free? No, Oliver Powers, MD, I'm afraid that's something you'll never be. But you *are* at liberty to traverse the roads and freeways unencumbered."

"Uh-huh. And you're *not* the cat letting the mouse run away so it can catch it again and rip its little head off. Gotcha."

"Goodbye, Oliver." Hark turns and walks down the drive toward the house.

"Nice try, Hark. What's the god-damn game here?"

He slows his stride, stops, and wheels about to face me.

"The *game*," he says, "is over. It really is. I've got no more cards to play. I tried everything in my bag of tricks. And still you remain... the way you are.

I'm played out. I'm tired. I want to go back to my life. I do have one, believe it or not."

He turns again and walks toward the house.

"You *can't* let me go," I shout after him. "*You* know it and *I* know it. I can identify all of you. I can have the police here in ten minutes. You'll all be arrested on the spot."

"Goodbye, Oliver," he repeats, continuing his trajectory.

"Where are you going? Come back here. Finish this."

He enters the house, leaving me on the road. Harkins Horvath, over and out.

So this is for real? I've been released from Odyssey House?

My left eye is already swelling from Bruce's punch, but I survey the dirt road through my open right eye and the narrowing left slit. To the west lies a wooded dead end; to the east, the road slopes down a gentle hill and hooks out of sight.

No houses are in view. It's hard to tell how close the nearest neighbor is, what with all the trees. But there's only one direction to walk in.

Tally ho, then? My house slippers may not be suited for distance hiking, but they'll get me far enough from *this* place to save my ass.

So why aren't my feet moving? Why am I rooted to the spot?

Fear of walking into a trap? Is that the source of my reticence?

I look back down the driveway at Odyssey House, and a pang of loss stabs my chest. Why? Why don't I want to leave? Am I like the prisoner who can't handle freedom once it's granted? Have I gone full Patty Hearst and bonded with my captors? Is there a part of me—a big part, perhaps—that knows their damn "treatment plan" is working and wants to finish what we've started?

I think the answer to all of the above is at least a partial yes. But a bigger factor looms above all of these.

Hark and company have access to Emmy.

Somehow.

And I can't walk away from that, can I? These people represent my one and only avenue to my daughter. Whether she's dead *or* alive.

Yes: whether dead or alive. That *is* the question, as a certain Danish prince might have framed it. And it is a question I must answer. For myself. Right here and now.

Which do I believe? Is Emmy dead or alive? Everything, it seems, turns on my reply.

I spot a tree stump down the road a bit, in a patch of wild grass. I walk to it, sit myself down, and gaze up at the crisp blue sky through the fullness of my right eye and the slit of my left. It sounds grandiose to say that destiny awaits my next move, but that's what it feels like.

*My* destiny does, that's for sure.

Logic tells me Em must be alive, despite the fact that my wife identified her body and I attended her funeral. My captors gave me the answer to a question only my daughter—no one else on Earth—could answer. Therefore, they spoke with her. Therefore, she is alive. The scientist in me is compelled to believe that. Compelled.

Decades ago, when I was in mental/spiritual crisis following Dr. Overtree's sweat lodge, I put all my chips on science and logic. And it saved my life. I bet on the interaction of chemicals and energy as the key to all of reality. I swore I would never look back, never reopen those doors to spiritual mystery I'd slammed shut. And that decision has served me well. The logic of organic chemistry has been the rock upon which I've built a career, a reputation, and a dandy Scottsdale lifestyle.

It didn't help me build a relationship with my daughter, true, but it kept *my* head above water. And what does that logic dictate now? The chips are mine to wager once again, it seems. Will I double down on chemistry and neurology? To which side of the table will I push the pile?

If Emmy is alive—flesh-and-blood alive—as she logically must be, then my only play is to run from here as fast as I can. Get hold of the police. Tell them my story. They'll come. They'll search Odyssey House. They'll confiscate phones. They'll go through call records, texts, emails. They'll find Emily, wherever she is.

But if I'm wrong...

If Hark and Anvita *have* been communicating with Emmy from "the other side," then by bringing in the police I will flush away my opportunity to contact her. My one and only channel for connecting to Emmy may close forever.

So the decision I make, right now, really is a black and white one.

If I slide the chips toward "the afterlife is real," my whole fortress of belief crumbles. I can no longer cling to the rock of rationality that has kept me safe and dry since college. I must take the plunge into the waters of mystery.

If I return to Odyssey House—I've probably blown my last chance, but if I do—it must be with full surrender, full humility, full openness. That's the only way they'll let me in the door. No more professional cynic, no more Doubting Thomas. I must go back with my teacup well and truly empty.

And if they do take me back, what then? The sweat lodge awaits. To go through that rite again may be to sever all ropes that have kept my ship moored to land lo these many years. Is the chance of talking to my daughter again worth the price of my sanity?

*What will it be, Oliver Powers? Which way will you push the chips?*

It comes down to one thing. One elemental thing. What do I believe in my gut is the truth about my daughter?

I stand up from the tree stump and take the most momentous step of my life.

# Chapter 35

The coyote-head doorknocker echoes within the front hall with a no-one's-home kind of sound. Clearly that can't be the case. I've only been gone fifteen minutes, and no one has left the property.

I knock again. Nothing.

I walk around the side of the house. The cars are gone! They were parked here only minutes ago, and there's only one road out of here. Gooseflesh blooms on my neck and arms. Oh wait: the attached three-car garage. I've never seen anyone use it, but maybe the cars are parked inside now. Why? Who knows?

The garage door has no windows for me to look in.

I return to the front door and knock again. This time I hear the patter of footsteps on the entry-hall tile. The door opens, and a slight, elderly woman I've never seen in my life stands in the doorframe. My mind blanks.

The woman appears to be South or Central American, and she wears a simple house dress. My first thought, an appallingly racist one, is that she must be the cleaning woman. During my time at Odyssey House, I never once saw anyone cleaning, and yet the place was always immaculate. Could she have been working here all along and I just never ran into her?

"Hello," I say to her. "Can you please tell Hark I'd like to talk to him?"

"Quién?"

"Harkins Horvath. *Mister* Horvath? Your employer?" She seems nervous; I can only imagine how I look to her with my beat-up face and swollen boxer's eye. "Can you get him, please?"

She stares piercingly into my good eye, moving her head from side to side as if to get a better view of what's inside my brain, and says, "Go. You. No business here. *Vete*."

"Please, ma'am. Just tell him I need to talk to him."

"Go! *Fuera de aqui!* I call police!"

"Ask Hark to come to the door, please."

"No Hock. You go. Police! No Hock."

She closes the door. No Hark. What did he do—*move* in the last fifteen minutes? I know the real estate market has been brisk lately, but really?

I march around the side of the house again, toward the back door—the door we normally used. I look in the side windows at the kitchen and living room. No signs of life. No traces of our breakfast meal. I'm getting that sick feeling in my chest again.

*The sweat lodge. Everyone's out back at the sweat lodge.* Yes, of course.

I head in that direction, but before I reach the angle from where I can view the full backyard, a fear seizes me and nails my feet to the ground. I'm *absolutely certain* that when I look into the yard, the sweat lodge will be gone. There will be no sign of the fire pit, no sign of the workers, no sign of the residents. Grass will be growing where the fire pit was. I'm sure of it.

I step backward, hauling in a breath.

I must prepare myself for that outcome, that impossible (but seemingly inevitable) outcome. If everything has vanished, that will mean only one thing. I'm back to brain-damage land. I'm back to lying in that hospital room. I'm back to all of this being some kind of fucked-up, hyper-realistic brain event—like my coma, but writ large. If that's true, how do I reboot reality? How do I get back to my real life again?

Cold terror sweeps through me.

I can't look. I literally can't look into the backyard for fear of seeing only virginal grass. Fighting my rising panic, I examine the house instead, scanning it for familiar cues. With my right eye—the left one is fully closed now—I take in the owl-shaped thermometer, the loose spline on the kitchen window. I remember those details. I've been *living* in this house for the past two days; I can recall my time here with granular specificity. It's been rather unforgettable.

A voice erupts from inside me like the howl of a wounded animal. "I'm sorry. Take me back." I'm not sure to whom I'm speaking; maybe the house itself. "Please." Talking to a building, not a top-ten sign of vigorous mental health. But it feels weirdly freeing. "I'm lost," I cry. "I don't know what I'm doing. I don't know what's real anymore. Take me back. I'm ready to see."

Who am I *really* talking to? God? Has it come to that?

"I'm ready to see." I drop to the grass on my knees. "To see my daughter. To see *everything*. Please, take me back. Give me another chance."

I pause. The air is perfectly still.

"Don't tell me it's too late. I'm ready to surrender. All the way."

A soft breeze blows up. It carries a scent that makes my heart swell. Burning wood. The fire pit? It's still there? I'm terrified to find out for sure.

I remain kneeling in the damp grass, afraid to move.

From out of the silence comes the *chunk* sound of a lock. The back door opens.

I never thought I could possibly be happy to see Harkins Horvath III.

"Get in here, Woggles."

We sit in a circle beside the hide-and-willow-branch sweat lodge, my four former patients and I. We're dressed in white bathing suits, provided by Hark, and draped in white towels.

"You knew I'd come back," I say, gauging Hark with my good eye.

"You are a loving father, if nothing else," he replies. "It's one of your most endearing qualities. Not that there's a lot of competition."

"So how do I do it? How do I make contact with her?"

All eyes look down.

"As you know..." Anvita lifts her head. "Your daughter reached out to me—*through* me—because she knew you were not ready or able to receive her. Had you *been* ready..."

"You could have saved us all a lot of grief." Hark barks a laugh. "None of this"—he tosses his hands open, signifying the whole crazy enterprise we've been embroiled in—"would have been necessary."

"Regrettably, it *was* necessary," Anvita adds. "Regrettably, it still is. For you are still not ready. The bread-dough of your soul is still proofing. We must see how it bakes."

"The sweat lodge," I say.

"The sweat lodge is merely an *external* stimulus. A catalyst. What happens *within you* is what will determine outcomes."

"Tell me one thing honestly." I study the ground, bracing myself for the answer. "Is this all just an elaborate way of preparing me to die? If so, I'm not afraid. I would just like to say goodbye to my wife. Is that what's happening here? Do I need to die in order to see my daughter again?"

"Yes," replies Anvita. "But not in the way you are thinking. The death you must die is the 'death before death.' The rarest kind of death—the most terrifying and yet the most extraordinary."

"What, please, is the 'death before death'?"

"It cannot be explained, it must be *undergone*. You will see... or you will not."

"Do I have to... lose my mind?" *As I very nearly did the last time I entered a sweat lodge?* my inner voice begs to ask.

"Yes. But again, perhaps not in the way you are thinking."

She bows her head. I move my sole working eye around the seated circle. Everyone looks solemn in their white garb. I wonder what *they're* getting out of this. Mary is fiercely Catholic. Why would she do a sweat lodge? Bruce has never affiliated himself with any spiritual customs. Anvita seems quite capable of tending to her spiritual needs without such extreme rituals.

The obvious dawns: they're doing this for me. They've been doing *all of this* for me. *For* me, not *to* me. They put their lives on hold and flew here to Arizona. Why? Vengefulness? Vindictiveness? Hatred? Those motives ring hollow now. Those motives don't explain what I'm witnessing here—the reverently bowed heads, the commitment I feel in the air. I recall what Hark said earlier: the opposite of love is indifference.

What I'm seeing here is not indifference. We don't invest in what we don't care about. And these people are invested.

"It is time to begin," says a voice above us.

I look up to see a small, thin woman in a beaded white robe, silhouetted against the bright sky. She is our shaman, our priestess, our ceremony leader. She is also the "cleaning woman" who greeted me at the door. *Another fine assessment, Ollie.* She looks into my non-swollen eye and does that odd side-to-side movement of her head again, as if trying to get a better angle on what's inside of me.

"You are ready now," she proclaims. She bends and enters the lodge, signaling us to follow.

• • •

We're twenty or thirty minutes into the sweat ceremony; hard to say, time breaks down within the lodge. The rite began with Sister Quilla—that's the name she goes by—explaining to us that the sweat is a purifying ceremony. For some, it can produce extraordinary experiences, for others it simply cleanses, heals, and prepares.

She laid tobacco leaves on the glowing hot stones piled in the center of the lodge, then lit a pipe of tobacco as we sat in a circle on the dirt floor and formed our intentions for the sweat. She passed the pipe to each of us. After that, she began ladling water onto the stones. The air became thick and hot with tobacco-infused steam, and then the drumming started.

The rhythmic sound continues now. It's coming from outside the animal-hide walls, and I think it's being provided by the three men who built the lodge. They're singing a native chant to the drumbeat. In combination with the lambent glow of the rocks and the intensifying steam-heat, the chant is having its intended effect. An avalanche of imagery bombards my mind. Flashes of scenes from my past intermingle with ancient symbols—a carved stone bird, petroglyphs on a cave wall. The heat is intense, the air hurts to breathe, and my swollen face is burning and throbbing, but I'm managing to endure the discomfort so far.

At some point, the drumming and chanting shift to a new rhythm, a subtler, more complex one, and my inner experience shifts along with it. Full scenes form in my mind now, and my emotions come alive. I see Emmy bent over a tidepool, showing me a tiny crab dancing along the barnacled floor. I see Hannah in our bed, smiling into my eyes, and feel her silken warmth as she wraps her arms around me. Love ignites in my heart, opening it wider.

From that wider heart place, I take in the presence of the people sharing the lodge with me. I sense no hostility from any quarter. Riding the chant, my eyes closed, I pull up a memory of the younger Mary sitting across my desk from me at Oakridge. We're playing cards—a regional game called Forty-Fives we both knew from our New England upbringing—and Mary is laughing shyly. I recall an aspect of her treatment I had forgotten: Mary did not always have an easy time with "Gadriel." In fact, the invasive presence was often quite troubling to her. I taught her some techniques for grounding herself in sense-reality and also extended an open invitation to her—if ever she was feeling unsafe and if I was free, she could come to my office and we would play cards together. Forty-Fives brought her peace.

We shared moments of genuine warmth and companionship during those card games. I recall fragile gratitude shining from her eyes on more than one occasion. How did I forget that?

Letting the chanting and drumming carry me, I move my heart-attention to Bruce. Again, memories flood in. There was a sort of friendship between *us* too. Most of our work together was actually fairly enjoyable and uncontentious. We often laughed about the absurdities of Newburyport social life and the local yachting set. In fact, I think it was the trust and affection we developed as two bros—not as psychiatrist and patient—that convinced him his life was going off the rails and he needed to rein it in. I understand now why he feels so betrayed. He trusted me—he *liked* me—and his life collapsed because of it, at least in his mind.

But the bond we had was real.

My chest opens, letting in more of the tobacco-rich steam. It burns, it cleanses.

Anvita, I'm buoyed along to Anvita. I met with her only that one time, when she was 17, and only for a few hours. But I now recall a mysterious connection between us too. She reminded me of Emmy, who had begun having her own life-struggles by that time. But it wasn't just that she *reminded* me of Em; it felt like part of her *was* Em, like there was some kind of cosmic overlap between the two. Venn diagrams intersecting. And when

I talked to that intersecting part, I was talking to both Emmy *and* Anvita. But I had no intellectual construct with which to frame such a thing. So I dismissed it, as usual.

But now it comes rolling back, the Emmy in Anvita—the reason I kept tabs on Anvita's life long after my one-time treatment of her.

The chanting has taken on a layer of harmonics, and now I'm riding only the harmonics. They sound like church bells, the bells of Sacred Heart, my childhood church.

I open my right eye—the functional one—and glance at Hark. His features are limned by the faded glow of the cooling rocks. He seems at peace, despite the sweat draining from his flesh. I close my eye again and let the harmonics transport me. An image of Hark—my tormentor, the perennial spear in my side—forms in my inner vision. Eight years younger, he is kneeling on the floor beside my psychiatrist chair in Andover. His head and shoulders rest in my lap, and he is sobbing. I am cradling him—a latter-day *Pietà*—and cooing words of comfort. "It's all right, Hark, let it out. Shh. Let it out, it's all right." In our session, he has come to the full realization of how unloved and neglected he was by Gumdrops, the only parent he knew for most of his life. And I have become, for the moment, his father—the universal father, the holder of boundless love and strength. And right now, I love this child. This poor, neglected, misbegotten child. I love this child so much, and I weep for him in my soul.

I had forgotten Hark and I had such moments. I had forgotten.

A soft bell rings, but not in my mind this time. It is Sister Quilla, calling us back to the here and now. The music and chanting stop. We open our eyes in the imperfect darkness.

"The time has come," says our shaman, "for the Speaking of the Sorrows. Who will go first? You, Oliver Powers, you will go first. You will speak your sorrows."

# Chapter 36

The "old me" would have asked for clarification on what the Speaking of the Sorrows meant, while composing a clever quip to show he was above all this stuff.

The old me is not present in the lodge.

"I betrayed you all," I say in the close-aired darkness. "And that is my sorrow. You trusted me. And I betrayed you. Just as I did my daughter. Why? Because you terrified me. On a level I couldn't even grasp. And I wanted to feel safe. That was the *real* reason I handled your treatment the way I did. All of you. My decisions were justifiable from a clinical angle, but I made them with the wrong intentions. Intention is everything."

Sweat pours from me like drizzling rain. "You don't owe me your forgiveness. You don't owe me anything. But I will ask for it anyway. Will you... *can* you... forgive me?"

Stillness fills the lodge. The ticking of water drops on packed earth is the only sound.

At last a female voice speaks. "Forgiveness is not something others can bestow on you." I'm not sure whose voice it is; in my altered state, it sounds like Mary, Anvita, and Sister Quilla rolled into one. Emmy too. "It is something only you can give yourself. To forgive is to lay down the burden of anger, blame, and bitterness. It is to say, 'I will not carry this load any longer.' Are you ready to do that?"

To forgive myself? Am I? Such a monstrous question.

I've been carrying this burden, this load of guilt and shame, for so long I cannot imagine life without it. It has become unbearably heavy in the months since Em's passing, but it is an old, old, familiar weight—like fifty pounds of body fat you learn to lug around unconsciously. The thought of shedding it feels almost like vertigo. Who would I be without it?

"Are you ready?" The female voice again.

"No," I reply. "But I'm ready to *try*."

"When the birds begin to sing, give your sorrows to the birds," says the female voice, now solely that of Sister Quilla, "and they will carry them away."

Wood flutes—two or three of them—pipe up from outside the tent, trilling like the warbling of birds. I close my operant eye. The sound becomes the *shrieking* of birds.

In my inner vision, I see myself sitting on a plain at sunset as a half-dozen hawk-sized birds fly toward me against the orange sky. The birds land on my lap, my shoulders, my arms. Their weight presses down on me as their talons dig into my skin. I smell their meaty breath. They peck at me with jerky motions, puncturing my flesh, pulling at something within. Then they flap their wings as one, rising into the air, their talons grasping onto black, stretchy tendrils attached to something larger inside me.

I feel something dense and sticky lifting out of me, like a heavy cloak, but one I've been wearing on the *inside*, not the outside. I know it's symbolic, but it feels like a visceral thing.

"Let it go," Hark says in a soft voice. "Let it go, Oliver. Forgive yourself."

I do. I forgive. I forgive the child who began weaving this inner "cloak" from fibers of shame because he thought he was a bad person who could hurt people with his thoughts. I forgive the young man whose childhood fears were reawakened through a sweat lodge ceremony and who chose the path of psychiatry to protect his fragile mind. I forgive "Doctor Powers," who for decades fought to keep the world safe for sanity by brandishing the sword of psychopharmacology whenever the cosmic chaos threatened to break through.

I release my inner grip on the cloak, woven from a million heavy strands of self-condemnation, and allow the birds to pull it out of me. Oh God, the pain, the release!

The birds fly away, carrying the black and rotten thing into the sky, and I feel a lightness beyond description. To be rid of this thing seems too good to be true. I feel a rush of gratitude toward my lodge-mates.

It comes out as a sob that wracks my torso from bottom to top.

"Shh," says Hark, comforting me as I once comforted him. "Shh, it's gone. Let it go."

The flute music twitters to a stop. Silence moves through me. I let the silence cleanse.

For the moment, I have no identity. No self.

"More rocks!" shouts Sister Quilla.

The entrance-flap of the lodge lifts, letting blinding daylight in. The young lodge worker with the bandana plows in, bent over, pushing a small wheelbarrow. He dumps a dozen yam-sized, red-hot stones onto the cooling rockpile in the center of the floor and exits.

The radiance from the new stones raises the temperature in the lodge by fifteen degrees. Not enough for Sister Quilla. She dips her ladle into the water bucket. "That was the preparation," she says and spoons more water onto the rocks. Steam erupts with a hiss, stinging my skin. She ladles on more water. And more.

The steam assails every cut on my swollen face like a harsh astringent. It scalds, it chokes, it is nearly unbreathable. My lungs wheeze in protest. One more ladleful will send me running from the lodge. I wonder how the others are able to stand it.

"Now we will journey," says Quilla.

The drumming recommences from outside the tent, but this time there is no musicality to its rhythm. It is a steady, fast, insistent beat. Almost a gallop. It is the beat that shamans around the world have used for millennia to trigger so-called "non-ordinary experiences."

Sister Quilla ladles more water onto the rocks. My skin, my lungs feel scalded. My swollen face wants to rupture. I can't take anymore. I'm seconds away from running out of the lodge. I *need* to escape this.

Or surrender.

Yes, I could try that.

Summoning the skills I learned in the Isolation Box, I plunge myself into a state of nonresistance. Putting my full attention on the drumbeat, I release all attachment to my bodily senses.

It works. My suffering dissolves, and the pain of the steam moves away to a distant and objective place. I can do this. I'm ready to continue. I'm ready for whatever comes next.

Sister Quilla instructs us to hold in our minds the image of a cave or a hole in the ground, one we have encountered in real life. I close my eyes and picture an old mine shaft I stumbled upon while hiking in the New Hampshire woods. Then, as the drumming pounds in its uninflected *bam-bam-bam-bam-bam-bam* tempo, she tells us to enter the cave—I do—and to find a tunnel within.

A tunnel forms in my mind, and I dive into it, head first. It twists and turns like a water slide in the semi-darkness. I smell the damp earth and feel the tendrils of tree roots brushing my face as I plunge downward, downward, downward. I feel like a giant earthworm, a living auger, pushing grubs and leaf-rot aside, plummeting to unknown depths.

At last I spot a glow of light ahead of me, and the bottom of the tunnel draws near.

My descent comes to a stop at a softly lit "exit." I push my way through dangling tree roots and climb out of the cave toward the light. I step out onto a carpet of spongy grass in a bright forest clearing. Flowers glow with impossible colors. Huge, mosaic-winged butterflies flutter about. Rabbit-like beings stare, wide-eyed, from the clearing's perimeter.

Is this the Lower World that shamans know so well and that Hark told me about so many times? Or is it the land they call the Upper World? I have no idea. But one thing is clear, this place is "real." As real as Buffalo on a snowy Tuesday.

Hark, Mary, Bruce, and Anvita step into the clearing from the opposite side. They wear beaded, cream-colored robes, as do I. They approach me, hands out in welcome. I know their real-life counterparts are sharing this experience with me, like avatars in the same videogame.

My four companions move in and flank me, the two men on one side, the two women on the other. They take hold of my garment and then, angling their bodies forward in an odd way, lift off the ground. I rise along with them, also angling my body to achieve flight.

We rise together to the treetops and soar out over the forest in a big, swooping arc. We're off—flying hot-air-balloon-high over lush landscape. Green forest whizzes by below us.

Our destination is clear: a plateau rising a thousand feet above the forest canopy. A tailwind kicks up and we arrive there in no time. My four friends—for that's what we feel like in this world—set me down near the farthest edge of this barren and lifeless plateau. My bare feet land on a surface that is cracked and sunbaked, hot to the touch.

A canyon as wide as a highway gapes before me, and another plateaued surface greets my vision on the other side. But the terrain on the opposite side of the canyon is not barren. It is lush with alien plant-life. Buildings constructed from impossible, MC Escher-like geometries loom in the distant mist. Avatar-Hark sweeps his hand toward the canyon as if to say *go that way*, and then he and the others bow and fly off, leaving me alone on the flat mountaintop.

My eyes fix on a crude stone shelter amidst the plants on the far side of the canyon. A figure steps out of its vine-draped doorway and walks down a short set of stone stairs. She, too, wears a cream-colored robe, but with a red shoulder sash, much like the one Anvita wears. Her hair is bright blonde with strawberry tones. She walks toward the canyon with a familiar, shoulder-swaying gait. As she nears the edge, the breath goes out of me.

Emmy. Alive. Before me.

She's close enough for me to see her smile, but too far away to see what *kind* of smile it is. She waves to me in her loose-elbowed way and beckons me to come to her.

I want to. With all my soul.

But of course, a giant canyon yawns between us.

I toss my hands up—*what do you want me to do?*

She shouts back, her voice drowned in the wind, something that sounds vaguely like *walk the plank*. No, I would really rather not. The wind dies down, and she repeats herself: "The walk of faith. You need to take the walk of faith."

I hope she doesn't mean what I think she does. I shrug my confusion.

"Walk to me," she shouts. "Don't look down. Just *know* you're going to reach me. Walk to me and a bridge will appear."

She's asking me to step out into the chasm, where jagged rocks gnash like alligator teeth a thousand feet below. She's asking me to abandon logic, reason, doubt, common sense.

This is the fulcrum moment of the sweat lodge for me, I realize. My call to action. The moment where I must... well, "take the plunge" is not exactly the ideal metaphor, is it? The moment where I must... *find new ground to walk on.*

Literally.

On the other side of the canyon awaits a new world. One where the old rules no longer apply. Once I cross, I may never be able to cross back. The last time I ventured across such a threshold, I very nearly *didn't* come back.

But *Emmy* stands on the other side, as real as my next heartbeat.

I step to the brink of the canyon. My toes can now curl over its edge. I dare not look down.

"Just know you can do it!" shouts Em.

Keeping my eyes fixed on her, I lift my left foot and step forward before thought can intrude. My heel comes down on a smooth, hard surface. Impossible. I'm beyond the edge; empty space lies below me. But somehow I feel solidness under my foot.

*Don't look down.* I step forward with my right foot. Rock-hard surface meets my bare foot again. Confidence swells. I step again. Success. And again. An unseen bridge forms beneath me. Again.

Em beckons me forward, waving encouragement. I take another step. Another.

Cables are snapping within me. Cables that have always kept me anchored to "this side of the canyon." I can almost hear them pinging and whipping about. But my center holds.

I can do this.

Another step forward on the invisible bridge.

And then... a hitch in my step. I glimpse motion in the stone shelter behind Em. A shadowy form passes a window. The doorway fills with darkness, and then a black presence *pours* out the door. A thing. *The* thing—from the stained glass window at Sacred Heart. The thing with the hyena-like neck and hunched shoulders that lodged itself in my childhood soul. The thing made of wriggling *absence*, with the glowing yellow eyes. The thing that came back to haunt me after that sweat lodge in college. The thing that spoke my name to Hark in his ayahuasca journey. The thing that has forever stalked the perimeter of my mind like a hungry dog around a campsite and that I have warded off again and again with the torch of logic.

The blackness-demon creeps forward, absorbing light from the air around it. Emily doesn't see it. I step up my gait, and the "bridge" continues to form beneath my feet. The beast is going to devour her!

But no. It slinks up beside her, almost like a familiar pet. She doesn't seem to notice or care. Or is she frozen with fear? I can't tell. I need to drive the foul thing away from her. Kill it.

Yes, kill it. But I lack a weapon.

I lack something else too.

Conviction.

The thought of tangling with the beast sends me spinning into a maelstrom of doubt. I doubt my power. I doubt my desire to cross the chasm. I doubt the false ground beneath my feet.

I look down and see only empty air and jagged rocks a thousand feet below me. The feeling of a surface beneath my feet vanishes.

# Chapter 37

I plummet toward the jumble of broken boulders, spread-eagled like a skydiver, the sickness of freefall in my belly. My virtual robe flutters and snaps like a flag in a windstorm.

Survival odds: zero. My lungs are frozen in my chest.

I tell myself this is only a "dream"—an altered state—but the hi-res texture of the rocks argues differently. I know for sure that when I hit those boulders, I will die. Not only in *this* dimension, but in reality (whatever that means).

It's said that in your final seconds, your life flashes before your eyes. Something very much like that does happen to me. The moment death becomes inevitable, acceptance settles in, and time stretches out, almost to eternity.

Three-dimensional scenes flush through my body like water through a pipe—going back to the moment of my birth. Me: standing in a stream, a kid. Jeans rolled up. Contemplating killing a frog with a rock. To see how it feels to take a life. Sickness in my gut. No, can't do it.

Me: in a church. Sacred Heart. My first time at a funeral. Standing by a coffin. My great aunt Bella. Believing I put her in the box. Not wanting to look up at that cursed stained-glass window. Knowing the demons will be winking at me.

My entire life, available for the plucking.

Oh. I think of something I *want* to see. *Need* to see. Near the end of my life-stream.

I "fast-forward." Found it. Me: driving in the desert. The Apache Trail. That pre-Thanksgiving trip. I'm following that mystery clue, whatever it is. My eyes pan the landscape. There! A crazily colored bird lifts off a cactus. I step on the gas, trying to pursue the bird, trying not to frighten it off the path it is navigating. Why am I following a—

The image shatters.

Rocks fill my vision. Sharp, ragged, huge. I'm half a second from impact.

Somehow I pull up, like a small plane, swooping away from the rocks, missing them by inches. And then I'm sucked backward and upward with astonishing g-force, my consciousness retracting, the journey-world receding from my grasp, shrinking and sealing up behind me like a geyser filmed in reverse, as a whole new reality fills in and takes its place.

*Whuup!* I'm back in the sweat lodge. Feeling like I've just landed from a fall. Panting and gasping in the tobacco-smelling darkness.

Pain attacks me. Real-life pain. Oh Christ! My lungs burn.

The steam! From the piled rocks. It's tea-whistle hot. My skin is literally cooking. I leap to my feet and burst through the door-flap, out of the lodge and into the cool, bright sunshine of the backyard.

I run across the grass, pulling fresh air into my lungs, devouring its coolness. Relief! My skin cries out in gratitude. I dance about in my white trunks, arms held high, bathing in the mountain air as if it were a lake.

God, it feels so good to be out of that lodge, like I've just escaped a burning building.

The joy doesn't last. The hammer of realization comes down.

My failure.

I ran. Ran from the lodge like a coward.

Failed the walk of faith. Failed my daughter. Lost my belief. Lost my conviction. Lost my chance to reunite with Em.

The others are still inside the lodge. How is it they've been able to endure the heat but I haven't? Even Mary—far from the hardiest of souls—has outlasted me. Am I that weak?

I look back at the dome-shaped shelter with my working right eye. Wispy tendrils of heat escape from between the overlapping animal hides like whispers of secrets still being told within.

Do I try again? Go back inside? Would I even be welcome in there?

I need a moment to gather myself. I go to the picnic table and sit.

Filling my lungs with precious air, I gaze up at the sky—a crystalline shade of blue I've never seen before—and then back at the shelter. The animal hides seem to bristle with life.

That's when I realize my senses are *electrified*. They're tuned to a whole new frequency. Everything seems to glow more brightly than usual. Colors are more vivid, forms less solid. Maybe the lodge wasn't a *total* failure. I feel an aliveness and openness I haven't felt since… after my *first* sweat lodge, the one I did in college. I have that same sense that doors have opened for me to step through, that I'm capable of new knowings. I should be exhilarated, but my failure presses down on me. Did I blow my one shot at seeing Emmy?

I rise from the table and look toward the lodge again. The fear of losing my mind wraps around me like a chill.

The door-flap lifts, and Sister Quilla steps out. She walks across the grass toward me with a stiff, almost processional gait. She stops. Examines me like a newly altered suit. Frowns.

"I know I failed," I say. "You don't have to rub it in."

"You do better than most," she replies. "Come, the others inside." She gestures toward the house, not the lodge.

The others are in the house? I was the *last* one out of the lodge, not the first.

• • •

"This way, Buffalo Bob," says Clem, his left eye puffy and red, matching mine, as I step in the door. He turns and strides off through the house. I follow him.

"Up here."

I ascend the stairs behind him, feeling that new sense of magnified power, and enter my bedroom as he directs.

"Drink that water and put on your street clothes."

I chug the tiny bottle of spring water on the dresser. It's about an eighth of what I need to replenish what I lost in the sweat lodge, but it tastes like nirvana. As I'm dressing in jeans and a sweatshirt, I catch a glimpse of myself in the wall mirror. I look like an extra in a *Rocky* film. The whole left side of my face is purple, swollen, and shiny, the left eye a split-top dinner roll.

I follow Clem downstairs, past Hark's office, and through a door I've never seen open. It leads to that three-car garage I've also never used. The three vehicles—the dark red GMC Yukon, the Cooper MINI, and the black Nissan Whatever—are parked inside. Hark paces on the far side of the cars, jabbering into his phone at someone. He's dressed in a turtleneck sweater, pressed pants, and a Brunello Cucinelli jacket. He gives me the "one sec" finger as he says to the phone, "Stand by, I'll call you one way or the other," and ends his call.

"Wogs!" he shouts as if he hasn't seen me in years. "We moved the cars in here just to fuck with you. Ha! Did it work?" Back to his asshole self again. *Que sera.* He grins, drumming the roof of the Yukon with his knuckles, then switches to a more businesslike tone. "I'm afraid our journey together ends today, my friend. You are moving on from Odyssey House."

He points behind me. Mary, Bruce, and Anvita file into the garage. They all wear street clothes now too. They line up, side by side, near the wall in a formal sort of way, hands folded in front of them. Something's about to go down. I feel strangely ready for whatever it is.

"Does this mean I'm 'graduating,'" I ask Hark, "or am I going the tulip-bulb route?"

"What did I tell you when you entered Odyssey House, McWags? I believe I informed you the program was pass/fail."

"I believe you did. And...?"

"Well... your sweat-lodge performance wasn't exactly a rousing success, was it?"

"I did better than all of you." Not a boast, just a fact.

"The sweat lodge wasn't a contest. But it *was* a test."

"And you're saying I failed it?"

"Get in the car, Woggles."

"No. I want to talk about this," I say. "I'm not ready to end things. Not like this."

"Still imagining you're running the clinic? The legendary Oliver Powers ego rides again."

"This isn't ego," I state, truthfully. "I came really close in there. I'm close *now*. I'm right on the brink of breaking through. Why end this now?"

Clem steps toward me, glowering. I turn to the others.

"I'm *this* close." I draw my thumb and forefinger together. "I swear. The sweat lodge wasn't a failure. It opened something in me. A new channel. What I said in there was the truth. I'm sorry for what I did to you. I really am. But I see now what you've been trying to show me all along. The thing I've been terrified of all my life is something in *me*. I've been afraid of my true self. My true power. I'm not afraid of it anymore. I'm ready to push through, all the way."

The three look at me with something bordering on empathy but are unmoved to speech or action. Clem opens the back door of the Yukon and glares at me through his bruised eye. *Get in.*

"No." I put my literal foot down. "Stopping my treatment now makes no sense. You go to all this effort—you put your lives on hold and take me through this elaborate process—only to give up on me when I'm *this* close to going the last mile?"

Clem grabs my arm, pulls me toward the car. Now fear does rise up. Not fear of dying, fear of losing my *chance*. I want to finish this.

"I've changed!" I shout at Mary, Bruce, and Anvita. "I can prove it to you. Just let me prove it. Don't abandon me now. Not now! Not now!"

Clem shoves me into the back seat, slams the door. He walks to a rack of outdoor tools on the garage wall. He grabs a long-handled spade and tosses it into the trunk.

Hark slides into the passenger side of the front seat. Clem sits behind the wheel and jabs a button on the visor. The garage door rises.

"I can prove it to you!" I shout at the others through the Yukon's closed windows. I don't even know what I'm promising I can prove.

Joanna enters the garage from the house, wearing a jacket and holding her car keys. She climbs into the driver's seat of a second car, the Nissan. Mary, Bruce, and Anvita get into the Nissan with her. Wherever we're going, they're all coming too.

I'm surprised to see Sister Quilla exit the house next. Her arms are wrapped around a clear plastic jug that looks half the size of her body. The jug is two-thirds full of murky green liquid that resembles swamp water. She gets into the back seat of the Yukon with me, arms around the jug, not acknowledging my presence.

Clem starts the car, and we head out. The gate to the road opens ahead of us as the garage door closes behind us.

I look out the rear window with my one good eye. The Nissan is following us.

No blindfold for me this time. They don't care what I see. The car rolls off the property, winding down the tree-lined dirt road I nearly escaped on. We pass a couple of cabins, a campsite occupied by three RVs parked in a triangle, a rundown hunting shack. After a mile or so, we turn. Another dirt road. The Nissan follows us.

I should be memorizing every turn, every detail. But my mind is on something more urgent: proving to my captors that I deserve to live, that I deserve another chance to see Emmy.

A realization dawns. What I need is my own elk-in-the-forest moment. A manifestation. Something dramatic and incontestable that can show them—and myself—that I've attained a new state of being. That I haven't failed.

An insane idea enters my head.

But it's doable, at least theoretically, I know it is. I know it from my medical training and experience. I've seen countless living examples of how plastic the human body is, how susceptible it is to the mind's influence. I've seen stigmata with my own eyes—people causing words and symbols to appear on their flesh. I've seen placebos heal. I've seen faith healings—diseases vanquished in a literal instant through belief. I always filed those things away in the "science will explain it someday" box, but now it's time to reopen that box.

I know my idea is possible.

All it will take is one-hundred-percent belief on my part. No, not belief. *Knowledge*. Knowledge that I can do this. Banishment of every shred of doubt.

Eyes closed, I go to work.

After several minutes, the car accelerates to highway speed, and I open my working eye to see a sign, "Tonto Natural Bridge State Park, 2 miles." Hannah and I visited that tourist site a few years ago. We must be on Route 260, northeast of Payson. I close my eye again and go back to my inner business: flooding my cells with visualized light.

Ten minutes or so later, the car slows and turns right. We're on dirt road again. A couple of miles farther along, we stop. I open my eyes, yes both of them.

We're in a field surrounded by pine forest. Hark and Clem climb out. Clem comes around to open my door, and as he leans in to grab me, he pulls in a breath and backs up. He shoots Hark a *WTF* look.

I step out of the car. Clem gives me a wide berth. The Nissan pulls up behind us and parks in the field a few yards away. Bruce, Mary, and Anvita step out into the sun. When Mary sees me, she tugs her head back in surprise. Anvita gives me a glimmer of a smile and bows slightly. Bruce looks at me, laughs, and says, "Okay, Powers, you've got *my* attention."

Hark walks toward me with a straight-legged strut, hands on his hips, smiling and nodding. He steps around me in a circle, looking me up and down in a theatrical way.

"Well, blow me down, laddybuck. Aren't you full of surprises?" He turns to the others. "What do you say, folks? Do we have an Odyssey House graduate on our hands?"

To my surprise, Mary, Bruce, and Anvita break into applause. I feel an unexpected rush of emotion. Love. Gratitude. And an almost foreign one for me: humility.

Hark taps his phone screen and hands the device to me. It's in mirror mode.

"Well done, Woggles," he says. "Well done." He joins the clapping.

I look at the electronic mirror and draw in a breath. It's exactly what I expected to see, but still the sight comes as a shock. My face is completely healed; no trace of bruises, cuts, or swelling.

Hark takes his phone back from me. He says to Clem, "You can leave the shovel in the trunk." Clem grunts. Hark steps a few yards away from the group and punches in a phone number. "Send it in," he says.

My three other ex-patients walk away from the car and stand side by side, facing the open field and gazing up at the sky. I join them, no idea what I'm watching for.

After only a couple of minutes, the sound of an engine ruptures the silence. The *whup-whup-whup* of a helicopter, flying low, fills the clearing with sound. The pine trees bow their heads as the craft approaches. It descends onto the field and lands thirty feet from where we're standing, its wind whipping our hair and clothes.

"What's this?" I shout over the noise, turning to Hark.

He shouts back, "Are you ready to see your daughter?"

# PART V
# Integration

# Chapter 38

Hark waves me toward the churning copter.

Over the din of the blades, I shout, "Where are we going?"

"What's with the *we*, Kemosabe?" He points to the others, waiting off to the side, no intentions of boarding. "Here's where the fare-thee-wells go down, Wogs. I'd like to say *it's been real*," he continues over the engine sound, "but that doesn't exactly encapsulate our adventure, does it?"

He laughs and holds his knuckles up for a bro-fist. "Maybe we'll meet again on the other side."

*The other side of what?* I lift my fist to meet his—why not?—and, for just a flash, his eyes betray the wounded child, about to be abandoned again. And for that one flickering moment, the father and therapist come out in me. I want to pull this sad boy to my chest, wrap him in strong arms, and tell him *there, there, it's going to be all right*.

I do the fist-bump instead.

I turn to the others, feeling a need for some kind of closure. "I know you won't believe me," I yell over the rotor, "But I tried to do right by you. In our work together."

I expect my words to ring hollow, but they surprise me by ringing true. Since this ordeal began, I've done nothing but castigate myself for my ulterior motives and my dishonesty—and deservedly so—but I haven't acknowledged one overriding truth: I tried to help these people. I did. The Hippocratic oath was always my ultimate compass, above and beyond any ethical sleight of hand. Help, not hurt. Always. That's why their cases were so damn complicated. I never, never intended harm.

"I cared about you all. I still do."

Mary stuns me by rushing forward and throwing her arms around me. Bruce grins at me in the old way he used to when we were friends as well as doctor and patient. Anvita bows from the waist, a true Namaste; the God in me sees the God in you.

"Goodbye," I say to the three of them, my voice pinching. I feel I should say more, but nothing comes.

I duck as I near the aircraft, even though the rotor blades are six feet above my head, then step up the entry rung into the cabin where two pairs of tan leather seats face each other. I choose a forward-facing seat. In the cockpit ahead of me, a helmeted pilot checks his gauges.

Sister Quilla comes waddling from the parked car toward the copter, her arms around the giant jug of sludgy green water. She stops at the copter door, slides the jug onto the floor of the aircraft, then departs without a word. Why is *this* stuff coming with me?

Joanna climbs aboard the chopper—damn—and takes the seat opposite mine, strapping herself in and placing a headset over her ears. And why is *she* coming with me?

"Buckle up," she orders, avoiding eye contact. I buckle my belt.

"Can I get some water?" I mime a drinking motion. I'm still massively dehydrated from the sweat lodge.

She points to my headset. I put it on, shutting out most of the engine noise. In the techno-quiet space, I repeat, into the mike, "Can I get some water?"

"No." Her voice comes through my headphones now.

Superb. Every cell of my body is screaming for hydration.

A few seconds later, Clem boards the copter, holding a small duffel bag. He sits next to Joanna, places the bag on the floor, and puts his headset on, stifling a wince of pain as the pad touches his bruised temple. They're both trying to project tough-guy nonchalance, but I can tell they're uncomfortable with me in the wake of my face-healing.

Clem reaches into the duffel bag and pulls out a black cloth bag with a drawstring. He tosses it to me. "Put this over your head... please."

No point making trouble. I obey, stretching the sack over the headphones.

"Cinch it and tie it."

"Before I do, can I *please* get some water?"

"Not permitted," says Joanna. "Sorry."

Alrighty, then. I pull the drawstring ends and tie them. Blackness effectuated.

I've never flown in a helicopter. Guess I'll be doing my maiden flight blind.

I *feel*, more than hear, the *thunk* of the door closing and the drone of the engine winding higher.

• • • •

We've been airborne for about twenty minutes, and Clem and Joanna haven't said a word. The blackness of the head-sack and the hush of the noise-canceling headphones create a sort of sensory deprivation chamber as the copter flies along. My instinct is to meditate, to prepare myself for whatever's coming next, but I'm too wired.

I have no clue where we're going, but dare I hope for the "unhopeable"? That Emmy *is* alive? After all, you don't use a helicopter to visit the "afterlife." Physical destinations are for physical meetings with physical people.

Mustn't allow hope to sprout wings, though. Not yet.

The far greater likelihood is that I'm still being messed with. We're probably flying in circles or heading back to Hark's House of Horrors for another spin on O'Halloran's Swing. Hark and the others *seemed* sincere about my sendoff, but "seems" has lost all predictive power.

Eventually I do settle into a meditative sort of wakefulness, letting my attention focus on the hum of the engine through the headset. I still feel charged up from the sweat lodge and my self-healing feat. I'm ready to step through a new doorway. Whatever it might be.

After what might be ninety minutes or three hours, our momentum shifts. The cabin starts to rock in a side-to-side motion. Are we descending? Apparently so. The landing-skids find ground, one-two, and the body of the copter settles. A minute later, the engine shuts off.

The voice of Clem through the headphones: "Take your shoes off."

Mine is not to reason why.

"Toss them to me. You can leave your socks on."

I do as I'm told.

"Take the blindfold off, please."

I untie the black bag and whip it off my head. The copter's rounded windows reveal a desert wilderness scene. Before I can speculate on where we are, or why, Clem pulls off my 'phones and walks me, sock-footed, to the doorway. Joanna slides the door open with a wheeze of sealed air. The desert sun hits my face like a floodlight. I blink the afterimages from my eyes as Clem leaps out ahead of me and grabs my wrist.

He helps me negotiate the step-down rung. Standing sock-footed in the warm, rocky dirt, feeling incongruously calm, I let my eyes adjust to the blazing sunlight. I look around and see only desert hills and vegetation. No buildings or vehicles. No roads, no trails. No trace of humanity.

Joanna steps out of the chopper with the plastic jug of green liquid and places it on the ground. She and Clem climb back into the aircraft. Clem tosses the duffel bag out. The two henchfolk stand in the open doorway of the copter, looking down at me.

"Welcome to Xanadu," says Clem.

"Looks more like Xana-*don't*," Joanna adds, yes she does.

Clem announces, "I have a prepared statement. From your host."

Cripes. Here goes.

"May I please have a drink of water first?"

"No, you may not," Clem replies.

He grabs a tablet device and holds it up for me to see. Hark's face is cued up on the screen. Clem pushes play. "Olliwog," says video-Hark. "So you were expecting maybe the Hacienda Del Sol? That wouldn't be very *on-brand* of me, now would it? You've come a long way in your inner journey, but I'm afraid you've only made it to base camp; the Matterhorn awaits. The location in which you find yourself is one of the remotest in the state of Arizona. You are *many* miles, in any direction, from the nearest road or trail. We are not coming back for you. You have been equipped with the following items: one flashlight, one blanket, one pair of plastic flip-flops from the Dollar Tree, and one jug of liquid refreshment, supplied by Sister Quilla. It is the broth of the San Pedro cactus, a powerful and sacred visionary medicine. You can try to walk out of here, but I wouldn't recommend it. If you wish to see your daughter, your only way *out* is *through*. Have fun, asshole, a-hyuck, a-hyuck."

Clem ducks inside and closes the copter door. The engine turns on and winds up. Survival-sense tells me to pound on the door and beg to go with them. I don't.

Clem salutes me through the glass. His gesture feels authentic, no sarcasm. Joanna frowns and bows her head, gives me a small wave.

The copter lifts off. I watch it rise, reverse direction, and disappear over the crest of a hill, the sound of its engine tailing to silence.

They did it. They flew off and left me here.

With a weird sense of acceptance, I stand up and walk in a circle, avoiding sharp rocks with my sock-clad feet and scanning the horizon. I'm in a roughly pie-plate-shaped "arena," about two hundred yards wide, surrounded by tall, rocky hills. Saguaro cacti dot the slopes. That means I'm back in the Sonoran desert, the southwestern quadrant of the state. I'll have to climb to the top of one of the encircling hills to get the true lay of the land, but my guess is Hark was serious: I'm in the proverbial middle of nowhere.

The sun is high in a cloudless sky and feels hot for January.

I dig into the duffel bag. The contents, as advertised: one four-inch "tactical" flashlight, one blanket, and one pair of flip-flops. The blanket is a high-quality, down-filled camping blanket that probably retails north of three hundred dollars. The flip-flops, on the other hand, are mint-green, palm-tree-patterned, and appear indeed to issue from a Dollar Tree, where they no doubt retail for the featured price of an unmarried George Washington.

The jug contains about two gallons of liquid the color of pickle skin. The thought of drinking it makes me gag. But I suppose that's the general idea. Thanks, Hark. How could I have thought he had changed?

I park my butt in the dusty dirt; no shade to be found. The sun beats down on me, unfiltered, and I'm surprised again by the heat. It must be ninety degrees out here; mild for southern Arizona for much of the year but hot for mid-winter, when the daytime temps usually max out in the sixties or seventies.

I'm already fabulously thirsty. Except for that little shooter of Poland Spring I chugged at the house, I haven't had a chance to replace the water loss from the sweat lodge.

Ah, Hark, you mad genius.

If what he said in the video is true, then here are the facts that now define my existence:

I am stranded in the desert wilderness, a great distance from civilization.

I have no food.

I have no water.

I am already dehydrated. And it's unseasonably hot out.

I have a bucket of green sludge that *can* provide hydration, but...

It's also a powerful hallucinogen.

For footgear, I have only the socks I'm wearing and a one-dollar pair of flip-flops.

The flip-flops will not carry me across miles of stony desert terrain. They are built for about five trips around a swimming pool.

The more I exert myself—by, say, trying to explore my environs or escape—the thirstier I will become and the more liquid I will need to consume. The more liquid I drink, the more I will trip my brains out.

And yet if I sit still and do nothing, I will die here in isolation.

It's a premise worthy of a Stephen King story. I laugh in spite of the circumstances and tip my hat to Hark. *Respect, dude. If I ever lay eyes on you again, I'll rip your god-damn head off, but mad respect.*

Of course, as always, there is the strong possibility Hark is just jerking me around, and that once I get past the hills encircling me, I'll find myself eighty feet from the back of the Casa Grande Mall.

Only one way to find out.

I'll have to tread carefully and pace myself, though.

I take off my socks, shove the little flashlight into my pocket, and put on the mint-green flip-flops. I set my sights on the summit of the most climbable-looking of the surrounding hills.

279

# Chapter 39

Climbing the hill is no small feat in my Dollar Tree footgear. I'm used to hiking on *trails*, with good shoes, and even then the Sonoran desert can be punishing on feet. Its terrain consists largely of jagged rocks of every shape and size, with an occasional thorn cluster thrown in for laughs. I'm lightheaded from dehydration too, so dizziness gives the climb an added difficulty rating. But after thirty minutes of sidestepping and back-switching, I reach the summit.

Fuck. Hark wasn't lying.

No Casa Grande Mall. This location is as remote as a Mars landing site. Distant mountain ranges serrate the horizon in a couple of directions, but I don't know which peaks they are. If Hannah were here, she'd tell me in an instant.

I know there's a huge native-nation reservation west of Tucson and south of Phoenix, one that sprawls for probably a million acres. There's also the Organ Pipe Cactus Wilderness and another big preserve bordering it whose name I can't recall. It dips way down into Mexico.

*Cabeza-Prieta*, that's it.

What difference does it make? The idea of hanging human syllables on a space so vast and wild seems laughable. Even more laughable is the notion of walking out of here in flip-flops with no food or water. The tiny mountain ranges taunt me from—fifty? sixty? eighty?—miles away.

I am well and truly screwed. Unless Hark decides to send the copter back. Which he said he would not do.

Panic wells up. I allow it to sink back down.

*Your only way* out *is* through.

I have no idea what Hark meant by that, but I shall cling to the belief that he meant *something*.

The hilltop I'm standing on is reasonably navigable as I pick my way amongst the scrub cholla and stubby barrel-cacti. Working my way to the far side of the crest, I make a discovery: a cave. On the side of the adjoining hill, fairly close to ground level. Dark and inviting under the cloudless sun.

I'll have to explore it ASAP. Yes, that feels like purpose.

Purpose will keep the panic at bay.

The afternoon heat is backing off just a tad. The sun is well into its descent arc. I probably have ninety minutes, at most, till sunset.

The climb, as predicted, has inflamed my thirst. A wave of dizziness moves through me, teetering me on my feet. The dehydration is going to cause some real damage soon if I don't address it. I left the jug of liquid down below. I may need to drink from it sooner rather than later.

Again Hark's mad brilliance emerges. He denied me all but a cup of water after the sweat lodge, knowing how dehydrated that would leave me. He has stranded me here in a state of acute thirst so as to exacerbate my need to consume the hallucinogen.

The man could accomplish world-changing things if only his father—and biochemistry—hadn't used his brain as a punching bag during his formative years.

• • •

After a gut-wringing descent (going *down*hill in flip-flops, when dizzy, is even trickier than going up), I pace around the jug of swamp-water, examining it as though it were an alien artifact. The container itself looks like one of those cheap plastic tubs used for selling cheese balls by the cubic yard in discount stores. As the late-day sunlight angles through it, I notice a clear glass ladle submerged in the brew. The liquid is a bit watery at the top, darker green at the bottom. Presumably, the darker the color, the more of the mescaline-rich San Pedro cactus rind it contains.

Maybe if I drink carefully from the top, I can ingest mostly water. For starters. That might allow me to stay relatively clearheaded for a while and get used to the potion gradually.

Worth a try. *Is it, though?*

The more immediate question is, do I *need* to drink now, medically speaking, or can I hold off till morning? My thirst is fierce. But so is my desire to remain non-psychotic.

I still sense that the sweat lodge has prepared me to walk through new doors. Perhaps the San Pedro cactus *is* that new door. *"Perhaps"? It might as well have Alice-in-Wonderland's "Drink Me" tag hanging from it.* But the thought of consuming the stuff terrifies me.

The San Pedro may be the key to whatever comes next, though. It must be.

*Your only way out is through.*

Fact: I will *need* to drink the cactus water if I want to survive. And likely if I want to see Emmy too—whatever form the "seeing" takes. Is putting it off till tomorrow just my fear preventing me from getting down to business?

I sit on the ground, lotus-style, in front of the jug. Speak to me, plant medicine.

I unscrew the red plastic lid. A dank, vegetative odor escapes—far from pleasant, but more "bad wheatgrass smoothie" than "stagnant swamp in July."

But hello, what's this? A folded paper is taped to the underside of the plastic lid.

I peel the tape free and find a handwritten note. I skip to the bottom to see the signature, "Sister Quilla," then read the note itself. Her written English is better than her speech.

*That was a powerful calling-forth you did, the healing of your face. But do not become spiritually arrogant. We call that "beginner's grace." Spirit grants us early successes to fortify us against the harder battles ahead. And make no mistake, a harder battle lies ahead for you. Here is where you Western healers have it wrong. You think* insight *is enough to change a human life. Insight and medicine from a factory. We who walk the old road know better. We know that when you have lost a part of your soul, as you have, you must go back and retrieve it. You must battle the entities that have taken possession of it and wrestle it from them. The plant medicine is the vehicle that will take you there.*

A chill blows through me despite the warmth of the desert air. I take a long breath, in and out, then read on.

*The plant spirits have always lived alongside us. They are the watchers, the still ones, our wiser brothers and sisters, and they are here to teach and heal us. The medicines you Westerners use have no spirit. But the plant medicine does. And it knows what you need. It will take you on the right journey, in the way you need to go. But you must respect it. Do not treat it lightly, but do not fear it either.*

Suddenly the idea of using the "plant medicine" for something as pedestrian as quenching my thirst seems almost dishonorable.

But my thirst rages. As a physician, I know how dangerous dehydration can be. It can lead to heatstroke, seizures, even hypovolemic shock, which can cause the blood pressure to plummet. I'm not in the danger zone yet, but I will be soon if I don't hydrate.

I sit there studying the jug. Ancient spirit medicine encased in throwaway plastic. Two disparate worlds, adjacent to each other, but not intermingling.

Physically, I am ready to drink. Spiritually, I am not.

I bow to the plant medicine, paying it respect, and rise to my feet.

I will go find the cave now. That is something I *am* ready to do.

I will walk slowly, without strain, so as not to tempt heatstroke or intensify my thirst. As I walk, I will prepare myself mentally—and, yes, spiritually—for the drinking of the medicine.

. . .

The cave can't be terribly far, maybe a couple of hundred yards, a distance I could cover in a jiff in my favorite Adidas hikers. But in flip-flops, picking my way over harsh terrain at a measured pace, the trek burns up a good chunk of my remaining daylight.

Edging my way around the base of the hill, I spot it on the neighboring hill. The cave. About fifteen feet above ground level. It looks deep, judging by the blackness within. And high and wide enough for a man, bending over a bit, to enter.

High and wide enough for other things to enter, too. Apex predators, for example. Bobcats, cougars, and even the occasional jaguar, the third largest cat in the world, are known to roam this region. If I were a jaguar seeking a lair, I could scarcely find a better home on cat Zillow.

Once my mind latches onto that possibility, it can't let go. There is a non-zero chance that a large carnivore lives in that cave—or at least a rattlesnake or two—and I had better approach it with due caution. I spend ten minutes searching for a defensive weapon. There are no branches or sticks out here, but I find a sharp-edged rock the size of an axe head and some smaller stones for throwing.

Desperation defenses only, but better than nothing.

I approach the area below the cave, treading quietly. Good news/bad news, there seems to be a dirt path leading up to the cave opening. The good news: I can ascend the path fairly easily. The bad: something *wore* that path in the dirt. Something a good bit larger than a kangaroo rat.

I look for signs of fresh footprints in the dust, don't see any.

"Hello!" I shout at the cave entrance—because wildcats speak English—then step back and freeze, raising the sharp rock. No sound comes from within.

I hurl one of my throwing-stones into the cave, my body tensing as it echoes off one rock surface, then another, and dies in dirt. I throw a second stone, at a different angle, and then a third and a fourth. No reaction from within the cave.

I remove the flip-flops and stick them in my pocket. My feet will handle the dusty ascent path better without them. Barefooting my way up the steep incline, I note a ledge in front of the cave-mouth. Again, couldn't be a cozier setup for a big cat. Silence issues from the cave. I take the tactical flashlight from my pocket, and, doing the cop-with-a-gun routine, aim the flashlight into the cave for a second or two, then duck to the side and mentally review what I saw.

Narrow entry "tunnel," rock walls, dusty floor, depth about twenty-five feet. No residents.

Emboldened, I bend and step into the cave with the flashlight on. Foot traffic of some kind has stirred up the dirt floor, but not recently. At the far end of the entry tunnel lies a larger chamber. Bent over, I make my way toward it, stepping over the bones of a raccoon-sized creature strewn in the dust. A former predator's lair, for sure.

The chamber at the rear of the cave is rounded and high enough to stand in. I raise the light beam and pull back in surprise—ancient petroglyphs adorn the rock walls. A stick-figure human. Spirals. A squiggly snake. Something shaped like a tiered wedding cake.

Was this room a temple? A "theater"? A clubhouse of sorts?

Do archeologists know about this place?

Panning the flashlight around, I see, over my head, two petroglyph-antelopes in the rearing-up position. They seem to come alive in the moving light-beam—and I haven't consumed a drop of mescaline yet.

On the wall to my left, a full scene is depicted. A dozen stick-figure humans huddle in a group. Standing apart from them is another human-like figure with special robes and a glowing sun for its head. Its arms are extended toward a nondescript four-legged animal with a sloping back. Are those ears or horns on the animal's head? The thing could be a buffalo, but with its oddly long neck, it looks almost—no, not possible—hyena-like.

I reject the notion. But still, my heart pounds like a skin drum.

The sunlight hitting the cave mouth has taken on an orange tone. I'm running out of daytime. Should I set up camp in this cave? Make it my home base? Seems like the ideal spot, even though the petroglyph scene unnerves me. I'm beyond lucky, actually, to have found a shelter like this.

Better go grab my stuff—my blanket and the "medicine"—while I still have daylight.

As a physician, I've made the executive decision that I can survive till tomorrow without ingesting fluid.

Tonight I will sleep.

Tomorrow, at dawn, I will drink the medicine.

# Chapter 40

My night is far from restful, though the dirt beneath me is soft and the blanket warm. In this ancient petroglyph theater, dreams and reality bleed together readily.

At one point, I sit up, seeing brilliant stars all around me. The cave has turned into a "planetarium." Then I realize the million points of light are glowing insects. They, too, disappear—apparitions. At another point I awaken to see the petroglyph scene on the wall light up and come alive. The figure with the sun for its head is a shaman, I sense, and he is keeping the hyena-beast away from his people. The beast advances, and the shaman trembles. I'm seeing this "animation" with eyes wide open, but then I awaken again. Dreams within dreams.

I wanted to be rested and clear-minded in the morning, but dawn finds me fragile and depleted. Not an ideal state for the drinking of the plant medicine.

I slip into my flip-flops. My mouth is dry as sandpaper, my throat caked with dust as I approach the mouth of the cave. The rising sun peeks over the hills to my left, but the sky is still half-dark, and the air is chill. The jug of cactus brew sits right where I left it last night, just inside the cave entrance. I slide it outside.

I will conduct my plant ceremony here on the ledge, as the sun rises.

No point delaying things. I know it's going to take an hour or more for the mescaline to kick in. I bow to the four directions, something I've seen Emmy (and Hark) do, then bow to the medicine itself and sit beside the jug.

I have one critical decision to make. How much to drink? Part of me wants to ease into this experience. Drink only a little at first.

I shine my flashlight through the liquid. The bottom has become thick green again, the top thinner and more dilute. Should I start with the dilute stuff? Take it slow? Fuck it; I open the jug and plunge my hand into the liquid, extracting the glass ladle and stirring up the brew.

Without ado, I pour a ladleful of the medicine, about three-quarters of a cup, into my mouth. Blocking the taste from my mind, I gulp down a second and a third ladleful. The hydration moves through me in a life-giving wave. Then the bitterness hits. Good God. My stomach convulses, and my gag-reflex trips. I nearly vomit, but somehow I hold the fluid down.

I'm glad I haven't eaten in almost twenty-four hours.

My stomach settles in a series of weakening spasms.

Now what? Sit here for an hour or two, watching the sun come up and waiting for the mescaline to kick in? Nah, too much nervous energy. I'll go down to the valley floor and do some exploring. Then, when I start to see symptoms, I'll come back up to the ledge.

I'm pretty damn scared.

. . .

Daylight is full now, and the air is warming fast. I'm down in my private valley, eyes on the ground, scoping out the flora and fauna, pretty much convinced that the San Pedro juice was nothing but a bad smoothie after all, when a prickly-pear cactus wearing a cowboy hat walks past me, whistling and twirling a lasso.

Holy crap, that came on fast.

I look up to see the desert vegetation all around me swaying in a dance rhythm. A drumbeat pounds from deep within the Earth, creating the tempo the plants are dancing to. Man, an easing-in period would have been nice.

An ecstatic charge shoots up my spine and bursts like a firework in my brain. Whoa. Buckle up, Oliver, your ticket to Wally World has just been punched.

When I make my way back to the cave mouth, a fat chuckwalla lizard is sitting on the ledge, bobbing up and down. It grins at me with a tiny rack of human teeth, then turns and waddles into the cave, its carrot-orange tail beckoning me like a finger.

I proceed to the chamber at the back of the cave, where my flashlight reveals new petroglyphs amongst the old ones, and they are all in full animation—spirals spinning, turtles swimming, hunters chasing herds of antelope. The sun-headed shaman throws bolts of energy at the hyena-beast as it chuffs and paws at the ground.

No sooner do I sit in the dirt to watch the "show" than the cave art disappears. And then the *rock wall itself* vanishes. Christ, I should have taken a smaller dose. I find myself in a mescaline-generated Imax theater. The ultrarealistic imagery surrounding me on all sides is New England forest and meadow.

I look down at my hands; they belong to a young man. I'm sitting on the edge of the frog pond behind the Godwin College campus—in that signal moment of my young manhood. I mean, I'm *there*, in full wraparound 3D, all my senses firing, though I know it's a memory too.

The scene is accurate down to the finest detail—the flattened Mountain Dew can sticking out of the mud, the crumbling barn foundation in the woods. And there it is: the *frog*, the one that triggered my near-breakdown at age twenty, sitting on its appointed rock.

*The frog winks and waves, as it did all those years ago, and again I know the gesture is meant for me. I receive that breathtaking insight that the frog and I are one and the same, and then I merge with the little man as it leaps into the water. We swim to the bottom of the pond, regressing through biological time as we do. We morph into primitive crustaceans, ammonites, crinoids, single-celled organisms, complex molecules. But every life-form is but a reshaping of the same source-essence, the same Oneness. I am flooded with direct knowledge that I am everything and everything is me; that all of eternity exists in every moment and that time is just a trick of consciousness allowing us to experience more and more facets of the One—like a CD that always contains every note of every song but can only be listened to sequentially.*

*I dive deeper than biology, into the heart of energy itself, into the soul of light. I travel back through the event we call the Big Bang and out the other side, racing through fathomless dimensions and universes, living complete lifetimes as formless light-beings that possess all knowledge. Eventually, the super-dimension I'm in flips itself inside out, and I find myself plunging back to Earth via some impossible wormhole in spacetime.*

*I land in my body again, sitting by the frog pond. But I'm far from "back to normal." My sense of Oneness still illuminates my being. I look around me, and I love every bird, every leaf, every insect my eyes land on. Love, I now understand, is nothing but the recognition of the One, the unbroken singularity. Fear is the illusion of separateness.*

*It strikes me that I am having a spiritual experience to rival those of the great spiritual masters. I laugh myself dizzy as I realize I have been avoiding this—the spiritual dimension of life—since childhood, out of fear. Fear! How could fear have ever gotten tangled up in something so spectacularly blissful?*

*Suddenly, as a twenty-year-old, I recall exactly how.*

*The 3D scene in the cave dissolves to my fourth-grade Catholic school classroom. I'm in that phase of my childhood when I believed—no, when I knew—I could affect reality with my mind. Sister Alice Marie is about to call on me, I sense it, so I mentally induce Gerard Pelletier to let out a giant belch—which he does, to his own surprise as much as the nun's. The class erupts in laughter, and Sister forgets all about me. Mission accomplished.*

That sort of thing, I recall, happened routinely for me at that age. When one day I tried to confide in my parents about my strange ability, they shut me down. Hard. With dark looks exchanged. The word *blasphemy* was introduced to my vocabulary.

As was the word *psychiatry.*

*The cave/theater transforms into Sacred Heart church. Fourth-grade me is sitting in a pew with my parents, trying to reconcile this ability I know I possess with the Catholic teaching that only God has such powers and that humans are lowly sinners. That is when the concept of evil first enters my heart and mind. Am I sinful for believing I have powers reserved for God? I try to concentrate on Father MacLean hoisting the host in his shimmery green robe, but my eyes feel drawn to that hated stained-glass window, the one with Christ blessing the*

*crowd and the demons giggling in the corner. I steal a look, can't help myself.*
*The demons are squirming in the glass, alive. One of them, with a weirdly long*
*neck and stooped shoulders, meets my eye and winks. And then... no god-damn*
*way... it drops out of the glass and onto the floor of the church, with a plop, and*
*scurries away—part of my real world now. No!*

I want to pull out of this 3D memory, but can't. I'm stuck.

I physically toss my body sideways to tear myself free.

Success.

I'm back in the plain cave, at least for the moment.

Good God. This San Pedro stuff is supposed to be a gentler experience
than ayahuasca, so why am I already at a thirteen on a scale of one to ten?
Because I have no idea how to titrate the "medicine," that's why. I took way
too damn much. I dash out to the ledge, ducking to avoid the long, low cave-
ceiling, hoping the brightness of morning will serve as a splash of cold water.

It does not. All the desert vegetation is still dancing to the drumbeat of
the Earth. No! I just want sanctuary. But there's none to be found, within
the cave or without. And I'm only at the beginning of this "adventure."

The entire desert scene changes to a black-and-white palette, and the
dancing of the plants takes on the trippy animation of an old Max Fleischer
cartoon.

Fuck this shit. I want to cry.

I duck back into the cave and return to the "theater" at the rear. Again,
the wall of petroglyphs comes alive, then fades away, and I'm back in the
world of virtual 3D memory.

*I'm at the pond again, twenty years old, trying to make sense of my*
*childhood memories in light of the mind-expanding experience I've just had*
*with the frog. From this college-age perspective, I recall another scene not long*
*after the church episode I just relived. I spin into another memory-within-a-*
*memory, another 3D scene.*

*I'm lying in bed, nine or ten years old, worrying myself sick that I've*
*committed mortal sins that will damn my soul for eternity, when I sense a*
*shuffling in the shadows of my bedroom. I know, without looking, that the*
*demon from the church window is in my room. Unable to resist a peek, I turn*
*and glimpse the silhouette of a figure against the window—semi-human, but*

*crouched on all fours. Sloping back, long neck. I whip my face away. Imagination, stop!*

*The thing whispers to me, in my mind. It tells me the goody-goodies are trying to take my power away, but that it—the demon—is on my side. It tells me I've only begun to explore my capabilities. It tells me I have the power to punish people who do bad things to me, to show everyone who's boss. Its words are terrible but oh so seductive. I imagine being able to focus my powers in a vengeful way. I imagine knocking Scooter Driscoll off the monkey bars with my mind the next time he makes fun of me. I imagine making...*

*The 3D scene dissolves and I'm in Sacred Heart church again. At my great aunt Bella's funeral. There's her coffin, only feet away, and she's inside it. Inside it. And I put her there.*

*Bella was a grandmother figure to me and would sometimes babysit me. Whenever we were alone together, her voice and face would change, and she'd make me do awful, semi-sexual things, like stand between her legs and read to her—words I didn't understand but didn't like. I hated her and wanted her dead. And then one day, after she made me "lick Jesus's pain" off the crucifix on her neck, I turned my desire into a focused wish. Die, Aunt Bella, die. Three days later, she slipped on icy steps and broke her neck.*

*And I did it. I killed her. I know I did. Guilt is a boulder in my chest.*

*I don't want to look up at that stained glass window, but I do. God help me, I do. The demons are dancing, celebrating my murderous act, trying to high-five me. No. I don't want to be on that team! The bad team. I will never use these powers again! I promise. Forgive me, forgive me, forgive me!*

*Back at the frog pond, I realize that was the exact moment my pliant young mind began to link spiritual empowerment with demonic evil and guilt. No wonder I ran from all things spiritual. No wonder I fell in love with math and the hard sciences.*

*I send love and compassion to the confused nine-year-old boy within me.*

*With a mind awakened by the frog experience, my twenty-year-old self sees that all my childhood fears were primitive and unfounded. Love is everything, and it has no opposite. All fear is self-imposed; it is fear of the magnitude of our own power. We are all gods-in-embryo, microcosms of Universal Mind, wielders of the same creative powers that give birth to cosmoses.*

*I rise from my pondside rock, the light of eternity beaming from my twenty-year-old eyes, committed to going forth and living in my glorious new power with no guilt and no fear.*

And that was exactly what I did.

For a while.

*The Imax cave-theater spins into montage mode. I relive a series of short 3D memories in rapid succession. Call it Scenes from My College Awakening: Me composing a sonata on the piano with no musical training. Me receiving an ovation from my Humanistic Psychology class for putting a poser professor in his place with masterful debating skill. Me willing Georgia Ball, the most beautiful woman on campus, to look up from her notes and glance at me across a classroom—and me knowing I would be sleeping with her within days.*

*Living in the zone, twenty-four-seven. Until...*

I roll to the side in the cave, breaking the spell of the 3D imagery and returning to "normal" reality. I know what's coming next in my Imax life-movie, and I don't want to see it. I run out to the ledge again, and the desert is swaying even more fluidly than before. The plants are chanting the same refrain as the fake Chimbu dancers in my "hospital room": *LooKAta LEE-dama—Look at the little man, Look at the little man.*

Fuck you, San Pedro. I duck back into the cave. The passage between the cave mouth and the "theater" provides a bit of sanctuary, though even there the rock textures are flowing and dripping. I don't want to go back outside. And I don't want to go back into the theater, because I know what movie will be playing next: my "fall from grace" at age twenty.

No, damn it, I don't have to see it if I choose not to.

*I'm* in charge of my mind, the San Pedro isn't. *I* get to decide which thoughts I entertain.

A sound to my right challenges this assertion. It is the sound of seeds being shaken in a dried pepper.

I turn to see a rattlesnake—a big fat diamondback—just inside the cave entrance. Its head is lifted, its rattle is vibrating, and its eyes are locked on me. It lunges, and I jump backwards, three feet deeper into the cave.

The creature is real, I think (whatever that means), not part of my San Pedro visioning.

A rattlesnake bite, out here, in the middle of nowhere? Oh God, that would be bad.

The snake springs again. I jump back.

Real or not, the snake is "herding" me back into the theater. Commanding me to finish what I started.

# Chapter 41

Backing away from the snake, I step into the domed cave-chamber and...

*I'm back in the virtual movie, twenty years old again. Now I'm at an outdoor party near campus. Private home, woodsy location. Music blaring—something from* Born in the USA, *as required by statute at the time. It's twilight. Sweatshirt weather in Massachusetts.*

*Georgia Ball is here. Tragically, so is her semi-boyfriend, Scott Perdue—quarterback of Godwin's pathetic Division III football team and world-class a-hole. Scott has always hated me, but since my "awakening," his hatred has reached fever pitch. And since Georgia began noticing me, it's been open war. He's been body-checking me in the halls, spilling drinks on me in the caf, all that good-time, testosterone-y stuff. I've been letting his high school antics roll off me. Until tonight. Tonight he means business. Each time I try to fill my cup at the keg, he or one of his Neanderthal friends smacks it out of my hand.*

*Something's about to go down; I can tell by the glances being exchanged.*

*Fine, I don't need an act of Congress. I'll leave. No chance I'm getting near Georgia tonight anyway, not with Scott around. I head off the property, walking down the long, wooded drive. I haven't gone fifteen yards when five guys step out of the bushes and block my path. They wear paper bags over their heads, for "disguise," but their identities are ludicrously obvious: the Godwin Bearcats' offensive line. Scott Perdue's sewing circle.*

*What I* should *do is bolt; I'd outrun these guys in a footrace. But instead, fueled by my sense of cosmic invulnerability, I decide to walk through their body-wall as if they don't exist.*

*Poor decision.*

*They grab me, haul me into brush, and slam me to the ground on my back, knocking the wind out of me. Four of them drop onto my thighs and shoulders with crushing weight, holding my mouth shut and my head still with their mitt-sized hands. I fight like a cat being forced into a pet carrier, but I don't stand a chance against these goobers.*

*IQ Giant number five crouches down, holding one of those thick, felt-tipped Magic Markers of the era—full of indelible ink. He studies my face as if it's an artist's canvas, then, pressing down hard with the marker, prints three or four huge letters on my forehead. He laughs at his handiwork and adds a couple of decorative flourishes to my cheeks.*

*A voice from beyond the bushes—Scott Perdue's—says, "Why don't you go make goo-goo eyes at Georgia now, Ass-Fuck?"*

*I wriggle in vain, trying to land at least one punch or kick, and then...*

*The ground beneath me falls away, and I plunge to yet another 3D scene.*

*A hotel room. Correction,* motel. *Its yellow plastic sign glows outside my window: The Blarney Stone Lodge. Fleabag joint with dive bar attached. I've rented a room here, because I can't go back to school, can't go back to my dorm room, can't go home to my parents.*

*Not until the ink fades.*

*I enter the bathroom and look in the mirror for the thousandth time. Scott's art brigade, in a fit of creative inspiration, wrote FAG! on my forehead in thick black letters. The matching male genitalia they drew on my cheeks actually look more like Civil War cannons, firing away. Maybe the guys are history buffs, I muse, not fucking morons.*

*Nah, I'll stick with fucking morons.*

*I can't be seen in public this way. A friend of mine, Toby, checked me into this room and went to Osco Drug to buy me the supplies that line the sink: baking soda, toothpaste, baby oil, rubbing alcohol. This is the pre-Internet era, so I can't google, "How to remove permanent marker from skin." I'm forced to rely on folk remedies.*

*My forehead is an angry pink from repeated scrubbing. FAG! has faded to a ghost of its former glory but still reads like a billboard. When it fades a bit more, I'll try masking it with makeup. Or some of that lovely Band-Aid-colored Clearasil they sell.*

*But for now, it's scrub and wait, wait and scrub.*

*I crack a Milwaukee's Best and flop on the bed to ruminate. How did my spiritual confidence betray me as it did? Maybe I betrayed it by letting it turn into arrogance. Either way, my encounter with Scott's goons has triggered a crash in me. I've fallen out of my state of grace, out of The Zone. Being stuck in this depressing, smelly motel room for the past forty-plus hours hasn't helped. All I've been able to do is pace the floors and think of ways to get slow, painful revenge on Scott Fucking Perdue. My mind has been sinking to dark places, and the external world has been reflecting my inner darkness back to me—car horns blasting, drunk voices raging, angry poundings on walls.*

*I shut off the bed-board light and press my back up against the thin pillows, fully clothed, listening to the blare of country music from the bar and the whine of truck tires on Route 110 through the cracked-open window. Where did my power go? How did everything turn so base and ugly? How did fear and anger get a grip on me again? Die, Scott Perdue, die.*

*My heart feels sick and shaky.*

*It's still early, nine o'clock at the latest, but I drift into a half-sleep.*

*Sometime later—not sure how long—a shadow moves across the bottom of the window. My muscles tense. I watch, pinned to the bed, as the window inches open wider. Something darker than night "pours" over the windowsill and coalesces in the corner of the room.*

*From within the pool of darkness, yellow eyes and jagged, rotten teeth grin at me.*

No! Not this!

*I thought I had rid myself of this thing, purged it from all but my deepest nightmares. I can't get a visual fix on it, but I know what it is: the thing from the church window, the thing that defiled my middle-childhood years. The demon.*

*It's back again—did it ever really leave?—and it has terrible business to discuss.*

Cut to:

*Blackness. A ringing phone. My eyes pop open and take in the red lighted numbers of the motel-room clock: 12:20. I must have fallen into real sleep. Somehow. I don't dare turn around and look in the corner of the room. The bedside phone rings again. Who could be calling at this hour? Why? Cellphones aren't a thing yet, and only Toby knows I'm here.*

*I grope for the receiver and croak a hello.*

*"Dude." It is Toby. "Did you hear? Scott Perdue, like, died. Wrapped his car around a telephone pole. Guess he was hammered. Going, like, ninety. I heard they had to search for his head. Dude? Olls? You there?"*

*I drop the receiver into its cradle. I force myself to flip around on the bed and look into the corner of the room. I can barely make it out, but it's still there—grinning mouth and yellow eyes bobbing up and down with laughter.*

*"GET OUT!" I scream into the darkness. "GET OUT! GET OUT! GET OUT!"*

The force of my shouting shatters the 3D scene. I'm back in the desert cave. Gasping for air. Staring at the rock wall.

Safe. For now. I think.

My breath settles into a calmer rhythm, and my heart-rate kicks down.

But then a sound behind me sends a jolt of cold electricity through me—something breathing, a few feet away, making a slight gurgle on the inhale.

I turn, and there it is. The thing.

Here. In this world. Now. In the cave with me.

The demon from the church window.

More precisely, the hyena-like monstrosity—sculpted from negative space—that my mind has twisted it into since childhood.

It crouches in the shadows, not five feet from me, breathing heavily, a dull expression on its "face," giving no indication of its intentions.

"Get out!" I yell, finding my voice. The thing tenses to alertness. Is it going to lunge? "GET THE FUCK OUT OF HERE!" Rage eclipses my fear. "GET OUT! GET OUT OF MY LIFE! GET OUT!"

The thing leaps past me with an abrupt, frog-like motion and scrambles down the cave passageway, crushing the rattlesnake as it passes. When it reaches the mouth of the cave, it springs like a giant bullfrog off the ledge. Into the world beyond.

I collapse against the cave wall, hyperventilating.

What the hell just happened?

Did I just pull a demon out of my mind and into reality? Have I banished it forever now, like a saint driving the devils away in one of my old catechism pictures? Or is it still...

Stop! I'm *hallucinating*. None of this is real. Not the demon. Not the dancing cacti. Not the crawling petroglyphs. Not the Imax theater of the mind.

I stand up and shake my head and arms. This is just a drug trip.

Not real.

A warm syrup of calm pours over me. I plop myself back down on the dirt floor.

Not real. None of this.

*But that's not quite true, is it?* a voice inside me answers back. The 3D theater may be an artifact of my drug-induced psychosis, but the *scenes it has been showing me* have been excruciatingly real. These memories of my life have been accurate in every photorealistic detail.

I had forgotten about that time in the Blarney Stone Lodge. But there it was, right down to the Bugles crumbs on the bedspread and the beer-stained copy of the *Boston Phoenix* with Bob Marley on the cover.

These memories are the *most real* thing in my world right now.

After getting that phone call from Toby, I recall, I left the Blarney Stone, in the small hours of night, and got into my car. I drove all the way to Gorham, New Hampshire, in the White Mountains, to the spot where my family used to rent a cottage every summer. I observed without emotion that the place had been turned into a Midas Muffler. Then I turned around and drove back, my mind in overdrive the whole time.

By the time I arrived at the campus in Massachusetts, in the cold light of morning, I had expunged the demon from my mind. I had dispelled all notions that I was the cause of Scott Perdue's death. I had pulled myself back from the brink of madness by an act of sheer will.

I had grabbed the reins of logic and vowed never to let go of them again.

Later that morning, I doctored my inked face with makeup from Osco Drug and sat down with my faculty advisor. I told her I'd made up my mind what I wanted to do with my life. I wanted to treat mental illness. I wanted to use the tools of science to heal the mind.

And my life would have proceeded on that chosen course until this very minute had not the universe, that Great Trickster, that mad Coyote, chosen to send me a daughter who was enchanted with all things spiritual. All of my conflict with Emmy, every bit of it, was a fight with myself. A fight to forget. To forget Scott Perdue. To forget Aunt Bella. To forget the absurd fiction that I had brought about their deaths.

Or worse, the deeper knowledge that I really *had*.

That I possessed such power.

. . .

No more 3D theater. Enough!

I'm out in the open desert, walking as briskly as flip-flops will allow. The dancing of the plants and the drumming of the Earth has settled into a gentle background rhythm. I'm scanning the horizon as I walk, looking for a sign as to where the San Pedro spirits will take me next.

Anything but that cave. That dark fucking dismal cave with its awful images.

Guide me, plant medicine. To new heights.

Guide me it does. On the highest of the surrounding hills, a band of bright energy, in the shape of an upside-down V, hovers above the ground, twinkling. Emmy used to wear a pendant with that same symbol on it. I never bothered to ask what it meant.

That is where I must go, of course, to that hilltop. From that lofty location, I will receive greater vision, literally and figuratively. I'm certain of it.

Standing at the base of the small mountain, looking up, I recall the difficulty of my previous climb. I glance down at my mint-green flip-flops, and a wild idea occurs. Can I use my current "mental plasticity" to my advantage? Conjure myself some better footgear?

Concentrating on my feet, I picture them clad in my cherished Adidas Terrex hikers. Like magic, the black canvas-topped shoes appear on my feet.

But then they morph into red clown shoes, honk at me, and walk away on their own.

*Imagining* isn't enough. I must *claim* my hikers with mental authority.

In my mind, I intone, *I am wearing Adidas Terrex hikers, I am wearing Adidas Terrex hikers, I am wearing Adidas Terrex hikers,* as if it were fact. I then repeat the words aloud, with feeling, adding, "They feel snug and solid on my feet."

Presto. The black shoes with the reflective diagonal stripes materialize on my feet, as real as the rocky dirt around them. I kneel and run my hand over them, feeling their fabric texture, smelling their new-shoe smell.

I climb the rocky hillside with a spring in my legs, crunching rocks beneath my Terrex-armored soles, feeling not a hint of a sharp edge. It's best not to think about what's *really* going on here; any trace of doubt may turn my shoes back to flip-flops—like that "bridge" that turned to empty space during my walk of faith.

The summit is an easy reach in my strong hiking shoes. The inverted V of sparkling light has vanished, but a stool-shaped rock sits beneath the spot where it hovered.

I plant myself on the rock and gaze out at the surrounding vista. The scale and luminescence of the landscape sends sparks up and down my back. Everything glows with inner light. I feel my vision expanding with the breadth of the land. It was smart to get out of that cave and that constricted little valley. I needed to see more, to open myself to bigger things.

Power rushes into me like water through a pipe, up from the Earth, up through my feet. Now *that's* what I'm talking about. Enough with the guilt and darkness.

*Open my eyes, San Pedro. Show me the way.*

"You are already walking the way," says a familiar voice. Sister Quilla. Her voice is only in my head, I know, but I turn and look for her anyway. She's not here. But her words linger in the air.

*Already walking the way?* What did she mean by that? I look down at my feet. The shoes. Yes, my shoe experience has something larger to teach me. Something vital.

But what?

*Stay with it, Oliver. Let it come.*

I stare at my Adidas hikers. They're so real in every detail, I have to remind myself I conjured them. When I recall the conjuring process, the shoes fade away, right before my eyes, and the mint green flip-flops return— beaten and dirty from the climb, sticky with blood from my battered, filthy feet, and missing chunks of their cheap plastic foam. My toes sing out in pain from multiple cuts and bruises.

I switch back to the Adidas-hikers "channel" (and that's exactly what it feels like: switching channels). The hiking shoes reappear on my feet, the pain vanishes. As I gaze down at my dusty hikers, a *memory* of acquiring them takes shape in my mind. Joanna handed them to me in the copter and said, "Put these bad boys on; they'll save your ass."

I switch back to "flip-flop" channel, and *the attendant memories switch too*. Now I remember video-Hark telling me the plastic sandals from Dollar Tree were to be my only footwear. I also remember the punishing climb my feet just endured in flip-flops.

My feet flicker between the two versions of reality. Hikers/flip-flops. Hikers/flip-flops. I realize it is *I* who is in charge of which version "locks in" permanently. And whichever version I choose will draw its own memory track to it, like a lightning rod drawing streams of electric current. And that memory track will cement itself in consciousness as fact. (*"That neural pathway will sheath itself in myelin,"* says the psychiatrist voice within me.)

I am being shown something vital about the way reality works. My heart races as I look out on the glowing vista and feel the sunlight pouring into my skin. The sunlight *is* knowledge, yes it is. I turn my palms upward, the better to receive the truth I feel is coming.

And boy howdy, does it come.

A "download" arrives, all at once, in my mind—a slate of connected understandings that steals my breath and floods my nerves with light. The knowledge doesn't come in a logical progression or a series of connected premises. It arrives full-blown. Omnidirectionally, not linearly. A total cognitive upgrade.

And it changes the way I see everything.

# Chapter 42

I can't emphasize enough: the mental download arrives as a gestalt, a whole, erasing my old knowledge like a computer file writing over an old one. But the only way I can begin to explain it—and *begin* is all I *can* do—is in chunks.

My talk with Anvita surely tilled the soil for this, as did my self-healing experience and the reliving of my spontaneous "awakening" at age twenty.

I see now that consciousness *is* reality. Period. When Anvita asked me if I had ever experienced anything outside of consciousness, I thought she was playing word games. But now I get that it's true—there is literally nothing *but* consciousness. Each of us is a witnessing node within a single, unified field of awareness that can look back upon itself. There are no external "things"; there are only waves in consciousness. It is our minds that convert these waves into a virtual world, a hologram, that we call real. Consciousness is not a product of the brain; the brain is a structure created and employed by consciousness. Like everything else is.

This glorious desert scene laid out before my eyes is *in me*, not out there.

Everything is wavy gravy—quantum clay—until we "freeze" it through the act of observing. Rocks, mountains, canyons—these are all acts of consciousness-freezing, not objects with independent existence. We make matter with our minds.

But we each do it uniquely. Our thoughts have frequencies, and we "light up" those bands of the quantum clay that vibrate to the frequency *we* emit. The world reflects back to us, like a giant 3D Rorschach test, *who we are* as the seer. When we hold a vibrational frequency—a thought, a feeling, a *belief*—we cause other vibrations in the field to resonate with it and track to it, like those memory tracks bending to whichever footwear I choose. The universe bends to us.

(*The target draws the arrow, Emmy used to say.*)

Thus we sculpt the future by the thoughts we hold. The beliefs.

But, of course, there *is* no future, because time is an illusion. Everything that has ever existed and ever *will* exist is already "out there" in potential form, like that CD my twenty-year-old self envisioned—waiting to be "lit up" by our observation and choice. At any point, we can hold a new thought, a new belief, and light up *the entire new universe* that branches off from that thought. That's how multiple universes work!

We are pure god-stuff, each of us.

I collapse in laughter as the immensity of this realization surges through me like electrically charged blood. I have always seen the task of modern man as one of coming to grips with our cosmic insignificance, our fall from the throne at the center of creation we thought we occupied until Copernicus and his pals came along to dethrone us.

Now I see we've been deluding ourselves indeed, but in the opposite direction. We *are* the center—of all creation—in a more intimate way than we ever imagined in our wildest geocentric dreams. We are the literal makers and keepers of reality.

Other insights crash in. From all sides. There is no time—or space— other than the eternal *now*. The past and future have no reality. Therefore, death is an illusion. Therefore, all fear is...

I can't hold any more. The rush of insights fuses with the luminous landscape around me, creating a dizzying, nuclear-powered mental explosion. Spiritual vertigo. I am having a peak experience in every sense of the term.

But then the words of Sister Quilla's note rush back to me, "... you Western healers get it wrong. You think insight is enough to change a human life."

Not *exactly* a cosmic buzz-kill, but a grounding reminder: Insight must be turned into action or else it dissipates. I don't want these insights to dissipate.

What can I do to cement them? What action can I take? There's no way I can act on *all* of this knowledge. It's too vast. So what specific angle will bear fruit?

I meditate for a minute—or an hour—and arrive at this. If *all* potential events already exist, and the past and future are an illusion, then theoretically it should be possible to alter the "past" by "lighting up" a different track, a different event-timeline, in the quantum clay.

But how?

The Imax theater of the mind, that's how.

Thus far, I have used my magic cave only as a passive device—to relive scenes from my past as 3D memories. Is there a way to use it more proactively? Can I, for example, go back to a chosen moment in the past and make a different choice than I originally made? See what new universe branches off from that choice?

Intuitively, I sense I can. Excitement courses through me. I know what I want to try. And it has to do with Emmy. All roads lead to Emmy, right?

I start down the hill toward the cave.

.   .   .

I'm halfway down the rocky slope when a shadow moves across me. How? There isn't a cloud in the sky. I look up to see a figure, blacker than blackness, standing atop one of the other hills that encircle my private valley. It has a hyena/human shape, and it looks like a hole in reality.

Fuck. So I didn't *defeat* the demon when I drove it out of my mind. I set it free, gave it independent existence. And now it is stalking me. The sculpture is stalking the sculptor. And it's twice the size it was when it scrambled out of the cave.

I know my mind is creating the beast; it always has. But—as insight has now shown me—my mind is creating the rocks and the valley as well. None of this stuff has independent existence. The demon is no more or less real than anything else I'm perceiving.

That should be a comforting thought, but somehow it isn't.

I run a few yards down the hill, and the demon makes a corresponding move down *its* hill, cutting off my escape route. It laughs at me in its mocking way.

A feeling of cosmic betrayal wells up in me. Why is it that every time I tap into my essential nature, my intrinsic powers, this monstrosity appears in my life, as if to say, "Don't be so full of yourself. You're nothing. You're a pus-boil, a plague." Self-pity stabs me like a crown of thorns. Why me, God? Why is it that others can have spiritual experiences that are rapturous and light-filled, but mine always devolve into terror and soul-nausea?

No! I refuse to give in to that kind of thinking. It will only pull me into a hole I may never climb out of. I must hold my center, my power.

I take Sister Quilla's note from my pocket and read: "when you have lost a part of your soul, as you have, you must go back and retrieve it. You must *battle* the entities that have taken possession of it and wrestle it from them."

I did lose pieces of my soul. Back in childhood, and again in my college years. When I let the demon win. And I need to get those pieces back. Reclaim them.

My mission becomes clear. *I must defeat this demon, once and for all.* That is why I am here in this valley. That is why I am on this San Pedro journey. I must defeat the thing, head on, before I leave the desert. And before it grows too huge to beat.

I'm not ready for that battle yet, but I must *get* ready. And right soon.

I'm going to need all the help I can get.

Looking up at the demon standing on the hill, I beam my defiance at it. It quivers with laughter, but it also slinks backwards, ducking behind the peak of the hill.

It has some fear of me too.

*You and me, asshole. Soon.*

Fuck.

I continue toward the cave. I've been knocked off my spiritual high with a nine-pound hammer, but I'm still committed to my plan: try to use the mind-theater in a controlled way.

Here's my idea. I will try to return to a past moment with Emmy—one of those all-too-frequent occasions where I ruined our encounter with my arrogance. If I can conjure up such a scene in the 3D memory theater, I will try to make a different choice than the one I made the first time around— light up a new universe from the quantum clay, ha.

I think it can work, as long as I keep my meta-awareness in the driver's seat and don't get too swept up in the momentum of past reality.

*Of course* it can work, I remind myself; this is *my* mind-trip. *My* reality.

I sit in the middle of the faintly daylit "theater" at the rear of the cave, fold my legs beneath me, and invoke the San Pedro. "Plant spirits, help me live the past in a new way."

A wisp of fresh air with a slight sandalwood scent—Emmy's incense— blows across my face. A cosmic green light?

The scene I have selected for my experiment is the one I recalled only a day or two ago—the one where I mocked Emmy for inviting me on a San Pedro cactus retreat and then proceeded to blast a canyon between us by getting incensed about her new tattoo. The memory is painfully fresh, and its San Pedro theme seems too significant to ignore.

I need a focal point, a mental vehicle, to transport my memory back to the scene. I close my eyes and picture the pan I was scrubbing in the sink at the time. That ribbed, bluish-gray broiling pan with the rows of holes in it. I scrub it in my mind, back and forth, back and forth.

*Success! I am in the kitchen, scrubbing the pan. Emmy stands beside me, loading the dishwasher. "So," she says with a twinkle of challenge in her eye, "Have you given any thought to that invitation I sent you?"*

*"You were serious about that?" memory-me replies. "Come on, Ems. Why would I spend fifty-five hundred dollars to fly us to Ecuador for five days of destroying our brain cells with substances science hasn't even begun to figure out?"*

*"I don't know," she says, reaching into the dishwasher. "Maybe to spend time with this inconvenient stranger who seems to think she's your daughter. Maybe to actually—"*

Stop. I've let the scene run too long already. Man, it's harder than I thought to stop the momentum of the past. Meta-me needs to climb into the scene sooner; activate my present intentions before my old, reactive, asshole self has a chance to drive the train.

Press restart.

I picture myself scrubbing the pan. The 3D memory begins again.

*"So,"* says Emmy, *"Have you given any thought to that invitation I sent you?"*

I have to fight through a magnetic "force field" of resistance to wrest control of the scene from past-me. But I am focused and determined this time.

I do it. Somehow. I wedge my way in. As present-day me.

Instead of firing back at Em with "You were serious about that?" I say to her:

*"Actually, I have given it some thought. Can we talk about it?"*

*She pauses in her dish-racking. "Talk? What do you mean, talk?" Suspiciousness flashes in her eyes.*

*"I mean have a conversation."*

*"As in... one of those things where two people exchange ideas in an equal and respectful manner? Where both of them actually* listen *to what the other party is saying?"*

*"I deserve that. Totally, Ems. But yeah, one of those things. A conversation."*

*She pauses with a dirty wineglass in her hand. "I'd like that, Dad. I'd like that a big bunch. Let's finish these dishes, and then we can—"*

*"The dishes can wait."*

*"The dishes can wait? Uh-oh. What trans-dimensional alien has taken control of this avatar that looks exactly like my father?"*

If she only knew.

*"I'll finish the dishes later,"* I tell her. *"Seriously. It's a beautiful evening. Let's go sit out on the patio and enjoy the stars and... each other's company."*

*"Okay, sim-father. Whatever you say. Shall I... grab us a couple of beers?"*

*"Absolutely. The good stuff, please."*

*As I watch my daughter walk to the fridge and grab a pair of Dogfish Head 90-Minute IPAs, I feel as if I'm flickering between two versions of myself, past-*

*me and present-me—almost the way my shoes flickered between flip-flops and hikers.*

My presence in the scene feels tentative, like it could slip away any second. I want with all my heart to stay in it, to ride the moment, but I want to ride it as present-me, not past-me with all his blind spots and knee-jerk sarcasm.

*Emmy steps outside, holding the screen door open for me, a crooked smile on her face.*

She has no idea of the immensity of the doorway she is opening for me.

*This is all in your mind*, an inner voice counters. *It doesn't mean anything.*

Bullshit. This *is* a "drug trip," yes, but my San Pedro journeying has been more real than anything I've ever experienced. The Emmy standing before me *is* the true Emily, the essential Emily, the Emily I know.

Oh God, the preciousness of this moment. Oh God, the preciousness of this opportunity. I am about to have a beer with my beloved Emmy. *Don't blow it, Oliver, don't blow it.*

# Chapter 43

*Emmy leads me out to the patio. She sets the two beers on the tile-topped table and stretches her arms to the night sky. It's a comfortably warm evening—i.e., downright arctic for summertime in the Valley of the Sun—with a nearly full moon. My mind is in overdrive. I want to milk this impossible opportunity to full advantage.*

*The main thing I long to know with every atom of my being, of course, is why she decided to end her life. But in this timeline, that event is still more than two months away. So what should I ask her? How should I steer the conversation?*

*How about not at all? It occurs to me that "steering the conversation" has always been my quicksand with Emmy. Cramming my agenda down her throat. Maybe I won't do that this time. Radical proposition, granted.*

*We sit at the table. I raise my Dogfish Head IPA, and we clink bottle-necks. She still has that faintly suspicious, what's-going-on-here lift to her brow.*

*Resisting the urge to infuse the air with the dulcet tones of my giant blowhole, I lean back and gaze at the stars—what few you can still see these days—letting the silence work its magic, giving her the chance to fill it, if she so desires.*

*"So..." she says after a verse or two from the night's cricket chorus, "shall we start with the elephant in the room?"*

*Which elephant does she mean? There have always been so many elephants.*

*She fans her hand toward her new tattoo—the sprawling rendition of the green, red, and yellow bird that now covers half her neck. "You've been staring at it all evening. Let's get the lecture out of the way first."*

*I'd actually forgotten about her new tatt. It isn't important to me anymore.*

*"Nice work," I say. "Dramatic, but restrained. Could have gone full Sedona crystal shop with the color scheme, but held back." Why the sarcasm, even now?*

*"Come on, Dad, say it. Tell me how it's an act of career suicide, how I'll never be able to set foot in a corporate boardroom, how I'm dooming myself to a life of making skinny soy lattes for people more successful than me. Come on, say it, you know you want to."*

*Now who's got an agenda?*

*"Actually, Ems," I say, admiring her ink. "I like it. It's rather stunning."*

*"I don't believe you, but thanks for saying so."*

*"Tell me about it. There must be a story."*

*She sips her beer, deliberating whether I've earned the intimacy. "Well... you know what kind of bird this is... or do you?"*

*"Lovebird, right? You have one on your keychain, your book bag..."*

*"The rosy-faced lovebird, to be specific."*

*"A type of parakeet, right?"*

*"Parrot, Dad. It lives in the wild, right here in the Valley."*

*"Wild parrots in Phoenix. I've heard about them. Never seen one. Pretty sure they're an urban myth."*

*"That's funny," she laughs. "I see them all the time. Literally. Once or twice a week. They show up at meaningful moments, whenever I need to see one."*

*"You do know there's a psychiatric term for that."*

*"Delusions of reference," she volleys back. At least she gets I'm joking.*

*I tilt my bottle, saluting her, and say, "Did you also know that in many indigenous cultures, birds are seen as emissaries between the spirit realm and the material plane?"*

*"I'm the one who told you that, Dad." She mock-salutes me back with her bottle. "The thing is, though, I actually believe it. Whenever I'm feeling lost or alienated, one of these little green guys shows up, as if to remind me of my connection to spirit."*

*She waits for my mocking commentary. I surprise her by offering none.*

She shifts forward, bringing me into her space. *"You've heard the story of the Arizona lovebirds, right? They're originally from, like, Namibia or somewhere, but they were brought here by pet breeders. A few decades ago, one of their aviaries got destroyed in a storm, and the birds got out and started breeding in the wild. Now they thrive here. Dig the poetics. They started off in the wild, then they lived in human captivity, and now they've returned to the wild. Happy and free."*

*"Sounds like you identify with them."*

*"Maybe I do."*

*"You've always felt a bit... imprisoned by this life, haven't you, Ems?"*

Her eyes meet mine in a testy way. *"Why do you say that?"*

*"Well, it's just that you're always..."* Don't say "always"; it sounds like an accusation. *"You have a... passion for seeking... 'exit ramps,' shall we say, from mainstream culture. Whether it's Buddhist chanting or shamanism or... substances or—"*

*"You've never understood that part of me, Dad. At all."*

*"I want to, Emmy. That's why I'm sitting here. I want to understand."*

*"You think I'm... a quitter, an escapist. That I can't handle reality. That I'm always looking for a way out that's easier and less painful."*

My silence is acquiescence.

*"But it's not like that. Okay, sometimes it is, but mostly it's... You're right that I've always felt—'imprisoned' is too strong a word—constricted by this life. But do you know why?"* She tilts her head, looks at me sideways, then straightens up again. *"Because we don't live truthfully in our culture. It's like we all just skate along on the surface of life, afraid to look at the deeper nature of things. We're like the walking dead. We've all been hypnotized into thinking and saying and striving for the same things. Wedding rings and babies and job titles. Is that really why we've been given the rather-fucking-astonishing gift of a human life? To replicate everyone else's life patterns?"*

*"I hear you."* I do. Maybe I didn't before, but I do now.

*"My motivation,"* she says, *"has always been about breaking the hypnosis, going to the heart of reality, not running away from it. It's the exact opposite of what you think."*

"I'm a stupid man, Sweetheart." I hold my arms open. "Make me smarter. Educate me."

"That's what I'm trying to do, thicko. That's why I invited you on that San Pedro cactus retreat—for, like, the third year in a row. But you still don't get it. In your mind, it's five days of recreational drug use, frolicking in the Ecuadorian rainforest. It's nothing like that. Nothing. It's about seeking truth in the most serious possible way. The San Pedro is a sacred plant, Dad; it has the power to help us see to the core of things."

I want so badly to shout, "I know! I'm on it right now!" But of course, I can't.

She goes on. "If you don't believe in plant spirits—which I know you don't—you can look at it strictly from a, whatever, a brain-chemistry perspective. These chemicals, mescaline and DMT, that show up in visionary plants have molecules that link up perfectly with receptors in the human brain, like a lock in a key. Don't you think that's more than a little strange? That something in a plant would be designed to interlock with something in a human brain to form a whole? And when that happens, our vision becomes whole too?"

"Sounds like the voice of first-hand experience."

"It is." She takes a long swig of beer. "You must know I've tried the stuff, Dad. Twice, in fact. And it's the best thing I ever did."

"So I get why you want to go to Ecuador," I say. "But why do you want me to come?" I almost say, "except to pay the bill." It's strange; I'm living the scene as the new me, but I can't stray too far from my old dick personality. It has its own weird momentum.

"I want you to experience it." She reaches out and touches my hand. "More than anything. I want you to do this so bad, Dad."

"It sounds important to you."

"It is. I mean... Can I just say...? You go around writing books and acting like an expert on spiritual experiences and the human brain, but—I'm sorry—you don't know what you're talking about. The San Pedro will change that. It will show you direct truth, it will rewire your belief system." She studies my face, sees something there she still doesn't fully trust. "But of course, Oliver Powers, MD, doesn't really want that."

"Why do you say that?"

"Oh, come on, Dad."

"What? Are you saying it would be bad for my brand if I were to expand my beliefs?"

"Wouldn't it? I mean, I would have preferred to say it in my own words, but—"

"Then do, Em. Say it in your own words. Please. Whatever's on your mind. Say it. I'll shut up. I promise."

"Dad..." She blows out a sigh. "We came out here to have a beer together and enjoy the evening." She leans back in her chair and opens her arms to the night sky. "Let's just do that. I don't want this to go the way it always goes."

"Emmy, I'm giving you a free shot at me, gloves down. I promise to listen and not react defensively."

"Let's just enjoy this excellent beer."

"Coward." I say, half joking, slumping back in my chair.

"Coward? Me?" She starts to lean back, then springs forward with almost vicious energy. "Okay, you asked for it. I've never met anyone more fearful than you. And it breaks my frigging heart. All I've ever wanted from you is your courage. But fear runs your life. Every choice you make, every word out of your mouth—fear, fear, and more fear."

I almost reply, "That's what I was afraid you'd say"—hardy-har-har—but blessedly, my mouth stays shut.

"That whole arrogance thing you do. The Dr. Experto bit. It's just you projecting your personal fears out into the world and then going to war with them. But the crazy thing—the part that kills me—is... that's not even the real you. If you knew the truth about who you really are, you would never be afraid again."

"What do you mean by—"

A violent force jerks me from the scene. It takes me a moment to realize my body is skidding and bumping through the dirt. Something has hold of my ankle. It's dragging me toward the mouth of the cave like an animal with its kill.

Adrenaline floods my system. I can't see what the thing is. It is filling the cave-tunnel like a piston filling a cylinder, blocking the light.

It drags me out onto the ledge, into the blinding daylight. It releases my ankle and leaps backward, a few feet away from me.

It is the thing, the beast, the demon. I have never seen it in the full light of day, only in half-formed glimpses.

It stands about six feet tall on its four legs—hyena-like in shape, but vaguely human too. Its "substance" is a churning mass of... inward-sucking *holes*. But it has a face. The face of my Aunt Bella. No, Scott Perdue. No, Mary Matheson.

No, it's the face of the exotic dancer I could have saved from being raped.

It's the face of a teenager who made me touch his erection in a railroad tunnel when I was eight or nine.

It's the face of the demon from the church window.

I try to focus on the shifting "holes" that make up the beast's fabric, but my eyes reject them, can't take them in, can't make logical sense of them.

They are puckering, blistering orifices.

They are railroad tunnels.

They are wormholes into non-Euclidean dimensions.

I can't look. I turn my body away. I know what this thing is, of course; I *am* a psychiatrist, after all. It is what it has always been: a projection of my inner fears. But it is standing before me now, in three-dimensional space. Demanding my engagement.

*It isn't real. It isn't real. It isn't real.*

But it is.

The thing rears up on two legs and lifts its "face" to the sky. It lets out a bellow that feels like it comes from deep within my spine, and then it beats its nonexistent chest like an inside-out mountain gorilla. It crouches again, looks me fully in the face—I can't make eye contact with it—and springs sideways off the ledge, landing on the ground below. It scuttles to the center of the small valley, then turns and faces up at me, waiting. The gauntlet has been tossed.

My time has come. My time to defeat this thing. This thing that has stolen pieces of my soul. I don't know how to do it. I don't even know what "defeating it" means. But I know my moment has arrived. The moment I cannot run from anymore. This must be what it feels like when death comes knocking at your door and you know you've run out of deferrals.

I step onto the path that leads down into the valley where the demon awaits. The instant my foot hits the dirt, the beast swells in size. It is feeding off my fear, as it always has. My fear is what gives it strength and substance.

By the time I reach it, it will have grown to the size of a city building.

Can I summon an energy stronger than fear to fight it with?

I take another step down the path. The beast swells.

Another step.

*Hate.*

Hatred is stronger than fear. And I hate this demon. Oh God, yes I do.

I step downward again. As my foot crunches the rocky dust, the descending path transforms into stone steps. My hiking shoes have been replaced by the flip-flops. No, not flip-flops. Roman sandals. Roman sandals walking down stone steps.

I focus on my feet, take another step.

My eyes sweep out over the land. The small valley has turned into a Roman coliseum: pillars, carved bleachers, huge blocks of sand-colored stone.

I'm a gladiator, descending into the arena for battle.

The awful beast bellows from a distance—a wet, hollow sound like a giant frog's, but voiced on the inhale.

Hatred is the energy I need to channel.

I *hate* this demon, this filthy fuck. For robbing my power. For depriving me of a childhood. For stealing my peace of mind. For poisoning my relationship with my daughter. For sucking the vitality out of my marriage to the finest woman on Earth.

Yes, hate feels stronger than fear.

I step onto the coliseum floor. The beast stands waiting for me fifty yards away. *Turn your hate into a weapon. Something you can fight with.*

If I'm going to play the Roman gladiator, I'd better not shy away from the heroic requirements of the job.

"Bring me a sword!" I cry to the heavens. "A sword of hate!"

No sooner do the words leave my throat than a small voice within me fires back, *Well, listen to you with your little Russell Crowe fantasies. Where's your faux-leather kilt?*

I know this voice. My inner critic—that snarky bully that resides in the back of my head, hurling insults. The superego's hit-man. It's been absent for most of my San Pedro journey. Suddenly it's back.

I look out at the coliseum floor, and the scene does that strange *flickering* thing—from coliseum to desert valley to coliseum again. Back and forth, back and forth. Two realities, switching channels. Both equally real. Both available for me to throw my belief behind. But the normal-reality channel seems to be gaining a stronger signal with each appearance.

Ah… I know what's happening here.

I'm coming down from the San Pedro.

# Chapter 44

Yes, that's what's happening. Each time the "normal" desert valley, with its scattering of juniper and creosote bushes, comes into focus, it looks denser, more nailed down, more filled in.

I'm coming down from the plant medicine, for sure.

The question is, do I want to? I have some rather urgent business to attend to here in San Pedro Land, don't I?

But the Arizona desert is calling me home. And I long to heed its call.

I look to the sky. The sun is past its zenith. *If I let the San Pedro wear off,* the growing voice of reason says, *I can spend the evening getting my head straight and preparing for tomorrow.* Rest, recover, and reevaluate.

Fight the demon tomorrow. When I've had more time to prepare.

Tomorrow.

With an effort, I flip the channel back to coliseum-world. The beast rears up and roars at me, its inward-pulling, death-wind voice threatening to flay my mind to ribbons. Yeah, no.

I allow the channel to switch back to Reality TV. The muted greens and khaki-tan colors of my barren but peaceful valley fill my vision. Easy choice. Reality wins. I'll come down from the journey for a while. Take a much-needed break. Muster my resources. Live to fight another day.

Agreed.

*Coward!* shouts a voice in my head. Emmy's. I see what I'm up to here. I'm actually trying to use *reality* as an escape mechanism. As a way to avoid facing the beast. If I allow that to happen, if I choose ordinary consciousness right now, I will be letting fear sneak in the back door to run my life yet again—putting off the showdown to yet another endless tomorrow.

Tomorrow is always better than today, right?

Fear always finds a way in Ollie World.

Can't allow that. Won't. This is my chance. My now-or-never moment. If I don't defeat this demon *right now*—not tomorrow, not someday—I never will. The demon will own me for life.

Fuck that. It ends here. It ends now. One way or the other.

I know what I need to do. Take *more* San Pedro. Fast. Before I come down completely.

I run back toward the path to the ledge before I can change my mind. With a concentrated act of will, I transform the sloping path into the stone steps of the hero's coliseum. My power to perform mental alchemy is fading fast, but I still possess it.

I dash up the steps to the ledge where the medicine awaits. I transmute the cheap plastic tub into a Roman urn. It changes back to plastic. I change it again.

My brain hurts.

*Come on, hurry. Do this.* I reach for the urn of medicine.

The psychiatrist in me stops my hand, making a final bid for control. He urges me to let my brain clear up. He tells me that consuming mind-altering substances is *never* an act of courage, that reality is *always* the braver choice.

*Thanks, Doc, but you're full of shit, and we both know it.* I dip the ladle into the urn and pour the bitter liquid down my throat.

I dip and drink again. And again.

Once more for good measure. Four ladlesful. I did three last time.

Fuck it, let's do five. I'm going in for the kill.

Ahh! I feel a resurgence of power. But that's probably just the H$_2$O kicking in. I've forgotten how dehydrated I am.

No, it's the power of the choice I just made.

Bring it on, Saint Pete, bring it on.

I stand on the ledge, hands on hips, facing out over the landscape. The desert valley looks wholly ordinary at the moment. It won't stay that way for long. With a tensing of my groin muscles, I *will* the coliseum to reappear.

Nothing happens.

The San Pedro takes time, I remind myself. *How* long when it's just a "recharge," not a cold start, I have no idea.

I descend the path. No stone steps this time. Only sloping dirt beneath my feet.

I march to the middle of the valley. When I reach the rough center, I spin around, 360 degrees. Everything looks natural, real, non-fucked-up. I don't see the demon anywhere. "Come out!" I yell, letting volume do the job of courage. "Show yourself!"

"Do you imagine *you* command the San Pedro?" says a voice to my left, startling me.

Sister Quilla sits on the ground, legs folded, three yards from me. She looks real in every way. Is she here? In flesh and blood? She must be; I don't seem to be visioning at the moment.

"Your arrogance has more layers than an oak," she chuckles. "Hear this: we humans do not command the plant spirits. *They* orchestrate the journey for *us*. And they always give us the journey we *need*, not the one we choose."

"I know what I need, Sister. I need to fight this battle. *Now*. I'm sure of it. I'm ready."

"Are you? Perhaps the kind of courage you are trying to summon is not the kind you need."

"What do you mean?"

Holes appear in place of her pupils, and for a second I can see out the back of her head.

"Perhaps it's time to let the snake devour you," she says.

*What?* I have no idea what she's talking about. But my chance to ask for clarification evaporates. The air around me darkens and thins. The little valley morphs into something new. Not a coliseum, not this time.

An alien world has moved into place. Jesus.

The outlines of the hills are exactly as they were, but now the vegetation—if that's what you call it—looks lumpy, pale, tumorous. The atmosphere takes on a cold ionic charge. A massive moon dominates the sky, but it is copperish in color and marked by deep gashes.

Something seems vaguely familiar about this world—as if I once lived a life here eons ago—and yet utterly outré. I am in a region of space inconceivably remote from Earth. And I am alone here in every way.

A train-sized shape, blacker than blackness, swells up from behind one of the hills. It slithers to a neighboring peak and sinks below it as if melting.

It is my demon. But it has changed. It has taken on spatial dimensions even more mind-scrambling than before. And the rules of engagement are different somehow. I am in *its* world now; it is no longer in mine.

A flash of movement catches my eye, forty degrees to the right. The thing appears from behind another hill, then ducks from sight again.

It is stalking me, encircling me. For sport. It owns me here in this cold place.

I am in its lair. Undefended.

I did this to myself. By being a cowardly piece of shit. I had my opportunity to defeat the demon earlier, and I *hesitated*. Lost the moment. Just as I did in my walk of faith. Just as I have done so many times in my life. And now I am in a situation far worse. As always.

The massive beast slithers out of hiding again and moves along the crest of the hills. It has a snake-like form now, not that of a hyena. It hides again, toying with me.

Sister Quilla's words come back to me: *let the snake devour you.* I recall that in shamanic lore, being devoured by the snake is an honor and a spiritual milestone. It signifies surrender to total transformation.

Now I get what Sister Quilla was telling me: I don't need the courage to *fight* this thing, I need the courage to *be devoured* by it. To let go of the familiar and embrace the cold vacuum of the unknown. To become something new, something *other*.

A chill moves through me, head to foot.

The idea of being devoured by a beast so soulless, in a place so alien, is infinitely more terrifying than doing battle with it.

But is that what I'm being called to do?

I wish I had some guidance. I didn't much care for those holes I saw in "Sister Quilla's" eyes. But perhaps that was her real message: *don't trust me, don't trust anyone.*

Trust only yourself. Trust only what your heart and gut are telling you.

The snake-demon—so impossibly *sunken* and lightless—plunges down a hill toward me. No more fucking around. It wants to feed. Now.

What *is* my heart and gut telling me to do? I receive no guidance whatsoever. Total flatline.

The beast is coming, like a freight train, that's all I know.

Let it eat me? Is that my play? Surrender to the unknown?

At some point, that's what we all must do, right? That's what death is. That's what transformation is. Letting go. Giving up the clinging. Dissolving into the chrysalis.

God, I'm so fucking scared.

But surrender *must be* the answer.

Anvita appears before me. She bows as if to affirm my conclusion. Then she transforms into Kali the Destroyer—grinning and wagging her tongue.

NO! A force rises up within me. My body rebels. Fuck this. I flee, in full retreat, toward the hill I came from. Toward the cave, if it even exists in this version of reality.

Toward the one place I *can* get guidance.

I race up the path to the ledge, never checking behind me, and—yes, there it is—the cave entrance. It still exists in this alien dimension!

I run to the chamber at the rear of the cave, ducking as I go. The rounded theater-room now glows with luminous alien petroglyphs, telling stories that blaspheme human sanity. I drop to the ground. I must get back to Emmy, find out what she was about to say to me before the demon ripped me away from her.

I know only one sure way to find her: re-enter the dishwashing scene. And finish it this time.

Speed is critical. The beast may come for me any second.

*Focus.* I lock my mind on that bluish-gray broiling pan in the sink. The scrubbing motion will again serve as my shamanic drum, my entry vehicle. *Scrub, Oliver, scrub.*

*Yes! I'm back in the kitchen with Emmy, scrubbing the pan. This time I will use my meta-awareness in a more muscular way. I will drive the scene. I won't allow myself to be ripped away.*

*Reciting the same lines I spoke to her last time, I force our dialog to replicate itself almost perfectly. Emmy fetches the beers; we sit at the patio table; we talk about her lovebird tattoo; we talk about my fears.*

*"If you knew the truth about who you really are," she says, as before, "you would never be afraid again."*

*This is the point where the demon yanked me away last time. I need to drive the scene further. "What do you mean, Emmy?" I say, rooting myself to the floor. "What truth?"*

*"That you're a—" She stops herself, thinks for a moment. "Do you remember my favorite movie as a kid?"*

*"The Santa Clause." Easy answer. She'd watch that stupid film as many times as we'd let her. She literally wore out the VHS version. I don't have time for nostalgia now, though.*

*"Do you remember what the movie was about?" she asks.*

*"Santa falls off a roof, new guy gets the job," I speed-reply.*

*"That's not what it was about to me. I saw it from Charlie's point of view. The kid. For me it was a story about watching your dad—your hero—deny his true nature and then finally accept and embrace it. ... Ever since I showed up on this planet, Dad, I've seen the true you. I just see it. And I see you not seeing it, and that is so damn frustrating. I think my whole reason for coming here, to this planet, to this lifetime, was to help you discover who you are. And so far, I've been doing a shit-tacular job."*

*"That's not why you were born, Ems. Jesus. You came here to discover you, not me. You've always shone brighter than me. Way brighter."*

*"Not true, Dad. The fact is... Are you ready to hear some really weird stuff?" I nod frantically.*

*"The fact is," she repeats, "I've only ever been in this life with one foot. The other foot has always been stuck in... the place we all come from. The place we never fully leave. The place where the actors go when they're not playing parts in the drama."*

*"The bardo?" The Tibetan concept of a realm between lives? Is that what she means?*

*She shrugs; close enough. "That's why I've always seemed... ill-suited to this life. But having one foot in each world lets me see things others can't. And I can tell you this. There are special souls who come to this plane—'next level' souls—that have the ability to move humanity to a new place. Jesus Christ was one. Buddha, Krishna. Amma—she's alive today; I've met her. Others. These beings are rare, but not as rare as we think. You're one of them, Dad."*

"For fucksake, Emmy, stop!"

"I'm not joking. Not even a little."

"I'm sorry, Sweetie, I refuse to accept that I'm some kind of—"

She cuts me off. "You see that? What you're doing now? That's your **real** arrogance, Dad. Always has been. What makes **you** think **you** get to set limits on your power? What makes you think your pathetic little ego has the right to put a ceiling on what you can become?"

Well, when you put it that way...

"You need to get out there, Dad." Now I feel she's talking directly to present-me, not past-me. "And you need to BE what you came here to be. You need to—"

Damn! It happens again. The demon yanks me from the scene. A tendril of icy blackness has wrapped itself around my shoulder. It pulls me backwards, dragging me toward the cave mouth. I still didn't get to say to Emmy what I wanted to say the most.

"I love you!" I shout toward the cave chamber, hoping the curtain hasn't closed on our father-daughter moment yet, but almost sure it has. "I love you, Em!"

My voice echoes lifelessly in the empty cave.

# Chapter 45

The tendril around my shoulder burns with the coldness of empty space. The entity drags me out the cave entrance and across the ledge. I am back in the Southwestern desert, not an alien world. A familiar sun lights the sky.

The beast drags me to the bottom of the path and along the desert floor for twenty yards, then releases me and scrambles across the terrain. It plants itself in the middle of the valley, wriggling and burbling and flashing in and out of existence. Here we go again. The battle resumes. The alien-world thing was just a test.

I guess I passed.

But why? Only to be devoured by the beast in a different setting?

No, there must be a way for me to triumph. Or else why are we doing this? Why would the plant medicine deliver this experience to me?

The beast, fifty yards away, stands as tall and wide as a four-story house. It no longer appears snake-like or hyena-like. It has become a shifting, writhing hole in reality's fabric, with no specific outline. It is no longer personal in any way. I can't mount any hatred toward it; it has robbed me of that power. It is a void, a gap in my world like a missing jigsaw-puzzle piece—consuming light like a black hole.

I take a few steps closer to the thing, keeping my gait steady and firm.

My mind reaches for what Emmy told me. Me, a "great soul"? A being of destiny? It's a laughable notion. But what if it were true?

I knew it as a kid, didn't I? I knew I was different from other kids. I knew I had powers no one else seemed to possess. Before I talked myself out of them.

*But every kid thinks that,* my inner critic shoots back. *Hell, every* adult *thinks it.* We all harbor fantasies that we're special. We all secretly think we're Superman, Wonder Woman, Black Panther. Or Christ or the Buddha. Or at least...

Stop. Stop the avalanche of doubt.

*There are only two possibilities. Either it's true—I am a mighty soul—or it isn't. If it isn't true, I'm screwed anyway. If it is, I must accept it in the deepest core of my being. I must be a believer. A* knower.

Am I capable of that? Have I ever once in my life held a *knowing* with absolute conviction and single-mindedness? Have I ever had the "faith of a mustard seed" for even a minute? Have I ever moved mountains?

Once, perhaps. When I healed my face in the car. *Do that again, then.*

I stand directly in front of the gaping entity and turn my full gaze upon it. God, it's awful. My eyes want to dance around it, avoid even *landing* on it. How am I to face down something I can't even look at? My head spins away.

I force myself to turn toward it again, to stare into the trans-dimensional chasm *(the void, the abyss, the pits of hell...).* The void is not empty, I see. Motion swirls within its blackness. Amorphous, wriggling shapes rush toward me and away from me simultaneously. They are repellent to my eye, sickening to my gut. I force myself to focus on one of these tumbling shapes—a brownish-gray blob with the vague contours of a twisted rag. A dizzying feeling opens up within my bowels.

*I'm in the railroad tunnel. The teenager exposing himself stands before me. I can feel two other teens flanking me from behind. The one in front of me says, "Now take it in your mouth, kid, or I'll put it in your bum. Do you want it in your bum?" My memory-legs fire like the hammer of a gun, and I'm off, running.*

Pulling in a breath, I focus on another shape in the void; long, pale, and tubeworm-like. I feel an iciness in my chest and shoulders. The cold shape slithers down into my groin.

*My great aunt Bella sits in her worn old armchair, beckoning me to approach her, twirling her crucifix, smacking her sticky lips, staring at me in a way no loving grownup should ever stare at a kid.*

God! I know what these shapes are. They are things never meant to be seen with the eye. They are fears internalized and held within the body. As a psychiatrist, I've often encouraged my patients to *feel the shape and color* of their fears—physically—and try to describe these feelings to me.

That's what these things are, these masses flying past me and around me, these clumps of purple, black, indigo, and gray—mostly amorphous, but some hard-edged and angular. Each one activates a feeling held deep within me, a pocket of pain or shame locked away in my body, marrow-deep. As the shapes bombard me, I hurt everywhere, as if my body is nothing but a storehouse of all the fear and pain I have ever felt.

I must *face* this churning chaos, face it like a warrior, but how can I when each tumbling shape opens up a new vein of fear I've packed away so tightly it's become part of my *biology*?

I think about the patients I've worked with over the years. How I encouraged them to find the buried pain or fear within themselves and to give it a shape and color and texture in their mind. And once they identified a feeling in this visceral way, to *be* with it, *sit* with it, *have* it, look it in the eye. Until it lost its power.

It was a good technique. People had breakthroughs. People were able to move on from massive traumas and avoidances. "You can't let pain *go* until you let it *in*" was my creed.

Can *I* embrace the pain of these squirming shapes swirling around me?

No, don't ask me to do that. Each one opens up an emotional abscess, a cyst of frozen suffering. Each one wants to bring me to my knees.

They are too many, they are too much.

Too much pain at once. I'm not big enough. No one is big enough to hold such pain.

No sooner do I register this thought than the void *multiplies*. Tenfold. I stagger backward to absorb its new dimensions. The chasm is now the size of a mountain. The forms and shapes barreling toward me and away from me are no longer just my own. They belong to every patient I ever treated. They awaken memories *that aren't even mine*. That corrugated, dark-ochre mass—that's Tom Clark being shaken as a baby. That bile-green, urchin-shaped thing—that's eight-year-old Mary Matheson watching the silhouette of a man creep into her bedroom at night.

I can't face this. It's too much.

Yes, I can. I must.

I *am* powerful. I *am* rooted. I *can* do this.

As if to say, "Oh, really?" the void swells and multiplies again. It takes over my *entire visual field*. I have to look straight above my head to see any remaining blue sky.

I try to step back from the swirling chaos, but it pulls me in, calling me to *feel* each flying shape and activate its story within me. Each one stabs, each one burns.

The pain is a thousand times more than I can hold. A million times.

The void is growing, blackening the sky, eating the earth, and I am powerless to stop it. The shapes now hold the fear and pain of more than just my patients; I am bearing witness, literally, to the suffering of all humanity. In its primal language. Every shape is a rape, a cigarette burn in the flesh, a vile humiliation. It's all pulling me in with more force than I can resist.

Now I can't take my eyes away. *But facing it isn't helping*. Facing it is making it worse, strengthening it.

I look up. The void is gobbling the last of the sky. The blue part is shrinking, shrinking.

I am losing the battle. Soon the whole sky and earth will be swallowed up, and there'll be nothing left but chaos and pain. I don't know what I'm being called to do!

I need Em again. One last time. She will know what to do.

I can't run back to the cave-theater. Don't have time, can't remember the way. Forget it—the cave is a crutch anyway! I must summon Emily from where I stand.

I conjure up the absurd blue-gray broiling pan again, using the scrubbing motion to power my way back into the kitchen scene.

*I appear at the sink, washing dishes with Emmy again. I don't have time to slog through our familiar lines. I need to get down to business NOW. I know I might traumatize her with what I'm about to say, but it's a chance I must take.*

*"So," she turns to me, "have you given any thought to—"*

*"Em!" I cut her off. "Sorry, but this is urgent and it's the craziest-sounding thing I've ever said." I try to show her with my eyes that I'm not kidding one tiny bit.*

*"You're freaking me out, Dad." She sets her glass on the counter, her hand shaking.*

*"Strap yourself in, Sweetheart, because it gets worse. There's no way to say this that sounds the least bit sane, but it's true, and you need to believe me."*

*Her eyes widen. "I'm listening." She is, I can tell.*

*"I've just stepped into this moment from a future time, Em, and I'm in the middle of a San Pedro journey, and it's the most intense thing I've ever experienced."*

*She has dabbled in plant medicine, so there's a chance she'll understand.*

*"Okay," she says, after only a brief hesitation, "I believe you." She takes my hand, presses it to her heart, and looks at me with the whole of herself.*

*God bless this human being I never deserved to sire.*

*"I've visited you a couple of times in this journey already," I say to her, "and you've told me you have... well, pretty high expectations of me and my life."*

*"I do."*

"I'm trying to live up to them, Sweetie, but I'm in the middle of a battle with something awful and the stakes couldn't be higher and I'm losing and I don't know what the hell to do."

"Okay, shhh, Dad. If we're going to do this, we need to do it all the way. Look at me." She holds my hands and rivets me with her gaze. A change comes over her. Her eyes become windows to a dimension of light and energy so primal it must be the place where universes are born. "You and I are playing roles here, in this life—father and daughter—but they're just roles. We've known each other much longer than this. Much longer. And our connection is much deeper. I don't have time to explain—you don't have time for me to explain—but listen. I know the battle you're fighting, and I know what you need to do. Are you listening?"

I nod furiously.

"Facing your fears—the fear and suffering of the world—is not helpful. That's a human myth. Facing fear just pulls you into its domain. What you need to do is go out there and be at a higher frequency than the fear is. I know you understand this."

I do. My download on the mountaintop taught me how things work. All is vibration. The inner creates the "outer." As within, so without.

"The frequency you need to find and hold—some call it Buddhahood, some call it Christ consciousness, Samadhi; it doesn't have a name. You need to become it."

"How?"

"I'll show you. But first there's a barrier in your way: you don't believe you have the worth or authority. You hate yourself too much. That needs to stop, right here, right now. So listen to me. You never killed anyone with your thoughts. Not your aunt, not Scott Perdue. Get over that. Now. You never ruined any of your patients' lives. You've actually helped a lot of people, despite your limitations. The healing work you've done is real. It's rippling out into the world this very minute. But you can't see it. All you can see is your failures, and they consume you. You need to hear this, and you need to trust me: you're a good man, Oliver."

*Wham. The words punch me in the solar plexus. Why? Why do tears rush to my eyes?*

*She takes my hands again and looks at me, this being that is no longer* just *Emmy but something much more. "You're a good man. Can you take that in?"*

*I nod, unsure.*

*"Then do it. Right now. Take it in. Fully and without reserve."*

*I let the idea sink in and fill me up. A sob rocks my chest. I feel like I'm going to shatter.*

*"Can you feel the worth you possess?" she asks.*

*"Yes."*

*"Then say it."*

*"I am worthy."*

*"Say it again. But mean it. Be it. In every part of yourself."*

*"I am worthy. I have goodness in me. I have goodness in me."*

*"Say it in the fullness of your soul. No fucking around!"*

*"I am good. I am good. I am good. I am good."*

*This time the words shake something loose in my bedrock. I feel something hard and dark cracking up and coming apart inside me. Shapes and forms—exactly like those in the demonic void—lift and swirl out of me, rising in a whirlwind and exiting at the top of my head. Light streams into me from below and fills me up, warming and vibrating every neuron.*

*"Now, take this gift I give you," the more-than-Emmy being says.*

*She closes her eyes and* becomes *a frequency—a set of frequencies—that is higher, more golden, more purifying than anything I've ever felt—by a hundredfold. It is love, yes, but only in the sense that the center of the sun is "warmth." I attune to her chord, like a guitar tuning up to notes it's never reached before. I'm a cheap old plastic K-Mart guitar, not a Gibson Les Paul, but I can hold Emmy's chord, damn it, if only imperfectly.*

*"Now go out there and be* that. *Be the blue sky. Don't look at the void that's eating the world around you, not even once; just hold this chord until your sky is all blue again and the cactus flowers and the birds return, brighter than ever."*

*"How will I know it's over if I'm not allowed to look?"*

*"You'll know."*

*The kitchen scene is shaking, wiggling, breaking up. I'm being pulled back to the desert. Only seconds remain until I'm whisked away.*

*"Before I go," I say, "can I talk to Emmy again, real quick? Just Emmy?"*

*"What is it, Dad?" Emmy has become my daughter again, only my daughter. She grasps my hand.*

*I want to tell her for the love of God don't kill yourself, but I can't find a way to frame it in the precious seconds remaining. "Whatever happens," I say to her instead, "I want you to know: you're my hero. You always will be. Don't ever forget that. You're my hero. I love you so fucking much, Em."*

*"I love you too, Dad. Go! Go! Go!"*

The kitchen breaks apart, and I'm back in the desert. The churning chaos has devoured everything but a patch of earth and a small circle of blue sky overhead.

I lock my eyes on that blot of blue sky and vibrate like I've never vibrated.

# Chapter 46

The black void with the tumbling shapes consumes the sky from all directions, but I pour my focus into that final, shrinking circle of blue. Vibrating the sacred chord and holding on to the blue is the most single-minded act of cognition I've ever performed. I may be as high as a lunar probe right now, but this is the realest moment of my life, bar none.

What I'm doing is so much more than concentrating on a patch of sky. I am seizing the authority to be a reality-maker. I am claiming the right to hold the center of my own existence. I am laying the foundation for a life in which I play the role of playwright, set designer, director, lead actor, and audience member, all at once.

I am doing the work of a lifetime in a single eternal moment.

The blue is the vibration, the vibration is the blue. Time and space spread out in all directions, becoming nothing but a dimensionless, all-conscious plane.

And then it happens. Doubt—duality—snakes its thieving hand in. The thought flashes in my mind, *I wonder how the battle is going.* My pure focus falters for just an instant. My eyes flick to the left to check the status of the demon-void.

Bad call.

The material world has begun to reassert its existence. But the demon is back.

And it is sentient again. Personal. It stands on the peak of a hill, glaring down at me with its bile-yellow eyes.

What happens next goes down in a fraction of a second.

A screech rips from the demon's throat, pulsating every molecule of air in the valley.

A glistening-wet tentacle—or is it a long neck with a head on it?—bursts from its belly and shoots toward me with the speed of a frog's tongue snatching a fly.

On the face-end of the tentacle is a mouth with slavering rows of shark teeth. The mouth opens impossibly wide and buries itself, sideways, in my thigh.

Pain explodes in my leg.

I scream. The sound reverberates around the valley.

The head—tentacle-end, whatever—locks its teeth in my flesh and gawps up at me with the rheumy, half-dead eye of a squid. The eye invites me to plumb its lightless depths. I want to fall into it and tumble back to the world of shame and shadow where I have lived my entire life.

But I don't. I shout, "Fuck you!" and smash my fist down on the head-like growth. Its teeth break apart and its screeching head retracts as if spring-loaded.

I shift my full attention back to the blue sky. I become one with it again. Time diffuses. I close my eyes. I no longer need eyesight to see. I vibrate the chord the Emmy-being gave me, and I make that chord my whole existence.

I am love.

I am.

Am.

. . .

My eyes open to a landscape bursting with color and birdsong. I'm back in my familiar desert valley, but the greens are more verdant, the earth-tones more radiant than before. The air crackles with light. Flowers of fluorescent pink, white, and red dot the cacti. Purple and yellow blossoms anoint the ground—the colors of Easter.

I am alive, awake, aware as never before. No trace of hallucinogen seems to remain. I am simply *in* the world in a fuller way than I ever thought possible.

I hear a *squeep* in my ear and feel the poke of tiny talons in my skin. A bird is perched on my shoulder. I can't see what it is. It flutters off and lands on a cactus a few yards away.

A parrot. Green, peach-orange, red, yellow, and blue.

A rosy-faced lovebird. Of course.

We make eye contact for a second or two, the bird and I. A knowing presence gleams from its eyes. My face stretches into a mad smile, and my heart inflates to fill my chest.

The lovebird flies off. It alights on the tall stalk of a mezcal plant fifty feet away. It waits for me to approach it.

I do. Tenderly, carefully.

The bird flies off and lands on the branch of a young mesquite tree, waits for me again.

I approach the bird, it flutters away again. I catch up to it. It flies once more.

The bird flits from landing spot to landing spot, across the floor of the green-quenched valley. At first I have to trot to keep up with it, then jog, and then I break into a full, joyous run.

The lovebird stays just ahead of me, dipping and weaving in the air, as my bare feet slap the ground. I look down to see I'm running in a wash now, its fine sand damp and packed as if from a recent rain. The brilliant-colored bird flies on.

The wash turns into a dirt road beneath my feet, bumpy and pebbly.

I run along the road, chasing the bird, and then suddenly I'm not running anymore. I'm driving.

In my car.

On the Apache Trail.

I'm on that pre-Thanksgiving drive—when I abandoned my Whole Foods quest for a quest of a different sort. I'm following the lovebird—*yes that's what I was doing in my car on that fateful November day*—astonished that it continues to lead me onward, farther and farther along the Apache Trail.

I'm back in the scene completely now. Driving my Land Rover. As with those 3D memories in the cave, all the thoughts and sensations of the original moment are active, but I also carry the second awareness of now-me.

My heart hovers in my throat as I navigate the meandering twists of the shockingly gorgeous mountain road with its sheer drop-offs on either side. I'm worried I will lose the lovebird any minute, that it will fly off in some random direction. But no, it continues to flutter ahead of me, resting on rocks and cacti, waiting for me to catch up to it. Leading me on. And on.

*How did I get here?* my meta-mind asks. What chain of events lured me to this very real road, on this very real day?—the question that has eluded me since this whole adventure began.

The memories, I find, are fully available to me now.

*At around two o'clock this afternoon—on this Wednesday in late November—I was driving along Shea Boulevard in Scottsdale, heading west from Fountain Hills toward the Whole Foods in north Phoenix. My mind was steeped in dread about spending Thanksgiving with Hannah's sister's family. It would be our first attempt at a social outing since Emmy's death. I knew how awkward the whole affair was going to be. Either we would all pretend not to notice Emmy was absent or we would "talk openly about it," either of which option would make me want to face-plant in the mincemeat pie and drown myself right there at the table.*

*I was missing Emmy in the pit of my belly as I drove along Shea, trying to whip up some excuse to weasel out of Thanksgiving. Wanting to spend the day with Em instead. Or at least with her memory.*

*A distinctly non-Oliverian thought formed in my head. I might even have voiced it aloud. "Help me, Emmy. Tell me what to do. Give me a sign."*

*Not five seconds later, I was signaling a right turn onto Route 101 North when I spotted a billboard for an online dating site over the 101 South exit. It showed two lovebirds cuddling on a branch, with the caption,* We're Not Saying. We're Just Saying. LovebirdsOnline.com.

*I'd asked for a sign, and here was a literal one; impossible to ignore, even for a dedicated nonbeliever like me. Lovebirds were Emmy's thing. She had a massive tattoo of one on her neck. She had lovebird earrings, a lovebird kimono, lovebird wallpaper on her phone.*

*I swerved left and turned onto 101 South instead. Heart pounding, but feeling calm, I drove south for several miles—and then I saw it again. The same billboard. Near the ramp to Route 60 East. I took the exit.*

*Proceeding east, I watched the scenery unfold for five miles, ten miles, looking for another sign, my doubt mounting with each passing minute.*

*As I was passing into Apache Junction, a motorcycle sped around me. Its rider, a young woman, wore a jumpsuit of bright parrot green, with blue-tinted legs. Her helmet was yellow at the base, fading up to peach-orange and then to red—the colors of a lovebird's head—and her long hair was blonde with strawberry highlights, like Emmy's.*

*She took the Route 88 exit. I followed her.*

*I stayed in pursuit of the green mystery biker for several miles, as she rode out along Route 88—where it turns into the Apache Trail—past the Superstition Mountain Museum and the Lost Dutchman Mine, and across the two single-lane bridges over Canyon Lake. She continued on to the little village of Tortilla Flat (pop. 6), where she parked her bike and headed into the Old West-style saloon and restaurant.*

*I parked my car and followed her as fast as I could, half-convinced she was Emmy.*

*I caught a glimpse of her disappearing into the restroom area. But after ducking into the men's room myself and peeing quickly, I couldn't spot her anywhere—not in the restaurant with the dollar-bill-covered walls, not at the bar with the saddle seats, not in the country store with the penny-flattening machine and jalapeño fudge.*

*I hurried back outside to find her motorcycle gone. Already? How? Why? I sat on the old wooden bench out front, unsure what to do next... and that's when the bird itself appeared.*

*I doubted my eyes. But there it was, hopping about in the strange evergreen tree across the street, its bright peach-and-red face and green wings* unmistakable. I crossed the road for a closer look—no doubt about it, a lovebird. (A rosy-faced lovebird, noted my second awareness.) Holy crap.

I knew of their alleged existence in the Phoenix area, but had never seen one. It fluttered off, toward the wilder reaches of the Apache Trail.

I ran to my car, my heart thwacking a lively bass-line, and jumped behind the wheel. Logically speaking, there was no chance of catching up to the bird and seeing it again, but logic was not at the helm on this day of mystery. I drove as fast as the road allowed.

The bird was waiting for me, perched on a signpost, as I pulled out of an S-curve a mile or two down the low-speed-limit road. It took off ahead of me, leading me on.

When I reached the spot where the blacktop gives way to dirt road—where the Trail begins in earnest—the parrot was literally hovering in air, a maneuver only hummingbirds can theoretically execute. It flew on. I steered my car after it, down the bumpy dirt road.

For the next hour-plus, I navigated the fifteen-mile-an-hour spaghetti curves of the trail Teddy Roosevelt once declared America's most magnificent roadway—through spectacular pink-rock cliffs, verdant washes, and stately stands of saguaro—as the lovebird appeared and disappeared, again and again, enticing me onward.

And now here I am, driving along the Trail in real time, the lovebird flying a bicycle's length ahead of my car. It flies, and I follow, kicking up a rooster tail of dust behind me.

At long last, the bird takes a swooping right turn and flies off the Trail into a dry ravine lined with small mesquite trees and glowing-green succulents.

I ditch the car on a rare stretch of road-shoulder and run off on foot to follow it.

There it is, the bird, a hundred feet off the road, perched on a cluster of two-foot-tall, column-like cacti sprouting from the bank of the ravine.

How close dare I get?

I creep within ten yards of the parrot.

Five.

The bird doesn't move.

Three.

I'm two feet away now, daring not to breathe, and still the bird hasn't budged.

I stand directly in front of the cactus cluster, looking down at the parrot. It gazes up at me, unafraid, uninterested in flight. Even Oliver Thicko Powers knows this moment is sacred.

*Hannah!* I must share this with Hannah. She's not going to be happy with me, gallivanting off on a chase when I'm supposed to be scoring last-minute victuals before the stores close early on this Thanksgiving Eve. But I *must* share this moment with her.

Lord knows we need it. I have been husband-*in-absentia* for most of these past couple of months—drinking alone, hiking alone, taking long, aimless drives. Avoiding closeness, avoiding conversation. Not because I don't want to be with Hannah, but because I don't want *her* to be with *me*. Scared to death of what will tumble out of my mouth, what holes I might pull us into.

But *this*—this is a Hannah moment if ever there was one, and she needs to be part of it.

Silently begging the parrot to stay put a minute longer, I slip my phone out of my pocket and dial Hannah on FaceTime. Her lovely, soft-but-angular face appears on the screen, complete with recently added creases under the eyes.

"Liv!" she says. "Where are you? You're supposed to be—"

"Shh. You're not going to believe this, Han. I'm on the Apache Trail. I've been following a bird since—well, since Scottsdale, in a way—and it landed right here."

I aim the camera down at the bird perched on the tall columnar cactus. Hannah gasps.

"You know what that is, right?" she whispers.

"A lovebird," I whisper back. "Emmy's bird."

"Oh, Liv. Oh, Liv. Oh, Liv," she says breathlessly. "What's that cactus she's perched on?" She answers the question herself—Hannah knows her plants. "It looks like the Organ Pipe, but why is it in bloom? It's not the right time of year for that."

I hadn't noticed the bright white flower atop one of the six-ribbed columns.

"Hang on," she says. I watch on FaceTime as she crosses the room to the bookshelf and reaches for her well-worn atlas of Southwestern plants. "Show me again," she says.

I aim the camera at the cactus cluster where the parrot is perched, and Hannah pulls in another breath. "That's not the Organ Pipe—you can tell by the starburst shape of the flower. That's the San Pedro."

"The hallucinogenic one?" I say. "The one Emmy was always pestering me to try?"

"The very one. But Liv, listen. The San Pedro doesn't grow native in Arizona. People do keep them as potted plants and put them in gardens, but they only grow native in South America—Ecuador, Peru."

"So... you're telling me the only wild lovebird I've ever laid eyes on just guided me to the only wild patch of San Pedro cactus in southern Arizona?"

"You have to do it, Liv," she says with reverent finality. I don't know what she means. "You have to take the San Pedro. That's what Emmy is telling you. You didn't accept her invitation when she was alive, but you *have* to accept it now. You *have* to."

"How?"

"We'll figure it out. When you come home." She looks beyond the camera lens, straight into my eyes. "We have a lot of things to figure out, Liv. Come home. We'll skip my sister's, tomorrow. We don't need anything at Whole Foods. Just grab a pizza or some Thai, and a bottle of wine, and come home. Come home, Liv, come home."

My breath hitches in my throat. No words come. I'm afraid I'll rupture if I speak.

Hannah and I disconnect—but only in a FaceTime sense.

Home. Yes, home would be good. So very, very good.

Before leaving the Emmy-spirit bird and the San Pedro cactus behind, I must take a video. Otherwise I'll talk myself into believing this never happened.

I locate the camera function and stand over the patch of tall, hexagonally shaped cacti. Aiming the phone downward, I find myself looking straight down the barrel of the tallest San Pedro stalk. From above, it looks like a series of concentric, rounded-edged Stars of David. My sense of dimension plays tricks on me. Instead of looking *at* an extruded column, it seems like I'm looking *into* a tunnel—a tunnel made of concentric stars that curve off into space and disappear into infinity. Like mirrors within mirrors.

The mouth of the "tunnel" opens like a flower, inviting me in. It grows larger and larger to my eyes, filling my field of vision. I want to enter it. I want to fall inside.

*Come home, Liv, come home.*

I topple into the tunnel and tumble through space. Falling, falling...

. . .

Lids flutter open. Light floods the eye. I jerk my head from the pillow with a neck-cracking start and haul in a breath. I'm back in the hospital room.

# Chapter 47

Harkins Horvath, there he is. Please no. Please not this.

But yes, it's him. Standing back, away from the bed, as if he doesn't want to be the first thing I see upon awakening. Too late. He flashes a pinched smile and casts his eyes at the floor almost demurely. A dusting of new beard darkens his cheeks.

Beard? How long have I been out *this* time? How long have I been back here?

I try to move, but a gentle hand presses my shoulder down.

"Liv, relax," says the most familiar voice in the world, to my right. Hannah.

*Hannah?*

A hundred gears spin in my brain, but none of them mesh. Why is *she* here? With Harkins Horvath? Is she in cahoots with my captors? Have they kidnapped her too?

My body lurches from the mattress, adrenaline-jacked. I try to dismount the bed. Hannah holds me back. Hark rushes in to help her as an accented female voice shouts, "Oscar! Fernando!"

Two male orderlies in white tunic shirts charge into the room. They hold me down, speaking gently in Spanish, and wait for me to stop thrashing and sputtering. I try to shove them off me, and a black sleep-mask flies from my hand.

"Sweetie," says Hannah, "you're safe. You're in a medical clinic, just like you wanted."

"Don't let them fool you," I tell her. "This place is an old hotel. ... But you must know that if you're here with them. Why are you doing this to me? Why are you working with them?"

"He's still coming out of it," says Hark from across the room. "It might take a while."

"This is a *clinic*," Hannah repeats. "In Peru. Aguas Calientes. Near Machu Picchu. You arranged to come here, remember?"

"Then what's *he* doing here?" I thrust an accusing finger at Hark. He lifts his hands in peace. "*What the fuck is he doing here?*"

"He's helping you," says Hannah. "Helping *us*. You reached out to him, remember? *We* did. He's the one who set all this up. He's the one who had the connections down here."

I retreat to the head of the bed, clutching the blanket around myself, waiting for Hark to burst out laughing and reveal the latest mind-fuck trick he's pulled on me.

"Sit up, look around, Liv." Hannah pats my leg. "It'll start to come back."

"You are still under the effects of the San Pedro," says the accented female voice, moving closer to the bed. I turn to see Sister Quilla standing on my left.

"This is Dr. Quintana." Hark gestures toward the Quilla lookalike. "She's a sacred plant practitioner. She does shamanic work, but she's also a medical doctor, like we arranged. You're under her care and supervision. This is her clinic."

"Come on, sit up, Hon," Hannah says. "Take your time. If you're not ready to come out of it yet, you can put the eye-mask back on and go under again."

I lift myself to a sitting position and take a good look around. Oh. This is *not* the "hospital" room I was in before. Although the ceiling, the avocado-gray walls, and the overhead light—the only features visible from a prone position—are exactly the same as in my fake hospital room, that's where the similarities end. This room is much lower-tech than the one in which I previously lay. The artwork has an Incan motif—no Dutch milkmaids, break my heart—and the wall has fewer power cords and outlets. The two or three pieces of medical equipment in evidence look like they were manufactured in 1975. There's even a glass jar of cotton balls. This is a clinic, not a full-blown hospital.

It's starting to come back, but I still feel like I'm straddling two worlds.

"You have been on a very powerful San Pedro journey, Dr. Powers," says Dr. Quintana/Sister Quilla. "You went deeper than most, deeper than perhaps I have ever seen."

"How long have I been here?"

Eyes meet around the bed.

"We came here a few days after Thanksgiving, Sweetie. Remember?"

"I arrived late to the party." Hark bows a small apology. "I wanted to be here for your 'sendoff,' but you were already journeying full-tilt by the time my puddle-jumper got me here."

"So, how long?"

"Do you remember the thing with the lovebird?" Hannah sits on the bed, takes my hand. "On the cactus? On the Apache Trail?"

I nod.

"When you came home after that, you were *on fire*. You wanted to try some San Pedro immediately—you were afraid you'd chicken out if you waited. But then you thought better of it and decided to try it under medical supervision. Hark helped us find Dr. Quintana."

The memories are stitching together, bit by bit. I'm having trouble integrating the concept of "help" with the concept of "Hark," and I still can't make sense of time, but I do recall a few things. Like coming *home* on Thanksgiving Eve—no kidnapping occurred. Like spending Thanksgiving at home with Hannah, bonding over our efforts to learn everything we could about plant medicine and how best to experience it. Like Hark coming into the picture in some way.

"But how long have I been *here*? In this room? How long have I been under the San Pedro?"

Eyes connect around the bed again.

"You've been on quite a journey." Hannah squeezes my hand. "It's been almost *nine hours*."

Nine hours.

Jesus. I know time behaves differently in non-ordinary states, but it's impossible to believe it's only been nine hours since I awoke under "Nurse LaTisha's" care—at the beginning of my journey. As I try to make sense of that fact, other details fill in.

*Yet another crack in the cosmic egg occurred on that pivotal Thanksgiving Eve. When I came home from the Apache Trail, Hannah and I spent a couple of hours talking about my "Emily encounter" and diving into our San Pedro research. Then, after we reheated the pizza I brought home, drank some wine, and made love, I went out to fetch the mail.*

*On top of the Kroger coupons and replacement-window ads was a hand-addressed envelope the size of a thank-you note, with a Peruvian return address. What? I ripped it open and read, "Dr. Powers, with Thanksgiving approaching in the states, I thought I'd reach out to thank you, after all these years. Putting me in the hospital and getting me on meds was the best thing you could have done. I don't blame you anymore for what happened to Lisa and the kids, and I'm sorry for the threats. I'm down in Peru and back on the spiritual path again, but first I had to get my head on straight. You helped me with that. May you and your family have a blessed holiday. Gracias y que Dios te bendiga, Harkins Horvath III."*

*Seriously? This had to be a joke. But the timing of it... the synchronicity.*

*I couldn't flip a mental switch to make myself suddenly start trusting Hark, the most dangerous patient I ever treated, but Hannah convinced me his letter's arrival was a sign. Using the address on the envelope, we found a phone number for him. Hannah made the initial call.*

*It turned out Hark knew the sacred-plant-medicine landscape better than anyone—Peru is its epicenter—and he couldn't have been more helpful. He steered us clear of the "ayahuasca tourism" posers and put us in touch with Dr. Quintana, a revered local shaman and MD, and probably the only person on Earth willing and able to conduct a sacred plant ceremony under controlled medical conditions. Within days, we were on a plane to Jorge Chávez International, there to begin our pilgrimage to Quintana's clinic in Aguas Calientes.*

*Working with Dr. Quintana, Hannah and I designed my "treatment plan": I would take the highest dosage of San Pedro allowable. I would mask my eyes so as to ensure an internal journey, undistracted by sensory data. Dr. Quintana would work with the plant spirits on my behalf the whole time; drumming, chanting, and doing soul retrieval work. (It must have been her drumming I heard in my journey, when the "Chimbu dancers" performed, and later in the sweat lodge and in the trippy desert scene.) A psychiatrist and poison control team would be on call just in case.*

· · · ·

Fully rehydrated now and having undergone Dr. Quintana's "reentry" protocol, I summarize my journey for Hannah, Hark, and Quintana. I'm still floored by the utter realism of it and the way it was built entirely on true details of my life. Dr. Quintana calls it a "Middle World" adventure and explains that the plant spirits gave me the only kind of journey my rational, psychologically oriented mind could grasp and extract truth from. I thank her and the others for their help in facilitating this signal experience that will take the rest of my life to unpack. But as I'm talking to them, I become aware of a gnawing pain in my leg. Intuition tells me to examine it in private. I ask the others for a minute alone to dress.

The moment they exit the room, I whisk the bed covers aside and see blood. My thigh is lacerated in a semicircle of puncture wounds—a huge bitemark. In the exact place where the "demon" bit me during my journey. The logician in me springs to life, reminding me once again how moldable the human body is by belief: the placebo effect; stigmata; the way patients with Dissociative Identity Disorder can exhibit scars for one personality state but not another. My wounds are of that nature, surely—a physical manifestation of an internal state.

But then I glimpse a ragged, yellow-white edge sticking out of one of the "tooth-marks." Clenching my jaw against the pain, I probe the wound with my finger and pull out an inch-long object: a broken tooth. Sharp, serrated, shark-like. As real as the wedding ring on my finger.

I slip the tooth into my pocket, press some gauze pads onto the wounds, put my day clothes on, and leave the room, making my getaway before anyone notices blood on the bed.

• • •

Hannah and I are quiet on the return trip to the states (which involves a long train ride and taxi to Cusco, a prop-plane jaunt to Jorge Chávez, and a many-hour commercial flight) and throughout our first day home. It's a respectful quiet, though, not one born of distance. Hannah knows I need time to process what I've been through. I'm calm on the outside, but internally I'm as restless as a tiger in a cage. I feel there's something that needs completion.

In the middle of my first full night home—around three o'clock—I awaken with urgency. Tuning in to my newly acquired inner guidance system, I head to my study and turn on a lamp. I pull a bunch of my old medical school textbooks from the bottom shelf of a bookcase, and there, against the wall, I find it. The journal. That fateful diary where I recorded my months of psychological *sturm und drang* following the death of Hark's sister. Yes, the journal is real, as are all the painful details contained within it—including those about Mary, Anvita, and Bruce.

I haven't opened the journal since I stopped writing in it seven years ago. As I lift its front cover with some trepidation, a textured blue envelope slides out. Its source is immediately obvious. Emmy liked to buy fine stationery and send handwritten notes.

So she *did* find my journal; that happened. And she left this envelope inside.

The handmade-paper envelope is sealed with red wax. Printed around the raised seal, in Emmy's fey hand, is "Open only if you have the key." Studying the wax seal in the lamplight, I see it is imprinted with the mark of a serrated-edged implement. I tiptoe back to the bedroom and fish in my jeans pocket till I find what I'm looking for.

The tooth.

I return to the study and lay the tooth in the imprint in the sealing wax. It fits *perfectly*, as if the indentation was *molded* by the tooth.

My hand jerks in shock—part of me still wasn't ready for such a thing— and I drop both items. I search the floor for the tooth, can't find it anywhere. Where could it have gone? It was right in my hand; it can't have vanished into thin air.

I pick up the envelope. The seal is broken, the wax crumbled. I sit on the floor and remove the sandalwood-scented notepaper from the envelope.

*Dad,*

*By the time you read this, I'll be gone (and so will the old you!). Don't grieve over what we didn't have. Please. Celebrate what we did have and what we are now. I know you will have trouble hearing this, but try: There's no such thing as suicide. Or maybe it's more truthful to say, there is ONLY suicide. What I mean is, on a soul level, WE choose the moments of our comings and goings. Always. We come when conditions are ripe, we go when our work is complete. There's nothing you could have, or should have, done differently.*

*I did what I came here to do.*

*Now it's your turn.*

*Eternal Love,*

*Emmy*

It's good that I'm on the floor; I would have collapsed here anyway. I read the note, over and over, sobbing my soul out through every pore. There is joy in my tears, as well as exquisite pain, in an oh-so-purgatory mix.

When I'm cried dry, I stand up. There's a new lightness in my bearing. I feel different.

I want to mark this moment somehow. My hand reaches for the bookshelf and plucks out my three remaining copies of *Spiritual Delusion: Man's Invention of Meaning in a Lonely Universe* by Oliver Powers, MD. I note, with a sting of shame, that one of the images on the cover is a group of Chimbu dancers in skeletal body paint. I know why the publisher chose it—to suggest superstitiousness, to imply that all spiritual belief is as "primitive" as the death dance of a New Guinea tribesman. I disagreed about the use of the image. To me, it seemed culturally obtuse and not terribly appropriate to the book. But I backed down. Why?

Why have I ever done anything?

Fear.

I place my journal atop the stack of published books and march out to the backyard patio, holding the pile. I grab a Scripto lighter on the way out.

Our gas grill could do the job, but I choose instead the handmade clay chiminea Hannah bought from a strange man selling wares on a blanket in Salt River Canyon. It feels more fitting for ritual work.

I drag the little terracotta stove up near the table, noting, with a laugh, that in classic Oliver Powers anal-retentive fashion, I've already prepped it for its next fire, with balled-up paper, wood scraps from the garage, and a small log from the hardware store.

I place the journal—my sole deep dive into the guilt and shame of a lifetime—along with the three copies of my book into the round-bellied stove, atop the log. Without sentiment or hesitation, I light the stack ablaze.

I sit at the tiled patio table, in the same chair I sat in with Emmy during our encounter in my San Pedro journey. Was that just a sophisticated hallucination or was it the actuation of a real timeline embedded in the quantum clay? My mind and my gut offer different answers.

The fire crackles. I lean back and gaze up. I have never seen so many stars in the Fountain Hills sky; maybe it's a three a.m. thing. Sparks from the chiminea rise into the heavens, the embers of my past claiming—for just a moment—equal status to the embers of stars that lived and died before the Buddha walked the earth.

I search for the right words to immortalize this moment, but no words rise to fitting. I look to my right and imagine Emmy is sitting in the other chair—no, I think I *really see* her there. Don't I? Look, what's that? On the table? Isn't that the silhouette of our two beer bottles? Isn't that the toss of her hair over the back of the chair? Isn't she leaning back now, grinning, gazing at the stars with me?

We don't need *words*, Em and I. Nah. We're good with silence. We both know what the fire represents, without naming it. We both know what I'm burning up in that red clay oven.

Tomorrow I begin a new life, one free from the clutches of demons. Tomorrow I set forth to uncover what Oliver Powers came to this good green plane to be and do. Tomorrow I sing the sacred chord. Tomorrow I step into the fullness of who I am.

But tonight? Ah, tonight, let me hang on to a thread of the past for just a while longer, just till the fire burns out. Tonight let me imagine I'm still a dad.

I take a sip of my beer and watch the sparks dance and expire, dance and expire.

Tonight, let me hold in a father's heart a coal of hope that in some timeline somewhere—one these aging eyes will never glimpse again—lives a daughter who knows she is my hero.

## END

# Epilogue

We're heading down to the Catalina Foothills northeast of Tucson, Hannah and I, for our fourth annual "pilgrimage" to El Santuario Catalina, our special getaway place. Every year since my San Pedro journey, we spend March 22nd there, no matter what day of the week it falls on.

For the first part of the drive, as we head out of the Valley, we talk shop. Hannah and I work together now. She dusted off her Master's degree and ran the obstacle course to become a licensed counselor in Arizona. We share a counseling practice, one that attracts a fairly particular clientele—people in spiritual or existential crisis, people trying to go deeper in their consciousness work, people who have glimpsed the "other side" and are trying to integrate it into their everyday lives.

I still practice a version of traditional psychiatry—even still prescribe medications occasionally—but my work now includes a fierce engagement with the "source dimension." (I use the word *spirit* only reluctantly in my practice and never the word *God*—it pushes too many buttons.)

Hannah and I work with a network of other healers—shamanic practitioners, energy workers, mediums; the very people I mocked in my previous life. I still make public appearances from time to time, and write books, not as a "reformed atheist"—as some have tried to pigeonhole me—but certainly as someone whose approach to counseling has deepened to include an understanding that consciousness is primary in this universe, not an "epiphenomenon of matter."

One thing that's become true since my San Pedro journey is that I no longer give a solitary fuck about trying to convince anyone I'm right. About anything. I just put my ideas out there, and people can take them or leave them. As Hannah says, bees don't try to convince flies that honey tastes better than shit. I'm not sure if my books are the shit or the honey, but I do know that the two I've published since my San Pedro adventure have each outsold *Spiritual Delusion* by a factor of about twenty-five.

That's a lot of bees. Or flies.

As we head out onto the long, flat stretch of Route 10 toward Tucson, our shop-talk peters out, and I reflect back on my San Pedro experience, as I often do. It will indeed take a lifetime to unpack. From any angle I look at it—spiritual, psychoanalytic, shamanic—it presents a more multidimensional package than anything my idiot mind could have conjured on its own. One thing I can say with certainty is that it wasn't a hallucination. My sacred plant journey was realer than reality.

The world I now walk in bleeds over into that realer reality. Synchronicities—"miracles," impossible coincidences—occur regularly for me, as do visits from green-backed parrots with rosy faces. I accept them with gratitude; I don't analyze them or try to prove them to anyone. If I were to even try, I would be diagnosed as Cuckoo for Cocoa Puffs, to use a clinical term, and my license to practice would be cheerfully yanked.

As for that stuff Emmy said, in my journey, about me being a special soul, I don't think that's exactly true. I think my ego was still in charge enough, back then, that I needed to *believe* I was an extraordinary being in order to defeat the demon my psyche had spent a lifetime growing and feeding. We are all extraordinary beings, that's my belief—we need only remove the clutter from our paths.

Hannah and I are driving in the Catalina Foothills now; we're up near Sabino Canyon, navigating a twisting mountain road. As we pull up to the office of El Santuario Catalina to check in, a sense of calm anticipation descends. This is our Emmy time, a private ritual we will probably repeat every year we're still pulling oxygen.

How did we find this place, and why did we choose it? It chose us, actually.

You see, Emmy and old Saint Pete had one last trick up their sleeve.

*A couple of months after Hannah and I returned from Peru, we finally got around to clearing Emmy's belongings out of the Dollhouse—so our hearts* wouldn't be put through a meat grinder every time we set foot in the place. There weren't many things to box. Em traveled light and never treated the Dollhouse as a permanent residence. Still, some stuff managed to accumulate, awaiting her next visit—a favorite pillow, a stuffed parrot (yes) from childhood, a hideous cat lamp she won at a carnival that we kept in use as a joke.

By the time cleanout day arrived, I had convinced myself the incident with the tooth and the sealing wax was not fully of this dimension, but rather a carryover from my San Pedro trip, a final hiccup of the plant medicine still in my system. After all, the tooth was never found, the bitemark on my leg healed almost overnight, and the wax crumbled in such a way that the mark on it could no longer be identified.

But it seems Emmy was determined to leave us a more definitive set of footprints. As I was cleaning out her nightstand, I found an issue of Arizona Backroads magazine with a sticky note on the cover, reading, in Emmy's print, DON'T THROW AWAY!

Needless to say, I didn't. But try as I might, I couldn't find anything in those pages that seemed significant. I read every word of every article, every travel tip, every cowboy-restaurant review, but came up dry. But then one night, half asleep, I tossed the magazine onto the sofa and something caught my eye: a detail in the full-page ad on the back cover announcing the Grand Opening of El Santuario Catalina near Tucson. The ad showed views from various parts of the hotel property. One of them featured a mountain foothill with an odd-looking cactus on it: hourglass-shaped with three upright arms that looked like they were holding a ball.

My heart stopped.

It was the cactus I committed to memory when escaping from the old hotel in my San Pedro journey.

The next morning I showed the magazine photo to Hannah and explained its significance. She said to me, "Do you know what today is?"

I had to think for a moment. March 22nd. Emmy's birthday. Oh, Jesus.

"Get dressed," Hannah said. "We're going to Tucson."

We did. When we found the aptly named El Santuario ("The Sanctuary"), tucked away in the mountains, in a scenic pocket of desert wilderness, I was hit by a punch-in-the-face of déjà vu like never before. The hotel. It was the same one in which my "hospital room" was located. The exact place. Fully refurbished, but instantly recognizable.

Impossible. Ridiculous. I'd only visited the place in my mind, right? Yet here it stood, in outer Tucson, in an area we'd never been to. Tastefully redone in adobe stucco, with a fountain out front, a cactus garden, and mosaic tile walkways.

I knew exactly what the interior would look like before we entered. It didn't disappoint. The layout, the floor tiles, the woodwork—all as I recalled them from when the place was only partially rehabbed. But again, that "memory" took place in mescaline-reality.

Hannah talked to the front-desk people and confirmed that the place had just opened after a remodeling—the old hotel had gone out of business seven years earlier and had stood vacant for six of those years. She told them I had "special memories" of the old place—that was an understatement—and they were gracious enough to let us snoop around.

We took the elevator straight to the third floor and turned left. Everything was repainted and recarpeted now, but it was the same hallway, I could feel it; the hallway where I made my escape in a johnny and a leg cast. In my mind I could still smell the musty, sunbaked air and see the dirty window at the end of the hall with the paint-roller swath across it—now bright and crystal clear. I had lived and breathed in this place. Not possible, but true.

When we had walked about half the distance from the elevator to the window, I stopped and faced left. The door to my captivity room, this was it. I had to fight to keep my knees from buckling. The room number? 322. March 22. Emmy's birthday—the present date.

We couldn't enter the room, of course. It was locked and probably occupied.

Wordlessly, we returned to the front desk. We inquired about vacancies, and they told us they were full. But no, wait, they did have one cancellation—a young couple that left for an emergency. We told them we'd take the room for two nights (we'd packed an overnight bag just in case). We knew before they handed us the keycards which room we'd be given. Anything but 322 would have been a physical impossibility.

*We unlocked the door of 322, and Hannah stepped in first. She put her hands out as if testing for rain and said, "Well, hello, Em. She's here, Liv. I can feel her, can't you?"*

*My reaction was a bit more complicated. I recognized the space instantly, even though nothing was physically the same. It was much bigger than my "hospital" room, but that was probably because my captors had put up false walls as part of their sham set.*

What captors? Your experience in the fake hospital room wasn't real, Oliver.

*But "real" had acquired a whole new definition since ol' Saint Pete and I had cut a rug together, hadn't it?*

*As I stood there inside the door, I could see "Nurse LaTisha" bustling around with her syringe and "Detective Pratt" pulling up a chair beside my hospital bed. I could feel the long hours I'd spent in this space, trying to piece my life and mind back together.*

*I sat on the bed, and my mouth fell open, and I started talking. Really talking, no holds barred, for perhaps the first time ever. Didn't even take my jacket off. Hannah and I sat there for hours, and I told her everything. I went through my entire San Pedro journey—my entire life—with her. I told her about all the guilt and fear I'd held since before I even met her; about the wrongs I'd committed; about the demon from the church window and how I'd let it burrow into my soul. I told her about my failures as a father, a husband, and a psychiatrist. I spared nothing. We ordered room service, and we talked and talked and talked some more.*

*We put our marriage back together in that room that day. Got to know each other again as new people, full of wondrous flaws, and we fell in love anew. Emmy's gift to us.*

*I remember lying back on the bed, Hannah warm against me, my throat hoarse from talking, and saying to her, "The best and worst two moments of my life took place in this room. The best was when I heard 'Carrickfergus' on the sound system and remembered Em. The worst was when I remembered she was gone."*

*"But she's not, Liv," said Hannah. "Nothing goes. You know that now. Close your eyes." I did. "Now put yourself in that feeling you had when you first*

*remembered Emmy singing that song. Just stay with that feeling. Don't follow it with the crash."*

*I did as she urged. I remembered the joy only. Held it.*

*"Feel that? You can still love her that way, Liv, even though she's not here in body anymore. You don't have to pinch it off. You can love her just as you always did. In fact, you can love her even more."*

*That was when the final floodgates burst for me. I realized what I'd been missing even more than Emmy's presence on Earth was the love I had for her. I thought it had to stop with her death. But it didn't. Hannah was right. I could keep loving my daughter. Without reserve. I could open my heart and let it flow. Oh God, the love didn't have to stop!*

• • •

So now, on this, our fourth annual pilgrimage to El Santuario, we check in at the desk and go up to the room, 322, our home away from home. Emmy is there to greet us, as always, along with the fresh flowers and welcome-champagne. Our daughter's not *physically* in the room, of course, nor is she present in any way we could prove to anyone. But she is here, we feel her. Every year she gives us a little sign to let us know we're not imagining it.

We will talk to Emmy throughout our visit, as we always do. We'll include her in our conversations. We'll invite her along on our Sabino Canyon hikes and our lunch excursions. We'll be a family. A weird damn family, but a family no less.

For me, the visits are a recharge and a reminder. This material world, with its shrieking opinions and frantic agendas, has a tendency to beat up on the spirit a bit. A visit to 322 always recalibrates me. And I always get an ass-kicking of love from Emmy that I carry forth into the world.

After all, if I can continue to love my dead daughter with a full heart, then I can love *everyone* who has passed on. My parents. My grandparents. My sister Lanie. My best friend Toby from college.

And if I can give unconditional love to those who are not even here anymore, I can certainly whip up a serving or two for those whose hearts are still beating. For my patients, my colleagues, my baristas, my fellow drivers. For that preening guy at the gym with the stupid neon-green shorts.

For telemarketers and ten-p.m. pollsters too. For talk show hosts and politicians; liars, cheaters, and criminals.

And sometimes, on good days, when the moon is just right, I can even eke out a little for Oliver Powers.

Miracles, I tell you, miracles.

# Acknowledgements

Endless love and gratitude to my wife and soul-partner, Karen, and to my wondrous daughters, Phelan and Quinn, for giving me the gift of fatherhood—the heart of this novel—among a billion other gifts.

Many thanks, Ken Laverriere, for your cherished feedback on two drafts of the manuscript. Thanks even more for the fifty years (did I just say that?) of friendship, love, and soul-nourishing conversation. This book would not exist without you, brother. Thanks, Sean Kavanagh, too, for your thoughtful reading of the manuscript, for your *nearly* fifty years of friendship, and for the laughs that lift my life and make me a better writer.

A shout-out to José Irizarry, my spiritual *hermano* in Puerto Rico. There is a lot of you in this book, amigo. Maureen, my sister, there's a lot of you in here too. Love and thanks. And thanks to my dear friends, Rosie and Mike, who inspire me always. Rosie, I learned about *good* mental health treatment from you all those years ago at Jackson House.

Much appreciation to my philosophy and theology teachers who, decades ago, got me thinking about the ideas that underpin this book—especially Joe Kelly of Merrimack College, who gave my narrow young mind a way of approaching spirituality that opened many doors.

Finally, very special thanks to my writers group, the Ahwatukee Writers Workshop. You were with me from the first word of the first draft, offering great advice and insight. To find such a talented and generous group of writers, even in one of the great literary cities of the world, would be rare. But to find it in the unassuming village of Ahwatukee, dangling out there on the south side of the mountain in Phoenix, is insanely fortunate.

# About the Author

*More from the Author*

Andy is the ghostwriter of over seventy fiction and nonfiction books, some for New York Times bestselling authors. His screenplays have been optioned numerous times in Hollywood. He has written/designed over 25 computer and video games, including many children's "classics" from the '90s and '00s, such as *Darby the Dragon*, *3D Dinosaur Adventure*, and *M&M's The Lost Formulas*. He is the author of the critically acclaimed thriller novel, *Fishermen's Court*, and the award-winning children's book, *The Girl from Glocken's Glen*. Andy has also written an award-winning stage play, *Empties*, and has done scriptwriting work for Disney, Blizzard Entertainment, and other media companies. He is a member of International Thriller Writers.

# Note from the Author

Word-of-mouth is crucial for any author to succeed. If you enjoyed *The Treatment Plan*, please leave a review online—anywhere you are able. Even if it's just a sentence or two. It would make all the difference and would be very much appreciated.

Thanks!
Andrew Wolfendon

We hope you enjoyed reading this title from:

# BLACK ROSE
## writing™

www.blackrosewriting.com

Subscribe to our mailing list – *The Rosevine* – and receive **FREE** books, daily deals, and stay current with news about upcoming releases and our hottest authors.
Scan the QR code below to sign up.

Already a subscriber? Please accept a sincere thank you for being a fan of Black Rose Writing authors.

View other Black Rose Writing titles at
www.blackrosewriting.com/books and use promo code
**PRINT** to receive a **20% discount** when purchasing.

CPSIA information can be obtained
at www.ICGtesting.com
Printed in the USA
LVHW052058281222
736011LV00002B/97